W̶H̶A̶T̶
CAN'T
BE SEEN

Pho

OTHER TITLES BY BRIANNA LABUSKES

Dr. Gretchen White Novels

A Familiar Sight

Stand-Alone Novels

Her Final Words

Black Rock Bay

Girls of Glass

It Ends With Her

To Megha Parekh
For being a steadfast champion of flawed and
complicated female characters.
This one's for you.

PROLOGUE

GRETCHEN

1993

Blood wasn't sticky like Gretchen had thought it would be.

It was warm and slick and thin, and something in her brain told her to bring her fingers to her mouth to taste it.

Her aunt Rowan watched her from the bed, her lips moving.

No sound came out.

Gretchen knew she should be calling for her mother, knew she'd get in trouble if she was found here holding the knife that had turned slippery in her hand.

But Gretchen couldn't step away, couldn't look away.

The moon was so bright that Gretchen could easily see the wounds left behind. Rowan's stomach, her chest, they were torn open.

Gretchen inched forward, fingers hesitant but curious. Something gurgled in the back of Rowan's throat, and Gretchen wondered if it was more blood, if Rowan was trying to tell her to stop.

It didn't matter. Rowan couldn't say anything anymore.

Gretchen watched her own hand reach forward, pinch the ripped skin, and *tug*.

A tap. A shuffle. A noise that shouldn't be there.

Gretchen whirled, holding the knife to her chest without thought. The blood soaked into the thin pajama top she wore, smearing onto her skin as it saturated the fabric, warm and wet and fascinating.

Despite the noise she'd heard, there was no one there. Just the shadows—and those were familiar to her, they were her friends.

By the time Gretchen turned back to the bed, Rowan's eyes had emptied. Her aunt stared at the ceiling, unblinking, unmoving except for the life still spilling out of her onto her mattress.

Gretchen had to get her mother now.

Before she could even take a step, the screaming started.

And then a voice, the horrified accusation behind it. "Gretchen. What . . . what have you *done*?"

CHAPTER ONE

GRETCHEN

Now

Pounding.

Music. Lights. The bass reverberating in her chest.

No. That wasn't right.

Gretchen White blinked, squinted against the harsh, bright white of the sun pouring into her bedroom.

Pounding.

In her head this time, not her chest.

And at the door.

The man lying next to Gretchen shifted, lifting up onto one elbow and scratching absently at the neatly manicured hair on his stomach. "Babe?"

"Not your babe," Gretchen gritted out as she sat up, her feet sinking into the plush carpet. "Don't panic. I don't remember your name, either."

The man groaned, head flopping back against the pillow, the shaggy blond hair spreading out against the pristine pearl-colored cover. He ran a knuckle down her bare spine. "Let's reintroduce ourselves then, why don't we?"

Without looking, Gretchen reached behind her, gripped his wrist, twisted until she heard the yelp of pain. Then kept going, longing for the pop of ligaments and the crack of bone. His legs kicked out as he tried to free himself, but he wouldn't be able to, not with the leverage she had.

Pounding.

Swallowing the primal scream that clawed at her throat, Gretchen finally let go of the man and stood. "I don't want to see your face again."

"How do I—"

"Window." Gretchen knew he wouldn't appreciate the helpful tip like he should. That suspicion was confirmed by the swears flung at her back as she stumbled toward the door, still naked. She ignored him, her memory already erasing everything about him other than how he'd made her body feel.

Pounding.

Briefly Gretchen contemplated grabbing her gun, but the better instincts that had kept her in check most of her life whispered from someplace deep in her chest. Now that she'd had a few minutes to process what was happening, Gretchen had a good guess at who stood outside her apartment.

And she had no desire to go to jail for shooting a member of the Boston Police Department.

Detective Lauren Marconi's fist paused, midknock, when Gretchen finally wrenched open the door.

The woman maintained her unimpressed expression in the face of Gretchen's nudity as well as her greeting that involved the most colorful combination of curse words in Gretchen's vocabulary.

"Delightful, as always," Marconi said, pushing her way into the apartment. "All right, it's been three months. You've sulked long enough."

Gretchen's hand found its way to Marconi's throat. In the next minute Gretchen had Marconi against the wall, teeth bared, her blood hot and thrumming with the beloved and familiar rage that she so rarely let herself feel.

The pounding was in her veins now.

"You think you know me," Gretchen whispered, white creeping in at the edges of her vision. "You think you've clipped my claws, little Bambi. But don't forget what I am."

Marconi didn't shrink beneath the implied threat, simply met Gretchen's gaze with those light amber eyes of hers. When she answered, her tone was dry. "A *nonviolent* sociopath, if I remember correctly."

Gretchen's thumb dug into Marconi's pulse, yet it still didn't race. Maybe that should have ignited even further the fury that simmered beneath Gretchen's skin, but for some reason Marconi's lack of fear was the ice Gretchen needed to get control of herself once more.

Still, Gretchen held her there for another long moment.

"Nonviolent by choice," she said, making sure the threat in each word came out weighted and dangerous.

Then she abruptly dropped her arm and walked toward the couch to snag the too-big sweater that hung there. Pulling it over her head, she then started toward the kitchen and the blessed relief of coffee.

Once out of sight of the living room, she heard the door slam and guessed her bedmate had taken his leave. She wished he'd tried dangling from the ledge instead.

"So is this what you're going to do with your life now?" Marconi asked, trailing behind Gretchen. "Aren't the drugs and sex a bit cliché, even for you?"

"Clichés exist for a reason, darling," Gretchen tossed back, but the heat had been sapped out of her. Now she just felt the ache in her muscles, in her bones. Once upon a time, after a night at the club, it would have been easy to roll into the next day, a mimosa in one hand and a baggie of suspicious pills in the other as she searched out more cheap thrills.

She wasn't used to that life anymore, though. She'd gone soft; the ability atrophied after years of impeccable self-control.

"You're too good of a psychologist not to know that you're acting out right now," Marconi commented from where she leaned against the kitchen island. Gretchen eyed the sleek stainless steel knives that sat next to her coffee maker, but the urge for caffeine had well and truly taken over any need to pierce Marconi through with a sharp object.

"You're lucky I have a headache," Gretchen muttered without bothering to acknowledge the accusation. Of course she knew what she was doing. She was not only a renowned psychologist but also one of the Boston PD's top consultants when it came to crimes and antisocial personality disorders like her own. Even if she hadn't needed to know everything about her own diagnosis to survive, she'd know it because she refused to be anything but the best when it came to her career.

She was spiraling. And there was exactly one person to blame for that.

The detective standing in her kitchen, hands shoved in her pockets, watching Gretchen like she had any right to be disappointed in her.

Gretchen grabbed her mug without offering anything to Marconi and headed toward the large window that overlooked her quiet street. It was in an exclusive part of town because Gretchen had never been shy about spending the vast fortune she'd inherited from her grandmother that made working with the police irrelevant, financially speaking. Curling up in one of the chairs placed strategically to catch the morning sun, Gretchen eyed Marconi.

She was wearing what Gretchen had come to realize was her version of a uniform: jeans, a dark button-down shirt, chunky boots. Her inky black hair was pulled back into a little ponytail, her bangs a harsh line above thick, unplucked brows. Gretchen hated that the look worked so well for Marconi.

"You need a case," Marconi said as she dropped into the second chair. In an uncharacteristically singsong voice, she added, "And what better case than your own?"

Gretchen looked away so that she wouldn't hurl her cup at Marconi's face. This suggestion that Gretchen investigate the murder that had haunted her since she was a child wasn't new. It was what had thrown Gretchen's carefully constructed world off-kilter three months ago when Marconi had slid that file across the table.

The one from 1993. The one with Gretchen's own name printed in stark block letters on the tab.

White, Gretchen Anne.

It seemed that for some reason Marconi wanted to rip Gretchen apart at the seams just to see her insides.

The impulse was one Gretchen understood better than most. That kind of emotional violence was stamped into the very foundational stones that made Gretchen who she was. But the strings holding her together—the ones that had never been strong in the first place—were now so frayed that she knew she'd never be able to stitch herself back up if Marconi was successful.

Even as a sociopath, Gretchen had long ago realized that if she lived driven purely by her urges, she'd end up with her freedom stripped away, either through jail or death. And she liked her freedom. She liked her life. So she'd developed a way to keep the impulses that came with her diagnosis under control.

And that life depended on Gretchen living in blissful denial when it came to her involvement in her aunt's murder.

Now after working a single case together, Marconi had decided she wanted to dig around in the past, convinced that they could clear Gretchen's name once and for all.

As if it was easy, an afterthought almost. Something Gretchen had forgotten about until Marconi barged into her life to press the issue.

As if the case hadn't shaped Gretchen's entire life.

She had known what she'd find if she opened the nearly thirty-year-old file. Though Gretchen couldn't remember the night her aunt died beyond fleeting images of flesh and shadows and screams, she had heard the recounting of it enough that the story felt seared into her bones.

A sensational murder, a budding sociopath, a rich family and too many headlines that had assumed guilt long before any charges were considered.

The victim of the vicious stabbing had been Gretchen's aunt, Rowan White.

The prime suspect had always been Gretchen, despite the fact that she'd been an eight-year-old child at the time of the killing.

Gretchen couldn't even blame anyone for the assumption. She'd been found holding the murder weapon, covered in blood, standing over Rowan's body, her fingers reaching out to prod the wound.

Rowan had died in her bed, and there had been no defensive injuries to suggest she had fought back. Rather, it looked like Gretchen had snuck in at night and stabbed her sleeping aunt.

Cold-blooded murder.

The stories had started coming out then. How strange Gretchen was, how verbally vicious she could be to classmates, how odd her teachers found her vacant eyes and predatory smile.

Detective Patrick Shaughnessy, the lead investigator on the case, might have pursued other leads—she didn't know. But he always came back to her.

No other viable suspect had ever emerged.

There had been no signs of forced entry, no signs of anyone else other than Gretchen's mother and sister—both cleared through forensic evidence—in the house that night. No prints on the murder weapon—a knife taken from the Whites' kitchen—beyond those of her family.

Maybe blaming Gretchen had been the easiest answer, but that didn't mean it wasn't also the right one. Not every murder was complicated; sometimes the death was exactly as it looked. If Gretchen had been given the case today, she would have put money on herself being the guy.

It should have—would have—been an open-and-shut case, her guilt obvious to anyone looking at the scene. But Shaughnessy had been stymied by Gretchen's influential family. Edith White, Gretchen's grandmother, had made a convincing case to the prosecutor that Gretchen could have simply stumbled onto the crime scene. Maybe that wouldn't have been sufficient for anyone else, but the Whites pumped enough political money into the city for the prosecutor to buy into the story.

That didn't stop the good people of Boston, and the rest of the country, for that matter, from speculating, their attention caught by the scandalous, titillating nature of the crime.

Even as the public moved on to whatever next lurid killing grabbed national headlines, most people believed Gretchen White had gotten away with murder.

To this day, after working with Shaughnessy for years in her role as a respected consultant for the Boston Police Department, the man never let Gretchen forget that he thought her nothing more than a killer who was rich enough to stay out of jail.

"Remember what you told me when I asked you why you were investigating the Viola Kent case?" Marconi asked.

Gretchen didn't dignify that with a response. Of course she remembered, as she remembered most things. The Viola Kent case was why Marconi was in Gretchen's life at all, and Gretchen dreamed longingly of an alternative timeline where she had never met the detective while standing over the body of Lena Booker, Gretchen's best friend. The question had been rhetorical anyway, so Gretchen simply sipped her coffee. Marconi was going to continue whether Gretchen participated in the conversation or not.

"You said, 'Curiosity,'" Marconi continued, as Gretchen had known she would.

"Make your point or leave," Gretchen said. "But you have until I finish this"—she gestured with the mug—"before I toss you out the window."

While the threat would have been more convincing had Gretchen lived in a penthouse instead of a converted town house, the salient part came through. *Get out of my house, or nonviolent classification be damned.*

Marconi cut her eyes to Gretchen's face. "Why aren't you curious, Gretchen?"

"Dr. White," Gretchen corrected. Marconi was already too comfortable around her, and they'd only ever worked together for the few days it had taken to unravel the Viola Kent mystery. Boundaries needed to be redrawn, reinforced, and maintained. They certainly weren't friends; they weren't even partners. They were simply two people who happened to have been thrown together over a dead body and a thirteen-year-old psychopath who had been framed for murder.

Nothing more, nothing less.

"Dr. White," Marconi parroted with a tip of her head. Gretchen searched the words for any trace of sarcasm or bitterness and found none. "Why aren't you curious about your own case?"

The answer, if Marconi thought about it long enough, couldn't be more obvious.

Because I think I could be guilty.

Gretchen had never—would never—admit that out loud. She'd never even hint at it. But in the quiet pocket of space within her where she held on to her truths, she knew that's what she feared.

Knew that's why she had never once, in the nearly thirty years that had passed since she'd been found standing over her dead aunt, tried to find another suspect. Knew that's why she had never even sought out her own file when she'd gained access to the police department's database.

With Gretchen's training, her advanced degrees in psychology and criminology, and her decade of experience as a freelance consultant with the Boston PD on cases relating to personality disorders, that one glance at the details of the case could prove her deepest fear correct.

To the world, Gretchen sneered at the idea that she was guilty of killing her aunt Rowan, mocked the detectives who had scapegoated an eight-year-old instead of doing their jobs, brutally cut out any cops who refused to work with her now because of her history.

In the darkness, though, Gretchen knew what she was capable of. Knew as a sociopath that the lure of blood, of torn flesh, of *violence* and ugly wounds was too compelling to believe she wouldn't have ever succumbed. She'd been a child, after all. Her reasoning and logic—the very things she relied on so heavily to keep her impulses in check as an adult—had been far from developed.

What did a young girl who had no fear of consequences know of restraint?

Shaughnessy had always viewed the fact that Gretchen couldn't remember anything from that night as more proof that she'd been the one to kill Rowan—the implication being that she was too young to come up with a better excuse for what she was doing in Rowan's room if she wasn't the one who stabbed her.

"There was no one else there?" he'd asked her relentlessly and in several different ways, as if changing the question would catch Gretchen in her lie.

"I don't remember" had been all she could ever offer, the family lawyer stone-faced beside her, ready to stop Shaughnessy at even the barest hint of a threat.

"Why were you in her room?"

"I don't remember."

"Why were you holding the knife?"

"I don't remember."

The interrogation had gone on like that, not only the first night when Gretchen had still had dried blood in the beds of her fingernails but also in the weeks after, when Shaughnessy had been desperate to make something stick. To break Gretchen.

It had been his first big murder case after all, a blotch on his record that he still probably hadn't lived down.

"You think you did it," Marconi finally said. It didn't sound like a revelation but rather a deliberate poke in a tender spot. "You think everyone thinks you did it, and that you just haven't been caught."

It had been one of the first things Marconi had ever heard Gretchen say, that last part almost word for word. And Gretchen wondered if, even after the Viola Kent case, even after how it had all played out, she still underestimated this woman.

And Marconi was right. Even though Gretchen hadn't looked at the file, she knew the facts of the case didn't exactly play out in her favor. It wasn't a lack of evidence that had Gretchen walking away without any consequences.

For some reason, though, Marconi was convinced of Gretchen's innocence. That pure optimism, that pure faith, was as addictive as any drug that Gretchen had ever tried. Could she really be blamed for wanting to inject it into her own veins?

"Tell me," Marconi said, nudging Gretchen's bare foot with her boot. "Make me believe it, and I'll leave."

Gretchen couldn't help but ask, though she despised being baited. "Tell you what?"

Marconi grinned. "Tell me you don't want to prove them all wrong."

CHAPTER TWO

SHAUGHNESSY

1983

Patrick Shaughnessy had learned to drive beneath the bright lights of the city. The first time he'd ever truly experienced pure darkness had been on a rare family trip to his grandmother's tiny cottage on the coast of Maine.

He'd hated it then, and he hated it now—that feeling of the void, the black consuming the air and space and earth until there was nothing left.

"Why are you driving like we're on our way to collect Social Security checks?" Detective Liam Boyd asked from the passenger seat. Shaughnessy glanced over but couldn't see much of the detective's face beyond the stark outline of his profile: the thick, prominent nose, the jutting chin. Still, he could picture the cocky smile that Boyd got when he thought he'd said something particularly clever.

Shaughnessy hated him almost as much as he hated driving out of Boston in the dark. He silently cursed the small sliver of jurisdiction that butted right up against the sprawling state forest where he was convinced no sane person should ever venture. He didn't bother cursing at Boyd. Shaughnessy was a rookie, fresh out of the academy, more a chauffeur than a partner. Boyd was the golden boy of the department, handsome, charming, and with an unerring ability to solve unsolvable cases.

If it got around that Shaughnessy couldn't take some gentle ribbing from him, Shaughnessy might as well switch states for all that he could recover from that reputation.

So instead of defending himself, he pressed on the gas, squinted into the nothingness in front of them, and prayed for the first time in months.

Boyd muttered something beside him, but Shaughnessy didn't take his eyes off the road this time. They accelerated around a corner. Headlights blinded him and his foot lifted from the pedal, then pushed down again.

White spots popped in his vision as the other car passed.

Darkness descended once more.

Shaughnessy wanted to double-check the map, actually make sure that this trek was necessary. But he knew they were on the right road.

It was their last call of the night, and Boyd had already complained multiple times about the date he'd be late to if this domestic-dispute complaint took any longer than knocking on the door to make sure everyone was still alive.

While Shaughnessy didn't know Boyd well yet, he'd guess the man thought the call beneath him. But they'd been in the area on a different case when it had come in, and even Boyd couldn't argue with the chief's orders.

"Christ on a cross, we're going to have gray hair by the time we get there," Boyd said. He might be a star detective, but Boyd wasn't exactly witty. Everyone laughed when he said things like that, but it was always faked. Shaughnessy didn't even bother with a polite chuckle.

They rounded another bend. Shaughnessy slowed on instinct, then sped up once he realized what he'd done.

"Just let me know if you need me to take over," Boyd poked.

Shaughnessy gripped the steering wheel, the silver of the guardrail making him blink as his brain tried desperately to orient itself.

Boyd was going for a rise now, probably bored from Shaughnessy's silence.

"No wonder you can't hold on to a partner," Boyd said casually. "You drive like a sissy little girl."

Heat crawled up Shaughnessy's neck, spreading along his jaw, behind his ears. He knew in the light the pink flush of anger would have been obvious. "Shut your f—"

The words died in the air between them as the car's headlights caught a flash of white.

A person. In the middle of the road.

Shaughnessy slammed on the brakes, the back tires skidding out to the side in protest. His eyes closed against his will as he waited for the thump of body and wheels.

Instead, the bumper stopped a whisper away from the girl's legs.

"Goddamn." Boyd sketched out a quick sign of the cross beside Shaughnessy.

But Shaughnessy couldn't tear his attention from the girl, her face pale white, her eyes deep, terrifying pools. A part of him cataloged that her arms were covered in blood, enough so that it dripped onto the pavement. A part of him cataloged that she was dressed in nothing more than a camisole and thin shorts despite the cold September night. A part of him cataloged where she'd come running from so that they could later try to trace her path.

Mostly, though, all he could do was stare at her mouth as she formed one word over and over and over again.

"Run."

Shaughnessy's legs shook as he heaved himself out of the car. Boyd was cursing behind him, and in the next moment they were both bathed in blue and red flashing lights, the colors flickering across the girl's pale skin, catching on the slick wetness trickling down her arms.

"Miss," Shaughnessy said, trying to be as gentle as he could, hating the hard Southie edge of his voice that caused her to flinch as he reached out to her. He froze, hands hovering in midair. "You're safe. You're okay."

He repeated the promises, shifting closer, trying to make his too-big body seem smaller.

She just blinked at him, still poised to flee.

"You're okay." He knew there were things he'd been trained to say in a situation like this, but all he could think of were soft reassurances. "Can you tell me your name?"

Haunted eyes that had been drifting toward Boyd snapped back to Shaughnessy. "My name," she said softly. Her voice was as delicate as the rest of her. "My name."

She said the words like she was just learning to speak.

"Do you know it?" Shaughnessy ventured, wondering what he'd gotten himself into here. Boyd was behind him with a blanket. But he, like Shaughnessy, seemed frozen, hesitant to spook the girl any further.

The girl exhaled, a shattered sound that broke something inside Shaughnessy.

"What's yours?" she asked instead of answering.

And that was one of those things he should have started with. "Detective Patrick Shaughnessy, Boston Police Department."

"Shaughnessy," she said, testing it out, his name coming out far more lyrical on her tongue than it ever had on anyone else's.

"That's right," Shaughnessy agreed with a little nod. "And what's yours?"

"Names, they mean something, don't they?" she said, blinking into the headlights, and for a desperate second he wondered if they should be checking for a head wound.

"I guess they do," he tried, inching forward. This time she didn't startle, didn't cower, and that small victory bloomed warm in his chest. Again he asked, "Can you tell me yours?"

She inhaled, wrapped her bloody and torn-up arms around herself, and whispered, "My name is Rowan White."

CHAPTER THREE

TABBY

1992

Tabitha Cross ignored the sound of her father's bottle of whiskey hitting the floor. It didn't shatter dramatically but rather landed with a thud. Sad and empty. Just like this house, just like them.

Levi Cross's hand dangled off the side of the couch, limp, his fingernails dirty and jagged where they brushed the hardwood. Once upon a time those fingernails had been neat, trimmed, and clean. Once upon a time Levi Cross had given a shit.

Then Jenny had died.

Tabby ignored the rumbling drag of phlegm and air against the back of Levi's nostrils and stooped to retrieve the discarded bottle of Jack, moving to the kitchen to line it up with its predecessors. Sometimes Tabby would collect them in plastic bags and drive them to gas stations' trash cans to throw them away so their neighbors wouldn't see the evidence of Levi's despair at the curb on garbage day.

It wasn't her father's fault. It was the fault of the monster who had killed Jenny. If he was caught, if he was punished, her dad would get better.

That's what Tabby had told herself, at least.

Once upon a time she'd probably even believed it. Certainly, she had when she'd been a ten-year-old kid, Jenny's death fresh and raw and painful. But that had been nearly a decade ago. Tabby was nineteen now, and Jenny's murderer had yet to be found in all that time. The cops had never even come up with a suspect beyond their father—who would have killed himself before ever laying a hand on Jenny—and a mysterious older boyfriend who had never materialized beyond whispers from Jenny's friends.

In her most brutally honest moments, Tabby could admit that her father was too far gone at this point, even if Jenny's killer was caught today. It wouldn't be enough to lure Levi back into the world.

Her father had died that same night Jenny had. Except that it was almost worse for him, stuck with the living, trapped in place, tortured with the knowledge that he was here and not with his daughter.

It had never seemed to matter that he still had one girl left. Tabby wasn't enough. She'd never been enough.

Tabby walked through their small house, turning off lights, collecting trash and laundry as she went. She lingered by Jenny's door—always, always, always closed. She'd gone in there once, when she'd been twelve. Jenny had been gone for two years, and Tabby wanted a book she knew Jenny had kept by her bed.

That had been the only time Levi had ever struck Tabby. Hard, across the face, the blow sending her to the floor. Levi had sobbed, staring at his own hand like it hadn't belonged to him.

She hadn't gone back in since.

But Tabby liked to stop here. Liked to remember the times she'd pressed her ear to the gap near the carpet to try to hear Jenny when she talked on the phone.

Once the cops had moved on from Levi to the mysterious-older-boyfriend theory, they'd asked Tabby time and again if she'd ever overheard Jenny call someone, a particular boy, perhaps hiding it from their father.

All Tabby had been able to tell the detectives was that there had been a man. He'd bumped into Jenny at her high school's Fall Festival, held just weeks before her disappearance. He'd talked to her, given her his number. But that hadn't been anything new.

Boys always talked to Jenny when she took Tabby to the mall, to the grocery store. The only reason Tabby had remembered the encounter at all when the cops had grilled her was because Jenny had lingered with him so long that the cotton candy vendor had been closed by the time they'd gotten there. Tabby had thrown a fit, and Jenny had called her a baby, which had made Tabby only cry harder.

The detectives had tensed at the story, their eyes hungry on her face.

Could she describe the person?

"Blond" is all she'd been able to offer. The man at the Phillips Academy's festival had been older, an adult, and kids don't remember what adults look like other than in broad strokes.

It had been enough to confirm what a few of Jenny's schoolmates had said—that she had met a new, older boyfriend at the festival. The same older boyfriend who they reported waited for Jenny after some of her field hockey practices. Including the one on the day she had last been seen alive.

Levi had gripped Tabby's wrists, his eyes scary, wide and dark, as he'd begged her to remember if she'd ever heard his name. That's all they needed, just a name.

Sometimes Tabby wondered if Levi blamed her for not knowing. Not intentionally, of course, but Jenny's murder had a way of bringing out her father's worst demons. Sometimes Tabby caught him watching her too closely, like maybe he thought she was hiding the answer, like maybe, if just in the smallest way possible, she was partly at fault.

He didn't seem to realize she would give anything to know.

Finally moving on past Jenny's room, Tabby headed for the broom closet–size office at the back of the house, the one she kept locked. Not that Levi really wandered beyond his own domains these days—the couch, the kitchen, the space outside Jenny's room. But she didn't want him stumbling in there.

She opened the door, sank into the chair behind the battered desk she'd rescued from the landfill one lucky day last year. Then she turned her attention to the police file on the desk, the one she had all but memorized.

It had been six months since she'd finally been able to get a fake ID so that she could get into a cop bar. She'd told herself she was going there because it was in her neighborhood, convenient, and she knew the bouncer never checked IDs too closely, because what underage delinquent would sneak into a place known to be frequented by BPD's finest?

But if pressed, she knew it was because she couldn't get the thought out of her head that there might be something in Jenny's official file, something that the cops might not recognize as important. If only she had that folder, she could solve the mystery of Jenny's death.

It had taken three months to catch the eye of a fresh-faced rookie, and then three weeks before she'd been able to talk him into getting her the file.

No one would miss it, she'd promised him.

Jennifer Cross was nothing but a cold case from the early eighties, after all.

There had been nothing new in the official details, because that was Tabby's life. Never lucky.

But the only thing worse than reading it again was not reading it again.

Levi wasn't the only one in the house who sought oblivion through self-harm. Tabby simply had different methods of chasing the pain.

Now, Tabby stared at the pictures of her sister's brutalized body and waited patiently for the familiar numbness to take her away.

CHAPTER FOUR

GRETCHEN

Now

"You brought Rowan's file, didn't you?" Gretchen asked. If Marconi wanted any other acknowledgment that she may have finally gotten through to Gretchen, she would be waiting a long time.

Marconi didn't say anything, just bent over to dig in her bag. She emerged triumphantly, file in hand.

Gretchen eyed the thing without taking it. "What does Shaughnessy say about all this?"

For the first time all morning, Marconi hesitated. After a beat of silence, she lifted one shoulder. "He's not a fan."

Considering he'd been the lead detective on Rowan's case, Gretchen guessed that was an understatement.

"You're not worried about that?" Gretchen didn't care what Shaughnessy thought, but Marconi was the man's current partner. And as an empath—the label Gretchen had learned to give "normal" people once they'd started calling her a sociopath—Marconi cared more than Gretchen did about interpersonal dynamics.

"I have vacation days for a reason," Marconi said without any inflection.

Gretchen laughed, making sure it had a cruel edge to it because she didn't like the unnamed flutter in her chest at the implication that Marconi cared about her. Sociopaths could have friends, as Gretchen had informed Marconi many times. They needed people in their lives who knew exactly what they were and didn't ask for anything more. But that didn't mean the process of making a friend was comfortable.

"If you're spending your vacation days on me, your life is even more pathetic than I'd guessed," Gretchen said, hard and derisive. "And that was already a low bar to beat."

Marconi rolled her eyes and flipped Gretchen off, a gesture that had become familiar after working only one case together.

Not that Marconi had left Gretchen alone the past three months following the Kent investigation. This wasn't even close to the first time that she'd badgered her way into Gretchen's apartment, trying to yank her out of the spiral Marconi herself had kicked off by forcing Gretchen to confront her past.

"What was that?" Marconi said, overloud. Gretchen winced as her hangover reared its head. "I couldn't hear you over the sound of *your* life spinning out of control."

"Please," Gretchen purred, amused now. "You haven't seen me out of control yet."

Marconi jerked her head toward the door, a subtle reminder that Gretchen had pinned her there earlier.

Gretchen laughed. "The fact that you'll have bruises instead of a gaping chest wound should tell you everything you need to know about my control."

A corner of Marconi's lips twitched. "My hero."

The easy dismissal would normally have grated on Gretchen's raw skin, but she was too tired from too many months of too much drinking and too little sleep. Walking the fine line of control had always been draining. But letting herself step off into the abyss, letting herself revel in her impulses instead of binding them tightly, had been exhausting. Not the bliss of release itself, but pulling back every morning. It had become harder and harder to remember that she liked her life more than she liked the rush of indulging.

"You need a case," Marconi said again, slapping the file down on the small coffee table between them.

Gretchen had started ignoring calls from the Boston PD the day Marconi had slid her file across the sticky table of the pizza place—the one Gretchen had been eating in to celebrate closing the Viola Kent investigation.

Eventually the calls had stopped coming, and Shaughnessy had started showing up in a dark sedan at the end of her street.

He'd been watching Gretchen almost her entire life, waiting for her to lose control again, a self-appointed guard despite the fact that she'd never been charged with a crime. As an adult, she'd used that obsession of his as motivation to keep her more destructive impulses in check. She'd led her life with one guiding principle—she refused to prove Shaughnessy right, refused to confirm his suspicions that she was nothing better than a killer who couldn't be caught.

But nearly thirty years of an *almost*-perfect record—she couldn't deny there'd been a time or two that she'd broken a few bones, a time or two she'd pulled out scissors with intent—and he still started sniffing around anytime she fell out of contact for more than a few weeks.

It hadn't happened in years, not since she'd more consistently been called on to help with the murder cases. They helped scratch her itch, took the edge off her need for violence and destruction, a fact she'd admitted to Shaughnessy.

Marconi was right, as much as Gretchen hated to acknowledge it. She needed a case.

For the first time in her adult life, Gretchen actually let herself consider the idea of her own innocence—and not just that knee-jerk, defensive reaction that had her mouthing off to Shaughnessy anytime he brought up the possibility that she was a killer.

"Tell me your theory," Gretchen demanded, instead of taking the folder.

A flash of triumph was quickly hidden behind Marconi's neutral expression. "Someone was setting you up to take the fall."

"Right," Gretchen said slowly, knowing the tone was obnoxious. If she wasn't guilty, that was the obvious alternative. "But who?"

"That's what I need you for," Marconi said, unruffled. "There's only so much I can get from Shaughnessy's account of the incident."

The incident. It was such a bland euphemism for the brutal murder of a woman who'd been killed in her own bed while she'd been sleeping. Presumably attacked by her unstable eight-year-old niece.

Gretchen stood up, the hem of the sweater brushing against her thighs. She nudged the curtain aside, swept the street, knowing exactly what she'd find. "You brought a friend."

"Here when I pulled up," Marconi corrected, like it was normal that Shaughnessy was staked out at the end of the block. The man had a solid track record as a cop, but that didn't mean he didn't have some disturbing quirks, most notably his obsessive nature that would cross the line to inappropriate for anyone who played by normal social rules.

"So he knows you're here."

Marconi shrugged again. "Like I said, I'm on vacation."

Why? Gretchen wanted to ask. *Why are you doing this? Why are you risking your career for me?*

She wouldn't, though. Gretchen had long ago given up trying to understand the motives of people with soft, squishy emotions.

Another question sat on her tongue. *What happens if we find out I really did kill Rowan?*

Again, she refused to give voice to it. Marconi was more rational than some of the other partners Shaughnessy had taken on over the years, could think in shades of gray rather than the black and white of most law enforcement.

Marconi had a moral compass, though, and it pointed north. She might seem to be on Gretchen's side now, but she'd be hard-pressed to walk away from solid evidence that proved Gretchen was guilty of cold-blooded murder, if that's what it came down to.

Maybe it was tempting to believe any evidence that emerged would point to Gretchen being set up to take the fall, but she was too realistic to actually think that would be the outcome.

It was entirely possible that instead they'd find something that would finally let Shaughnessy arrest her. His biggest dream come true.

Without taking her eyes off Shaughnessy's car, Gretchen asked, "Where shall we start?"

"We need to figure out who would have known to frame you, for one," Marconi said. "And then who would have motive to kill Rowan."

Gretchen held back the snarky response to the obvious little to-do list. Instead, she simply nodded. "Those would be good places to start."

Marconi rolled her eyes at the tone. "Let's start with everything you know. About your aunt, about the murder. About your family."

Gretchen shifted, deliberately dropped her eyes to the file, then raised one brow. All the details would be there, and they both knew Marconi had pored over the thing until she knew it word for word.

Marconi shook her head. "No. Tell me what *you* know. Not what the police report says."

"How about you do your job and ask me specific questions instead of me having to do all the work," Gretchen suggested.

It had taken years of research, of watching movies and soap operas and YouTube videos, reading books about body language and facial expressions, more recently listening to psychology podcasts, before Gretchen could confidently navigate social situations without people seeing that she was all smoke and mirrors, hiding a void where a personality and emotions should reside. Through hard trial and error, she'd managed to figure out how to strike the right balance, how to utilize sarcasm and irony to soften her edges.

And she knew—*she knew*—that on top of the rest of the jabs from the morning, that remark had been too harsh, too much of her unfiltered thoughts without the light teasing that made it socially acceptable.

Marconi studied her instead of flinching back, instead of leaving. She was wearing that careful expression of hers that gave away nothing of her thoughts.

Careful.

It was strange that that was the best word to describe Marconi when she actively aligned herself with a sociopath, never showing an ounce of fear. But Gretchen had noticed it before, and she noticed it now. Marconi didn't move through the world like most other people Gretchen had encountered, with seemingly uncontrolled reactions. Everything anyone got to see of Marconi was vetted, deliberate.

For the span of a heartbeat, Gretchen wondered how and why Marconi had so much practice hiding her thoughts. It wasn't just that she was a cop—Gretchen had known plenty of those who couldn't control themselves for all the money in her bank account. It made her pause. Though Gretchen had been insisting Marconi didn't know her well enough to assume certain behaviors, Gretchen had forgotten that the opposite was true.

Any other time, the curiosity would have bloomed, deepened, grown claws and dug in to well-armored flesh. But Gretchen had more pressing matters to deal with.

"Here's the deal, because I know this is harder for you than you'd ever dare admit," Marconi said, her voice even but firm. "I'm going to give you a pass on a few of those. Let's say two a day for the foreseeable future."

Gretchen smirked because she enjoyed this side of Marconi. She'd once seen the woman nearly strangle a sleazy tabloid reporter without breaking a sweat because he'd hit on her. "Careful" did not mean that Marconi was lacking a spine. "And then?"

Marconi's eyes narrowed, like she could sense that there were few threats that would actually intimidate Gretchen. Other people's consequences mattered little to her. It was the ones she imposed on herself that kept her in line.

"And then I'll stop telling you what I think," Marconi said, the smallest trace of arrogance in her voice.

Marconi sat back, taking Gretchen's silence for what it was—victory. But she didn't waste time gloating. Instead, she did what Gretchen had asked in the first place. And that's why they worked well together. Marconi could hit back when needed, but she didn't hold grudges; nor did she cut off her nose to spite her face.

"Why was Rowan staying with you the night she was murdered?" Marconi started, probably thinking it was a softball.

The memories weren't easily accessible, though, even the ones before the actual night her aunt had died. Gretchen had built a wall around them, had hidden them away in the darkest, most secret part of her mind. They didn't dare creep into her present, not even when she let her attention drift, not in the boring moments, nor the ones that might remind her of her childhood. The closest they'd come to knocking through her defenses had been when Viola Kent had burst into the headlines.

The case had been so similar to Gretchen's own—a young girl with a personality disorder accused of brutally stabbing her mother—that it had taken a three-day binge to properly lock the memories up once more.

Normal people might be able to see a therapist, perhaps slowly work through the trauma. But Gretchen simply wasn't equipped with the ability to process it.

"Rowan was living with us back then," Gretchen finally answered. "She was . . . My father called her the black sheep of the family. But we were all terrible, I think."

"What do you mean?" Marconi asked.

Gretchen swallowed the last of her coffee, staring longingly at the bottom of the mug.

Then she sighed, and all her carefully constructed walls crumbled into dust.

CHAPTER FIVE

SHAUGHNESSY

1983

Rowan White had gone catatonic by the time they reached the police station, and Shaughnessy wanted to follow suit.

She sat silently in the cold metal police chair next to his desk, staring at the wall behind him.

God, he was too new for this. They'd given him his badge and his gun all of six months ago. He stared at the paper in front of him, the one with all the blank spaces he should have been able to fill out an hour ago when he'd first started questioning her. The words blurred, and he pressed his thumbs into his eyes.

A medic had seen the girl, at least. The source of the blood on her had been deep knife cuts all up and down the outside of both her arms. The bandages were now hidden beneath the blanket she was still clutching with a death grip.

She was a delicate thing, her bones fine, her features carved from expensive marble. Rich, Shaughnessy guessed. She made him feel clumsy, made him aware of all the calluses on his hands. Made him feel like she would break apart if he even thought about touching her.

Her ice-blonde hair hung limp around her shoulders, her frost-coated blue eyes dim and vacant. And yet he could tell she was beautiful underneath the layer of grime and exhaustion and what looked like torture.

If he had to guess at her age, he'd put her around seventeen. Only a handful of years younger than he was.

"Miss White," he said, as gentle as his thick, rough accent would allow. He glanced around the mostly empty room like it would offer some relief, wondering where the hell all the senior officers were. "Can you tell me what happened to you?"

He half expected that the girl wouldn't react at all. But at the question, her attention slid to him and she blinked in that slow, dazed way of hers.

Then she leaned forward, crooking her finger to get him to do the same.

When he was close enough, her lips brushed against the shell of his ear. "They're going to lie."

He flushed hot, then cold, fighting the urge to recoil. "Who's going to lie?"

Before she could answer, the door leading from the station's lobby hit the wall as it opened.

Rowan didn't flinch, didn't cower, didn't even drop to the floor or take off for an exit, which is what Shaughnessy would have put money on given the apparent state of her nerves.

Instead she froze, only her eyes darting across the room to the woman who stood backlit against the hallway light.

Shaughnessy found himself on his feet, blocking Rowan, without even thinking about it.

The woman's attention flew to him, and he knew whom she was here for. The two could have passed for twins had the girl been a little older and the woman a little younger.

"Officer," the woman said, the honorific dripping with a disdain Shaughnessy was used to from his teenage years, catering parties thrown by the rich. "I'm Mrs. Edith White. Thank you for finding my daughter. I can take it from here."

"Uh," Shaughnessy stuttered. "We're going to need her to answer some questions, ma'am. She was in quite a state."

Edith's chin lifted, her eyes narrowing. But he could actually see her reining in the desire to thrash him for getting above his station. His badge might be shiny and new, but it came with some power at least.

She glanced behind him to Rowan, who sat rigid in the seat, any color in her cheeks gone. Then Edith took his elbow, pulling him aside. "This isn't the first attempt at"—her lips pressed together—"taking her own life."

If she'd punched him in the gut, he would have been less surprised.

"Ma'am? You're saying this was a suicide attempt?"

She reached into her bag, pulling out a card. "This is her psychiatrist. We had hoped her stint at the facility had helped, but"—her eyes slipped to the girl—"one step forward, three back. You understand."

He fingered the card. It looked professional.

DR. ANDERS WHITE, PSYCHOANALYST.

White. Did that mean he was related to Rowan? Was that ethical to treat someone you were related to?

They're going to lie.

Shaughnessy shoved the card into his pocket. "She'll still have to answer a few questions."

Edith's demeanor softened so suddenly Shaughnessy fought the desire to step back. She blinked up at him, long, pale lashes aflutter against porcelain skin. "She's fragile, you have to understand. She creates stories, thinks they're real. Anything she could tell you now would likely be pulled from her imagination. Perhaps at a later date? After you've talked to her doctor."

Before he could argue further, Rowan stood up, the blanket pooling at her bare feet.

"She's my mother," she whispered, though her voice carried in the otherwise silent room. "It's all right. I've been foolish."

Shaughnessy opened his mouth, though he didn't know what he would say. She stopped him from having to come up with anything, placing a hand on top of his. "Truly, I'll be fine."

Not sure what else he could do other than arrest both of them and hope for the best, Shaughnessy gave a curt nod and stepped back.

"There's a good girl," Edith said. It sounded kind, the tone gentle and fond. But Shaughnessy couldn't help the shiver that rolled through his muscles, nor could he completely quiet the need to grab the girl and hide her away from the person claiming to be her mother.

Rowan's answering smile was wan but seemed about as genuine as possible given the situation.

Maybe the hostility between the two was all in his imagination. After the night he'd had, Shaughnessy couldn't even blame himself for seeing ghosts where none existed.

Before Rowan let her hand drop from Shaughnessy's, though, she tucked her fingers into his palm.

Only when she moved away did he realize that she'd slipped him a piece of paper.

He watched the pair depart; then he sat back down, smoothing out the ripped message, the one Rowan must have scrawled when her mother's attention had been on Shaughnessy.

There in the blue ink of the pen that still rested on the corner of the desk closest to her chair was a simple message.

There are more girls. Find them.

CHAPTER SIX

GRETCHEN

Now

"Perhaps the first thing you should know is my family is fabulously wealthy," Gretchen said. She'd gone for a refill of her Irish coffee, and Marconi still hadn't said a word about it.

At that statement, though, Marconi snorted out a laugh. "Yeah, I didn't think you'd bought that Porsche with your police consultant money."

The car was a luxury that Gretchen had allowed herself. She enjoyed the power, the speed, the way people watched her when she drove it. More than one detective had lobbed a snide insult at her about it, but the comments were rooted in a jealousy that was almost as addictive and thrilling as the murder cases themselves.

"It was my grandmother's money," Gretchen said.

"Your grandmother?"

"Edith White. Her father was an oil baron and she was the sole heir, much to his everlasting disappointment, I'm sure." While Gretchen had never met him, she'd long suspected the rotten genes in their family had come from the old man. In the portraits throughout the White town house, his hands were big, meaty, with knuckles that looked like they could deliver cruel blow after cruel blow without remorse.

"Edith married Theodore White, who did his best to burn through the inheritance in the year between their wedding and his death," Gretchen said. These were easy facts so far. It would get harder soon.

"Did she kill him?" Marconi asked, her slightly raised brows the only noticeable hint of surprise.

"Of course not," Gretchen said with an exaggerated wink, pitching her voice to overly innocent. "She would have been charged if she had."

"Right," Marconi responded, drawing out the word.

"Between the drinking and whoring, he did manage to get her with child before he departed the earth," Gretchen said. "My father, Anders, was born six months after Theodore died."

"Anders White," Marconi said to herself, like she was getting familiar with a cast of characters and it helped saying their names out loud.

"Dear ole Daddy," Gretchen said. "Rowan didn't come along until Anders was twelve."

"Big gap," Marconi commented absently.

Gretchen ignored the obvious statement. "No one talks about who her father was."

"And there's no chance that mystery man is a player here?" Marconi asked.

Her knee-jerk reaction was no. But . . .

"Never say never," she said with a little shrug. "I don't think he's involved in Rowan's death, though. From what I could tell, it sounded like a one-night stand where Grandma went slumming with the normal people. Which of course is horribly embarrassing for Edith to admit, so no one ever talks about it."

Marconi accepted it easily but did jot something down in that little notebook of hers. "Okay."

"Edith hated them both," Gretchen continued. "Anders and Rowan."

"Why?"

"She wasn't exactly the maternal type to begin with. I think had she been an animal like a lion, she would just as soon have eaten them as raised them," Gretchen said, amused at that thought. "But the socially acceptable excuse for hating them? The one she probably told herself? We were an old-money family; reputation was all that mattered to my grandmother. And pretty much since her birth, Rowan did her best to run the family name into the ground."

"How'd she do that?" Marconi asked, and Gretchen wondered if she was thinking that Gretchen pretty spectacularly had taken care of that in one swift move.

"Rowan was in and out of psychiatric facilities when she was a teenager," Gretchen said. "I didn't get the sense it was voluntary."

"There's no shame in that," Marconi protested, like Gretchen should have guessed she would.

Gretchen rolled her eyes. "You're talking to a psychologist with an antisocial personality disorder diagnosis. *I* know there's no shame in that. Tell that to a woman who thinks being spotted in sweatpants is a crime worthy of disownment."

Marconi accepted that with a nod. "What was she in for?"

"Depression, mainly," Gretchen said. "I think the last one before she came of age was for a suicide attempt that was rather dramatic."

"Dramatic how?"

"The cops were involved," Gretchen said. "Which would have made Grandma Edith's head explode."

"When was this?"

Gretchen did the math. "Eighty-three, I think. It was only ever referenced in vague, passive-aggressive asides during fights."

"So it's safe to say she was a troubled teen?" Marconi asked.

"Troubled." Gretchen rolled the word around. For some reason, that didn't sit quite right.

"No?"

"Does reality matter?" Gretchen asked, with a little shrug. "Or just the stories we tell?"

"What do you mean?"

"If you tell the world someone is crazy enough times, the world stops believing them when they say they aren't," Gretchen said, lifting one shoulder.

"That's how it was with Rowan?" Marconi pressed.

"I don't know," Gretchen admitted, one of her least favorite phrases. But everything she knew about her aunt's life had come secondhand from people who had an agenda.

"All right, what about Anders?" Marconi asked. "Why did Edith . . . ?"

"Despise him?" Gretchen finished the question for her when she paused. "Maybe she sensed the darkness."

"But she left *you* all her money?" Marconi winced at the implication once the question was out. As if Gretchen would be insulted.

"Her attempt to restore the family name, if you can believe it," Gretchen said. "She thought if she left me the inheritance, people would at least start to wonder if I was innocent after all. The fact that it screwed her children over was probably an added benefit."

"She was alive when Rowan was killed," Marconi observed. "Who did she think did it?"

"Me probably." Gretchen shrugged. "Like I said, she only cared about perception, not the truth."

Marconi hummed out a little sound but moved on. "Speaking of siblings, you have one, don't you? A sister."

Gretchen's nails dug into the soft flesh of her palm, and she welcomed the pain. "Fran," she managed, through a clenched jaw.

"I take it your relationship wasn't rosy?" Marconi asked in a voice far too gentle, far too understanding. It made Gretchen want to scratch either herself or Marconi until blood spilled onto the floor. She didn't care whose it was.

"Those inductive skills of yours are nearly Sherlockian," Gretchen bit out, the tone too mean. But she couldn't help it. Her brain wasn't designed to truly factor in consequences.

Marconi sighed. "That's two."

The self-destruct button that was always lit up with flashing neon signs beckoned. Gretchen had been jumping on it with abandon as of late. If she was going to go down this rabbit hole that was her past, and it seemed like she was, Gretchen needed to find that rigid self-control again.

The socially appropriate thing to say here was obvious, even to her, so she forced it out. Marconi was lucky she'd proven herself useful enough for this. "I'm sorry."

Marconi's nose wrinkled. "That felt . . . wrong in so many ways."

Something within Gretchen relaxed, and she laughed genuinely for the first time in what felt like months. "Think of how it felt to say it."

"I don't need your fake apologies," Marconi said. Then she narrowed her eyes, her scrutiny intense but not as unwelcome as earlier. "Do you want to do this?"

A small part of Gretchen hated Marconi for making her admit it. And so she held on to her answer until the silence grew awkward. Finally she relented. "Yes."

Marconi studied her for another long minute before she nodded. "Then cut the shit. You're not five—you're a grown adult who knows how to be civil. Act like it."

Gretchen yanked on the urge to lash out once more, wrapped the figurative leash around her hand, held firm. "Fran is the perfect one. My mother's mini-me."

"Your mother?" Marconi asked, no longer hesitant or gentle. She'd learned her lesson as well. "Tell me about her."

"Bardot White," Gretchen said. "Née Bisset."

Marconi squinted into the middle distance. "French?"

"Somewhere in her family tree, sure," Gretchen said. "More importantly, upper-class Bostonian."

"But your grandmother didn't approve of her?" Marconi asked. "Even with that pedigree?"

"Approve and like are two different things," Gretchen said, and congratulated herself on hitting light and amused rather than condescending and derisive. Three months might have made her rusty, but a lifetime of honing the skills that she needed to pass as normal didn't just disappear overnight. "My father managed the seemingly impossible feat of marrying someone nearly as monstrous as he is."

Marconi's eyes dropped to the file. "He was a psychoanalyst?"

"Is."

Marconi's chin jerked up at that. "Excuse me?"

It was better than *What?*—a response that Gretchen hated—but only slightly. Gretchen didn't bother repeating herself; Marconi had heard her perfectly fine.

"Your father is still alive?" Marconi tried again, more precise this time.

"Yes?" Gretchen said, both confused and intrigued by the apparent surprise. "He's nearing his seventies but still kicking, much to my everlasting disappointment." She paused. "So is my mother, just in case that wasn't clear."

"But . . ." Marconi stopped herself, shook her head, looked back down at the file like it would offer answers. "You don't . . ."

"I don't visit them?" Gretchen asked on a laugh. "Why on earth would I do that?"

"They might have an idea who actually killed Rowan," Marconi said slowly, like she was talking to an imbecile.

Gretchen decided not to mention the fact that her father had considered having her institutionalized following Rowan's death. Anders had been just as convinced as Shaughnessy of Gretchen's guilt. It had been Edith who had saved Gretchen from that fate. "You're going to want to talk to him, aren't you?"

"Why yes, yes I am."

"I'm going to need more whiskey for this," Gretchen said on the final swallow from her mug. She could feel Marconi's eyes on her back.

"You really don't like your family, do you?" Marconi said. "Is this a sociopath thing or a Gretchen White thing?"

Gretchen lifted her brows. "Can you stand your family?"

"Maybe if they were alive," Marconi said. It sounded empty, but not as if she were devastated. Tone, at times, could elude Gretchen, as could emotional nuance, but she didn't think any layers existed beneath Marconi's *just the facts ma'am* answer.

"All dead?" Tact wasn't Gretchen's forte on the best of days, and this was far from the best of days.

"Just me left," Marconi confirmed, and again Gretchen shoved aside the curiosity with both hands.

"Ah, the dream," Gretchen mused. If only the rest of her family were dead. Maybe the case would be harder to solve, but that was quite literally the one downside Gretchen could see.

Marconi shook her head as if exasperated, but to Gretchen it seemed more perfunctory than actually annoyed.

"How were they 'monstrous'?" Marconi asked instead of scolding her.

"Anders is . . . mercurial," Gretchen said. "Edith did a number on him, I think. Made him obsessed with the family name, always trying to please her, failing miserably."

"Mercurial," Marconi repeated. "Bipolar?"

Gretchen contemplated that. "He's never been diagnosed with anything—would probably cut off his own tongue before letting himself be evaluated."

"But what do you think?" Marconi pressed. "You said Edith might have sensed a 'darkness' in him."

"Possibly some personality disorder, but there was no mania or depression," Gretchen said, trying to unwind the facts of her childhood from her inevitably biased version of it. "Sometimes terrible people are just born terrible."

Marconi was quiet beside her. And then: "Would he have had motive to kill Rowan? If he was that concerned with what people thought about your family. Maybe she did something that was his final straw."

"Does it matter?" Pointless theoretical discussions were a waste of time unless they moved the case forward. It hadn't been Anders. "He'd been away at a conference in Texas at the time of Rowan's death, which was verified by countless eyewitnesses and security video from the hotel."

"He could have hired someone to kill her," Marconi suggested. "Maybe that's why he got out of town. Set himself up with a perfect alibi."

Gretchen shook her head. "If he was going to kill her, he would have wanted to do it himself."

"That kind of sounds like a psychopath," Marconi pointed out.

Gretchen spared her a smile, pleased her lessons from months earlier had stuck.

Most laymen use the words "sociopath" and "psychopath" interchangeably, though neither are very technical terms. The way Gretchen had explained it to cops whose eyes glazed over when she started dropping scientific lingo was to think Wall Street bro versus Ted Bundy.

A significant percentage of sociopaths passed for normal—they were CEOs of Fortune 500 companies, politicians, defense lawyers, the like. Some didn't even realize why they never quite fit in, existing on the outskirts, maybe getting fired more often than their peers, maybe ruining a few more relationships than would generally be considered normal. But it was a leap for the average person to add all that up and diagnose themselves as a sociopath. After all, they'd probably never murdered anyone, and that's what the media and pop culture told people sociopaths did.

Psychopaths, on the other hand, landed in jail more often than not. Not all killed, but there were plenty of ways to inflict violence even if it never turned fatal. It wasn't *if* a psychopath would be consumed by the flames, but *when*.

Gretchen had trouble picturing Anders White as the latter, but she was enough of a scientist to admit to her own blind spots.

"Maybe he is." Gretchen lifted one shoulder. Maybe those tight reins she so prided herself on were as genetic as the darkness that lived inside her. "All I know is our particular gene pool should be heavily diluted with bleach and then drained."

"Okay, we'll move him to the back burner for now," Marconi said with a decisive nod. "Your mother. She was there that night Rowan was killed."

"She was also cleared by Shaughnessy," Gretchen said. "She's strict, holds herself and others to nearly impossible standards."

"That must have been a fun household," Marconi said.

"Genetics loads the gun, environment pulls the trigger," Gretchen drawled. "You've heard me say that."

"Sounds like you could have ended up on the far end of the spectrum," Marconi said. Like most things, sociopathic tendencies presented on a spectrum, one that included lack of remorse, delusions of grandeur, a repeated failure to accept responsibility. Gretchen scored just high enough for a diagnosis, but the fact that she was on the low end helped her move in normal society with an ease those on the upper end couldn't manage. "Is Bardot like you?"

"A sociopath?" Gretchen hadn't actually thought about it before—she tried to think about her family as little as possible. "She certainly has some traits. But I'm not sure the answer is as easy as that."

"There are cruel people who aren't sociopaths," Marconi said. "Would she have had a motive to kill Rowan? She was the one who found you, right?"

"They didn't get along," Gretchen said, something tickling at the back of her skull. *The one who found you.* That didn't sit right for some reason. But of course it had to have been Bardot who had screamed. Fran had slept through the murder, and there had been no one else in the house. "I find it hard to imagine Bardot getting her hands dirty like that, though."

"Got it," Marconi said, though more in neutral acknowledgment than in agreement. "What about your sister?"

"Personality-wise, Fran's the same as Bardot," Gretchen said. "Her little clone. But no disorders." Gretchen paused. "Though that seems unlikely given our family. So I'll amend that to 'none that I know of.'"

"Is she still in the area?"

"In Waltham, married with two point five perfect children," Gretchen said. "Living off Bardot's trust fund and whatever the bland potato she married does."

Marconi pulled out her notebook, jotted down God knew what. "I take it you're not in contact?"

"As last I checked, hell had not frozen over," Gretchen said. "That would be no."

"And your parents are . . ."

"In Cambridge," Gretchen supplied. "Anders still guest lectures at Harvard."

Marconi went quiet, long enough to get Gretchen to look over, to identify and then understand the doubt in her expression.

"You don't believe me," Gretchen realized. "About what they're like."

Marconi opened her mouth, closed it, opened it, and still nothing came out.

"Yes, a delightful impression of a fish, dear," Gretchen said.

Rolling her eyes, Marconi shifted forward in her seat a little like she was trying to soften a blow. "I believe you're a self-proclaimed sociopath, and that might not give you the best reading of your family's personalities."

And that shut Gretchen up.

"It's still helpful to hear about them," Marconi said, like some kind of offering.

Gretchen waved a careless hand in her direction. "I'm not insulted. I was merely impressed by your reasoning."

Marconi gasped, loud and overdramatic, clutching her chest. "Be still my heart. A compliment from Gretchen White."

"Don't get used to it," Gretchen said with a proper amount of irritation. But her lips twitched, and for the first time in three months she felt on almost-solid ground.

Gretchen stretched her neck, rolled her shoulders. It wasn't just the easy banter with Marconi that had her feeling like she was no longer a hairbreadth away from an abyss she couldn't come back from. Talking about her family for the first time in decades felt like pus being let out of a rotting boil. The sour smell of it was almost too much to take, and yet the relief was there, just out of sight. A promise.

Then Marconi went in with her knife one more time. "All right. Now tell me about Rowan."

Gretchen thought, *I wanted to kill her before I even understood what killing was.*

Gretchen said, "To be honest, I don't remember her at all."

CHAPTER SEVEN

TABBY

1992

Tabby paused outside the door of the diner, plucking at a loose thread on her fingerless gloves. Her breath puffed out, dissolved, and she found herself wanting to follow its lead.

But Nick had caught sight of her already. She'd always thought the phrase "face lit up" was a silly cliché. Except there was no other way to describe what Nick's expression did whenever he looked at her.

There was no good cliché to describe how much she hated it.

What he saw, she didn't know. Her thick mahogany hair was the one feature that made her pretty, and so she tended to wear it tucked up under a knit hat anytime she met with Nick O'Leary. The rest of her was *fine*. A pale, round face, brown eyes, a body that was exactly average. She could dress it all up and draw a few glances, but no one else would have called her beautiful—let alone captivating—the way Nick did.

She pushed into the diner.

He stood to greet her, his metaphorical tail all but wagging. His wet lips dragged against her cheekbone, and she fought the instinct to swipe at the saliva left behind. He would never say anything, but he'd give her that kicked-puppy look that always had her wanting to screw him just to make it go away.

After they ordered, he leaned forward, his eyes darting around. "So did you find anything in the file?"

And that's why Tabby put up with him. Nick was a lowly uniformed cop with big dreams that made him easy to manipulate. He'd been the one to finally smuggle her Jenny's official file. Tabby didn't ask how he did it, and he didn't offer. She guessed it wasn't any kind of impressive feat, otherwise he would have bragged about it.

Tabby dug a thumb into the soft spot of her temple, wondering for a strange, curious moment if anyone had actually died that way. Such a vulnerable spot, right there, waiting to be exploited.

She sighed, dropped her hands to the table. "No, nothing new in there. Not really."

Nick blew out a breath and sat back. He'd wanted to be the hero, she knew. Wanted to somehow provide her with the key to unlock a mystery that would change her life.

But she doubted anyone had that. Jenny was just another cold case in a long list of cold cases. Just another dead girl in a seemingly endless series of dead girls throughout history.

The only reason Tabby had been holding on to hope that she might solve the crime was the official file, and that had been a bust. She'd go out with Nick a few more times because she didn't want him to realize she'd used him. But then? Maybe she'd actually have to move on with her life.

The waitress deposited their plates with a weary "Enjoy" before heading back to the kitchen.

"Maybe we could talk to some of her classmates from the Phillips Academy again?" Nick offered up as he dipped his fork into his runny eggs. "That school is full of ruthless, rich brats who would probably kill someone just for the fun of it."

"They didn't know anything then," Tabby pointed out, and shoved the buckwheat pancakes she'd ordered toward Nick. He'd eat them without really realizing she hadn't had anything. He wasn't the most observant cop on the block.

"Maybe one was lying," Nick said, eyes wide. He thought they lived in a cheesy made-for-TV movie.

Tabby didn't have the heart to tell him they were in a Stephen King horror flick instead.

She lifted one shoulder and stared out the window. Nick filled the silence with idle chatter because he was one of those people who hated silence. Tabby actually liked the quiet, liked how it almost buzzed and sank into the creases in her skin and those spaces in her body that ached to be filled with *something*.

Nick paid for the meals—both of which he'd consumed—and kissed her on the cheek again, hot and wet and open. Why hadn't he ever learned that wasn't appropriate? Maybe it was the same reason she never slapped him on the wrist for it. Those puppy dog eyes and sweet, earnest face let him get away with a lot.

When she started down the sidewalk back to her house, she caught sight of a man in her peripheral vision. He was leaning against a car, his legs out in front of him, one corner of his mouth crooked up, sunglasses hooked into the vee of his shirt.

Tabby glanced over her shoulder to see if Nick had disappeared around the corner. The coast clear, she sidled up to the man, tugged off her knit hat so that her hair spilled out and over her shoulders, tumbling down her back.

His smile widened.

Then slowly, ever so slowly, he reached out and brushed the pad of his thumb over the exact spot Nick had kissed, like he was wiping away the memory of it.

"Better," he said, his eyes soft, affectionate. Tabby had fallen for his eyes first, then his face, then his laugh, then the way he touched her body.

He'd found her in a grocery store two months ago staring at the empty cereal aisle at 2:00 a.m., numb after reading Jenny's file for the first time. He'd asked if she'd needed help and then called her a taxi and even paid for it ahead of time—which had been good because she would have had to dash out at a stoplight otherwise.

Before the taxi had driven off, he'd slipped her a card with his name and number.

Cal Hart.

It sounded fake, and so she assumed it was. She called him "baby," if she had to call him anything, because tasting something like "Cal" on her tongue always left her jittery and nervous. He called her "darling" even though she'd given him her real name.

Even on the off chance that Cal was the name he'd been born with, she still wasn't part of his real life. She knew that with the certainty in which she knew just how many bottles of liquor her father could get through in a week.

Tabby was Cal's dirty little secret, there was no doubt about that. They had sex in hotel rooms, he'd never introduced her to his friends, and he gave her rules on when she could contact him. She would be utterly naive to think that meant anything other than that she was the mistress in this little affair.

But Tabby didn't care. When he touched her, she forgot about Jenny, forgot about torn-up skin, forgot the laugh that should have faded from her memory by now, forgot the way Jenny had tugged on Tabby's hair when she'd teased her.

She didn't love him, but whatever she felt came damn close—a twisted, toxic, rotten kind of love maybe. Because no one else had ever given her that kind of peace before.

At her most paranoid, on the nights she stared at pictures of her murdered sister, Tabby wondered if it really had been a coincidence that Cal had found her in the grocery store that night.

Sometimes Cal would smile and Tabby would remember that Fall Festival, the older man, the flirting, the way he'd slipped a card to Jenny just like Cal had done to Tabby. Her young mind had painted the stranger in broad strokes, but those strokes fit Cal like a well-worn jacket. Blond. Handsome. Charming.

Sometimes she wondered at the timing of it all. How she'd asked Nick to get Jenny's file and then how a few nights later Cal had stumbled upon her.

Sometimes she wondered if she would live the rest of her life paranoid, looking for connections that didn't exist. No one told you that's what tagged along with a brutally murdered sister.

Cal smiled at her now, his big hand wrapping around the nape of her neck, bringing her forward. And she let herself chase oblivion once more, this time in the plush give of his mouth.

When he kissed her like this, she didn't care who he was.

Names were overrated anyway.

———

Tabby smiled into the lackluster hotel pillow as Cal walked his fingertips down the knobs of her spine.

She had always had the impression that Cal was well enough off that he could afford better accommodations than the budget chains he'd always taken her to. But something about the choice felt right. She was a budget chains kind of girl, and she might have fled if he'd tried to take her somewhere fancy.

It was stupid of her, but she liked that he seemed to know her that well.

"Was that your boyfriend?" Cal asked.

"Like you would care," she said, no heat in it. They both knew what this was. And it certainly wasn't exclusive.

He smiled, almost to himself, and traced his way up her back, his fingers tangling in her hair. "He's a cop."

"I'd noticed, believe it or not," Tabby said, wiggling free of his grasp and sitting up. There was no reason to loiter. "I didn't think he wore that uniform because he has a kink."

He stared at her, unnaturally still. "You're using him for something."

Again, that thought niggled at the dark corners of her brain. The one where he'd found her so close to her asking Nick for help with Jenny's case. She dismissed it as easily as it came, hating this version of herself, hating that she always saw monsters where there were just shadows.

Cal was just a rich guy slumming it to get off, nothing more, nothing less. Or maybe he was a rich guy dabbling in the shadier side of the city, padding his bank account in a not quite legal way. She'd been with a few men like that—they always kept their eyes on cops whenever they happened to share the same space with them.

"What makes you think that?" she shot back.

Another long beat passed, the silence taut enough to get her to look up. He watched her until she met his eyes, and then he looked away.

"I could help you instead," he offered, quiet and shy in a way she'd never seen him before.

"Oh yeah?" Tabby said, almost laughing at the absurdity of men. They always thought they could help. "You have an eyewitness to my sister's murder hiding out somewhere?"

They didn't talk about these things with each other. Hardly ever got through a *How are you* exchange before their clothes came off. But he didn't flinch at the verbal jab.

Instead his eyes narrowed. "So I'm right. You're playing Nancy Drew."

"What if I am?" Tabby said, angry, defiant, and chafing at the underlying condescension in his assessment. He didn't need to know she had gotten exactly nowhere in her attempt at amateur detective work. Didn't need to know that earlier that day she was thinking about giving up completely. That one blunt, condescending assessment did it, though—it relit the fire Tabby had kept simmering for a decade. Maybe the file was a bust, but there had to be something else Tabby could try.

She tilted her chin up now, challenging. "What business is it of yours?"

"Girls who play Nancy Drew get murdered," he said, his light tone contrasting with the loaded warning.

"Yeah, well, girls get murdered for just being girls," she said on a tired sigh, the fight going out of her, thinking not only of Jenny but of all the ones who came before and after her. So many. Why'd there always have to be so many murdered girls? "At least I'll have known I tried."

CHAPTER EIGHT

GRETCHEN

Now

"How was there not another viable suspect?" Marconi asked, ripping her napkin into tiny pieces that were accumulating into a small mountain on the table in front of her.

Marconi had suggested they seek out food, and Gretchen had readily agreed. The greasier the better, considering the state of her blood alcohol level.

Gretchen smiled sweetly at the waitress who was busy sending her dirty looks from across the room, possibly for smelling like a distillery at eleven in the morning, and took a large bite of her burger. Around a mouthful of food, she pointed out the obvious. "I was found with the murder weapon."

"I mean, all I've ever heard of the case was that an eight-year-old was the only plausible suspect," Marconi continued, as if Gretchen hadn't said anything. "But it sounds like every person in your family could have been a suspect, along with a host of other people. Your aunt disappeared for years, right? What was she doing during that time? Did she make enemies in the facilities she was in and out of as a teen?

There're so many angles to pursue that make more sense than a nonviolent kid stabbing her aunt to death."

Gretchen raised a brow in a carefully practiced move. "I was found over her bed, covered in blood and still holding the knife."

"Right," Marconi said, drawing out the word. "But was that reality, or was it a story being told? You know as well as I do that you would have been a perfect scapegoat for any murderer who wanted to get away with something."

That was easy enough to say in theory, but the scene had been damning. There was no use pretending otherwise just because Marconi had taken a liking to Gretchen for some reason. "And sometimes everything really is as it seems."

Marconi drummed her fingers on the table. "Who called the police?"

"My mother."

"Bardot Bisset White." Marconi said it quietly, like she just enjoyed hearing the name. "And then Shaughnessy gets his first big homicide case, makes all the headlines, but can't quite pin it on his prime suspect. You." She paused. "If the case was so open-and-shut, why didn't it stick? Why weren't you charged?"

"The prosecutor was afraid of my family." Marconi knew as well as Gretchen did that there was a different justice system for rich people. "Said Shaughnessy didn't have enough hard evidence."

Without her permission, Gretchen's attention drifted over Marconi's shoulder to where Shaughnessy sat parked outside in his sedan, not even trying to blend in. Gretchen shot him a jaunty salute and was disappointed that the angles hid his reaction. "You said . . ." Gretchen shifted her focus back to Marconi. "You said he wouldn't let me consult on cases if he actually thought I did it."

"He wouldn't," Marconi said, not an inch of budge in the assurance. "You have to be around him for about one day to realize that he wouldn't compromise cases like that."

It was true. Gretchen rarely had to testify as a witness for the prosecution, but it wasn't unheard of. Most people had learned to keep their mouths shut about her history, but desperate defense attorneys had been known to open that line of attack if they thought it would serve their client.

She had to be above reproach, impeccably so, if she wanted to still get calls from the Boston PD. And until three months ago, she'd been doing a decent job of it, all things considered.

Gretchen tapped the table. "Give me the file."

Without a word, Marconi slid it over. Gretchen had déjà vu from that pizza place three months earlier. Her hands had been just as sweaty then.

She opened the folder, began to read.

"At 11:37 p.m. on August 11, 1993, Bardot White called 9-1-1 to report a stabbing. The victim was her sister-in-law Rowan White, age twenty-seven. When asked if the victim was still alive, White said she couldn't get close to her."

"'My daughter has a knife,'" Marconi quoted, without taking her eyes off Gretchen's face. "That's how Shaughnessy came to find you still in the room."

Blood. Hot. Wet.

The slippery hilt.

The tree at the window. Beating against the glass.

Rowan's eyes. Still open.

A shadow in the corner.

What . . . who . . . ?

Welcoming numbness called to Gretchen with outstretched arms. It waited, ready to wrap a blanket of fog around the memories so they could be forgotten once more.

Gretchen fought it. This wasn't her case. This was just *a* case. That's how she had to look at it.

An eight-year-old found standing over a bleeding woman, knife in hand.

"Why didn't Bardot just overpower the girl?" Gretchen murmured, only realizing she'd spoken out loud when Marconi sat back, eyes a little wide.

"The girl?" she asked.

Gretchen shook her head. "Me."

A pause, an expression Gretchen couldn't name. But then Marconi let it go. "I wondered that, too. The normal reaction would have been to rush in, grab the knife."

"I was a . . . strange child," Gretchen admitted slowly. "People were . . . scared of me. Even then."

"Had you ever hurt anyone?" Marconi asked, her tone clinical rather than accusatory. "Seriously I mean. Not normal kid stuff."

"Myself, sure," Gretchen said, with a shrug. When she caught Marconi's surprise, she almost laughed. "I wasn't a cutter, nothing like that. I just didn't have any fear or concept of consequences. And that leads to injuries. It's quite common in young sociopaths."

"But your sister? Your friends?" Marconi pressed. "Violence escalates, right? Shouldn't this have started somewhere smaller? If you really did kill Rowan."

"No friends," Gretchen said, her chin going up. "I hadn't learned . . ."

"How to fit in?" Marconi guessed.

"Kids know," Gretchen managed to force out. "When you're not quite right."

"They do indeed," Marconi agreed. "Your sister then?"

Fran.

I'm telling! I'm telling, I'm telling, I'm tel—

No you won't.

"She'd say I did," Gretchen finally said, dancing around the answer. Gretchen had a fast-and-loose relationship with the truth, an even more casual one with lies of omission. But Gretchen wanted to get ahead of whatever narrative Fran had crafted for herself. And Gretchen supposed they would be speaking with her eventually.

Marconi guessed at what she wasn't saying anyway. "So what's the truth?"

Gretchen lifted a careless shoulder. "We hurt each other."

"But she's not"—Marconi waved at Gretchen—"like you?"

Marconi did that sometimes, hesitated to stick a label on Gretchen, like she didn't quite believe it was true.

"No, she's just a bitch," Gretchen said, amused when Marconi wrinkled her nose at the word.

"Where was she that night?"

"Sleeping," Gretchen answered even though that information was in the file.

I want to hear it from you.

Gretchen wondered if Marconi was more interested in the inconsistencies than anything else.

"Was there anyone else in the house?" Marconi pressed. "Staying with you? Visiting? Did Rowan bring home men with her? Was she dating someone?"

The shadow. In the corner of the room.

Gretchen shook her head.

"I don't know," she admitted, again disliking the truth of those words. Gretchen was used to being the one who knew things.

"Okay," Marconi said. "Was there a phone in Rowan's room?"

Gretchen's lip curled back in contempt. "How would I remember that if I don't even remember killing her?"

"Were there phones throughout the town house?" Marconi reframed the question without flinching.

"Not in the bedrooms," Gretchen realized, and ignored the flare of appreciation for Marconi's line of thinking. This had been before the time of cell phones.

"So Bardot ran to go call the police, leaving you alone in the room?" Marconi asked, eyebrows raised. "With Rowan, who was, I presume, dead?"

"She must have," Gretchen said instead of having to admit that she didn't know. Bardot had been the one to call the police—the transcript was right there. She wouldn't have wasted time waking up Fran to come have her supervise her dead aunt and her dead aunt's killer.

"Okay," Marconi said once more, easily. "And Shaughnessy showed up quickly because he'd been in the area when the call came in."

"According to him," Gretchen said.

"He found you in the room still? Clutching the knife?" Marconi asked, and Gretchen nodded once. "Did he say anything? Right in that moment?"

Her head pounded in a dull throb as she tried to remember. "I don't know."

"What's the next thing you remember?" Marconi pressed. "Anything from that night?"

"The station," Gretchen said, not willing to share the blurred memories before that. The shadow in the corner of the room. Was it even real? A horrified voice. *Gretchen, what have you done?* None of that was going to help anyway. "A uniform took me to an interrogation room. My mother called our lawyer, and Shaughnessy questioned me that night."

The interview must be in the file. Marconi likely had it memorized. Still, she asked, "Did you tell him anything?"

"Nothing," Gretchen said. "Quite literally nothing."

"He must have loved that," Marconi said, breaking some of the tension at the table. Gretchen tipped her head in acknowledgment.

"We had a few more chats," Gretchen said, deliberately downplaying the interrogations. "But I couldn't remember anything from that night, and he couldn't believe that."

"He thought you were lying?"

"Yes," Gretchen said, without a trace of doubt. Looking back, she could tell what he'd been doing—changing questions just slightly to trap her in a lie. It was a favorite technique of his.

Marconi's mouth twisted, but she moved on. "Was Rowan living there permanently or just visiting?"

"Living," Gretchen said even though she hadn't realized she'd known the answer. The memories were creeping back, taking up space in her present. "Like I said, she'd disappeared for a few years in her twenties. When she showed back up, she said she was on consistent medication and seeing a therapist."

"You remember that, or you were told that?" Marconi asked.

An answer sat there at the ready. *Yes, I remember.* But she didn't. Not really. There were feelings Gretchen couldn't ignore. *I wanted to kill her before I knew what killing was.* That resentment bordering on hatred had roots that went deep even if Gretchen didn't know the origin of that particular seed.

But everything she "knew" about Rowan had come from her parents, her grandmother. The press, even. They'd all been building a story about Rowan's life that Gretchen had internalized as *real.*

She shook her head instead of giving an answer. For once in her life she didn't have one. Marconi hummed in that considering way that Gretchen was starting to find grating.

"She showed up again in the spring of '93?"

"Summer," Gretchen corrected.

Marconi drummed her fingers on the table, staring out the window at Shaughnessy's sedan. "And then a couple months later, she was dead."

CHAPTER NINE

SHAUGHNESSY

1983

Shaughnessy smoothed a thumb over the ripped edges of the message he'd memorized the first time he'd read it. This had to be the hundredth time, the thousandth time.

There are more girls. Find them.

"You need me to pass a note to your crush, Shaughnessy?" Boyd dropped a heavy hand on Shaughnessy's shoulder and squeezed.

Shaughnessy didn't shake him off. And he didn't react to the weak taunt. Instead he directed his energy toward curling possessive fingers around the message, trying not to be obvious about it.

"What can I help you with, Detective?" he asked, his tone as civil as he could make it.

Boyd propped himself on the edge of Shaughnessy's desk, looking like he was settling in for a good gossip session. "What happened with that ghost girl from the other night?"

Ghost girl. That seemed appropriate. Rowan had appeared in the road out of nowhere, pale as anything. Shaughnessy shook his head.

"Troubled teen. The mother came to pick her up, said she's being treated for depression."

He thought about the card Edith White had given him. Rowan's psychiatrist. Dr. Anders White.

Shaughnessy had gone as far as to search the man's name in their databases, and had come up with a clean record beyond two speeding tickets. He'd even dialed the number on the card only to hang up when a pleasant voice had informed him that Dr. White was in an appointment but he'd be happy to return a call if Shaughnessy wanted to leave his name.

It had all seemed legitimate, aboveboard. Yet still, he couldn't shake the feeling that he shouldn't have let Edith White walk away with Rowan.

Boyd scratched at his chin, stretched. "Still seems odd."

The man's personality sometimes rubbed Shaughnessy the wrong way, but Boyd did always have a sense for when things were off. "Yeah."

"Let's take a drive," Boyd said, clapping Shaughnessy on the shoulder once more. "You have their names?"

Shaughnessy scrambled to his feet, eager like a pup given a treat, grabbing for his jacket, his keys. "A name, not an address."

"Pam," Boyd called over to the buxom woman manning the scanner. "Get us an address, love?"

"For you, doll, anything."

Ten minutes later, they were in Shaughnessy's car, heading back out toward the state forest, the roads innocuous in the daylight.

They didn't speak until they pulled up to a mansion, gated and everything. They had to be buzzed through after holding up their badges to the high-tech video camera mounted to the guardhouse.

"Money," Boyd commented idly as Shaughnessy braked behind a high-end Beamer.

Shaughnessy wanted to throw out a *No shit, Sherlock*, but since Boyd did actually seem to care about what had happened to Rowan, he kept his mouth shut.

When had Shaughnessy started thinking about her by her first name?

Rowan White was a victim, someone they'd helped during a shift, a tragic but sadly common tale. Rowan, on the other hand, was the girl with scared eyes who'd slipped a message into his palm.

Edith White waited for them at the door, her shoulders a tense line, her thin lips all but gone. She held her hands locked in front of her stomach like ladies in old-timey photographs.

If Shaughnessy could have sketched a picture of "wealthy Bostonian," it would be her.

"Mrs. White," Boyd drawled in greeting. He'd come to Boston by way of Texas, and he liked to lean heavy on the accent when he prepared to charm someone. "If you would indulge us?"

Edith's mouth pinched in farther. But she turned without slamming the door in their faces and led them to a small room off the foyer. A salon, Shaughnessy thought. That's what rich people called living rooms.

He felt too big, too clumsy, just as he had staring across his desk at Rowan.

"My daughter is ill, you understand," Edith said, directing her full attention to Boyd, easily reading him as the more senior detective here.

"Of course, of course." Boyd's tone was sympathetic, understanding. "If we could just ask her a few questions."

"I'm afraid that's not possible, Detective," Edith said. "We've decided Rowan needs full-time care again. We're simply not able to deal with her unique situation here."

"And what is that situation?" Shaughnessy cut in. If Boyd hadn't nodded along with the question, Shaughnessy wondered if Edith would have been struck with a case of selective hearing.

But she subtly worked her jaw and then turned to address him. "To put it bluntly, Officer?" she started, making it clear she knew exactly where he ranked. "Suicide watch."

Shaughnessy had been expecting that. Not the first time. That's what Edith had claimed back at the station.

The only thing was, Shaughnessy had seen plenty of suicide attempts. None of those people had tried cutting their upper arms. Shaughnessy pulled out his notebook. "And what facility is she in?"

"I don't see how that's any of your business."

"Resting Meadowwoods," came the answer from the doorway.

"Anders," Edith murmured, clearly dismayed. As dismayed as she could show in front of company.

Shaughnessy's eyes slid toward the newcomer.

Dr. Anders White.

He was fussily dressed in a neat vest and trousers, and had the same ice-cold coloring as Rowan, the same delicate features, though he still came off as masculine. Handsome rather than pretty. A Greek patrician carved from marble.

Resting Meadowwoods. Even after jotting it down, Shaughnessy stared at the name, wondering if it was a joke, like something *Saturday Night Live* would come up with for a psychiatric facility.

But both Edith and Anders wore straight faces.

"Mother," Anders replied in a conciliatory tone, "these fine police officers are clearly concerned with Rowan's well-being, just as we are. They should be commended for going above and beyond."

As Anders drifted closer, Shaughnessy's spine straightened, his thighs bunched. The way prey would ready themselves to run when sensing a predator.

The fight-or-flight instinct was fleeting enough, but it left Shaughnessy sweaty, uncomfortable.

No one looking at Anders White would categorize him as a threat—he looked like he'd go down with one punch that landed solid enough. But he'd commanded the room from the second he'd spoken, competing with even Boyd and Edith, both dominating presences in their own right.

"She was in quite a state." Shaughnessy found himself repeating what he'd told Edith that night, helplessly. He couldn't say, *We found her quite a bit tortured.* That wasn't actually accurate, nor could a rookie cop six months out of the academy go around accusing the Boston Whites of that. Even he—ignorant as he was of all these political games—knew that.

"Rowan didn't react well to her latest change in medication," Anders said. "I had been treating her myself"—he held up a hand as if they were about to protest—"unorthodox, I know. But Mother didn't want to draw even more attention to the problem."

The corners of Edith's eyes tightened, but she didn't contradict the sentiment.

"I may be at the top of my field, gentlemen," Anders continued, somehow managing to strike the right balance between self-deprecating and arrogant, "but even I have my limits. We've had success with Meadowwoods in the past. We decided it was worth taking her out of school for full-time care."

Shaughnessy tapped his pencil against his notebook. All this rang true. Even six months on the force and he'd already seen a handful of similar cases. Troubled teenager, a concerned family unable to control them. It all wrapped up nicely in a neat bow.

Still . . .

They're going to lie.

"What school?" he asked, just for something to ask.

A pause as mother and son exchanged glances. But then Anders answered. "The Phillips Academy."

Shaughnessy wrote it down, then grasped in the darkness for a thread to pull, anything that would get this perfect little story to start to unravel. "Her father?"

Beside him, Boyd coughed. But he didn't go so far as to wave away the question.

Edith's knuckles went pale where she had them clasped in front of her.

Anders, however, kept that gentle, understanding smile on his face. "Not in her life anymore. Left a few months after she was born."

Edith blinked fast, too fast. But still she didn't say anything, didn't contradict Anders's version of the facts.

"A name?" Shaughnessy ventured, feeling reckless, feeling brave. Feeling absolutely stupid beyond belief. What was he doing risking his badge for this girl?

For the first time, Anders seemed thrown. He hesitated, glanced at his mother, then back to them. "I don't see how that's relevant."

Because it probably wasn't. Shaughnessy just didn't know what else to ask. In desperation, he glanced at Boyd, who just lifted one shoulder.

"She said there are more girls," Shaughnessy blurted out, nearly wincing once the words fell with a heavy thud onto the pristine carpet of the room.

Edith sighed and exchanged a look with Anders, who nodded once.

"My mother mentioned that she told you about Rowan's overactive imagination," Anders said smoothly. "Anything my sister might have said about—what was it? more girls?—is just a product of bad medication." He paused, his face the perfect picture of concern. "But rest assured, we're addressing that mistake now."

Again, that sounded plausible. And yet it sat wrong for Shaughnessy. Only, he didn't know what to do about that feeling.

"Well," Boyd said after a beat of silence. "Everything seems in order then. Shaughnessy here will give you our information. If anything should arise . . ."

"Of course." Anders stood. Edith stayed seated.

Shaughnessy didn't bother with the polite goodbyes beyond handing over a card with his contact details on it. Anders took it with a vague smile, slipped it into one of the pockets of his fancy vest. Most likely it would soon find its way into a trash can.

Only when they climbed back into the car did Boyd shiver, overdramatic. "Ten bucks says that creep has her chained up in the basement."

Any air left in Shaughnessy's lungs got punched out of him. He wanted to double over, to scrape at his skin just to make sure it was still there. Instead, he stared at the mansion in front of him blankly. "We really can't do anything?"

Boyd yawned, stretched, and then sprawled against his door, settling in for the drive back into the city proper. "Sorry, kid. Not until she turns up dead."

CHAPTER TEN

GRETCHEN

Now

"Gut instinct," Marconi called from Gretchen's living room. They'd migrated back to Gretchen's place, the papers from the file spread out all over the carpet, two separate laptops open with old news reports from the murder.

Gretchen hesitated, her hand on the wine bottle. But she grabbed the water instead and walked back toward where Marconi sat on the carpet. Gretchen loomed silently until Marconi twisted, squinting up at her face like it was difficult to look at.

"Gut instinct," Marconi repeated at normal volume. "Who killed her? And don't say you."

"Anders," Gretchen said as the plastic seal gave way beneath her hand. "Going by statistics, it's most likely to be the man who was in the house. A close relative at that."

"But Anders was on a business trip in Houston," Marconi pointed out. "And time of death was confirmed as shortly before Bardot's 9-1-1 call."

"I know," Gretchen said with a shrug. That was partly why the viable alternative to Gretchen had winnowed down to zero. "Bardot was checked thoroughly for spatter."

"What if she changed?" Marconi suggested. "Out of her clothes, I mean. The death wasn't immediate—Rowan bled out."

"So you think Bardot stabbed her, ran to change, and then lured me into the bedroom while Rowan was dying?" Gretchen asked, pitching her voice just right so Marconi would pick up on how far-fetched that sounded.

"Why not?" Marconi pushed back. "They get in an argument, Bardot snaps and then panics. Shaughnessy is distracted by the scene. It took an hour to get uniforms to search the premises."

An hour. Someone could do a lot with that time if all eyes were directed elsewhere.

No. This was a dangerous path to walk. At the end of it lay something far too tempting. Hope could derail even the most objective investigators. She had never let herself believe she was innocent, not fully believe it. She wouldn't start now, despite Marconi's earnest little face.

"There were no other fingerprints in the room."

"That almost makes it more likely, though, right?" Marconi asked. "If I dusted a place and found only the victim's prints, I would think the killer cleaned up."

"Her prints and mine," Gretchen corrected.

Marconi just shrugged at that. "I'm not arguing that you weren't there, just that you weren't the one to stab her."

"Shaughnessy noted that it was unlikely Bardot could have both cleaned herself up and erased anything she'd left in the room before making the 9-1-1 call within the window the coroner gave for TOD," Gretchen said.

"Unlikely isn't impossible," Marconi countered, unruffled.

"Unlikely is unlikely," Gretchen said, harsher now. She rolled her shoulders, trying to release the knot that had coiled at the nape of her neck.

"If it wasn't Bardot, then it's someone else." Marconi's chin tilted up like she was about to fight someone.

"Me," Gretchen said quietly.

But Marconi wasn't listening. "We should figure out what Rowan did with those years she dropped off the radar."

"Pointless," Gretchen said, hearing the petulant stubbornness in her own voice and not caring that she sounded like a child.

"Put your computer wiz on it," Marconi suggested. "It's not like you can't afford a pointless expense if that's what it turns out to be."

That wasn't a terrible idea. Gretchen palmed her phone, scrolling to Fred's number.

Gretchen had few friends, but she did have a network of people who tended to be helpful when she was consulting on a case. Ryan Kelly, the tabloid reporter Marconi had nearly strangled, was one of them. Fred—full name Winnifred James—was another. And probably her most valuable. The woman fell high enough on the antisocial spectrum that her threat to stab Gretchen in the carotid artery should she ever call Fred by her full name rang true.

"Long time, Dr. White," Fred said when she answered. "And here I'd dared to hope you'd lost my number."

Gretchen didn't rise to the bait. Fred liked to pretend she was the long-suffering half of this arrangement, but Gretchen knew she subsidized much of Fred's rent.

"Can you find a trace of someone who dropped off the map for a couple years?" Gretchen asked without bothering with the banter.

"Depends on a lot of variables," Fred said. "But, short answer, yeah."

"It would have been in the late '80s, early '90s." Gretchen wondered if that would be a deal breaker because that was before most people had a digital footprint, but Fred just hummed.

"A challenge. I like it."

"It's doable?" Gretchen glanced over to find Marconi watching her intently. Gretchen sent her a sarcastic thumbs-up, and Marconi rolled her eyes.

Computer keys clacked in the background. "Name?"

Gretchen hesitated. There was no way around this. "Rowan White."

All noise from the other end of the line stopped. Then Fred whistled low and long. "Shit, Doc."

"Yes, that about sums it up," Gretchen said. "How much?"

"Seven K," Fred tossed out without missing a beat. She wasn't one to let sentimentality or empathy stand in the way of a profit, and she knew how deep Gretchen's pockets were.

"Five, and only if you find something." Gretchen negotiated because Fred would take her for all she had otherwise. The two-thousand-dollar difference was a drop in the bucket of her wealth, and she wouldn't blink at paying the higher sum. But it was the principle of the matter.

"Five no matter what, eight if I find something," Fred countered. "And ten if it's good."

"If it's good, the bonus will be better than that," Gretchen agreed. Positive incentive tended to work well with Fred.

She hung up without giving any further instructions. There was enough information out there that Fred wouldn't struggle with where to start.

Marconi had leaned back on her hands and was watching Gretchen again. "I hate to say it, but I think we've gotten what we can from the files."

Which was nothing. Except maybe the realization that Shaughnessy hadn't been as incompetent as Gretchen had liked to pretend. "Shaughnessy won't talk to us."

"If we make enough trouble, he'll have to," Marconi said, mischief in the slant of her lips, her brows.

Treat it like a stranger's case.

What would get Shaughnessy riled enough to step in?

Gretchen sighed. "I guess it's time to visit dear ole Daddy."

CHAPTER ELEVEN

TABBY

1993

Tabby could recite the facts of her sister's case like some could recite Bible verses and others epic poems. The words were far from religious or lyrical, but when she said them out loud, they seared into her soul like both.

Jenny was a scholarship student at the prestigious Phillips Academy, where she was more an acquaintance than friend of her fellow classmates.

She had been sixteen when she'd been killed.

There were a few phone calls on the Crosses' bill from a number that their father, Levi, hadn't been able to identify. It had been tracked to a pay phone near the mall ten minutes away, out of sight of any security camera. No one who worked at the mall could remember seeing anyone use the booth with any frequency.

A dead end.

Jenny's field hockey teammates said that she'd been picked up from practice by an older man in the weeks before she'd disappeared. She would blush when questioned about who it was. No one had ever gotten a plate number, and the make had been generic. When asked about the color, the girls had shrugged. Black? Dark blue?

No one ever got any look at him? No, but one girl remembered Jenny mentioning the Fall Festival in passing, thought that's where the two might have met.

Jenny was quiet, kept to herself mostly, they all said. She didn't gossip about her exploits—not that there were many.

She was found a week after she'd gone missing, her body dumped in the woods in a shallow grave. Her arms had cuts on them, all up and down the outside, from shoulder to wrist. The coroner hadn't known what to make of the wounds. They didn't seem to serve a purpose—even as a method of torture, it would have been ineffective.

Cause of death had been blunt force trauma to the back of her head.

There were no signs of rape. No semen. No fibers. No other girls in the morgue or local hospitals with similar injuries.

No one in the houses nearby had seen or heard anything. But they were all mansion-type places, with gates and long driveways and as much distance between themselves and their surroundings as possible.

The cops had wasted weeks trying to track down the mysterious car just to look like they were doing something.

They couldn't admit they had nothing else to chase.

A cold case. That's what the detectives called it when they thought they were out of earshot of Tabby.

Now, Tabby listened for another minute for her father's snores coming from the couch. Then she touched her fingers to Jenny's doorknob like it might burn her.

It didn't; of course it didn't.

The idea of going inside still scared her. But now that the file had let her down, this remained the last stone unturned.

After this, she would give up, move on, finally come to grips with the fact that Jenny's murder wasn't ever going to be solved.

Tabby nearly laughed at the thought. How many times had she said that already in her life? Another stone always seemed to show up. She wondered if she would ever be free of Jenny's ghost.

She stepped into the room, and only realized once she was inside that she'd closed her eyes, bracing for a blow. None came; her father slept on below. The world kept turning. Jenny was still dead.

The cops had asked her father for Jenny's diary, and he'd handed it over as quickly as possible. But Tabby wasn't looking for her sister's account of petty grievances and crushes. That's not what told the story of a girl's final days.

People had a way of lying in those pages, even when the audience was just themselves.

The fact that the cops hadn't found anything in it seemed to prove Tabby's point for her.

Even though Jenny hadn't been friends with her shallow, rich schoolmates, they'd gotten at least some things right. Jenny was quiet, studious, kept to herself. Especially at that academy. She hated everyone there, she'd always said, but she'd jumped at the scholarship once it had been offered.

Because Jenny had always wanted to get out. She'd looked around their modest house in a modest neighborhood and this modest life that she was destined to live out and had refused to settle. Tabby had always known that she herself would end up in some dead-end job living paycheck to paycheck.

But Jenny? She'd had big dreams. And she'd known just how to fulfill them.

That wasn't by drawing hearts around boys' names in her diary. It was by meticulously scheduling her homework in her planner.

If the cops had really wanted to know what Jenny had been thinking about during her last days, her last hours, they should have looked at her school papers; looked at the Post-it Notes Jenny had loved leaving for herself, all curling at the edges but still clinging to the wood nearly ten years later. They should have looked at her essays and her field hockey playbook, which lived in its prominent place in the top drawer.

When cops saw a murdered girl, they looked at the extremes—the boys, the fights, the drugs, the sex, the shame.

But Tabby couldn't shake the feeling that the answer was far more mundane.

Tabby sat in the desk chair her sister had decorated with childish stickers when she'd been all of ten years old and had never peeled them off. She picked up the closest bundle of papers, a group project about the Founding Fathers and the Revolutionary War—a subject Boston schools never tired of teaching.

The group had gotten an A.

Tabby would have never expected less of Jenny.

Beside her sister's name was one that sounded almost familiar to Tabby.

She ran her finger over the ink, chasing a memory that was probably imagined.

It was a pretty name, old-fashioned but light and melodic, and Tabby repeated it to herself even as she moved on to the papers beneath it.

Rowan White.

CHAPTER TWELVE

GRETCHEN

Now

Gretchen rapped her knuckles against the sedan's driver's side window.

Shaughnessy heaved a sigh that she could see even if she couldn't hear, and hit the button, the glass whirring laboriously as the decade-and-a-half-old Crown Vic attempted to follow commands.

Bending down, Gretchen leaned on the door with one hand and gave him a smile that carried that same attitude as the jaunty salute from earlier. "Detective, sir, I'm wondering if you could help me."

He glared, clearly knowing he was being played. "What." It came out a demand, rather than a question.

"I have a stalker, it seems," Gretchen said.

"Or maybe you have a guard making sure you don't go off the deep end and kill someone," Shaughnessy groused back.

Gretchen pretended to ponder that. "Hmm, yes, seems just as likely. In that case, I've come to help you out."

Eyes narrowed, Shaughnessy shifted back. "In what way?"

"We're headed to Cambridge."

Something clicked behind Shaughnessy's eyes, and his face went carefully blank. "Anders."

"You're a quick one, Detective. Don't let anyone tell you differently," Gretchen said. Then before he could even react to that, she let the hilt of the knife she'd kept tucked up against her forearm drop into her palm. With a flick of her wrist, she sank the blade into his front tire, slashed down to truly shred the rubber. "*Just* not quite quick enough."

Shaughnessy started cursing and didn't stop even when she was halfway back to her Porsche, Marconi already buckled into the passenger seat.

"He could arrest you for that," Marconi commented, though she didn't sound particularly perturbed.

"I'd love to see him try," Gretchen said as she revved the engine. Historically, Shaughnessy had granted her more leniency than she'd expected on the few occasions her impulses had gotten the better of her. But this time she almost hoped he'd complain. Then he'd have to explain what he was doing to his chief, who, she guessed, had no idea one of his top homicide detectives was wasting time tailing one of his top consultants. "Then we wouldn't have to visit Anders."

She shot Marconi a glance. "What do you make of his current behavior?"

Marconi ran a hand through her hair and looked out the window, protecting her expression. "Maybe he's just trying to keep an eye on you."

Maybe. That tracked with his past actions whenever he started getting twitchy about what Gretchen was doing. But . . . there was something particularly agitated about Shaughnessy lately. This wasn't just about an old case. This was about a case that might have defined him as much as it had defined her.

"He went into our house that night without waiting for backup," Gretchen said, ignoring that fair point. Shaughnessy did like to lurk in general.

"It's unusual," Marconi agreed. "But not unheard of, if what he says happened was true."

Shaughnessy's official story was that he had been heading home when the emergency operator relayed the details of Bardot's call. He just happened to be a handful of minutes away. By the time other detectives arrived, Shaughnessy had entered Rowan's room and disarmed Gretchen.

"He didn't follow protocol," Gretchen said.

"Well, you still had the knife and there were other potential victims in the house," Marconi said, reasonably. "Including your sister, who was . . . how old?"

"Fifteen."

She didn't particularly enjoy admitting it—and wouldn't do so out loud—but Marconi was right. It wasn't inherently suspicious that Shaughnessy had gone in early and alone. The reasoning might give out if pushed in court, but Shaughnessy's reported assessment that there was still an active risk covered a lot of otherwise questionable behavior. And anyway, it had been the early '90s, long before cops had standardized crime scene procedure. That had come along with the O. J. Simpson debacle.

"Plausible enough to be true," Marconi said, echoing Gretchen's thoughts. But she sounded hesitant.

"You don't think it is?" Gretchen pressed. "Do you think he knows something? That he's been hiding something?"

"Maybe," Marconi hedged. "But at the end of the day I still can't reconcile the fact that Shaughnessy would let you work on murder cases if he thought you'd killed someone. And . . ."

Gretchen tried to rein in the irritation in her voice when Marconi trailed off. "Don't start sentences you can't finish."

Marconi slid her a look. "Between the two of you, you're the only one who told me that he thinks you did it."

"Explain," Gretchen bit off.

"The jokey stuff at crime scenes where you call yourself a murderer and he doesn't disagree," Marconi said so slowly Gretchen was tempted to slam on the brakes to startle her into spitting it out. "The banter, all that. He doesn't talk like that when you're not around."

Gretchen flew through a red light as she contemplated that. She hated moments like these, where she knew she was being told something important but her brain didn't let her recognize the significance of it. Finally, she gritted out, "Get to your point."

"It's just a theory," Marconi said, staring out the window again. Gretchen wanted to shake her, slap her. Something. "You think Shaughnessy thinks you got away with it. But I think that might be the story you've told yourself and not reality."

"The police report says differently," Gretchen said, and she despised the fact that for a minute she'd thought Marconi would say something life changing. "Not exactly a brilliant theory, then."

"The police report—and the interviews the tabloids got ahold of back then, before you say anything—was written thirty years ago," Marconi said with a shrug, her voice still calm, unemotional. "He tells people off at the station if they gossip about you at all."

Gretchen swallowed, not sure what to do with that information. It sat on her strangely, a borrowed coat that was too tight in all the wrong places.

"Maybe he's convinced himself that it's justified because I was a kid and it was a onetime thing," Gretchen offered up. She'd found that people were incredibly talented when it came to mental gymnastics and rationalizing things that they wanted. For Shaughnessy, that was solved cases. In the years she'd been working with him, his reputation had drastically improved. And that was in no small part because of the expertise she'd offered him during investigations.

"You know he doesn't think like that," Marconi countered. "If you killed Rowan in cold blood? I don't see him writing that off. Even if you were a kid when it happened."

Gretchen stared at Marconi's profile for so long she had to swerve to avoid catching the side mirror of a parked car. "Would you work with me if it had been a onetime thing?"

"A onetime thing," Marconi repeated under her breath with both amusement and disgust. "It doesn't matter. You didn't kill her."

"You're going in with just as much of a preconceived bias as Shaughnessy did," Gretchen pointed out, not willing to let this drop now that she'd started picking at the wound. Heat flushed up her neck, down her chest, her fingers gripping the wheel.

No matter whether Gretchen believed she was actually guilty of killing Rowan—something she'd wavered on over the past thirty years—the murder, the suspicion, the talk, and the looks and the consequences of being the prime suspect in a murder investigation had shaped her entire life. They were part of her bones, the cornerstone from which she'd built everything else.

She'd left primary school early, had graduated college when she was a teenager, had decided to study criminology and psychology so that maybe she could better understand why she was an endless void of nothing where everyone else seemed to be filled with *so much.*

Gretchen had refused to be chased out of her city because of her reputation, had thrown that very past in the faces of anyone who said she couldn't become a leading expert on crimes and antisocial personality disorders. Even Shaughnessy's obsession with her had worked to mold what others would call a *personality* and she would call her *outward behavior.*

Had he not been there watching over her shoulder since she was eight years old, would one of those times she'd been nearly driven to violence by her impulses have won out? Would she be in jail or dead because she had never learned how to control the darker side of her nature?

Even as she loudly declared her own innocence to anyone who would listen, in truth she had created a life shaped around the idea that she'd killed Rowan.

Who was she if she wasn't the child who had gotten away with murder? What would she be if that wasn't her history?

For the longest time, she had been telling herself that she hadn't looked into the case once she'd become a consultant for the police because she was scared of being barred from helping on criminal investigations; she'd told herself she was scared of jail; she'd told herself that the consequences weren't worth her sated curiosity.

But really what she feared was that the one traumatic event that had built her might not have actually happened. When she'd been younger, she would have given anything to shed the dark cloud that followed her no matter how far she ran. As an adult, if she were being honest, she didn't think she would change the past even if she could.

What would happen to her carefully constructed life if by some miracle they found evidence exonerating her completely? Would everything change? Would anything?

Marconi was watching her from the passenger seat, and Gretchen brutally yanked on her control to hide whatever was going on with her face. People thought sociopaths didn't have emotions, but that wasn't quite true. Gretchen could attest to that fact at the moment. And she had no desire to show her hand to Marconi.

"If you killed her, there's a reason for it," Marconi said, sounding so much more decisive than she rationally should.

"Why do you have such faith in someone who, by all accounts, doesn't have a moral compass?" Gretchen asked, despite herself. She should just shut up and let Marconi help her. If the woman got burned in the process, that wasn't Gretchen's fault. She'd been properly warned, after all.

Still, curiosity was a beast she could only sometimes ignore.

"Because, from what I've seen, despite the fact that you're a sociopath, you still end up doing the right thing nine times out of ten anyway," Marconi said. "Isn't that almost more impressive than doing it because you're born with the correct wiring?"

"Maybe eight times out of ten," Gretchen said to ease that damn flutter in her chest.

"Sure. Eight out of ten," Marconi said, some kind of annoyingly knowing smile lurking behind her voice. "Even seven out of ten puts you above average in my experience."

Gretchen didn't have a clever reply, and Marconi grinned. "Oh, have I finally left you speechless?"

She wasn't proud of it, but Gretchen reverted to Marconi's favored rude gesture as a response.

"There's that infamous wit," Marconi quipped. But she shut up after that, keeping quiet as Gretchen slid in and out of the lanes, dodging cars at thirty miles over the speed limit. Careful, but trusting.

Gretchen found herself in the unique position of not wanting to exploit Marconi's faith in people even as she cataloged it for herself to use later should the need occur. Just like she had during the Viola Kent case.

After they crossed the bridge out of the city, Marconi shifted in her seat, not seeming uncomfortable but rather thoughtful. "You said if Anders had killed her, he would have wanted to be the one to do it."

"Yes," Gretchen agreed. "He's controlling, if nothing else."

"Those wounds, they were overkill."

A *tug* on ripped flesh. "Yes."

"This wasn't a paid hit, and this wasn't defensive, because Rowan didn't have a weapon," Marconi continued, her voice distant, like she was working through something. "This was rage or sadism."

Marconi had seen pictures of the body, just like many others had. "The easy answer was sadism, of course," Gretchen said with a little wave at herself.

"But if it wasn't you . . . ," Marconi said, again more like she didn't mean to say this out loud. "That could bring rage back into play."

"I suppose."

"Do you think anyone else in the house would have gotten off on torturing Rowan just to torture her?" Marconi asked.

"No," Gretchen said. "Unless Bardot or Fran is a secret serial killer."

"Let's go with the assumption that they're not," Marconi said. "That leaves rage."

"So we're going about this wrong," Gretchen said, slightly mortified she was only now catching where Marconi's thought process was headed.

"We don't need to find the suspect," Marconi said, eyes big, body all but vibrating with excitement. "We need to find the motive."

Gretchen turned onto a residential street she remembered too well despite the fact that she hadn't been there in twenty years. She stopped by the curb instead of pulling into the driveway. A quick exit strategy was crucial when dealing with Anders and Bardot White.

"Well," she said, opening the car door. "We're about to get a houseful of them."

CHAPTER THIRTEEN

SHAUGHNESSY

1984

It had been nearly four months since Rowan White had dashed in front of Shaughnessy's car, and he still couldn't get her out of his mind. The memory of her face had become hazy and soft, more an idea than an actual likeness.

The lilting voice, the way her fingers tucked into his palm for one instant—those had been seared onto his skin. Indelible.

He'd told himself to let it go. There was nothing there to find. But he'd never been good at that.

Shaughnessy had finally given in and called the facility the Whites had mentioned, only to be blocked by the receptionist.

"It's a rather pressing issue, ma'am," he'd said.

"And I'm sure you'll be able to convince a judge of that" had been the frosty reply.

After that, all he could do was wait, keep an eye on police reports from the surrounding districts, and hope that the next time he saw Rowan it wasn't her lifeless face staring back at him.

"She got in your head, didn't she?" Boyd asked, propping a hip against Shaughnessy's desk, tapping on the file that sat precariously close to the edge. Shaughnessy cursed himself for leaving it out for anyone to see. "That's dangerous, my friend."

Shaughnessy fought the urge to hide the folder in his desk—that would only bring more attention to his behavior. "You saw her arms."

"Yeah, not the first girl to find herself a razor blade," Boyd said, mostly bored but with a hint of curiosity that he seemed to be fighting. "Come on, we're getting a beer around the corner."

Shaughnessy shook his head. "I'm good."

Boyd shrugged into the jacket he was carrying. "You just gonna sit here and obsess about ghost girl?"

"She came flying out of the woods like she was running from someone," Shaughnessy said.

"Which she could have done during a psychotic break," Boyd countered. But he wasn't walking away, and Shaughnessy was reminded of his nickname. Bloodhound Boyd. Once he caught a scent, he tended not to let it go.

"She told us to run," Shaughnessy tried.

"I didn't see that." Boyd shrugged, and Shaughnessy knew he was playing devil's advocate.

Shaughnessy searched for another reason beyond *that family seemed creepy and you know it*.

"She said there were more girls out there," Shaughnessy muttered.

"And, again, we have an explanation for that." Boyd pushed off the desk, checking the readiness of the rest of the guys. Someone had gotten caught up talking to the chief, which was probably the only reason Boyd was still lingering. But Shaughnessy could tell his attention was already fading.

Desperate, Shaughnessy leaned forward to draw Boyd's eyes back to him. "You said we couldn't do anything until she turned up dead."

That did get Boyd to glance back over. And he sighed, seemingly unable to help himself. "What's your grand theory then?"

This was a risk, Shaughnessy knew. Because his theory sounded crazy, even in his own head. But he was getting nowhere by himself.

There are more girls. Find them.

He hesitated for a second longer, long enough for Boyd's eyes to drift away again, before he reached into the bottom drawer of his desk.

And he pulled out his collection.

Magazines, newspaper clippings, ripped-out pages from books and psychology journals. There was no dearth of material these days. They lived in a nation obsessed with these monsters.

Serial killers.

Boyd stared down at them as Shaughnessy spread out some of the covers. The Zodiac Killer, John Wayne Gacy, David Berkowitz.

"Are you shitting me?" Boyd asked, voice low and urgent as he shifted, his body blocking Shaughnessy's desktop from the rest of the cops milling by the door. "Christ, man. You realize people around here already think you've got a screw loose, right?"

A muscle in Shaughnessy's jaw jumped. He wasn't an idiot. It was a leap to go from one girl running out into the road to serial killer; Shaughnessy knew that.

And he also knew what the other cops said about him. It wasn't as if he hadn't heard it before.

His ma had warned him about the way he'd get when he had a new obsession.

"Focused," she'd called it.

His siblings hadn't been as kind.

"Creepy," Brenna had said.

"Psycho," Mick had added.

"Sinister." That had been Saoirse. He hadn't taken it too hard, because she fancied herself the smart one in the family and had been practicing for her SATs at the time.

His pop had always pulled him aside whenever the kids started in on him, though.

"A good cop." That's what pop had said time and again. *"You got a nose for it, Patrick. Don't let no one tell you different."*

Whenever Shaughnessy went home for Sunday dinner these days, he tried to make his job sound more impressive than driving around older detectives and sitting at speed traps and DUI checkpoints. Brenna and Mick and Saoirse never bought it, but his pop, his pop would look at him with something terrifyingly close to pride.

"I told ya, didn't I?"

Maybe he didn't have any real cases under his belt. But he still knew *something ain't right* when he saw it.

And Shaughnessy couldn't shake the memory of Rowan's arms. They were weird, out of place. They didn't make sense.

They seemed like a signature in the making.

Added to the fact that she'd looked like she'd just escaped from a basement in her underthings and then warned him that there were more victims out there—could he really blame himself for spinning out a story?

"Tell me that her cuts didn't strike you as a ritual," Shaughnessy said in a hushed voice, his own eyes slipping past Boyd. The guys at the door were getting restless now, one of them breaking away and heading toward them.

"What, you work for the Eff Bee Eye now?" Boyd said, the letters elongated until they were caricatures of themselves.

Shaughnessy's shoulders lifted defensively as he gathered up all the papers. Boyd was right about one thing: he didn't need the other detectives gossiping about what a loony tune conspiracy theorist the rookie was. "I'm not asking for your help."

He knew it came off with the bitter hurt of a teenager, but he couldn't stop it. When anyone else paid attention to his—*obsessions,* some voice in his head whispered; *interests,* he corrected—he tended to get too excited, too eager, a kid showing off his work.

"Look." Boyd sighed. "I'll poke around for anything weird, similar cases or what have you. But you're not going to get anywhere without solid evidence."

"I've tried." Shaughnessy shook his head as Boyd shifted toward the rest of the detectives. "What should I do?"

"Go get laid by someone who's not a ghost girl," Boyd muttered. And then sighed once again. Because Shaughnessy wasn't the only cop that could get a little too invested in a good mystery. "All right, panties unbunched, please. You're not getting into that house again, and you're not getting anything from the psychiatrists."

Shaughnessy knew all this. "Right."

"So what does that leave?" Boyd asked, leaning in close.

Irritation threatened to wipe out all logical thought, but Shaughnessy pushed it aside. Instead he remembered slamming on the brakes, remembered what he'd thought about.

"The woods."

"Bingo, bango, baby," Boyd said.

"But what am I going to find there?" Shaughnessy couldn't help but ask. It wasn't far from the mansion. More than likely she'd been running from the house.

"I don't know," Boyd said, shrugging one shoulder. "But you won't find anything at all if you don't look."

CHAPTER FOURTEEN

GRETCHEN

Now

One of the benefits of an obnoxious cherry-lipstick Porsche was that it helped Gretchen make an entrance.

That's the only reason Gretchen could figure that Bardot herself answered the front door rather than having one of her maids there, either to usher them in or send them away. Gretchen wouldn't put money on one outcome over the other.

"Darling." Bardot leaned forward to kiss the air far, far away from Gretchen's actual cheeks. "How good of you to stop by."

She said it as if they'd seen each other even once outside the lawyers' offices following the reading of Edith's will.

"Mother," Gretchen said, deliberately adopting Bardot's tone. "We were in the neighborhood. Lauren here insisted she meet the parents."

Gretchen lingered over Marconi's first name, intimate in the way she rolled her tongue to give her mother the exact wrong impression. Everything about Bardot—from her carefully pinned-back coffee-colored hair to the single strand of pearls she wore at her neck and the pristine off-white skirt suit and matching pumps—made Gretchen want to catch her off guard, made her want to ruffle that unrufflable persona.

Bardot flicked Marconi a look, her attention darting back to Gretchen as fast as hummingbird wings, like lingering any longer would give Marconi the idea that she was actually welcome.

"I'm sorry, darling, we may have to reschedule this visit." Bardot managed to sound almost genuine. "The DAR ladies will be here shortly."

Marconi shifted beside Gretchen, digging in her jacket for her badge. "Actually, ma'am, I'm Detective Lauren Marconi with the Boston PD. I was wondering if you could spare us just a few minutes?"

Gretchen smirked as Bardot's Botox was put to work. If there had been an unparalyzed muscle left in her mother's face, it would have twitched and seized in a way that surely would have horrified Bardot. All the more reason to take pleasure in it.

"Gretchen, what were you thinking? You brought the police to our house?" Bardot said, once again ignoring Marconi, who was busy moving forward in that way of hers that no one else really seemed to notice until they'd already let her in the front door.

Bardot, despite her indomitable presence, was no different. In the next second, all three of them were standing in the marble-floored foyer of her parents' house, Marconi's eyes sweeping over the two Monets, the Degas, the Tiffany chandelier, and the Dior chaise nestled into the far corner. Gretchen had her doubts that Marconi could actually identify the pieces, but the room screamed wealth, and Marconi was too good a cop not to pick up on that.

Anders and Bardot may have been cut off from the hefty White trust fund, but that didn't mean they were hurting for money.

"We'll be happy to return some other time, if you can't fit us in now," Gretchen offered, like she was being helpful. "Perhaps even stay for the night?" She turned to Marconi with wide eyes. "Or the weekend. Doesn't that sound divine, darling?"

Marconi met her gaze with a flat look, then shifted her attention to Bardot. "Ma'am, this shouldn't take too much time."

In the face of the alternative, Marconi's implicit offer of a quick departure seemed to finally win over Bardot.

Glancing at the delicate gold watch on her wrist, Bardot hummed. "I think I can fit in a few minutes."

"And Anders," Gretchen interjected. "He'll be joining us, yes?"

"Your father is in the greenhouse," Bardot commented, which everyone knew wasn't an actual answer. But then she leaned into a doorway as they passed. "Jane, will you let Dr. White know we have company, please?"

A young woman dressed in an outdated maid uniform ducked around the three of them and headed toward the back of the house. Bardot gestured toward another doorway, just short of the kitchen. "In here."

As they followed Bardot, Marconi caught Gretchen's eye and mouthed *Calm down.*

Marconi had a point. Gretchen didn't feel completely in control of herself, but she was losing sight of why she should care about that. "You know, Mother, you don't have to dress those poor women like that just to indulge your French maid kink. It would be much simpler to hire an escort."

Marconi looked skyward before visibly composing herself.

"You'll have to excuse Gretchen," Bardot said in an aside to Marconi, who seemed to have won her over on the sheer fact that she wasn't Gretchen. "It's not her fault. She has very little self-control, as I'm sure you've noticed."

Instead of readily agreeing as Gretchen would have expected, Marconi leveled Bardot with something that came precariously close to a glare. "Actually, I've found her to have extraordinary self-control."

Gretchen tried not to smile smugly as she sat down. Something about Marconi coming to her defense soothed the lightning storm that had been racing beneath her skin ever since they'd pulled to the curb.

"Now, if we could—"

Bardot cut Marconi off. "We'll wait for Dr. White."

They then proceeded to sit in silence for seven minutes and forty-five seconds. The tension in the room coiling tighter, tighter, tighter. For anyone other than Gretchen, it would likely have been unbearable, but she found the whole thing highly amusing. She even made a game of it, studying each tiny flinch when Bardot had to keep herself from fidgeting, counting each time Marconi crossed and then uncrossed her legs.

"Ah. Guests," said a voice coming from the doorway. It slithered into all the cracks Gretchen pretended she didn't have. She didn't turn toward Anders, simply waited for him to cross the room to stand behind the couch where Bardot sat.

Even coming from working in the greenhouse, Anders was dressed impeccably, his crisp white shirt rolled up to his elbows but tucked into beige linen pants. His hair—mostly silver with the memory of blond threaded throughout—was thick and pushed back away from his patrician face. Wrinkles were more acceptable on men, so they lived there in the corner of his eyes and mouth, though they were not as deep as they should be.

Positioned just so, the two looked like an expensive family portrait come to life. Gracefully aging with the help of wealth.

Anders dropped a well-manicured hand on Bardot's shoulder as his eyes landed on Marconi—instead of the daughter he hadn't seen in years.

There was an obvious reason for that, though. Marconi read easily as a cop. Anyone with even a semblance of self-preservation tracked her when she moved through crowds. And Anders was interested in nothing more than he was in self-preservation.

"My apologies for keeping you waiting," Anders said smoothly. "May I ask"—for the first time his attention slipped to Gretchen, before returning to Marconi—"what this is about exactly?"

Gretchen's nails dug into her palms. The sight of him made her want to lob bombs, and so she did. "Did you kill Rowan?"

It was almost impressive the way Marconi sighed in exasperation without actually making a sound. But . . . she didn't cut in to soften the question, an action that would have undermined Gretchen.

The question had been designed to shock a reaction out of one of them, but neither even blinked. Years of training.

"Darling." Bardot's mouth pinched in concern. "Darling. Hasn't this gone on long enough?"

"And what, pray tell, is that?" Gretchen asked. She knew, but she wanted them to say it out loud. They'd always danced around the topic, all of them pretending it hadn't happened.

Anders deliberately looked at Marconi before returning to Gretchen. "Do you really want to do this now, Gretchen?"

Gretchen raised her brows. "Yes, I believe I do."

Bardot's mouth pressed into a thin line. Anders's fingers squeezed as if conveying support. Gretchen nearly scoffed at the theatrics of this all. Every hesitation, every movement a clear performance. For Marconi.

Who was watching it all with that careful attention that meant she was missing nothing.

"Darling, I was there," Bardot said, in a quiet, halting voice. "Please, if you want to get help, we've been telling you all your life we'll support your decision."

That was a lie, or enough of a misrepresentation to count. Being forced into an institution didn't count as "getting help." They both knew Gretchen couldn't be cured in the traditional sense of what society meant by those words. What they'd wanted was her out of the way so they didn't have to deal with all her complications. If Shaughnessy had ever gone through with arresting her, they would have gotten their wish.

Instead they'd gotten stuck with their strange child in an attempt to placate Edith, and hadn't even gotten a payout for it.

Gretchen stared at both of them dead in the eyes. "You haven't answered the question."

She still didn't think it was Anders who had orchestrated Rowan's death, but that wasn't the point. The point was to get a reaction, see which way they dodged the bombs. That could be more telling than anything else.

"It's not a question that needs answering," Anders countered before Bardot could say anything further.

Marconi shifted, a subtle request that could easily be ignored. Gretchen chewed at the inside of her mouth until she tasted copper, but then sat back. It was enough of a signal for Marconi to speak again for the first time since Anders had come in.

"I just have a few details I'd like to get straight about that night," Marconi said, pulling out that notebook of hers. Gretchen doubted she actually needed it to remember any details, but it was an effective prop. Marconi gestured to the couch beside Bardot. "Would you mind having a seat?"

If someone didn't know Anders well, they would have missed the way his shoulders rolled back at the command, phrased as it was as a question. Anders wasn't told what to do in his own house. But he was also trying valiantly to play a role, one of the concerned, helpful gentleman. So, after an almost imperceptible pause, he rounded the end of the sofa to lower himself to the spot next to Bardot. They clasped hands without even looking, an obvious show of unity and partnership.

The theater of the absurd.

"Mrs. White, could you take us through the evening, prior to the stabbing?" Marconi asked, pen poised.

Bardot drew in a breath, patted her hair as if even one strand were out of place. "It was a normal night, other than the fact that Anders was away. The girls had been put to bed."

The phrase struck Gretchen as . . . off. In the same way Marconi's earlier *She's the one who found you* had.

Gretchen turned the words over, pulled them apart, and put them back together.

Put to bed.

The room seemed to shrink, the world shivering and then crystallizing around Gretchen. *Christ,* how could she have forgotten? "The nanny."

Marconi shifted next to her. "There was a nanny?"

Although her voice was neutral, Marconi had to be thinking the same thing Gretchen was. There had never been a nanny mentioned in any of the police reports.

Bardot's eyes darted between them, but her expression remained placid.

"We always had a nanny," Gretchen said. Why hadn't she realized this before? Bardot never let the position sit empty for more than a day. God forbid she be forced to deal with her own children. "There was always a live-in nanny."

"Yes," Bardot said, as if it were a minor detail she'd forgotten to mention. "I suppose that's true."

Marconi glanced down at her notebook as if it held any kind of information other than the blank page Gretchen knew she was staring at.

"Was she there during the stabbing?" Marconi asked.

Bardot inhaled audibly, like she was startled it would be put into such blunt terms. "She must have been."

Marconi glanced at Anders, who nodded and added, "Unless she'd asked for the night off . . ."

Gretchen ignored that nonanswer. "What was her name?"

"It was thirty years ago, Gretchen," Bardot snapped. Anders patted their joined hands with his free one, and Bardot visibly composed herself. "I would have to look it up."

What have you done, Gretchen?

That question. It had come in a voice that hadn't been her mother's. Younger, shocked, and horrified.

The nanny.

Gretchen glanced at her father. "You don't remember, either?"

He shrugged. "To be honest, I can't even remember meeting the girl. Your mother handled the nannies. And"—he paused, delicately and deliberately—"we tended to have quite a bit of turnover."

Gretchen scoffed at the implication that she was at fault for that. If any staff lasted around her mother for longer than a month, it had been cause for celebration. But Anders and Bardot so loved making themselves the long-suffering heroes of this particular tale.

"You'll call me with the name," Gretchen said, and it wasn't a request. "You'll look it up once I leave and call me as soon as you find it."

"Fine, though I can't imagine what good it will do," Bardot said as if the information was inconsequential, as if Gretchen hadn't run over the list of people who'd been in the house—herself, Bardot, Fran—time and again unable to come up with another suspect. Bardot just lifted her brows. "Shall I continue?"

Marconi waved magnanimously.

"The nanny took Gretchen up to bed at around eight o'clock," Bardot said. And with just that sentence, Gretchen realized Bardot had deliberately been avoiding mentioning the girl before. She had been so careful in her phrasing—just not careful enough.

The question was, *Why?* Was she protecting the nanny from something? Or herself?

"And Fran?" Marconi asked.

"Fran was old enough to see after herself."

"Right," Marconi said after a strange pause. "She was fifteen, correct?"

Anders and Bardot exchanged a look that Gretchen cataloged for later. She wasn't sure why the moment had become fraught, but both her parents and Marconi seemed poised at the edge of something.

It was Gretchen who answered. "Yes."

Everyone else seemed to exhale. It was one of those times, the ones where Gretchen felt her diagnosis most acutely. Something was layered beneath the surface that she couldn't understand. The words, sure. The body language—*that* she could discern. But what it added up to, she was missing.

Marconi sent her a half smile, but her eyes remained flat. "And you, Mrs. White, what were you doing?"

"I had a glass of wine in the study," Bardot said. "Read for a few hours—"

"What book?"

Bardot faltered. "How does that matter?"

Marconi held up a hand in a placating manner. "Just trying to paint myself a picture here."

Bardot glanced at her watch. "Well, while you're doing that, your time is running low. Are these really the questions you want to be asking, Detective?"

With more social grace than Gretchen would ever be able to muster in her life, Marconi looked down at her notebook, then back up. "So shall I put that you don't remember?"

"Put whatever you like," Bardot snapped.

"All right." Marconi scribbled something. "And then what happened?"

For some reason, the exchange seemed to have rattled Bardot. Anders must have sensed it as well because he shifted closer, his thumb rubbing over her knuckles. But he had very publicly and officially not been there that night, and so he couldn't jump in. Not without shifting into a more antagonistic tone.

"Around eleven thirty, I believe, the nanny started screaming," Bardot finally continued. "I went upstairs to find the poor girl outside Rowan's bedroom."

"And the door was open?"

"Yes," Bardot said. "The light was off, though. I could see . . ."

Gretchen raised a brow. "Me."

Bardot swallowed. "Yes. Holding a knife. And Rowan, as well. On the bed."

"And no one else in the room, correct?" Marconi checked.

"No, of course not," Bardot answered, almost defensive. "No one else was in the house."

"The nanny was there," Marconi pointed out. "In fact, she was the first person at the scene, if your account is accurate. That seems to have been omitted from the police reports."

Bardot blinked, lashes heavy with mascara. "What does that matter?"

"Do you remember, was there any blood on her?" Marconi asked. "On her hands or clothes? Maybe even on her shoes?"

"Of course there wasn't," Bardot said, though she sounded more confused than anything, as if she truly didn't see the point of their interest in the nanny.

Gretchen knew what Marconi was getting at, but the timeline Bardot gave rang true. The nanny had screamed right away. And she hadn't been the shadow in the room that Gretchen was still trying to force into the shape of a person.

"All right," Marconi said. "The knife, it was one from the house?"

"Yes, from the set in the kitchen," Bardot said. "It was quite expensive, which was how I was easily able to identify it."

"And you decided against entering the room to check on Rowan because . . ." Marconi's eyes dipped down to her notebook. But Gretchen got the sense that it was performative rather than necessary. "You were scared Gretchen was going to hurt you as well?"

At that, Anders seemed to finally see his opportunity. "You have to understand what Gretchen was like at the time, Detective."

"She had been previously violent?" Marconi asked, her tone carefully even.

"Yes," Anders said without a hint of shame. Not that Gretchen would expect anything else from him. "She hurt her sister, her mother, herself." His attention landed on Gretchen, who rolled her eyes at the way he was making a few slaps and bruises sound like torture. "We tried to help you."

"All right," Marconi said, again so easily. So nonthreateningly, if you didn't know her better. "What phone did you use to call the police, Mrs. White?"

Bardot hesitated, but then lifted her shoulder. "The one in the study."

"So you left the nanny and Gretchen upstairs to—"

"Run down to the study, yes."

"Right, right." Marconi agreed with a nod. "And your older daughter, Fran, slept through all this? The scream that was loud enough for you to hear downstairs?"

And, *ah*. Gretchen finally realized what the tense moment from earlier had been about. Fran had been in the house, too. If Gretchen had been old enough at eight to be a suspect, Fran at fifteen was an even better one. If you ignored the fact that it had been Gretchen holding the murder weapon.

Anders shifted forward. "What exactly are you trying to get after here, Detective? We all know what happened that night."

"Well, I'm not quite sure that's accurate, Dr. White." Marconi's smile was as pleasant as ever. "Could you answer the question, Mrs. White? Fran slept through all this?"

"She was a deep sleeper," Bardot said, recovering gracefully during the brief reprieve.

"Sure, same here," Marconi said. But she wrote something down. Gretchen almost wished this was being recorded. The whole conversation was turning out to be far more enjoyable than she could have ever expected, and she would have taken deep pleasure in watching it back. "Did you return upstairs? After you called the police."

"They wanted me to stay on the phone with them."

"So . . ." Marconi drew the word out. "No?"

Anders bristled once more. "Detective, I'm going to have to ask you to watch your tone. We're being more than cooperative here."

"Just trying to establish an accurate timeline," Marconi said, placating and apologetic. "And how long did it take for the police to arrive after you called them, Mrs. White?"

"About . . . I don't know, Detective. It was nearly thirty years ago."

"An estimate," Marconi pressed.

"I don't know, maybe ten minutes?" Bardot said.

"Leaving Gretchen, Fran, and the nanny all upstairs, unmonitored, with the victim," Marconi said softly, as if to herself, but everyone in the room heard.

This time Anders actually stood up. He wasn't a large man by any stretch, but he knew how to carry himself with a confidence that filled the space. "All right, I'm going to have to ask you to leave now."

Marconi glanced at him as if startled, as if she hadn't been poking at them for the past few minutes trying to get a reaction.

"If you have any further questions, you can direct them to our family lawyer," Anders said. "I'm sure Gretchen remembers his name well."

"Yes, I do actually," Gretchen said as she stood. "From when you tried to convince the judge I was mentally unfit to handle Edith's fortune."

Anders's eyes slid to the window, to where they could see the tail end of her Porsche, the message clear that he still held that opinion.

Marconi broke the moment by flipping her notebook closed and putting it away. "We'll be doing that. Thank you for your time. And we'll need the nanny's name the minute you find it."

Then, somehow, she managed to maneuver Gretchen out of the room without further incident.

Neither of them spoke until they were once again in the Porsche.

Gretchen slid her a look. "I didn't know you had that in you," she admitted. "I feel like I should be clapping."

Something hard had settled into Marconi's expression, but at that she grinned. "One of these days you'll stop being shocked I'm not as incompetent as you first thought."

"Perhaps," Gretchen acknowledged as she gunned the engine out onto the quiet street. "But today is not that day."

After several miles of silence, Marconi said quietly, "The nanny."

Gretchen's tongue traced over the fresh scar on her inner cheek. "There are two options here."

"Either your family hid the fact that there was someone else in the house," Marconi said.

"Or Shaughnessy lied about her presence in the official police report," Gretchen said, finishing the thought.

"Bardot didn't want us to know about her," Marconi said, and Gretchen wasn't surprised she'd picked up on that as well. "I've read her transcribed testimony from '93, and she didn't mention a nanny."

"Maybe," Gretchen said. "But it just as easily could have been Shaughnessy who kept her out of the report."

Marconi was a cop down to her bones, and while Gretchen was far from surprised that Shaughnessy might have been something less than completely honest, she could see Marconi struggling to wrap her mind around the fact that her partner might not be who she thought he was.

But then Marconi's chin tipped up, just slightly, like she was readying for a fight. "Well if it was him, it's time we find out why."

CHAPTER FIFTEEN

TABBY

1993

It took a month for Tabby to effectively work her way through Jenny's room—and all the papers she'd kept tucked in her desk.

One name kept cropping up over and over again in the weeks before Jenny's death.

Rowan White.

The mentions started with those group projects for their shared history class. But then Rowan was being penciled into Jenny's calendar, her initials scribbled on a Post-it. She even got a mention in the margins of the field hockey playbook.

Rowan getting a ride with Anders.

Tabby didn't understand what that meant—but she made sure to remember it.

When Tabby had been younger, she'd become obsessed with the microfilm machines at the library, in awe of how much information you could get from spending time there. But, searching now, they had been mostly useless when it came to anything on Rowan White. On a whim, Tabby had also searched for *Anders*—if that even was a real name—but had likewise found nothing.

So Tabby turned to the place that had been the connection between Rowan and Jenny.

She stepped into the principal's office at the Phillips Academy and immediately hated everything and everyone in sight. Tabby hadn't been smart like Jenny, hadn't earned any kind of scholarship—wouldn't have, even if she hadn't been distracted by the overwhelming and crushing grief of her sister's death.

But all principals' offices felt the same, and this one reminded her so strongly of JFK High over on Boyle Street that she ducked her head, expecting a reprimand simply for being there in ratty jeans and scuffed boots.

Mrs. Martinez, the principal, greeted her with a warm smile, though the kind people wore whenever they heard of her tragic backstory. Tabby played it up when she wanted something, and right now she wanted something.

She pinched her thigh through the pocket of her jeans and let her eyes go watery. "Just want to see the yearbooks . . . if you have them . . . Don't mean to be any trouble."

Mrs. Martinez's face went—if possible—even softer as she led Tabby to the library. A shelf off to the side held every yearbook going back several decades, and Tabby had to work to keep the triumph out of her expression until the principal backed away with quiet instructions to let the librarian know if she wanted to make a copy of any of the pages.

Tabby ran her finger along the neat spines of the yearbooks, plucking out the one for Jenny's junior year. Her last year.

With a quick glance to make sure no one was secretly watching, Tabby searched out the farthest, darkest table.

Timeless graffiti had been etched into the wood, and Tabby almost smiled as she touched CALL SUSAN FOR A GOOD TIME. No number—that was too much work to carve probably. Kids were so ridiculous and predictable.

She sat and flipped through the yearbook that would have had pictures of Jenny. There was a whole page dedicated in memoriam to her, with classmates performing grief for themselves, their parents, the masses. None of these people had actually known Jenny; none had cared about her.

Tabby found the generic class photo of Jenny, with her subdued smile, frizzy brown hair, and big glasses. The chunky striped turtleneck she had on was out-of-date even for nine years ago, and her two front teeth overlapped just enough to make it noticeable. But, God, she'd been pretty. Far prettier than Tabby.

Blinking hard, Tabby flipped the page until she got to the *Ws*.

Rowan White.

The girl was beautiful in an icy way. The picture was in black and white, but Tabby could tell Rowan had white-blonde hair cut in a bob just around her chin. It would have been strange, back then, to wear it like that.

There was something hauntingly dark about the girl's eyes. Probably it was because of the gray scale, but also Tabby had seen plenty of girls with sad eyes. Enough to recognize what it meant when she saw the bruises beneath them. Not all was right in the world of Rowan White.

Tabby spent the next half hour paging through the yearbook, searching for Rowan, in the posed club pictures, in the background of candid shots. There was a page dedicated to the Fall Festival, but there was no sign of Rowan, no sign of Jenny, and no sign of a handsome older man who might have been caught in the corner of a snapshot.

If only Tabby could be that lucky.

There were no mentions of anyone named Anders, either.

Checking once again to see if anyone was watching, Tabby snuck the disposable camera she'd brought out of her jacket pocket. She'd marked each page where Rowan had been mentioned, and she went through them now, snapping pictures. Even though the principal had assured her she could make copies of what she wanted, Tabby was feeling paranoid. She had no interest in anyone seeing whom she was focused on.

Once done, she slotted the yearbook back into place and eyed the librarian. She was on the younger side—maybe midthirties if Tabby had to guess. Jenny's murder had been about ten years ago, which meant she might know something. But it was more likely Tabby would get information out of the older woman who had been stationed outside the principal's office.

The place had only become more chaotic in the hour since Tabby had been in the library, but she spotted the dragon at the gates without a problem.

Mrs. Simmons—Gail Simmons, if her nameplate was to be believed—clearly reigned over her little fiefdom, but for some reason those types of women were always taken by Tabby. Maybe they recognized themselves in her hard exterior, in her take-no-shit expression. Whatever it was, Tabby wasn't going to question it.

She lingered by Mrs. Simmons's desk until the woman shot her a look over thick bifocals. "What?"

"I'm looking for information," Tabby said, straightforward without any hemming and hawing. That was always a good first step. "About a student named Anders."

Mrs. Simmons's mouth pursed, but she didn't immediately shoo Tabby away. That was a positive sign.

"You don't look too cut up about your sister," Mrs. Simmons said, blunt like Tabby should have expected.

And she had, honestly. Women with deep, weathered skin and eyes that had seen too much tended not to beat around the bush. "Yeah, well, it's been ten years."

Mrs. Simmons nodded once in acknowledgment of that fact. "That it has."

"Anders?" Tabby prompted.

"Not supposed to be giving out students' details willy-nilly," Mrs. Simmons said, sounding like she didn't care all that much for propriety but liked playing these games.

"For a student who has long since graduated?" Tabby asked, trying to suss her out. Either she just liked to gossip—which wouldn't be surprising for a woman in her position—or she wanted a bribe. If Tabby misjudged, she had the feeling it would backfire immediately.

"Anders White, and that's all I'm telling you," Mrs. Simmons said.

"White?" Tabby asked, straightening. "Related to Rowan White?"

"Brother," Mrs. Simmons said, in a strangely dark voice. Her salt-and-pepper brows had collapsed into a deep vee over the rims of her glasses. "Don't ask me anything else."

"What year?" Tabby couldn't help but press her luck.

Mrs. Simmons studied her and then heaved out a sigh big enough to make her substantial bosom roll with exasperation. "A decade or so before his sister?"

"Thank you." Tabby slid a wrapped caramel across the desk. A gesture that demonstrated gratitude and respect but didn't demean Mrs. Simmons's position with something so crass as cash.

"Humph." But the candy disappeared into Mrs. Simmons's palm as she sent Tabby a wink.

Tabby smiled at the ground as she made her way back to the library. She spared a wave at the librarian, but tried not to make it too familiar.

A decade or so left a lot to be interpreted. But Tabby pulled off four yearbooks in about that range. It took a while, but she made her way through all of them until she found Anders White.

It was his senior year picture so it was in color instead of black and white. He wore a nice suit with a silky green tie that brought out the deeper hues in his frozen-lake-blue eyes. He was almost as beautiful as Rowan, although Tabby was sure men didn't like to be described that way. It was true, though. Plush lips; a swoop of blond hair; a straight, strong nose; a straight, strong jawline. His mouth curved in that same smirk as Rowan's had, but his eyes weren't sad, and so the effect was different.

His charisma all but radiated from the page, like he would step out of ink and pixels and become real flesh and blood if only she closed her eyes and believed enough.

None of that was what caused her blood to rush against the thin skin of her wrist.

She swallowed, trying to even out her breathing, despite the sweat gathering at the nape of her neck, at the small of her back, in the dips of her palms.

She'd come to the library braced for the idea that she might recognize Rowan.

What Tabby hadn't been prepared for was the fact that she recognized Anders.

CHAPTER SIXTEEN

GRETCHEN

Now

It was late by the time Gretchen and Marconi crossed the bridge back into downtown Boston, and Shaughnessy had ignored all ten of Marconi's phone call attempts.

"He's going to avoid this as long as possible, you know," Gretchen pointed out.

Marconi's eyes were locked on something in the distance. "God, did he do it? Did he frame you?"

The shadow in the corner of the room as Rowan's life seeped out of her. Gretchen tried to make it look like Shaughnessy. "I wouldn't put it past him."

Marconi twisted in her seat. "You're taking this awfully well."

Gretchen lifted one shoulder. "The perks of being a sociopath. The betrayal thing isn't really a factor for me."

"No, I call bullshit." Marconi tried pointing a finger in Gretchen's face, and Gretchen snapped her teeth at the thing. "You get mad at me when I say 'What?'" She waved to the space between them. "You nearly just bit my finger off because I pointed at you. And you're not angry at the fact that Shaughnessy might have framed you for your entire life? I don't believe it."

"Like it's really that strange not to enjoy fingers near your face," Gretchen said, amused at Marconi's obvious exasperation. "And even as someone who appreciates a good leap of logic, the one you're making is about the size of the Grand Canyon. We don't even know if it was Shaughnessy who left the nanny out of the report. Even if he did, it might have been incompetence."

Marconi ignored Gretchen, her voice rising in the most entertaining manner. "You pinned me against a wall because I even mentioned this investigation."

Gretchen wished she didn't have to keep at least half an eye on the road. She was sure the flush along Marconi's neck would be intriguing to watch blossom into something deeper.

"You spun out of control for three months because I brought this case up," Marconi continued, far more agitated than Gretchen had ever seen her. "And now Shaughnessy might be involved—the man you say is the reason you have this insane self-control in the first place—and you don't even blink? I don't buy it. I don't."

"Maybe you should *calm down*," Gretchen said.

"See." Marconi almost pointed again but wisely dropped her arm. "You're pissed that I told you to calm down at your parents' place. You may be able to keep it hidden, but your temper is literally hair-trigger. There is no way you're not upset about this."

Something clicked.

"Oh," Gretchen said. "You're getting emotional on my behalf again."

It had happened before, and each time it did, it delighted Gretchen.

Marconi slumped back in her seat, like her strings had been cut. "The nonreaction is freaking me out."

"You barely react when I threaten people with violence, and yet it's the fact that I'm not about to kill someone that's troubling you?" Gretchen checked.

"Well when you put it like that, I sound—"

"Let's go with irrational, shall we?" Gretchen cut in. "And anyway, Shaughnessy never framed me."

Gretchen held up a hand when it looked like Marconi was about to get riled again. "I wasn't arrested, which he could have done even if he knew I wouldn't be charged. He didn't frame me. At most, he tried and failed."

"But . . ." Marconi floundered. "You've dealt with the suspicion your whole life. Even now some cops won't work with you."

"Are you trying to make me angry?" Gretchen asked, curious mostly.

Marconi all but threw up her hands. "Yes."

Gretchen glanced over. "I could probably pop out a few tears if that would make you feel better."

Marconi flipped her off, and Gretchen laughed.

"You said Shaughnessy is your line in the sand," Marconi said, slightly more subdued, more serious. "You said he's your moral compass. So what happens if we find out he's not quite as good a person as you might have believed?"

While it was a myth that sociopaths were all mindless killers, it was still a dangerous diagnosis. The uncontrollable urges, the inability to weigh consequences, the thrill-seeking behavior to alleviate boredom, they all primed a person to commit crimes of varying degrees. Sociopaths, especially those on the less severe side of the spectrum as Gretchen was, realized that those symptoms could have a negative effect on the lives they enjoyed. So they created anchors, guideposts, lines in the sand they wouldn't cross. Anything that would tether them to appropriate behavior to allow them to function in society.

For some, that was religion—a clear set of rules often proved extremely useful. For others, it was the penal code—maybe allowing themselves to rack up misdemeanors but making sure to steer clear of felonies.

It had taken a few years of trial and error—and a brief stint in what she now realized was a cult—for Gretchen to recognize that she kept coming back to one thing.

Shaughnessy.

She had no love for the man. Grudging respect would be as far as she went. Maybe, on a good day, an acknowledgment of their mutually beneficial relationship. But on most occasions when Gretchen's impulses had flared bright and big and almost impossible to put out, she'd seen Shaughnessy's face. The smugness that would come if he ever had the chance to arrest her and actually make it stick.

Now she wondered if she'd been misreading the situation all along.

That, in and of itself, wouldn't be shocking. Gretchen often misread the nuances that motivated other people—that was as much a part of her diagnosis as the desire to floor her Porsche through every red light in Boston. She relied on stereotypes and clichés even more than the average person, fell back on the broad generalizations that made sitcoms so watchable and body language tutorials universal.

Gretchen had always read Shaughnessy's watchful behavior as suspicion. That's how cops would act in those murder-a-week procedurals.

But maybe it was something else. Something she could neither read nor understand.

You said he's your moral compass. Marconi had just thrown that down like a gauntlet. But was it true any longer? Gretchen thought about the way the Viola Kent case had played out, thought about the way Marconi had kept showing up at her door, the way she'd bullied Gretchen into trying to clear her own name. That was more than Shaughnessy had ever done in the past thirty years they'd known each other.

"Well, now I have *you* for that, don't I?" Gretchen tossed out lightly, not quite meaning it but not fully teasing, either.

"But I've never thought you killed anyone," Marconi countered. She knew it wasn't Shaughnessy's *opinion* that mattered to Gretchen, it was proving him wrong.

"Yes, but you would give me those disappointed eyes," Gretchen said on a shudder, "if I ever did something you didn't agree with."

"I'm pretty sure you've done plenty I don't agree with."

Gretchen shot her a look. "But nothing that would make you stop working with me."

"And that matters to you?"

"I told you, life's all about the cost-benefit ratio," Gretchen said with a careless shrug that belied the importance of the conversation. "The benefit you bring to this partnership—like making Bardot look like she wanted to shit bricks right there in her perfect little living room—outweighs the cost of not killing someone just because I feel like it."

"I'm honored," Marconi said dryly. But if Gretchen was forced to guess, she'd say there was some truth beneath the words. Marconi glanced at the time, sighed. "Drop me at home?"

Gretchen pulled to the curb of the next empty spot. "Your observation skills are the real reason I keep you around."

Marconi jerked and then glared up at her own apartment building like it had betrayed her. When she glanced back at Gretchen, she studied her for a long second. "I'm not going to wake up to news that Shaughnessy's been killed in his sleep, am I?"

The question surprised a laugh out of Gretchen. "If I ever killed Shaughnessy, it wouldn't be in his sleep. It would be long, painful, and there would be some symbolism involved, without a doubt."

"I feel so reassured," Marconi muttered, but then grabbed her bag and hauled herself out of the Porsche. "Just remember, I won't help you hide this particular body."

"Oh," Gretchen crooned. "But others?"

"Depends on the cost-benefit ratio to me," Marconi said, slamming the door behind her.

Gretchen rolled down the window to shout, "We'll make a proper sociopath out of you yet."

Marconi didn't even bother to look as she flipped Gretchen the finger.

Gretchen laughed off and on for the ten minutes it took to drive to Shaughnessy's apartment. She parked in the shadows, dug for the knife she'd used to slash the man's tire earlier in the day, and stroked the blade with the tip of one finger as the darkness fell around her.

CHAPTER SEVENTEEN
SHAUGHNESSY

1984

The ice-crusted snow crunched beneath Shaughnessy's boots.

Some part of him recognized it as beautiful, this winter wonderland. But all he could really concentrate on was the fact that snow had a way of hiding evidence.

Not that Shaughnessy thought he'd actually be successful on this goose chase. This was stupid, pointless. But that hadn't stopped Shaughnessy from driving out toward the woods, looking for something, *anything*, that would prove his theory right.

The rising sun caught the edge of something metal in the distance, and Shaughnessy caught his breath. The light splintered so that he couldn't see what it bounced off, but he started in the direction anyway.

Up. Just a small hill, but enough of a rise so that it made sense Rowan had headed down, in this direction.

He blinked, panted, slid, and then righted himself, holding his hand up flat so that he could make out the silhouette of . . . something.

A shed.

When he got to the top of the hill, he shifted so that the rising sun was to his back, the small structure spotlighted by its rays.

It had narrow windows on each side, high, toward the roof so that they'd be hard to climb out of if someone were trapped inside. It was neither abnormally small nor overlarge. The paint had chipped in some spots, but in general the thing looked well maintained.

A padlock hung against the door.

There are more girls. Find them.

Shaughnessy gripped his Maglite, glanced around. He hadn't crossed any property line that he could tell, though he was close enough to the White mansion that he knew he could feasibly be on their land.

Still. There was no sign. There was no fence.

He chewed on the inside of his cheek, his fingers going numb around the heavy flashlight.

Shaughnessy tried to ignore the echoes of his family's taunts, but couldn't quite silence them.

Focused.

Creepy.

If he broke the padlock, nothing he found in the shed could be used in an actual case. If he broke the padlock and the chief found out, he'd likely be fired. At best.

Shaughnessy closed his eyes, as if he'd be able to hear the screams of some phantom victim locked up in those walls. Nothing but the wind greeted him.

He could try to look into the windows, but the shed was just tall enough that he'd need a ladder to really get a good view.

There was nothing in there anyway. He was being ridiculous.

Maybe if he just broke the damn thing he'd be able to get on with his life, forget about that night, forget about Rowan White.

The padlock cracked before he even realized he'd raised the heavy flashlight.

He stared down at it. It had been so easy. Too easy.

No one would ever have to know.

Shaughnessy watched as his gloved hand reached out, knocked the stray pieces out of the lock, pulled open the door.

It was the metal chains this time that caught the rising sun. And then the knives on the wall, their blades slick and shiny.

Just as his hand dropped to his radio—to do what? call this in?—the unmistakable sound of a rifle cocking had him whirling around.

Anders White stepped from the shadowed trees.

"Officer Shaughnessy." Anders greeted him like he would have if they'd just bumped into each other in a coffeehouse in the middle of Boston, that same pleasant smile on his face from when they'd met six months ago. "Would you care to explain exactly what you are doing on my property?"

The question punched the air out of Shaughnessy's lungs and every single doubt he'd had about this little trip rushed into the emptiness left behind.

But if he went on the defensive here, he knew he'd never recover his footing. "You want to explain your little sadistic chamber?"

Anders followed Shaughnessy's gesture back to the open shed. "I'm sure you had a warrant to look in there, Officer. I can't imagine a fine, upstanding member of Boston's Police Department actually breaking and entering on private property."

"Probable cause," Shaughnessy offered up with a confidence he was mostly faking.

The corner of Anders's mouth lifted, like he was more amused than irritated by all this. "And yet we offered you a perfectly good explanation for why Rowan was in the road that night. What other probable cause could you possibly have?"

Something about the phrase "offered you a perfectly good explanation" hit Shaughnessy wrong. Like Anders knew it was bullshit, but also knew that on paper it held up. "I heard screaming."

Anders relaxed out of his hunter's stance so that the barrel of the rifle pointed at the ground instead of Shaughnessy's chest. "From the road?"

Shaughnessy could play this game, too. "I was on a hike, didn't realize it was private property."

Tilting his head, Anders asked curiously, "What do you want, Officer Shaughnessy? What purpose could this have possibly served?"

"I'm looking for more girls," Shaughnessy said. The only way to get guys like this to flinch was to rush at them, knock them off their feet before they could twist you up in slick words and fancy distractions. "You may have started or finished with Rowan, but she's not your only victim, White."

"More girls," Anders echoed, slowly, like he was tasting unfamiliar words. Then he sighed. "Oh. Rowan really did get in your head, didn't she? You think I'm one of those . . . those serial killers."

Know it, Shaughnessy wanted to correct, although he knew this was madness, knew this was a terrible misstep. He couldn't quite seem to shut his goddamn mouth, though. Never in his life had someone raised all his alarm bells like this man did.

"Want to explain the sadistic chamber?" he asked again instead of confirming or denying Anders's guess.

Anders laughed lightly. "Not a hunter are you, Officer Shaughnessy?"

Shaughnessy shot him an incredulous look. "Yeah, didn't really get to that badge in the Boy Scouts."

"You know what?" Anders said with a magnanimous smile and a wave toward the shed. "Have at it."

Shaughnessy knew Anders was smarter than he was, knew he could easily be played by this man. He tried to imagine any way this could be a ploy—would Anders lock him in once he turned his back? But that seemed unlikely. So he nudged the door open as carefully as possible, then stepped inside.

It took ten minutes, but he had to admit after thoroughly searching the small square footage that there wasn't anything damning in it, either.

"Can I explain to you what you're about to think?" Anders called in that crisp, condescending voice. "Since I am a trained psychiatrist."

Shaughnessy grunted as he reinspected a crack in the concrete floor, wondering if there was blood down there he just couldn't quite get to.

"You won't find anything in there, but that won't matter. You'll move the goalposts," Anders continued. "You'll think that I must keep my serial killer den somewhere else. It's how conspiracy theories work, Officer."

Nothing goddamn *theoretical* about a clearly abused girl running out into the middle of the road in the middle of the night. But Shaughnessy didn't waste his breath arguing.

"And when you don't find it—or any other victims for that matter—you'll simply think I've gotten away with some heinous crime. That I'm a genius so I can clearly outsmart anyone investigating me. You will never be convinced that I'm innocent," Anders said, not sounding too ruffled about the possibility. In fact, his voice had taken on a curious, academic tone, like Shaughnessy was a case study. "There will be no convincing you otherwise, even if I gave you free rein to search the mansion. Even if we let you talk to all of Rowan's psychiatrists who will swear up and down that she's suffering from depression and delusions."

Because you treated her, and the rest would be all your buddies was what Shaughnessy thought as he stared at the weapons strapped to one of the walls. Knives. Deadly, damning, and yet ultimately pointless to his investigation. They could certainly have made the cuts on Rowan's arms. But even if he proved they were used, Shaughnessy couldn't prove the wounds hadn't been self-inflicted.

Everything was circumstantial here. Everything had a *perfectly good explanation* attached to it.

"You have no proof of anything, Officer," Anders said. There was no hint of malice underlying the words, no challenge even. He was being reasonable to a fault. If Shaughnessy was watching this play out from the outside, he'd think himself the crazy one here. "And I wouldn't mind except that I have a feeling you'll be bothering Rowan in the future. I can't let you do that."

Bothering Rowan. She might be eighteen now, and be able to have a say about her visitors, even if she was being held in a psychiatric facility. Shaughnessy kept his expression flat as he finally stepped out of the shed. "Is that a threat?"

Anders held up his free hand, palm out. "I wouldn't dream of threatening a law enforcement officer. But I will be informing your chief about this little incident."

Shaughnessy nodded. He'd expected no less. He thought about everything he'd read on serial killers, how the ones who were smart and controlled liked to brag about everything they'd gotten away with, how many of them secretly wanted to get caught. "I get it. I'm not clever enough to catch you, White. But you know what?"

"Hmmm?" Anders encouraged, clearly still amused.

"Someday someone will be," Shaughnessy said. "And when that day comes, you'll pay for everything you've done."

"Everything I've done," Anders said, almost beneath his breath, his eyes on the ground.

And for the first time since Anders had stepped into the little clearing, the mask dropped.

What lay beneath wasn't fear or ego or pleasure, like Shaughnessy would have expected.

No. In that flicker, that brief second where Anders seemed unable to school his expression, what showed on his face was deep, profound sorrow.

CHAPTER EIGHTEEN

GRETCHEN

Now

Gretchen had never killed anyone. Not that she could remember, at least.

There were a few times in her life when her rage had burned bright and deadly, but she'd never taken that final, irreversible step.

Perhaps it wouldn't take much to kill Shaughnessy, just a blade drawn across a neck. It didn't seem like an impossible feat. But Gretchen had never been inherently prone to vicious attacks—urges and impulses alone did not equal real violence.

Although she'd been born without the ability to care about the innate sanctity of other people's lives, Gretchen had no actual desire to take one. Especially not Shaughnessy's, who even with his flaws had proven, on the whole, mostly beneficial to her life.

Gretchen watched from the driver's seat of her Porsche as the lights in Shaughnessy's apartment flipped on, the knife she had been twirling now resting against the pad of her thumb.

It was hard to make out anything more than a dark outline behind the curtains, but Gretchen saw Shaughnessy in her mind, moving through the rooms, putting some old record on the ancient vinyl player he kept next to his portable bar. Pouring himself something brown and medium priced because that was a splurge for the man.

One time, Gretchen had bought him high-end Scotch for Christmas, and she thought it was the closest he'd come to ever crying in her presence.

She tapped her phone to check the time. It wasn't much past midnight, but Shaughnessy wouldn't be going to bed anytime soon. He suffered from insomnia, a fact that she'd used to her advantage before when she'd wanted to catch him at his weakest.

The whole time she'd known him, she'd thought he was just *that* moral, thought the cases he'd never been able to solve weighed at the soul he put so much stock in. Now she wondered if there was another reason he couldn't sleep at night.

The problem was that Gretchen had just spent the past three hours trying to figure out a reason for him to lie about the nanny's presence that night.

She couldn't come up with one reasonable justification. That didn't mean there wasn't one, of course. Gretchen knew better than most that people tended to think they could guess every motivation and outcome even when the amount of knowledge they had was a mere crack in the door. She was prone to falling into that trap, especially given the delusions of grandeur that came with her diagnosis.

But Gretchen kept getting stuck down logical dead ends.

Had Shaughnessy known the nanny prior to finding her at the scene of a crime? That would keep him from including her in the report unless for whatever reason it made her look suspicious. But how suspicious could anyone look standing next to a blood-covered girl holding the murder weapon?

Had Bardot shuffled the nanny out of the house even as she ran to the study to call the police? In theory, in a panic the entire time after finding her sister-in-law brutally stabbed by Bardot's young daughter?

That made slightly more sense than Shaughnessy lying on an official police report, but that was a low bar to pass.

And why would Bardot shuffle the nanny out in the first place? She had no loyalty to anyone but herself and her husband.

Three hours in, Gretchen started poking at the possibility that Shaughnessy and Bardot somehow conspired together. That's when she realized she was getting nowhere.

The picture of the two of them working for a common purpose was almost laughable. She wasn't even going to start dreaming up motivations for why they would do that.

For now, she didn't have the right pieces to figure out what had really happened. Whatever secrets Shaughnessy was keeping, he'd held on to them for three decades. She wasn't going to find any answers here. Not tonight.

So Gretchen drove away from his apartment, the lights still blazing, the smudge of a silhouette firmly ensconced in the armchair in front of the window.

There was no point to going home, as late—or early—as it was. Gretchen wasn't going to be able to sleep, so she wound through the streets as the city started to slowly awaken. She flirted with tight corners and nudged the speedometer ever higher, her thoughts as restless and unsettled as her trajectory. But eventually she ended up at Marconi's, and she wondered idly if that meant something important.

Outside, she texted, and Marconi must have been waiting for her because she was swinging through the building's door only two minutes later.

"No body to bury, I guess," Marconi said when she climbed into the Porsche.

"It's cute that you think you would know," Gretchen retorted, sipping on the coffee she had picked up for herself but not for Marconi. Marconi glared at the cup, then dug out her own thermos from her oversize bag, a cocky little twist to her mouth like she believed she'd one-upped Gretchen by predicting her thoughtlessness.

"So I went through the police report on Rowan's death again with the idea that it was incomplete," Marconi said as Gretchen started driving without a destination in mind. "And I realized the detail about the nanny isn't the only thing missing."

Gretchen shot Marconi a look. But she wasn't about to be baited into asking *What?*

Marconi smirked, clearly hearing it in the silence anyway. "The coroner's report was missing a page."

"Which page?" Gretchen asked, already making a U-turn to head in the direction of the medical examiner's office.

"Second to last."

Which meant it might not be anything important. "How can you tell?"

"It was hefty enough that I never noticed it went from page seventeen to page nineteen before." Marconi sipped her coffee. "The information is all—I don't know what you'd call it with coroner's reports, but for lack of a better word—B-matter."

Gretchen shook her head, not getting it. "Come up with a better word."

"You know what I mean," Marconi protested. "It was noting things like her thyroid and fractures from when she was a kid. Background information that's not really pertinent to the current investigation."

"But a page was missing from there," Gretchen said, more to herself than Marconi. She rarely needed things repeated.

"Yeah. Someone wanted to hide something from the official report," Marconi said.

"Guesses?"

Marconi seemed to think on that. Lifted a shoulder. "Scars maybe? From abuse when she was younger?"

"But you said the fractures were mentioned." Again, it was more thinking out loud than anything else. "Why would someone take that out if it was just more of the same?"

"Whatever it was they removed, they were damn lucky."

"How so?" Gretchen asked.

"It's not jarring at all, the missing page," Marconi said. "It reads as if it's not there. I wonder if it was a completely separate notation."

Gretchen eyed Marconi, and after a beat of silence grudgingly tossed out, "Good work."

"Oho!" Marconi laughed. "Did that actually hurt for you to say? It looked like it hurt."

Gretchen's mouth twisted to show she was annoyed, but a smile lurked behind her teeth, and she guessed that Marconi realized it. "Don't ever say I never gave you anything."

"Right, because your praise is worth its weight in gold," Marconi snarked back.

"No use arguing with the truth," Gretchen said, and Marconi laughed again, a deep sound that easily filled the interior of the car. Marconi was lighter these days than she had been when they'd first met. She had defenses, like an old castle with its moat and drawbridge, its high walls and turrets. Gretchen wondered if Marconi may have let Gretchen inside at least a few of them.

How many more existed?

Marconi did her very best to blend with the background, even though objectively speaking she was gorgeous—all curves, dark hair, pale skin, and impossibly light hazel eyes—intelligent, and a fairly competent detective. The combination would have normally wreaked havoc on Gretchen's carefully ordered world, jealously and bitterness layering into every interaction. Gretchen was not one to take to competition well.

But for some reason, Marconi seemed to fit up against Gretchen's jagged edges. She never reacted the way Gretchen would predict, and for that, she kept things interesting.

The worst thing for a sociopath was boredom, and Marconi certainly wasn't boring.

Gretchen pushed the thought aside as they pulled up to the medical examiner's office.

"Oh look, it's your favorite place," Marconi said, and she wasn't joking.

Despite the fact that Gretchen might not be built for murder herself, she was a sociopath. She was drawn to death, to shredded flesh and sour wounds and bodily fluids that had nowhere to go but *out*. Gretchen had once stood over her best friend's dead body and admired the way her muscles twitched from rigor mortis.

The morgue scratched every morbid itch that burrowed into her skin, and she loved it.

But even more than she loved the place, she loved Dr. Leo Chen, perhaps Gretchen's favorite person in the entirety of the Boston Police Department. Not because he was professional or kind or smart—though she knew that people said he was all of those things. Instead it was because he shared her delicious fascination with dead things.

"Gretchen," Dr. Chen called, elbow deep in someone's belly. Through glasses covered by bug-eyed lenses, he watched her and Marconi cross the room. When they stopped beside the examining table, he kissed the air in the direction of Gretchen's cheeks, his hands still buried in the organs of his current cadaver. "And Detective Marconi. What a pleasure, what a pleasure."

"A bad time?" Gretchen asked. The corpse was stiff and pale, as most corpses were. A young man riddled with obvious bullet holes. She didn't think it took an advanced degree to figure out what had happened to him.

Stab wounds were far more intriguing. She didn't want to think about the why of that; it would likely lead her to her own history and also far too close to Dr. Freud's theories. And she'd written that man off as a hack about twenty minutes into her first Psychology 101 class.

"Never a bad time to receive a call from my favorite visitor," Dr. Chen said, beaming at Gretchen. The coroner was nearly old enough to be her grandfather and preferred male partners, but they did enjoy flirting. "I suppose this isn't a social call?"

On Friday nights, when Gretchen was feeling in a particular mood, she'd come down to Dr. Chen's to pore over historic photos of medical oddities while drinking his expensive port. It was often the highlight of her week.

"Sadly no," Gretchen admitted with a little pout. Dr. Chen finally pulled his hands out of the dead body, but he was so smeared in blood and entrails neither Gretchen nor Marconi moved any closer. "You weren't the lead coroner for my aunt's death, correct?"

Dr. Chen sighed, loud and long. "Oh that I could have been. But tragically, no. That was my predecessor. I was but a mere assistant at the time."

"Did you participate in it?" Gretchen asked. Dr. Chen always seemed older than God, but she wasn't sure of the exact date he'd been hired in Boston.

"I did indeed," Dr. Chen said, shucking off his gloves after giving the corpse's flank a pat. "An honor of a lifetime, getting to work on that case, though I did not realize it at the time."

"Because of its connection to me?" Gretchen grinned.

"Why else?" Dr. Chen tossed her an exaggerated wink.

Marconi bit off an "Oh my god."

"Don't mind her," Gretchen said. "She has no appreciation for the dramatic."

Dr. Chen, who had been somewhat won over by Marconi in the past, swooned. "That will never do."

"Tell me about it," Gretchen agreed.

"I feel like I should be defending myself," Marconi cut in. "But I really can't argue with the facts."

"Do you remember it well by any chance?" Gretchen asked. "Rowan's autopsy?"

"I'm sorry, I do not. Not any particular details, at least." Dr. Chen hung his head, a kicked puppy dog. "I could refresh my memory if it's important."

"With the official report?" Marconi asked.

That got Dr. Chen's attention. "Of course."

"The report's been tampered with," Gretchen told him.

Dr. Chen actually took several steps back, clutching at his chest. "Sacrilege."

"My thoughts precisely," Gretchen said. "Is there any chance there's a handwritten backup?"

"Oh dear," Dr. Chen murmured. "In the archives, perhaps. There was a fire in '97, so I can't guarantee it's there, but that would be your best bet."

"It's accessible by us?"

"Not an official case, I presume?" When Gretchen nodded once in acknowledgment, Dr. Chen glanced around. "Then, no. Not in theory."

"But?"

He stroked his chin. "I have been looking for a project for my interns. Perhaps organizing the archives would prove educational for them."

"Have I ever told you you're my favorite person in the world?" Gretchen asked.

"Not nearly often enough, my dear," Dr. Chen said, a blush crawling into the crevices of his wrinkles. "Now shoo. I'll call if we find anything."

As they stepped back outside, Marconi nudged Gretchen's shoulder with her own. "What are the chances they'll find something?"

"I'd give it thirty-seventy of not," Gretchen said. "But it's not looking good for Shaughnessy's innocence here. It's not as if my parents would have had access to the coroner's office."

"I wonder how easy it would have been to bribe someone, though," Marconi pointed out, and Gretchen had to admit that was a possibility. Her parents were fantastic at throwing money at a problem. It probably wouldn't have taken more than a couple of hundred bucks in those days, and that was essentially pennies to her parents. Or even Edith.

That reminded Gretchen that she still hadn't heard from Bardot about the nanny's name. She dialed the numbers for both the house and her mother's cell phone, but both went to voice mail. That was strange. There was always a maid around to answer the main line, at least.

Was Bardot avoiding the question?

Marconi drummed her fingers on the roof of the Porsche after Gretchen restashed her phone. "Shaughnessy's also been dodging my calls since yesterday."

They could chase him down, Gretchen supposed. But what would he even tell them if he was this determined not to talk to them?

"Fran?" Gretchen suggested despite the sour taste it left in her mouth.

"Yeah," Marconi said slowly. "But while we're in town, I may have another idea first."

Gretchen considered objecting just to be contrary, but Marconi was usually a go-with-the-flow partner. That meant if she was trying to suggest something, she thought it would truly help. "All right."

"Just like that?" Marconi asked, rocking back on her heels. *Surprised,* Gretchen's brain supplied.

"No, not just like that," Gretchen replied.

Marconi was trying to hide a smile, and Gretchen glared.

"What?" Gretchen snapped out.

"You trust me," Marconi singsonged, like an insane person. "You like me."

"Don't get ahead of yourself." Gretchen rolled her eyes, dropping into the driver's seat.

"You can't fool me anymore," Marconi crowed, as she buckled up. "You want me around."

Gretchen heaved a sigh but didn't deny it. "Where is this brilliant idea of yours taking us? And please believe me you'll never live it down if it's a terrible suggestion."

Some of the sunshine seeped out of Marconi's expression, and she slid Gretchen a look. "You're not going to like it."

"Off to a good start," Gretchen muttered.

Marconi chewed on her lip. "Lachlan Gibbs."

When Gretchen started cursing, Marconi held up her hands. "I said you wouldn't like it."

"Not liking it and not wanting to get arrested are worlds apart." Gretchen jammed the key in the ignition. Lachlan Gibbs was a hotshot in Internal Affairs, and he had annoyingly strong opinions about sociopaths being used as police consultants. "Galaxies."

"Lachlan is not going to arrest you."

"Darling"—Gretchen revved the engine—"trust me when I say don't bet on it."

Marconi's eyes slid toward Gretchen and she grimaced. "Okay, yeah he might. But it could be worth it. If there are any inside rumors about Shaughnessy and Rowan's case—he'll have heard about them."

Gretchen sighed and pulled into traffic. "You're paying my bail."

CHAPTER NINETEEN

TABBY

1993

Tabby stared at the business card Cal had given her that first night, pressing the tips of her fingers into the points at the corners.

Girls who play Nancy Drew get murdered.

She glanced toward the living room where her father was passed out on the couch and then grabbed the phone, tucking it between her ear and shoulder.

When Cal answered on the third ring, Tabby squeezed her eyes closed, letting his voice wash over her. "Can we meet?"

There was a pause. Then: "Everything okay? You sound strange."

"Yeah, yeah of course," Tabby said, her fingers getting caught as she ran a shaky hand through her thick hair. "I don't know, I think I . . ."

"What?" he prompted when she didn't continue.

"Found something?" she said, hearing the doubt in her own voice. "I don't know. I'm probably just being stupid." She paused, and then asked again, "Can we meet?"

Another heavy silence fell. But then he gave her a time, before hanging up without saying goodbye.

It wasn't that strange. He was probably angry she'd called him in the middle of the day. That always seemed to get his temper up. But she didn't care. She needed something to get her mind off the afternoon, the yearbooks, Anders and Rowan White.

Cal picked her up in a beat-up trash heap of a car that Tabby wouldn't be surprised to hear he'd stolen from some junkyard.

She wondered if his real car was something like a BMW.

The passenger side door had a dent over the joint so that it took three pulls for her to get it open. Once she'd slid in, Cal roared away from the curb.

"I told you not to call me during the day" was the way he greeted her. She'd been right: he was pissed.

Tabby curled in on herself, pulling her legs up to her chest, resting her forehead on her upturned knees, as if making herself small would make her less irritating to him. She didn't apologize. She didn't say anything.

They just drove.

It took twenty minutes for Cal to decide on a motel. He didn't bother telling her to wait in the car—just got out, slammed the door behind him, stalked off to the little building that housed the check-in desk and not much else.

Why had she thought this was a good idea?

Because she wanted to not think, and Cal helped her not think.

He was angrier than he should be, though.

And that paranoia crept in as she replayed their conversation. *I found something . . . Can we meet?*

Cal knew she was investigating her sister's murder. He'd introduced himself to her only days after she'd gotten the file stolen from the archives.

Stop it.

God, she was so sick of herself. Of this constant buzz beneath her skin that told her she needed to flee, to hide. A shrink would probably slap a fancy word on her behavior, but Tabby didn't need a diagnosis to know this feeling wasn't rational.

But still, as Cal walked back to the car, Tabby had to tell herself, *You're not scared. He's not going to hurt you.*

There was nowhere to run anyway. They were in the middle of nothing, the only things around besides the motel were a dubious-looking McDonald's and an unlit gas station with boarded-up windows.

He picked this place for a reason.

Tabby tugged at her hair, *hard*, to get that stupid voice to shut the fuck up.

She repeated the mantra to herself when he stopped by the trunk, opened it, and pulled out a bag.

They didn't do overnights. They got together for a couple of hours, screwed, and then went on their merry way.

Why did he need a bag?

Tabby chewed on her lip, pulling her legs into her chest.

I think I found something.

When she stepped out of the car, his entire demeanor shifted. He shot her a smile and lifted the bag. "I have dinner plans. Didn't want to go home in between."

The throbbing ball of anxiety in her chest didn't loosen, but Tabby tried to pretend it had. She smiled back, nodded. Couldn't imagine how she was going to get through sex with him. What would he do if she pushed him away now? If she told him she'd changed her mind.

Swallowing, she eyed the little lobby building that was so far away, eyed the McDonald's one more time. Would she be able to make it to either before he was on her?

Stop it.

Why was she thinking like this? She was so exhausted from living a life shaped by Jenny's murder.

So instead of letting that fear dictate her actions any longer, Tabby gave Cal a real smile, stepping close to hook two fingers in the loops of his belt. She all but felt him falter at this new welcome, but his charming expression didn't flicker. Neither of them would mention the odd strain between them, it seemed, even after it dissipated.

"Hey," she said, sultry, so she sounded pleased to see him. Fake it till you make it.

He studied her for a long minute, and then he gave her a tentative half smile. "Hey."

There was almost a question mark at the end of it, like he was riding this emotional roller coaster as much as she was.

Tabby pulled away, sending him a look over her shoulder, a classic come-hither. She saw him hesitate for one second when his eyes dropped to the bag in his hand and then slid back to the trunk.

You're not scared.

Then as if the pause hadn't happened at all, he grinned and sauntered after her.

Cal dropped the bag by the door once they stepped inside. The room was typical for them—shitty and smelling of smoke and pot. The TV was a decade old, and she was certain the mirror in the bathroom would be cloudy and cracked. The familiarity of it soothed her nerves. This was fine. They'd be fine.

She stretched, then plopped on the bed, grabbing the remote in an effort to actually calm down.

A small part of her brain registered that Cal didn't take his shoes off like he normally did.

It was a habit of his, slipping out of his loafers and leaving them by the door. He did it without fail.

Tabby kept her attention on the TV screen that was now flashing with some kind of infomercial, all bright colors. It would be loud if she hadn't muted it first.

Loud enough to cover any struggle that might occur.

She turned the TV off.

Cal leaned back against the door, his arms crossed over his chest, face casual. If she didn't know him at all, she'd think him relaxed. But she could see the strain in the way he held his shoulders, in the grip of his hands against his elbows.

Her eyes slipped to the bag, and when she glanced back up, she could tell he'd noticed.

"You found something?" His voice was controlled but not defensive. She shook herself. This was him asking a simple question, nothing else. It's what she said to him on the phone. She would expect anyone to be curious.

"I thought I recognized . . . ," Tabby started, stopped herself. Stupid. She looked away. "No, it was nothing."

"You sounded upset on the phone," he pushed, like she'd expected him to.

Tabby pressed her lips together. "I just want to forget about it for now."

Without thinking about it, she noted the closed curtains, the windows that were probably sealed shut with neglect and age.

Cal was blocking the only exit. He'd brought her to a motel in the middle of nowhere, and he was blocking the only exit.

You're not scared. You're not . . .

Her lungs burned, and it was then that she realized she was taking increasingly desperate gulps of air. Her shoulders heaved, her heart beating fast enough that she could feel each pulse.

"Here's the thing, Tabitha," Cal said, reaching down to his bag. "I don't believe you."

CHAPTER TWENTY

GRETCHEN

Now

"You're sleeping with Gibbs," Gretchen figured out as she maneuvered into the parking lot of the police station. "You're messing around with the future director of Internal Affairs."

Unflappable as Marconi usually was, she got weird about sex. At the question, she actually blushed. "I am not."

Gretchen laughed, now convinced she was right. "You are. You called him Lachlan."

"Foolproof evidence," Marconi said in that tone of voice that was the equivalent of an eye roll.

"When was the last time you called a detective by their first name?" Gretchen said, smug and amused now. Her favorite combination. It took the sting out of the fact that they were headed to Internal Affairs.

A beat passed, and then Marconi winced.

"Aha!" Gretchen poked Marconi's shoulder and got swatted at in return. "What exactly does your moral compass have to say about all this?"

"We're just friends. I think he could have some insight about Shaughnessy," Marconi said, but her tone was too ruffled, too defensive for her to be anything but embarrassed. "He's pretty anal-retentive about keeping tabs on all the officers here."

"Oh, I'm sure he has plenty of 'insight' to offer," Gretchen said.

"That doesn't even mean anything," Marconi muttered.

Gretchen continued as if she hadn't heard her. "And he thinks I'm the one who doesn't have any ethics."

She wasn't exactly in the habit of making friends with Boston's finest—Marconi being the exception rather than the rule—but many of the seasoned detectives found her useful enough not to make a fuss about her history.

On the whole, she found that logic extremely satisfying to her nature. She appreciated people who understood the cost-benefit ratio, even if she didn't actually *like* them.

But that didn't mean she didn't have plenty of enemies within the department. Or at least people who treated her with far more suspicion than respect.

Lachlan Gibbs, well set on his path toward taking over IA, was the man at the front of that charge, handing out torches to anyone with a similar opinion.

Gretchen didn't know if IA had enough influence to keep consultants off cases, but she wouldn't put it past Gibbs to do everything in his power to try.

A bad influence, that's what the department thought of her. At least that's what she'd gathered over the years of mutual distrust.

"You *don't* have any ethics," Marconi countered.

"Fair point, but clearly neither does he," Gretchen said, as they climbed out of the car.

"Sheathe the claws if you can. Gibbs"—Marconi cut her eyes toward Gretchen, probably to ensure she was making note of the use of the detective's last name—"might talk off the record about Shaughnessy."

"If I can? Please." Gretchen stopped to study Marconi, who wasn't meeting her eyes. "What do you think Gibbs will know?"

"I have the sense that Shaughnessy has a reputation," Marconi said slowly, carefully. "I didn't pay it any mind before—you know cops gossip worse than high schoolers. But now I'm curious. Especially since the police report's been tampered with. Maybe Gibbs will know something off-the-record about Shaughnessy's role in the investigation. It was his first big case on Major Crimes, after all."

"And Gibbs will know about this reputation?" Gretchen asked. She herself was bad about keeping track of the interpersonal dynamics of the BPD apart from knowing who would and wouldn't work with her. And, of course, knowing that keeping the walls up to protect the brotherhood was far more important than any bad feelings between individual cops.

The exception to that rule being Internal Affairs.

"He's the only one I trust to ask," Marconi said with a shrug. "Maybe he won't know anything, but it won't hurt to try." She held up a hand when Gretchen shot her a look. "Between the missing nanny and the missing page, and the fact that Shaughnessy went in alone?"

"None of it damning in itself, obviously," Gretchen said. "But death by a thousand cuts."

"And . . ."

When Marconi didn't continue, Gretchen poked her again. "I don't like when you trail off."

Marconi rolled her eyes. "Noted."

"So?"

"Shaughnessy's obsession with you . . . ," Marconi said, hesitant now, like she was feeling out a half-formed idea. "I know you've always thought it was because he considered you the guilty party. But I don't think that's quite right."

Gretchen stilled. "What do you think it is then?"

"Remove your own expectations from the behavior, and . . ." Marconi took a breath. "It's almost like he knows you might have seen something you shouldn't have."

Gretchen exhaled like it was punched out of her.

The shadow. The person?

"He's sitting in his car outside your apartment," Marconi said, grimacing. "That's not behavior you associate with innocent people."

"He's always been overzealous." Gretchen tried to rewind the past ten years she'd worked with him and then the past twenty before that. What if he'd covered something up that night? What if he'd been living his life terrified she'd remember whatever it had been?

Why was he avoiding their calls now?

If it had been Bardot who had erased the nanny's presence that night, wouldn't Shaughnessy be eager to hear about it? Even if he didn't know that they'd found anything, wouldn't he want to know if the Whites had given anything away?

Or was he just that sure of Gretchen's guilt that he couldn't imagine any new evidence emerging?

"Maybe," Marconi said, her posture rigid and uncomfortable. She hated thinking this about her partner, Gretchen could tell. But she would poke at this wound anyway. For Gretchen. Or perhaps just because it was the right thing to do. Sometimes she had to remind herself that people did the right thing for that reason alone.

"Well, let's get this over with."

"Gibbs is not going to arrest you," Marconi promised.

Gretchen's mood soured further. "You've talked to him about me."

"No, believe it or not, the world doesn't revolve around you," Marconi said with enough attitude that Gretchen actually believed her. "But he's not an idiot. You haven't done anything wrong, and you've solved more cases for the department than half the detectives on staff."

Gretchen slid her a look. "If you're trying to butter me up with compliments, keep going, it's working."

Marconi rolled her eyes again, but some of the unease bled out from the air between them.

They turned as one and started toward the door.

"What's it like?" Gretchen asked. "Being his partner. Shaughnessy's, that is—obviously."

"You would know better than I," Marconi countered, cutting in when Gretchen went to argue. "It's true. You guys have been working together for a decade at least. Known each other for a lot longer. So, what's it like?"

It was difficult to think of her relationship with Shaughnessy in the same way that it was strange to think about breathing or blinking or swallowing. It just happened, it was just there. It had been since she was eight years old.

Shaughnessy was a constant presence, one that she didn't try to deconstruct all that much. The idea of him had kept her wilder impulses under control, and she had to admit they worked well together. She didn't *like* him, because that didn't even feel like an option.

Family, she realized, and something hot and uncomfortable fizzled beneath her skin. She'd consumed enough media, read enough books to know this was what many normal people felt about their families.

Thinking of Shaughnessy as family, however, did little to calm her down. It itched, settling like someone else's uncomfortable realization.

"He always wants to find the truth," Gretchen finally said. "If he thought I was onto something, he'd support me until I figured out the answer."

"A good detective then," Marconi said, with a little nod.

"Maybe," Gretchen said. But her worldview was unstable.

They came to a stop in front of Lachlan Gibbs's office, Marconi letting Gretchen take the lead. After one deep breath, Gretchen pushed inside without bothering to knock.

Lachlan Gibbs was a beautiful man with dark skin, deep brown eyes framed by long lashes, a strong jawline, and high cheekbones.

He stared at her from behind his desk, unimpressed, because he was always unimpressed when he stared at her. Then his attention slipped behind her to Marconi.

"Lauren." He greeted her warmly, and Gretchen's eyes widened. She shot Marconi a smug smile, but the woman brushed by her without comment.

"And Dr. White," Gibbs said, finally acknowledging her, his tone about ten degrees cooler than when he'd addressed Marconi. "To what do I owe this . . . pleasure?"

"See," Gretchen said beneath her breath to Marconi, who gave her a look Gretchen was realizing meant *behave* in Marconi-speak.

"I need a favor," Marconi said.

Gibbs put down his pen in a manner that was too deliberate. "I thought you were on vacation."

"You know her schedule well, then?" Gretchen asked and was summarily ignored by both parties.

"I am," Marconi admitted. "We're looking into Gretchen's case."

"The one where she murdered her aunt?" Gibbs asked. Marconi's hand jerked out to grab Gretchen before she could leave.

"The one where someone murdered her aunt and possibly framed her," Marconi corrected.

"You're putting quite a bit of faith in a murderer," Gibbs said quietly, as if Gretchen couldn't hear.

"Yes, because it's sociopaths who have cornered the market on terrible behavior, clearly," Gretchen said. "What is it exactly that you do again? Because I'm pretty sure you're not irrelevant here."

"Yes, I catch bad cops," Gibbs said, finally turning to Gretchen. "Me thinking people like you have no place in the department and getting rid of corrupt detectives aren't mutually exclusive. In fact, they line up pretty well, don't you think?"

"Your bad cops are greedy, lazy, and—or—racist," Gretchen fired back. "Not sociopaths."

"Not exactly giving me reasons to trust *you*, though, are you, Dr. White," Gibbs said. When people voluntarily used her honorific like that, they were usually mocking it. Gretchen wanted to stab him in the throat with the pen he had placed on his desk. She thought that might mean Marconi would stop working with her, though. So she refrained.

"Lachlan," Marconi cut in. "Detective Shaughnessy. Can you tell us about him? I already know there are some rumors that he had a rocky start when he was a rookie. Back in the eighties."

He stared at Marconi for a long time, his gaze flicking only once toward Gretchen. Then he stood, grabbed his coat. "Let's walk."

None of them said anything else until they reached the park three blocks over. Gibbs bought a hot dog for himself and a bottle of water for Marconi. Not that Gretchen would have taken anything from him, but he didn't even bother to offer.

"Lauren, you know this is a dangerous path," Gibbs said, as they found a bench. He let them sit and he hovered, half his hot dog already gone.

"You're making me think we're on the right one, though," Marconi said quietly, and Gretchen made a helpful, agreeing sound. Which, again, was ignored by both of them.

He sighed loud enough that Gretchen knew he wanted them to hear his exasperation.

"The biggest red flag is that he can't hold on to a partner, which is why he came to my attention in the first place." Gibbs let his eyes rest on Gretchen before swinging back to Marconi. "But . . . now I have a file."

"On what?" Marconi asked. "His behavior?"

Gibbs swiped his thumb over the corner of his mouth, catching the mustard that had lingered there. Gretchen had been finding it amusing.

"Actually, it's about a girl, a cold case," Gibbs said. "She was murdered in the early eighties."

"Name," Gretchen demanded.

Gibbs's jaw worked.

"Is it classified?" Marconi asked, gently, like they'd actually back off if the answer was yes.

"I guess not," Gibbs said, rolling his shoulders. He was the picture of discomfort. Gretchen wondered what was layered beneath—fear? He was a consummate professional, with his eye on the highest position in Internal Affairs. That ambition was what made her the most surprised when it came to a potential relationship between him and Marconi. Perhaps no one else was as observant as Gretchen, and they were getting away with it now. That wouldn't last forever. And maybe interoffice romance wasn't officially banned, but it couldn't help either of them.

"Lachlan . . . ," Marconi said, a plea in her voice.

He finally relented. "Jennifer Cross."

"It was Shaughnessy's case?" Gretchen asked.

"No, that's the strange thing," Gibbs said, shoving his hands in his pockets. "It was long before he made Major Crimes. It's like you said—he was a rookie doing traffic stops at the time her body was found."

"Then how was he involved?" Marconi asked.

"You have to understand what it was like back then," Gibbs said. "It was the golden age of serial killers, even more so than now. That wasn't long after the FBI Behavioral Analysis Unit started up—all those guys were making the news every other week. I even took a class about it once, taught by some guy who'd made his fortune writing about it all."

"Zachary Daniels?" Marconi asked, and the name rang a bell that was confirmed by Gibbs's answer.

"Yeah, former FBI guy turned sellout." There was some kind of bitterness, some kind of derision there. Gretchen wondered if Gibbs ever got sore up on that high horse of his.

"This is relevant how?" Gretchen asked.

"Everyone back then—"

"Wasn't that before your time?" Gretchen interrupted, and Marconi shot her a disappointed look.

"Yeah, but reputations have a way of sticking in police departments," Gibbs said, unruffled. "Everyone said Shaughnessy caught the bug."

"The bug?"

"The serial killer bug."

Gretchen wrinkled her nose. "That's a thing?"

"In that era? Yeah it was." Gibbs shrugged. "Everyone wanted to be the cop who caught the next guy."

"So Shaughnessy thought this cold case, Jennifer Cross, was a victim of a serial killer?" Gretchen asked, following the logic. "That would be incredibly rare, statistically speaking."

"You are correct," Gibbs said with a little bow of acknowledgment. "Everyone knew he was crazy about it, but he was on Vice at the time he got caught up in the case. What could he really do but make a little trouble?"

"How do you know all this?" Gretchen checked again. Reputations were one thing; this was something more than that.

"Like I said, he's raised red flags for me before." Gibbs started pacing again, just the small distance from one end of the bench to the other, which made his movements appear all the more jerky. "And then he was working with you. Forgive me, but I wanted to know all I could about him."

Gretchen lifted a shoulder. "Smart."

Marconi brought them back on topic. "Tell us about Jennifer Cross."

"Her body was found in the woods in 1983," Gibbs said without hesitation. Rumor had it that he had an eidetic memory, but Gretchen wondered if that was a case of laymen not knowing what the hell they were talking about. Instead, Gretchen guessed from what she'd previously observed that he had an echoic memory, which meant that he remembered everything he heard rather than everything he read. That would be an invaluable asset for a member of Internal Affairs, where investigations relied heavily on interviews and confessions. "She went to one of those fancy schools but was a scholarship student. Cause of death was blunt force trauma to the back of the head."

"And he thought she was the victim of a serial killer why?" Gretchen asked.

"The girl was found with cuts on her arms," Gibbs said, heavy and grim.

Gretchen glanced at Marconi, who shook her head. She didn't get it, either.

"And that's meaningful because . . . ?" Gretchen wished they weren't dealing with someone who hated doling out any information no matter the reason. Internal Affairs tightwads. They thought their lips were Fort Knox.

He rubbed his thumb over the shell of his ear and then met her eyes. He was trying to decide if he should share something, she realized.

Gibbs heaved another one of those sighs of his. "Your aunt came in around the same time Jennifer's body was found. Same kind of cuts on her arms."

The information was so unexpected that Gretchen was reduced to a "What?"

Gibbs looked between them, and Gretchen knew Marconi was wearing a similar expression to her own.

"Your aunt, Rowan White, was found by Detective Shaughnessy in the middle of the road one night when he was, I don't know, six months on the force," Gibbs said slowly, like he thought they were tricking him and couldn't quite figure out the how or the why of it. "Her arms were all cut up." As they continued to stare, he ran a hand over his face. "And you didn't know this already."

Gretchen didn't bother responding. Their reactions were obvious enough. "Excuse me, when was this exactly?"

"Around that time," Gibbs said. "Something like 1982, '83. I could look it up. It's in the file because it led to his only official slap on the wrist from the department." He paused. "I'm sorry, how did you not know this?"

"And why wasn't this in the report about her death?" Even as Gretchen said it, she wondered if this was the information they would have found on the missing page.

Eighty-three. That must have been the last suicide attempt that Gretchen's family always brought up in those passive-aggressive fights. The one where the cops had been involved.

"That first night was marked as a suicide attempt," Gibbs said, confirming her guess. "It wasn't relevant to her death ten years later. Everything was paper files . . . things were forgotten in the archives. The only reason I know about both of them is because I made it a point to pull all the cases Shaughnessy was the lead on."

The blasé manner in which he said it had Gretchen fighting for her self-control.

"Wasn't. Relevant." She let the disdain do the work her hands couldn't. His face went carefully blank, and she knew her condemnation had landed.

"It wasn't my case," Gibbs said, sounding defensive for the first time since she'd been introduced to him years ago. The problem with high horses was that the fall was a long way down.

She, personally, liked the view from the mud. You didn't bruise as easily.

"They both had the same cuts on their arms?" Marconi asked, again reeling them in.

"Once Shaughnessy got ahold of that detail, he was relentless," Gibbs said. "But rumor has it he thought there was something fishy going on in that family long before he knew Jennifer Cross's name."

Gibbs had the good grace to wince a little at "that family." But then he barreled on. "That was the reason for his probation. Anders White—"

"My father," Gretchen cut in for no other reason than to drive home how ridiculous it was that no one in the department had found this history noteworthy.

"Your father," Gibbs acknowledged. "Filed a complaint on Shaughnessy that he was trespassing on his property, looking for evidence that Anders was, and I quote, 'one of those crazed serial killers.'"

"Yikes." Marconi slid Gretchen a look from the side of her eye. "Interesting to note that his obsessive nature didn't start and stop with you."

Maybe it started and stopped with her aunt, though, Gretchen realized. If all this was true—and from the look on Gibbs's face, it was—Shaughnessy had been tangled up in Rowan's life for ten years before her death. The fact that Rowan was his first major case as a homicide detective no longer looked like a coincidence—it looked like he had been in the area when the call came in.

Perhaps even in the room itself.

Christ. Gretchen didn't even know what to do with this information.

"So what happened with the Jennifer Cross case?" Marconi asked, as if she knew Gretchen was beyond forming questions.

"Nothing," Gibbs said. "Shaughnessy was obviously grasping at straws, the case stayed cold, and everyone moved on. It became a footnote in an Internal Affairs file and forgotten about." He paused, then waved at them as if to say their very ignorance of the investigation was evidence of this. "Clearly."

"What do you think?" Marconi stood so that she bumped elbows with Gibbs. "Was it a serial killer?"

"The cuts were weird, I won't deny that," Gibbs said slowly. "But similar cuts don't a serial killer make."

"Wow, what would the Boston Police Department do without observations such as those," Gretchen said, feeling mean and cornered.

Gibbs ignored her. "It's just not my area of expertise, to be honest."

"But bad cops are," Marconi jumped in before Gretchen could lash out any further at such an easy opening. "So, what do you think of Shaughnessy?"

Gibbs grimaced. Even Internal Affairs hated ratting out someone in the brotherhood of detectives. "It's concerning that he found Rowan both nights."

"The night she was cut up and the night she was murdered," Marconi clarified.

"If I had been here then, I would say it's enough for me to open an investigation," Gibbs said. "Now? He hasn't had any complaints about him since. Seems like he learned a lesson."

"Tell me, Detective Gibbs," Gretchen said. "What's the statute of limitations on bad cops' behavior."

"I'm not going to hold a little passion against a new cop trying to prove something," Gibbs said. "That's all it looks like right now."

"But you were worried enough to start a file on him," Marconi pointed out. "Doesn't that mean something?"

"I have a file on about twenty cops in there," Gibbs said, jerking his head back in the direction of the department. "It's my job to keep an eye out."

"Can we see the file?" Gretchen asked, knowing what the answer would be.

"No," Gibbs said without missing a beat.

Before Gretchen could argue, Marconi pressed her elbow into Gretchen's side.

"How do we get more information on this Cross case?" Marconi asked.

Gibbs studied them, and then everything about him sagged forward as if in defeat. "I'll write you a pass for the archives. You won't be able to take anything out under your name since you're officially on vacation. Just . . . try to be subtle about it, okay? I don't want this getting back to me."

Gretchen glanced at Marconi, and then said in a loud aside, "You must be *fantastic* in bed."

Marconi smiled, but it was more a baring of teeth than anything else. "And you wonder why he wants to arrest you."

CHAPTER TWENTY-ONE

SHAUGHNESSY

1984

The trip into the woods near the White residence cost Shaughnessy an official letter in his file, a week suspension without pay, and a dent in his reputation, which seemed to be going downhill fast.

He watched himself through it all as if he were standing outside his body, unable to stop the slide into the ditch. He watched himself dig around in cold case archives, spend countless weekends at libraries parsing through old newspaper articles, contact the DMV for information on Anders's car. And he just didn't seem to be able to stop himself. He was an addict.

Shaughnessy got better at hiding the obsession, though. When Boyd had asked about it in February, Shaughnessy had shrugged and parroted his partner's earlier response—*can't do anything else until she's dead.* When the chief had checked in with him three months after his suspension, Shaughnessy had truthfully assured him he hadn't been back out to the mansion. When his family had asked if there were any interesting cases he was working on, he'd ducked his head and admitted to being stuck on traffic duty.

But in March, his work paid off because he found her.

Jennifer Cross.

Her body had been found about six months prior in the woods, less than a month after Shaughnessy had first met Rowan. Jennifer's arms had been cut up, in the same way Rowan's had.

Modus operandi. That's all Shaughnessy could think, his mind catching on the foreign phrase that was so often used by the FBI agents who hunted serial killers these days.

The girl could be the game changer he needed.

Two victims. People could write off Rowan, because she was still alive. But a dead girl? One who had garnered national media attention? That would be harder to ignore.

If Shaughnessy could convince anyone to see the connection.

In a rare bit of good luck, the week after Shaughnessy found Jennifer's case in the archives, he heard about a lecture being held by retired FBI special agent Zach Daniels.

Shaughnessy took it as a sign, rented a sedan, and drove the fifty-one miles to Providence on a random Wednesday night, lying to the chief about a dentist appointment so he could leave early enough to make the talk.

Daniels had been making a name for himself up and down the New England circuit. After he'd retired early from the FBI, he'd written four bestselling books about the serial killers people couldn't seem to get enough of and the victims they left behind.

As the lights dimmed, a murmur of anticipation rippled through the crowd. It built to a roar as Daniels walked onto the stage, waving into the darkness, a rock star for those recently exposed to just how evil humans could be.

If Shaughnessy was being honest, the talk itself was a letdown, for the most part broadly rehashing the information that had been well covered in the man's books. But Shaughnessy wasn't there for the lecture.

When Daniels began wrapping up, Shaughnessy ducked out.

He'd bribed one of the security guards into showing him the door where the talent came and went. Shaughnessy leaned against the brick wall just out of the glow of the bare bulb that offered the suggestion of security without actually offering any security.

A half hour later the door pushed open, and Daniels stepped out. Shaughnessy shifted so that the light caught his face, and, more important, his badge.

"Buy you a drink?" Shaughnessy asked.

Daniels hesitated, glanced back to where a handful of people hovered behind him. Then he shrugged, nodded.

They didn't have to walk far to find a bar, and Shaughnessy tried not to wince when Daniels ordered the most expensive whiskey on the menu.

"You get this a lot, don't you?" Shaughnessy guessed as they settled into a back booth.

"It's a rare stop that I don't." Daniels swirled the drink, watching it closely, far more interested in it than Shaughnessy. Daniels smirked, though, and Shaughnessy could tell he found this all very amusing. "Tell me about your serial killer."

Something about this man set Shaughnessy on edge. "How do you know I have one?"

Daniels shot him a look. "Everyone has a serial killer these days." He paused, set the glass down, leaned his forearms on the table, actually meeting Shaughnessy's eyes. "Do you know how rare serial killers actually are?"

Shaughnessy licked his lips. He knew the statistics. And just like everyone probably before him, he knew he defied them. "There are one hundred forty-seven active serial killers operating this year. Give or take."

"Well, at least you know your shit," Daniels said, leaning back. But he didn't sound impressed, only tired. He picked up his drink, downed the entirety of it, then motioned to the waitress. "You think you've stumbled upon one of those one hundred forty-seven."

"Give or take," Shaughnessy said, because he wanted to poke at this man. In his books, Daniels came off as dedicated, honorable, courageous. That wasn't the man in front of him.

Daniels laughed at that, tipped his new glass at Shaughnessy. "You got me there."

"I'm not sure he's a serial killer yet," Shaughnessy admitted. He held the file loosely between his hands. All of a sudden it felt so thin.

"One victim?" Daniels asked, with a knowing twist to his mouth. He reached out, snagged the waitress by the wrist. "Doll, can you get us some food. Surprise me and put it on his tab."

"Two victims," Shaughnessy said, managing to get out once the waitress sauntered away, a new swing in her hips. "Well . . . no. Yeah, two."

That seemed to get Daniels's attention. "You don't sound so sure there, buckaroo."

"One dead, one tortured," Shaughnessy said, trying to inject some confidence into his voice as he slid Daniels the file. The man actually took it, and while he studied the pictures, the carefully compiled information on both Rowan and Jennifer Cross, Shaughnessy thought he saw the ghost of something in the man's serious expression. Maybe the lingering echo of a version of him when he still cared. "Both with the same distinct injuries."

"This doesn't look like the same guy," Daniels said. But he was still reading.

"One of the victims is his sister," Shaughnessy said, his words a little rushed. "I think he might practice on her, but doesn't want to kill her."

Daniels nodded, absently. "She's his true victim, but he doesn't want to lose her yet. So he finds substitutes."

"Yes," Shaughnessy breathed. "Yes."

"One problem with that theory." Daniels closed the file with a decisive slap. "They don't look alike."

"But there are serial killers who—"

Daniels cut him off with a raised hand. "I'm not saying *serial killers* don't deviate from a victim profile. I'm saying if this guy—White—is finding a substitute for his sister, then they would have at least passing similarities. Sorry, kid."

Shaughnessy winced when the waitress brought Daniels a new glass along with every appetizer on the menu. "I can't do anything?"

Daniels shoved a handful of fries in his mouth and shrugged. "Come back to me when you actually find something."

Shaughnessy dug out his credit card and tried not to think about all the ways this had been an utter disappointment.

Instead, he took Daniels's command as a challenge.

Find something.

Find them.

It took Shaughnessy two months after that drink with Daniels to find Jennifer Cross's father and then get the man to talk to him. A part of Shaughnessy knew he should have given up after the first phone call, when Levi Cross had hung up on him in a rage that Shaughnessy had even mentioned Jennifer's name.

But Shaughnessy hadn't been able to ignore the connections.

Focused. *Creepy.*

A part of him wondered what thousand-dollar word Saoirse would label him with now that she had a fancy college degree.

Fixated.

Bedeviled.

Haunted.

Levi finally agreed to a meeting on the first day that the sun was shining in Boston in weeks. Shaughnessy sat awkwardly on a plastic-covered sofa in a small but tidy house that straddled the edge between a middle-class and a poor neighborhood. It was hard to believe that a girl from this family had moved in the same circles as Rowan White.

The man was large, big-boned with some cushion to go with it, the buttons on his shirt and the seams of his khakis both straining. He had a neat, well-trimmed beard and empty eyes.

He reeked of alcohol even at nine in the morning.

His bear-paw hands cradled a yearbook, but he hadn't opened it yet. "She was a scholarship student. Everyone thought we were rich or something, but Jenny worked her butt off to be there."

Shaughnessy fought the urge to pull out his notebook and pen. He didn't want to startle Levi, who looked about one stiff breeze from fleeing to somewhere dark and safe and far, far away from cops with questions about his dead daughter.

"At the Phillips Academy." It wasn't actually something Shaughnessy needed clarified; he knew far more details about Jennifer Cross's life now than he probably should. But he wanted to ease Levi into this conversation.

Levi nodded, still staring blankly at the carpet.

"Sir, I know you've been over this many times," Shaughnessy said, as delicately as he could. The only other instance he'd interviewed any-one like this was when he'd been at the White mansion months ago. This wasn't the same thing. This was far from the same thing. "But is there anything you remember, or have thought of since . . ."

"Do you think if I had any information that would help find my daughter's killer, I wouldn't be banging on the police chief's door?" Levi asked. The question should have been burning bright with anger and resentment. Rather it was hollow, dejected. This was a man without hope.

Shaughnessy tried to say something, couldn't think of any words. So he closed his mouth.

Levi opened the yearbook, handed it over to Shaughnessy. "They always used that one picture of her that her mother gave the press, the glamour one where she was all dolled up in lipstick." He tapped the photo. "But this was the real Jenny."

Shaughnessy knew exactly what picture the man was talking about. He'd found it in a *People* magazine of all things. And she'd looked like the perfect, popular, pretty girl whom Shaughnessy could easily imagine being friends with Rowan. He'd thought the pair of them seemed more like actresses on a teen soap opera than real students.

The photo of Jenny in the yearbook, though, was different. She looked ten years younger, wearing a striped turtleneck and big glasses that hid those eyes that were startling in the magazine. Her hair frizzed about her face, and two pimples drew the eye to her chin. She was still pretty, but she looked like the girl she was instead of a woman dressed in teenage clothing.

As he studied the picture, Shaughnessy fought the urge to flip through the pages to find Rowan White.

"Was Jennifer seeing anyone?" Shaughnessy asked, suddenly feeling too big for this house, suddenly feeling like he was all elbows and thick tongue. He was trying for gentle, but what did he know about gentle?

Levi's mouth pinched at the corners. "Jenny was a good girl."

Shaughnessy nodded, at a loss for what to ask next. A flush of heat crept up his neck as Levi seemed to realize Shaughnessy didn't know what the hell he was doing here.

"You're not on my daughter's case," Levi said slowly. Like he was putting something together for the first time.

"I'm just closing the loop on another investigation." Shaughnessy rubbed at his pants with a damp palm. The explanation did nothing to appease the man, whose ruddy cheeks deepened to an upsetting color.

"Why would you do that to me?" Levi asked with the breathlessness of someone who'd just been punched in the gut. "Why would you bring this all up again? If you don't have something new about Jenny's case?"

Shaughnessy swallowed, but the saliva caught in his throat. What the fuck was he doing here? Why had he gotten so caught up in this wild-goose chase that was nothing? Nothing.

Focused. *Creepy.*

He stood, his shins knocking into the coffee table, sending his ignored cup of tea sloshing.

"Get out of my house." The command came as a roar, a bellow from the man's chest, no longer hollow but filled with the rage of a grieving father. Levi stood, his fists bunched.

Shaughnessy stumbled, caught himself on the squeaky arm of the plastic-wrapped couch.

That was when he saw her.

A girl.

She had slotted herself right up against the wall, her face pale, her lower lip trembling. But she held his eyes, her little pointed chin tilted up.

Shaughnessy wasn't good with kids, wouldn't be able to tell if one of them was five or twelve if there was a gun to his head. But he guessed this one was about ten. She had the same deep brown eyes as Jenny, the same dark hair—though hers was shot through with red and braided into two plaits that hung over her skinny shoulders. She was built like a willow reed, with knobby knees and all.

Behind Shaughnessy, Levi seemed to lose his fight with just the sight of her.

"Tabby," he whispered.

But Tabby didn't take her eyes off Shaughnessy. "Do you know who did it?"

Shaughnessy couldn't answer. Saying no felt like a lie, but saying yes would be dangerous. So he just stared at her and she stared back, undeterred.

Tabby just nodded, like she wasn't surprised. "Will you catch him?"

She looked and sounded so much older than her age. But living in a house with the ghost of a murdered sibling made kids grow up real fast. He might be young and inexperienced, but he knew that for certain.

Shaughnessy didn't have any second thoughts when he answered, "Yes."

CHAPTER TWENTY-TWO

GRETCHEN

Now

The archives were as dusty and dark as the name suggested.

Gretchen had never ventured into the belly of this particular beast because she had Fred, and because this work was so far below her pay grade she would have quit a case immediately if it had been forced upon her.

But circumstances were what they were, and they demanded the visit.

A kindly old man with thick glasses and a bad comb-over had scrutinized the slip that Gibbs had written and then had pointed them in the right direction.

Jennifer Cross's evidence box was surprisingly light for how much national attention the case had gotten.

"So Shaughnessy thought this girl was a victim of your father's?" Marconi said as she donned latex gloves like the good little detective she usually was. "You think there's anything to that? Anders being some kind of serial killer?"

"Seems unlikely," Gretchen said, though she heard the silent echo from their earlier conversation. Unlikely isn't impossible. "Who were the detectives?"

"No one." Marconi's head tipped. "I mean no one associated with the rest of this. Shawn Jones and Grace Li."

Neither of the names rang a bell, but Gretchen made a mental note to have them checked out. "Give me the details."

"Jennifer Cross, last seen getting into a dark-colored four-door sedan on the evening of October 12, 1983," Marconi obediently read.

"So she knew the guy," Gretchen said, more to herself.

"Must have," Marconi agreed. "Her father reported her missing that night, but none of her friends knew anything and no one had gotten a license plate."

"No top suspects?" Gretchen asked, because while those were often kept from the media, they'd be noted in the report.

"The father, of course," Marconi said. "But no one really thought he did it. One of the girls reported that Jennifer had a boyfriend. Though they also said that she'd never mentioned his name, or what he did. Only hinted that he was older."

"And no cell phone records back then," Gretchen said. "No texts, no emails, no digital footprints."

"I don't know how they solved cases," Marconi said.

"Did they?"

Marconi rolled her eyes. "Your insults are getting lazy. That's just blatantly untrue."

"Not my best effort," Gretchen agreed absently, glancing around. The old man was hunched over his desk, not paying them any attention. "Cover me."

"What? No, Gretchen," Marconi protested, but it was too late. Gretchen was already slipping down the next row and then the next until she found the letter she was looking for.

W.

She trailed a finger over the labels.

WHITE, ROWAN J.

Gretchen hefted the box off the shelf and toted it back to where Marconi stood. "Don't give me that face."

"I'm not going to stop Gibbs when he tries to arrest you for this," Marconi said, but she was already straining to get a look at what Gretchen had grabbed.

"The only way he finds out is if you tell," Gretchen said, her voice dripping with saccharine sweetness. "And you know better than that, don't you, darling?"

Marconi eyed her. "Why do I have the feeling you just slid a razor blade against my neck?"

"Oh good, that's what I intended," Gretchen said brightly, before flipping open Rowan's file. This wasn't the original of that copy Marconi had been carting around. This one was from the earlier incident all the way back in '83. "What was the date Jennifer disappeared?"

"October 12, 1983," Marconi read, though she probably knew Gretchen didn't actually need it repeated.

"Rowan was brought into the station on September 28, 1983."

"What," Marconi said, but it wasn't a question, more like confusion made verbal. She shook her head. "So Shaughnessy found Rowan only two weeks before Jennifer disappeared, and both girls had the same cuts on their arms? That timing seems too tight to be a coincidence, right?"

"Could mean something," Gretchen said, but then added, "could mean nothing."

"How could it mean nothing?" Marconi asked, a little edge to her voice.

"Just because *you* can't come up with another explanation doesn't mean there isn't one," Gretchen explained, mostly distracted, her attention on the file. "When assessing any given situation, we're limited to our own experience, logic, or creativity—but there's a world of causes and effects out there that you simply *can't* imagine. Not understanding that is why some people fall into conspiracy theory rabbit holes."

"Thank you, Dr. White," Marconi said, and Gretchen could all but hear the eye roll.

Gretchen shrugged. "I've said before you're good at making connections—your job depends on it. But that leaves you prone to creating links for things that might not actually be related."

"Still think that timing is weird," Marconi said. "Maybe I could see their injuries being a coincidence if it was years apart, but two weeks?"

"It's another data point," Gretchen agreed. "So is Shaughnessy's involvement with both cases, for that matter."

"Okay, Rowan ran out in front of him that night," Marconi said. Gretchen recognized it as her way of getting the conversation back on track.

"Right. Shaughnessy and a Detective Liam Boyd were in the area, checking out a domestic disturbance call. That's . . ." Gretchen trailed off, considering. "What are the odds?"

"Of what?"

"That Rowan just happened to run out in front of cops," Gretchen mused. "On a dark road outside the city."

Marconi hummed. "Maybe . . . she was the domestic disturbance? Maybe Anders really was torturing her, and she put up a fight, the neighbors called it in. She got herself out of his control and ran for the road?"

Maybe, was all Gretchen thought. It was an intriguing theory, but she still had doubts that Anders was a psychopath who'd tortured his sister in the first place. If that were the case, Gretchen would have expected some kind of violence during her own childhood. Beyond the emotional abuse both her parents liked to dole out.

"My grandmother signed Rowan out from the station," Gretchen said. "If Anders was torturing Rowan, Edith would have had to be in on it."

"That wouldn't surprise me," Marconi said, her eyes returning to Jennifer's file. "The mothers are often abusers themselves."

"Oh, thank you, I'd never heard that very basic fact about serial killers while getting my doctorate in serial killers," Gretchen drawled.

Marconi looked up. "You can get a degree in serial killers?"

"No, I was doing a"—she waved, and finished lamely—"bit."

"Bummer," Marconi murmured, lips twitching as her attention slipped again. "That would be cool."

Gretchen's eyes narrowed. She hated that Marconi could be so immune to her sharp edges. But she also acknowledged that it was why they worked well together. She decided to write the exchange off as a draw.

"I could see Edith trying to save the White family name," Gretchen said. "That would be a reason she would cover for Anders."

"While throwing Rowan under the bus," Marconi added.

"Girls in rich families are meant for marriage and being quiet until they walk down the aisle," Gretchen said, lifting a shoulder. "It doesn't matter how bad their male siblings are."

"Lovely," Marconi said. "So Jennifer Cross went to the same school as Rowan, disappeared a little over two weeks after Rowan was seen fleeing from the woods in her underthings. And she was found with the same cuts on her arms as Rowan."

"Who says 'underthings'?" Gretchen asked, amused.

"You really know how to focus on the important things," Marconi said. "It's that keen insight of yours."

Gretchen flipped her off, but agreed. "Too many connections."

"Or are we looking at this with hindsight and a tendency for our brains to make patterns?" Marconi asked.

Gretchen's brows rose with an approval that she refused to make verbal. On the Viola Kent case, Gretchen had warned Marconi about the human propensity to find connections where none existed. Pareidolia was the technical name for it, and it was the same thing that made kids find shapes in clouds or adults see faces in inanimate objects. Evolutionarily speaking, the impulse was extraordinarily important to humans, whose survival relied on social connections. But it did make people take leaps in connecting unrelated things and could lead to dangerous conspiratorial thinking.

"The Phillips Academy connection alone would be enough for me to link them," Gretchen said. "Which is probably what Shaughnessy thought, as well."

"He must have come up against a dead end, though," Marconi pointed out. "Case still isn't solved."

"If you were starting the investigation today, what would be your first step?" Gretchen asked. "Jennifer Cross's, that is."

"Do I know about Rowan?"

"No," Gretchen answered, curious to see how Marconi would approach it.

"The witnesses said Jennifer might have met the boyfriend at the academy's Fall Festival," Marconi said slowly. "I'd pull a roster for volunteers, security, teachers, anyone who was listed as being there. Put a team of uniforms on interviewing them, check if anyone saw anything suspicious. And have them scour the photos in case Jennifer was caught in the background of any with this mysterious older man."

Gretchen crossed the small space between them and hooked her chin over Marconi's shoulder so she could read the file. "The sister said it might have been a blond guy."

"That fits Anders," Marconi offered.

"And Shaughnessy."

Marconi went still beneath Gretchen. "Huh."

Gretchen poked her in a tender spot beneath her ribs, and Marconi flinched.

"What are you thinking?" Gretchen asked when she still didn't say anything.

"Connections," Marconi muttered, deliberately putting more space between them. "There's nothing else about Jennifer's death that screams serial killer."

"Just the cuts," Gretchen agreed.

"Which is the only other link back to Rowan," Marconi said.

"Wrong. Look at the location where her body was found." Gretchen tapped the file. "My family used to live less than a mile from there."

Marconi just blinked at her, and Gretchen heard the *What?* in the silence.

"We moved when I was . . . six or so," Gretchen said, trying to recall the exact date. "Into a town house in the city." Gretchen jerked her chin toward the desk. "Jennifer's body was close to where Shaughnessy found Rowan that first night, too."

"What is going on?" Marconi said, beneath her breath.

Gretchen had no desire to admit that she didn't know. But thinking about the town house let her direct her frustration to an easy target. "Bardot still hasn't given us the name of the nanny."

"Hmm," Marconi hummed, mostly distracted. "Wonder if the nanny's living down here, too."

With Jennifer and the rest of the cold cases.

"With how cagey Bardot is acting, I wouldn't be surprised," Gretchen said, as she pulled out her phone, found the right number, and pressed call.

A maid answered the phone, even though it was Bardot's cell, and Gretchen wondered if she'd just earned herself a pink slip.

"The nanny's name," Gretchen demanded as soon as Bardot took over.

There was a pause that went too long to be natural. But then Bardot cleared her throat. "Yes, yes. I don't see what this has to do with anything."

The deflection sent a frisson of curiosity down Gretchen's spine. She had truly thought that her mother might not have remembered. But this reeked of protesting too much. "That's not for you to worry about."

"Let's see," Bardot said, the sound of shifting papers in the background. "Ah, yes. Tabitha. Tabitha Cross."

Gretchen's eyes pressed closed. "Repeat that."

"Tabitha Cross," Bardot said with exaggerated emphasis. "Now, if that's all?"

As an answer, Gretchen hung up.

When she opened her eyes, it was to find Marconi on high alert.

"What's the name?" Marconi asked, but Gretchen was already calling Shaughnessy.

He didn't answer; she hadn't expected him to. Still, she left a message.

"I need you to call the archives and have them release Rowan's evidence box from 1983 into my custody, as well as Jennifer Cross's cold case file," Gretchen said into the phone. "We don't need to talk about it, we don't need to hash it out, I just need you to do it."

Gretchen hung up, watching the old man now.

"You think that's going to work?" Marconi asked, but she sounded curious rather than skeptical.

Over at the desk, the old landline phone jangled, and Gretchen grinned.

"Yes."

"Gretchen," Marconi said. "Who was the nanny?"

Gretchen hefted the box onto her hip. "Jennifer's sister."

CHAPTER TWENTY-THREE

TABBY

1993

Cal loomed over Tabby, the light behind him so she couldn't see his face. He held the rope he'd withdrawn from the bag in his hand, the loop of it resting against his thigh.

"What did you find?"

Black spots popped in Tabby's vision as she tried desperately to control her ragged breathing. There was too much air coming in and then not enough.

Her eyes flew to the door.

"No," she managed. "I just . . ." *Pull yourself together, girl.* Her teeth chattered like she was cold, and her pulse beat in the soles of her feet. "I got in a fight with my dad—that's why I sounded so strange."

That didn't make any sense, she knew that. Tabby had admitted to finding evidence on the phone; she couldn't erase that fact. But she couldn't think clearly enough to come up with something plausible, either.

The silence stretched between them, unbearably uncomfortable. Tabby counted the steps to the door. Four, maybe. He'd be on her in an instant, hand tangling in her hair, yanking her back.

"Tabitha, why do you keep lying?" His terrifyingly calm voice slithered over her skin. Her palms, her armpits, the nape of her neck went sweaty.

She was going to die here in this shitty motel room.

Somehow it was almost fitting.

Cal was on top of her in the next second, pressing her back into the bed, forearm closing off her windpipe.

Her lips moved; her legs kicked out but didn't catch on anything. Her fingernails found skin, scraped, drew blood.

"Bitch," he cursed, easing up, his lip pulled back in a snarl.

When she sucked in desperate gulps of air, the man laughed. No longer Cal. No longer anyone or anything she recognized.

He let her go.

Oxygen. Pure, beautiful, addictive. It flooded her lungs and then her bloodstream. Her hand found the bruises that were already forming on her skin as she watched him.

Slowly, but with the confidence of a man who'd done this before, he once again reached for his bag.

Cal might be strong, but Tabby was quick.

And she might be able to take him by surprise. If she moved *now*.

The door. Freedom. Safety.

Or the relative safety a barren stretch of highway offered her.

She'd take it. She'd take anything over this.

He bent over, his attention diverted, more vulnerable than he had been since they'd walked in the room.

Tabby pressed herself up on her elbows, got her feet planted on the ground.

She counted her breaths, tried to control them, tried to make sure her lungs were ready for this.

One deep inhale. One more.

And then . . .

The doorknob cold under her hand.

Cal's shout behind her.

Cement and then pavement.

Cars. Two, three. All blurring by.

No one would stop.

Don't stop.

The McDonald's.

Cal behind her.

Just cross the street.

Her lungs screamed, hollered, almost collapsed.

The door.

Push.

A kid. Pimpled, with a straggly mustache.

"Your phone," she managed to get out.

Cal stood outside. Pacing. Glancing in.

The boy's eyes darted between them.

Then he pointed to the wall.

Tabby slipped behind the counter with a shaky "Thanks." The girl manning the fryer watched her, eyes impossibly wide as she dumped french fries in oil.

The phone. Tabby touched it and closed her eyes. The plastic felt like salvation.

She thought back to that day in her living room, years and years and years ago.

The man had promised her something, his voice fierce, his stance oh-so steady.

Will you catch him?

Yes.

Tabby dialed information. When the operator answered, she knew what she needed.

She opened her eyes, saw Cal's shadow waver as he crossed beneath the streetlamp.

"Detective Shaughnessy," she whispered into the phone, sinking down to the floor as she did. "Detective Patrick Shaughnessy. Please."

CHAPTER
TWENTY-FOUR
GRETCHEN

Now

Gretchen allowed her mind to go blank as she dropped Marconi off, as she drove home, parked, made her way to her apartment, poured herself a large glass of wine.

When she sat on the floor, she spread the contents of Rowan's and Jennifer Cross's evidence boxes out in front of her.

According to the medical examiner's report, Jennifer's state of decomp matched the time she'd gone missing—meaning that if she'd been held alive somewhere, it hadn't been for long. There had been no skin beneath her fingers, nor signs of any defensive wounds.

There had been some debris in the cuts on her arms to suggest she had been moved postmortem, but it had matched the gravel and dirt that was common in the woods where her body was deposited.

Jennifer's case had caught the national media's attention. She'd been featured in *People* magazine, probably because she'd been pretty, white, and navigating in social spheres above her own. Yet, past the initial flurry, the investigation had hit a brick wall. Then it had effectively died.

That struck Gretchen as odd because that's not how people worked. Brains, even neurotypical brains, hated the *not knowing*. People were still obsessed with JonBenét Ramsey, D. B. Cooper, and, even most famously, Jack the Ripper.

If a mystery existed, it had to be solved.

And if it couldn't be, the mystery didn't just disappear. It became infamous.

Yet there were no answers for who had killed Jennifer Cross. The girl lived in a dusty box in the basement archives of the Boston Police Department, and that was it.

Gretchen guessed that others might find this all very sad, but she found it curious more than anything. National attention meant pressure on the police chief, and a police chief under pressure rarely had tolerance for detectives who couldn't turn up even a stray hair or a partially credible suspect.

There could be a few reasons for that. It was the eighties in Boston, and the police department's attention might have been focused on trying to control the mobs. Jennifer's death was long before the ability to use DNA and other technology, and so murder investigations relied heavily on relentless footwork that might not have been there to spare.

But Gretchen could also see another possibility beneath the ice that had settled in the nooks and crannies of this case.

Someone had had an active hand in shutting down this investigation.

If that was the truth, logic dictated that the person who had done so had been the killer. Who else would have benefited from this turning into a dead end?

Gretchen took a deep swallow of wine and then flipped Rowan's 1983 file open.

All she could think was . . . two dead girls, a decade apart. A missing page from the police report and, even more damning, a witness who had been left out of the file. A witness who just happened to be the sister of one of said dead girls.

They were connected, there was no denying that. But were they connected because *Shaughnessy had caught the bug*, as Gibbs had said, or because they were victims of the same perpetrator?

A classic chicken-or-egg question.

Could the cuts on their arms have been a coincidence? Even though they went to the same school and Jennifer's body had been found near the White family mansion? Had Shaughnessy drawn lines that didn't exist, setting in motion whatever the sister had been doing by applying for the nanny position?

Or had it been Shaughnessy who killed both girls?

First Jennifer and then Rowan, when she'd discovered what he'd done ten years later.

The sister had said Jennifer had had an older boyfriend who fit Shaughnessy's description—no matter how vague it might have been.

That description also fit Anders, though.

What if Gretchen was wrong, and he really was a psychopath who'd practiced on Rowan and then moved on to her classmates? What if Shaughnessy had actually been onto something with the idea that Anders was some kind of serial killer, first in training and then in reality? What if Anders had to silence Rowan once Jennifer's sister worked her way into his household, looking for evidence of what she knew he'd done?

A picture of Rowan stared back at Gretchen. It wasn't a mug shot—Rowan had never been arrested. Instead, it was a clipped photocopy of a gossip column.

She thought about Marconi's observation—rage had driven the murderer's hand.

Rowan had been stabbed, viciously, more than once. Enough so that it had looked like Gretchen had wanted to see her aunt's organs, touch them, revel in it all.

If all the murderer had wanted to do was frame Gretchen, the wounds had been overkill. Gretchen hadn't had a history of violence.

At most, she'd been the strange kid with blank eyes and no sense of self-preservation. There'd been no dead animals, no tortured classmates with fresh bruises and cuts on their bodies. Her sister may have walked away from a skirmish with a broken wrist once, but that had been as much her fault as Gretchen's.

Again, Gretchen tried to remember Rowan divorced from her brutal end. Her aunt hadn't been living with them long, hadn't come back until the summer of 1993, only about three months before her death.

Gretchen hadn't understood how to read interpersonal dynamics back then, though. She remembered whenever Rowan was in the room with Anders or Bardot everything went sharp and staticky between the three of them. But was that Rowan's doing, or was that because she'd been scared of her brother and sister-in-law? Maybe she'd had nowhere else to turn—especially if Edith had cut off her funds—and had to put up with living in fear in exchange for a roof over her head.

What Gretchen did know was that Rowan had taken attention away from anyone else, and to a child, that felt like an assault in and of itself.

The resentment had been a slow burn. It had started as an annoyance that Rowan, with all her problems, was dominating everyone's attention, and it had crystallized into something sharper over the three months Rowan had lived with them.

I wanted to kill her before I knew what killing was.

Gretchen couldn't deny that sentiment had come from somewhere. But . . .

The fact that Rowan had been found in her bed without any defensive wounds had always struck Gretchen as odd if she had been the one to kill her aunt. It was true that Gretchen had a hair-trigger temper at times. Her urges were always in the moment, though, an immediate reaction. She wasn't cold-blooded; she didn't stalk sleeping prey. Her anger might burn bright, but it also burned quickly. Gretchen didn't hold grudges, and she wouldn't have snuck into her aunt's room hours after an argument only to stab her prone form.

Deep down, Gretchen knew this didn't look like her handiwork.

I was framed.

It was a powerful thought, one that almost knocked the breath out of Gretchen despite everything that had happened since Marconi had knocked on her door. There was a difference between projecting the idea that she was innocent and actually believing it.

For the first time in her life, Gretchen let herself think, *I'm innocent*, and it didn't come with the sour aftertaste of a pleasant lie.

The idea brought her back to rage.

If the murder had been premeditated, there were easier ways of shifting blame than framing an eight-year-old child without a history of extreme violence.

For one, Rowan had a well-known history of mental illness—not only mental illness but actual attempts at suicide. If someone had wanted to kill her and get away with it, it would have been simple to make her death look self-inflicted.

What this seemed like was panic.

And if that was the case, it did exonerate Anders, who'd been away on business.

If there truly hadn't been anyone else in the house that night and the shadow in the room really had just been Gretchen's imagination, that left Bardot, Fran, the nanny, and Gretchen as suspects.

Fran and Bardot had been cleared by forensics.

But Tabitha Cross hadn't been.

CHAPTER
TWENTY-FIVE

SHAUGHNESSY

1984

Shaughnessy met Donna Sanders at a Memorial Day barbecue hosted by a guy in Vice. The only reason Shaughnessy had decided to go was because he'd gotten word he was being considered for a position on the beat, and while he would have preferred Major Crimes, he desperately wanted to get off traffic duty.

Donna had come with another officer's girlfriend. She was pretty in a plain way, with a round, freckled face and teased, bleached-blonde hair that, given the shade, had come from a bottle. Her nose turned up at the end too sharply, but Shaughnessy liked the way his hand fit against her hip, his thumb tugging at a loop at the waistband of her cutoff whitewashed jean shorts.

A week and four dates later they were officially dating, and the boys at the station were giving him shit when he came in late one morning with a hickey on his neck too high up to hide.

It had been a few months since he'd been chased from Levi Cross's house, more than six months since Anders White had held a shotgun on him. Most days he could forget about Rowan and Jennifer; most days he could pretend that he didn't see Rowan's face before he went to sleep every night.

And Donna helped with that. She gave him an air of respectability that he hadn't realized he was missing. The cops at work would slap his shoulder and buy him coffee these days rather than sliding him suspicious looks whenever he spoke.

There were times, though, when he had Donna sitting in his lap, his earlobe caught between her teeth, and all he could think about was the way Rowan had said, *"Run."*

"I have a late shift tomorrow," he said, and she hummed, working her way down to his shoulder, his collarbone. She smelled of peppermint, like she always did when she tried to cover up the fact that she smoked like a chimney.

"I thought you were going to take me to that restaurant you liked." The pout in her voice made him want to push her off his lap, see her sprawled on the floor like the child she sounded like.

"The next day, baby," he promised.

"You should talk to the chief—he's giving you too many late-night shifts," she said, but she was already distracted with the buttons on his shirt. He hoped she wouldn't talk to that friend of hers, Gina. The one who was seeing that guy in Vice.

Because Shaughnessy didn't have a late shift. He just got tired of her sometimes in a way that he knew was inexcusable.

But she listened when he nudged her hands away from him, and she left his place, like she always did when he got like this. He did like that about her.

The knock on his door came twenty minutes later, just as he was about to pour himself a drink. He glanced at the clock on the mantel.

It was late, past the time when a neighbor or friend would drop by unannounced. He thought about his gun, but then dismissed the worry. A criminal wouldn't knock.

He opened the door.

The closest streetlamp to his place had been busted for weeks, but even without its weak glow he would recognize the figure shivering in the heavy rain anywhere.

"Miss White," he said, thinking *Rowan* instead. The name tasted like sugar and copper, sweet and metallic at the same time.

"I didn't know where else to go." Rowan's voice quivered in the middle, then steadied itself like she was trying to be strong while on the brink of falling apart. "I didn't—"

He cut her off before she could apologize. He never wanted her to feel bad about seeking his help. "Come in, come in."

She hesitated, then with a quick little nod crossed the threshold, dripping on the floor. Shaughnessy directed her to the stained flower-print sofa he'd never replaced after the previous owner had left it behind. A flush worked up his neck as he wondered what she must think of his place.

"Towels," he managed to get out, stepping just into the hallway to fetch a few from the linen closet. Rowan accepted one cautiously as he draped another around her shoulders. Some long-buried instinct prodded him to rub her arms, warm her up.

He stepped away.

The room devoured her small frame, everything too big, too bright, too much. The rain had given deep honey-brown highlights to her hair, the strands plastered to her face, her neck; it had softened the fabric of her shirt so that the material clung to her body. The cold had teased a pink stain into the pale skin of her cheeks.

Shaughnessy looked away, after his eyes lingered for just a second too long on her flat stomach, the gentle curve of her hips.

"I'm glad you came," his voice rasped out in a rough scrape of sandpaper and gravel.

He wondered if she could tell that he was watching her now just like he had that night—like she was spun from gossamer-thin glass, about to shatter. And only he could prevent it.

It was probably written on his very skin, but somehow by instinct he knew he had to hide the affection, the tenderness that he felt toward this skittish girl. Otherwise she would run, and run fast.

Rowan sat on the edge of the couch, poised to bolt, like she was proving his point for him. "I didn't come at a bad time, did I?"

Shaughnessy thought about what would have happened if she'd knocked on the door only a half hour earlier. What would Donna have said in coming face-to-face with the woman who'd become his obsession for the past year? "No." He lowered himself onto the arm of the thread-bare chair that he never used. "No, this is . . . this is good."

Rowan's eyes dropped to his empty left ring finger, and he was suddenly thankful that she hadn't come three months from now when there would be a gold band there. "I didn't know where else to go."

He crossed his arms over his chest, unsure what to do with his hands all of a sudden. "Did something happen?" Her head hung, her drying hair hiding her face. When she didn't answer, he prodded as gently as he knew how. "Rowan?"

Her head jerked up at her name, her mouth working. "I'm eighteen now."

Shaughnessy swallowed, looked at the wall instead of the way her shirt had plastered itself to her body. "I'm not sure how that's relevant."

"Aren't you?" she asked, softly though, so he wasn't convinced he'd been meant to hear. Louder, she continued, "No. It's harder to force me into the facility now."

"Okay," he said, trying not to step on any land mines here. "Do you need help?"

"Just a place to stay for a few days," Rowan said, her chin dipping once more as she seemed to wilt beneath his gaze.

It took only a handful of seconds to make the decision to kneel in front of her, at a distance, but lower than she was so she didn't feel overwhelmed.

"Rowan, did someone hurt you?" He paused. "Your brother?"

Once again, her eyes snapped to his. "N-no. Never."

He wanted to argue but didn't. This wasn't the time to focus on his pet theory. It seemed even more absurd in the quiet space between them. "Your mother?"

She shook her head, her eyes slipping back to the floor. The denial meeker, more hesitant. He didn't know what that meant.

"Tell me what to do," he said, a little helplessly.

Rowan licked her lips and then pushed the towel from her shoulders. Her eyes were red rimmed but no less beautiful for it, her lashes dark from the tears. She placed delicate hands on his shoulders, and he waited for her to push him away.

"Keep me safe?" The question—the plea—broke him, destroyed him. He shook his head, a bit helpless. "That's all I've ever wanted to do."

———

Rowan White slept curled in the fetal position, her knees pulled in close to her body.

Shaughnessy watched her from the guest bedroom's open doorway the next morning, debating whether to wake her.

Just as he had the thought, her eyes opened wide, met his. It wasn't slow and groggy how most people woke up, but rather fast and all at once on alert. How soldiers slept in the middle of a war zone.

Rowan exhaled as she took in her surroundings, sat up, let the blankets fall to her waist. She was wearing one of his shirts—her own in the dryer—and he hated the possessive jolt the sight sent through him. She'd come to him for help; he had no business looking at her like this.

"Go back to sleep," he said as quietly as possible so as not to startle her. She shook her head, the corners of her mouth tipping up shyly as her cheeks flushed pink.

The pale light of morning slipped into the room and then into the private space between her collarbone and shoulder, and he couldn't help but ask, "Why did you come here?"

Uncertainty flickered into her expression. "You were nice to me."

"Is that such a rarity?" he asked.

"You would be surprised," Rowan said with a little laugh that lacked any humor at all. "It's hard when you're the crazy girl in the family."

His gaze dropped to her arms where he could see the thin white lines that served as a reminder of the night they'd met. "You tried to hurt yourself."

He didn't know why he said it. Maybe he wanted to force her to tell him the truth. Or force her to confess that she hadn't been the one with the blade at all.

Rowan's hands cupped over the scars as if she could actually hide them now. "That's what they say."

"Your family?" he asked.

"Everyone," she whispered, her shoulders rounded.

"Not everyone," Shaughnessy said. "Not me."

She lifted her head slowly, a flower seeking the sun, and smiled. Warmth bloomed in his own chest, and he wanted to make a vow to her right then and there to slay every dragon in her path.

"Breakfast," he said, before anything emotionally revealing could spill out of him. He turned and walked away because lingering in her carefully limited happiness was too tempting.

When he was cracking eggs over the skillet, he thought about her phrasing. *That's what they say.*

If people thought Rowan was crazy, they'd never believe her testimony.

That was the most obvious reason why her family was screwing with her sense of reality.

And by now he was sure they were. She could deny it all night, but he heard in the hesitancies, the pauses, the way her chin dipped and her hands covered her scars. The *That's what they say*, which was just as soft and lilting as *Names, they mean something, don't they?*

None of that mattered, though, if they couldn't even get Anders on the hook in the first place.

There wasn't enough evidence to pin Jennifer's death on him, and Anders had made sure anything Rowan said would be discounted by a jury.

What they needed was a new body.

A new victim.

As he set Rowan's plate down in front of where she'd just come to sit at the table, his eyes traced the vulnerable curve of her neck, focused on the fluttering pulse there.

His mind echoed with Boyd's resigned voice: *Sorry, kid. Not until she turns up dead.*

CHAPTER TWENTY-SIX

GRETCHEN

Now

"We're stuck," Gretchen admitted in a rare show of vulnerability. Instead of making a big deal of it, Marconi simply nodded sleepily over her coffee as the rest of the customers in the crowded Dunkin' Donuts pressed in around them.

"We need to find Tabitha Cross," Marconi said.

"I have Fred on it," Gretchen said, throwing an elbow into the ribs of a middle-aged man who was standing obnoxiously close to her as she pushed her way toward the door.

They stepped out onto the sidewalk, and Gretchen's eyes automatically found Shaughnessy lurking in his sedan. "Call Gibbs."

"Why?"

"I want to know about the three detectives," Gretchen said. "The two who were on Jennifer Cross's case and then also Liam Boyd."

Marconi had already fished her cell out of her pocket. "The detective who was with Shaughnessy the night in '83."

Since Marconi already had her cell pressed to her ear, Gretchen didn't bother confirming her guess as they both climbed into the Porsche.

When Gibbs answered, Marconi put him on speakerphone and asked about the cops.

"Shawn Jones and Grace Li have spotless records," Gibbs said after some keyboard clacking. "Li retired two years ago and moved to California. Jones is still on Major Crimes and has one of the best solve rates in the department."

"Except for Jennifer Cross's murder," Gretchen said just loud enough so Gibbs would hear.

He didn't acknowledge her, but then again she hadn't expected him to.

"And Boyd?" Marconi asked.

The silence this time was longer. "Looks like he resigned in '93."

The year caught Gretchen's attention. "What month?"

"August."

The same month Rowan had died.

Marconi's eyes snapped to Gretchen's. "Where is he now?"

"Uh," Gibbs hedged. "Fell off the radar."

"Wouldn't he still be in the system?" Marconi asked. "For his pension, at least."

"There weren't really digital records back then," Gibbs said, but Gretchen detected something in his voice that she'd rarely heard from him before. Doubt.

"Can you find out what happened to him?" Marconi said, reading Gretchen's mind.

"I can try," Gibbs said, and Gretchen wiggled her eyebrows. Marconi shoved Gretchen's shoulder and hung up with a perfunctory thanks.

"That's strange," Marconi said, tucking her phone back into her pocket.

"The dates," Gretchen said.

"The people, is more like it," Marconi muttered. "Rowan White runs out into the middle of the road in front of two cops. One is the lead detective on her murder ten years later, one resigns the same month of her death."

"But Boyd wasn't on Rowan's case," Gretchen said. "Not in '93."

Marconi's eyes drifted to the rearview mirror.

"You're thinking something," Gretchen prodded.

"Boyd knew," Marconi said, after she'd taken a long sip of her coffee. "No one put it together back then. At least, that's what it seems."

"That Shaughnessy knew Rowan before he led her murder investigation," Gretchen said, following Marconi's train of thought. "But Boyd had been in the car with Shaughnessy that night."

"Cops don't fall off the radar," Marconi murmured.

Gretchen was already dialing Fred. She wasn't about to rely on Gibbs to find something. "Can you do a search on a Detective Liam Boyd?"

"Your tab for this case is going to be longer than a CVS receipt," Fred griped, but didn't hang up. After a handful of minutes, she continued: "Looks like a fairly normal history until August 1993."

"Normal how?"

"Middle-class family on the outskirts of Boston, they moved here from Texas. He was a football star at his high school, joined the academy after graduation," Fred rattled off. "Nothing else major pings."

"And then he just disappears?" Gretchen guessed.

"Got it in one," Fred said. "Resigned early from Boston PD and then radio silence for the past thirty years. And you've got to work hard not to have a digital footprint these days."

"Could he have died?"

"If there was no one to report him missing?" Fred asked. "Sure. But that's your arena, Doc."

Gretchen hung up without any pleasantries and stared out her windshield, not really seeing anything.

"What are the odds he didn't have any close friends or family to report him missing?" Gretchen asked. And she was genuinely curious for the answer. She thought maybe Marconi would notice if she disappeared, and Shaughnessy would obviously notice as well. How many others would just assume she'd dropped contact with them? She guessed most would just shrug and move on.

"It's not unheard of that cops have trouble with their personal lives," Marconi mused.

Gretchen elbowed Marconi. "Not you."

Marconi rolled her eyes so hard it looked like it hurt. "What are you thinking? About Boyd, not my very uninteresting romantic life."

"Game it out," Gretchen said, after thinking it through for a minute. Anything was possible here. "If Shaughnessy got tangled up in Rowan's death somehow, maybe he panicked when Boyd called him on the connection."

"So he killed him and faked a resignation letter?" Marconi asked, her voice dubious. "That would have to be some resignation letter for the chief to just accept that Boyd was no longer there."

"Family emergency, had to move that weekend out of state, blah blah." Gretchen twirled a hand in the air. "It was the '90s. It wasn't as easy to drill holes in things like that."

"You really think Shaughnessy's capable of killing at least two people and he's just been, what? Living with it for the past thirty years?" Marconi asked. "That would make him a psychopath, wouldn't it?"

"Ted Bundy's neighbors loved him," Gretchen said, though she was with Marconi on this. Because it also stood to reason that Shaughnessy hadn't stopped at two, but rather three. Jennifer Cross.

And while Gretchen struggled to understand empaths, she had made a career of understanding people with personality disorders.

Shaughnessy didn't raise any flags for her. Not the kind that would signal he'd been capable of murdering at least three people.

He was clearly hiding things, but Gretchen was having a hard time imagining him as the guy.

"He's involved—I just don't know how." Gretchen's eyes flicked to the rearview mirror.

"This is starting to give me stalker vibes," Marconi said. "I saw it a lot when I was a beat cop working the night shift."

"Stalker vibes," Gretchen repeated, a little derisive of the imprecise terminology, but also a little intrigued. "That might round some of the pointed edges that didn't quite fit with this case."

Marconi nodded. "A lot of times stalkers will idolize their victim, maybe even see themselves as their savior. They love them, they want to protect them. Or at least that's what the stalkers tell themselves."

"They build up their own reality," Gretchen said. This wasn't her area of expertise, but she knew enough about general abnormal behavior to understand where Marconi was headed. "It becomes all important to them."

"And then the victim does something that either challenges that reality or deviates from this paragon of perfection the stalker has made them into," Marconi continued. "And the stalker snaps. It makes more sense than him being some in-the-closet serial killer."

Gretchen chewed the inside of her cheek, thinking about the conversation with Gibbs. Thinking about the way Shaughnessy had parked outside Gretchen's place. Thinking of the times he'd been there when she left for school as a teen, when she'd come home late from a night of partying in her twenties. "Shaughnessy *is* predisposed to creepy behavior."

"I don't know if he's predisposed to fictionalizing women from afar, though," Marconi said. "He's a cop who views it as his duty to protect people. When does it become a pathology?"

"When someone ends up with a knife sticking out of her chest, I presume," Gretchen said.

"It would be nice to stop it before it got to that point," Marconi said, something darker than humor layered into her voice. "So, why then? He'd known her for ten years."

"What was the trigger?" Gretchen asked. "Rowan coming back into the house where the man who Shaughnessy thought was a serial killer lived."

"It feels like it would have been more immediate in that case," Marconi said. "She'd been there for three months."

"Waiting for an opportunity?" Gretchen suggested. "It would answer some questions I've had about the rage."

"The disconnect between the fact that Rowan was lying in bed and the violence of the wounds has always been weird to me, too," Marconi agreed. "If he felt wronged by her, that could have been building, and could explain the intense emotion on the attacker's side of things."

"So where do the Cross sisters come into this?" Gretchen asked, knowing it was a wrench in their little scenario.

"Maybe that was the trigger." Marconi tapped her finger on the side of her cup. "Tabitha."

Gretchen let the thought derail the narrative she'd been weaving for herself. And it tracked. Tabitha's new presence in the White household could have easily set something in motion.

"She was too young at the time of Jennifer's murder to investigate anything," Gretchen said. "But she was getting close to uncovering something in '93."

"Cold case families . . . ," Marconi said. "They're their own special breed. They do a lot of weird things, especially if they think the cops have forgotten about their loved one."

"Tabitha wasn't wrong there," Gretchen couldn't help but note.

"So she starts digging into her sister's murder, Shaughnessy finds out—"

"The killer finds out," Gretchen corrected. When Marconi shot her a look, Gretchen shrugged. "I'm not defending him. But we already have an entire boatload of preconceived bias on this case. We don't need more."

"The killer," Marconi continued with exaggerated emphasis. "Goes to shut Tabitha up and . . . what? Rowan got in the way?"

"Tabitha was the one who found me in Rowan's room," Gretchen said. Even though last night she'd been thinking that forensics had never ruled the girl out as the killer, Gretchen was still struggling with the logistics of it all.

And the only way to get answers was to go to the source. "We need to meet with Tabitha Cross."

Marconi voiced what Gretchen was already thinking. "If she's alive."

CHAPTER
TWENTY-SEVEN

TABBY

1993

It took three tries and forty-five minutes to get Detective Shaughnessy on the phone, and by the time he answered, Cal had long given up his pacing in front of the McDonald's and the boy with the pimples had gone back to his comic books.

"What happened?" Shaughnessy asked after she'd told him her name. His voice was so gentle, like he was talking to that scared child she almost couldn't believe she'd ever been.

"My sister, Jenny, was murdered."

Silence. And then a deep, weighted exhale. "I know."

Tabby sagged against the wall, that sticky fear gone from her body so that she was just left with a tired ache.

"You said you were going to catch him." It sounded so small, like she was ten years old again.

"I shouldn't have promised that," Shaughnessy confessed on a sigh. "I didn't have perspective—it's one of the reasons I've tried to move on from her investigation."

The words pressed in against tender skin, and Tabby barked out a humorless laugh. "Must be nice. To be able to make that choice."

"I'm sorry."

That apology was what Tabby was used to; it's what everyone said when they heard about Jenny, if they could bring themselves to say anything. Some couldn't stand to be so close to tragedy; some couldn't stand the shame they felt at being happy it hadn't happened to them. And the others were at a loss beyond empty phrases trotted out because no one in their goddamn society had ever learned how to address grief.

"This is stupid," Tabby muttered, but didn't move to hang up.

"What happened tonight, Tabitha?" Shaughnessy asked, with that same gentleness with which he'd answered the phone.

And so Tabby told him, because what did she have to lose? She told him about hanging out in cop bars, about picking up a rookie and taking him home. About having him get Jenny's file, and then meeting Cal only a few days later. About how Cal would ask her about Jenny's case, all casual like. How he'd warned her to stay away from investigating the murder.

When she looked back at the sequence of events, it was so painfully obvious what had happened.

"You think it's a fake name?" Shaughnessy asked. And try as she might, she couldn't hear any scolding behind the question.

"I had thought that," Tabby said. "Now, I'm sure."

A beat. "Why?"

"Why would he try to kill me like that?" Tabby asked. "While using his real name?"

"People do all sorts of stupid things," Shaughnessy muttered. And then louder: "What set this 'Cal' off?"

Tabby took a breath. "I found yearbooks."

"You recognized him."

"No," Tabby corrected the obvious assumption. "But I saw someone I recognized. A man named Anders White. It . . . rattled me."

"Come again?" Something about the way his voice tightened made her think he'd heard her just fine.

"Anders White, he was the brother of one of Jennifer's classmates," Tabby said. "I recognized him because he came to Jenny's funeral."

Shaughnessy exhaled, low and controlled, like he was making an effort. "What?"

"He showed up at the church," Tabby said. "He sat in the back row. Alone."

"Jesus."

"My dad had him and a couple other people kicked out because he thought they were gawkers," Tabby continued. "Anders didn't fight it or anything. He just left." She paused. Waited. "Does it even mean anything?"

"Maybe, maybe not," Shaughnessy said, and she couldn't tell if he was lying to her.

Tabby ran a hand through her hair. "It just startled me, is all. Remembering him. Knowing he was there."

"Yeah, of course," Shaughnessy said, like it made total sense. "Did the security record their names anywhere? Is it on record that he showed up?"

"I don't—I'm sorry I don't," Tabby stuttered out, feeling like she was that child again, disappointing everyone because she didn't have the answers they so desperately needed. "I don't know. I'm sorry."

"No, no," Shaughnessy rushed to reassure her. "No. That's understandable. I don't suppose your father—"

Tabby made a little hum of dissent.

"Ah, okay, well," Shaughnessy trailed off, sounding a little helpless.

"I can ask," she offered up.

"Sure, sure, let me know," Shaughnessy said, now sounding half-distracted. Then, with a tentative inhale: "And you decided to tell . . . Cal," Shaughnessy said slowly, obviously trying to piece together her reasoning. "Why?"

"I didn't . . ." Tabby bit off a frustrated noise. "I just wanted to forget for a little while. He helps me forget. Helped me."

He didn't comment on the obvious fact that she was sleeping with the man, and there was no judgment when he asked, "What did you say when you called?"

"Just that I'd found something. It was vague—it shouldn't have spooked him," Tabby said. "He must have been on edge."

"If he was waiting for you to remember something . . . ," Shaughnessy said.

"Then he was paranoid already, and I freaked him out," Tabby finished the thought running a hand through her hair. God, Shaughnessy must think her so stupid. *Girls who play Nancy Drew get murdered.* And this was why. What had possessed her to think she could investigate a murder?

"I'm sorry I have to ask," Shaughnessy said slowly, interrupting her internal strife. "Cal isn't Anders White, correct?"

"No." The denial came punched out. Her surprise had to be evident in case Shaughnessy had any doubt. "You thought . . ."

"I thought it could be him with a fake name, yes," Shaughnessy said. "What does this Cal look like?"

"Blond, handsome," Tabby said, knowing it was inadequate. Wondering if she would always fail this test. Blond, handsome. There were a surprising number of men who fit that description. "I always had the feeling he was well off, too."

"What gave you the impression he was rich?" Shaughnessy asked.

"He never hesitated at a cash register."

People like her hesitated. People who didn't know if they had quite enough money, who calculated each purchase down to the penny to avoid embarrassment. Cal had never worried about that. Maybe that didn't make him rich, but it made him comfortable.

"Okay," Shaughnessy said, contained and controlled, like he was trying not to take his frustration out on a young woman. "I'm worried that Cal might be Jenny's killer. But we don't have nearly enough evidence to go on."

"You said . . ." Tabby cleared her throat. "You said you knew who did it. Back then."

"I was young."

"Does that mean you don't know who it was?" Tabby asked.

The silence dragged until he said quietly, so she nearly missed it, "I've long since realized I don't know anything at all."

He sounded lost, hopeless. But she remembered how his voice had gone taut at the mention of Anders White. And the inevitability of it snuck in, not like a blow but a realization you hadn't known you'd already had. "Did you think it was Anders White?"

"Maybe," he hedged. "But if that were the case, then who is this person trying to kill you?"

"And," Tabby asked for both of them, "what does he think I know that makes me so dangerous?"

CHAPTER
TWENTY-EIGHT

GRETCHEN

Now

Before Gretchen could check to see if Fred had a current address for Tabitha Cross, her phone rang.

Dr. Chen.

Gretchen answered with "The missing page?"

He was one of her favorite people in part because he didn't bother commenting on her lack of social manners. "It's your lucky day, my dear."

"You found it." Her fingers tightened around the wheel. She ignored the look Marconi shot her from the passenger seat as the Porsche's engine roared, reflecting Gretchen's excitement.

"I would of course love to take the credit," Dr. Chen said, "but it was an intern who did the work."

Gretchen thought the appropriate thing to do here was to make sure Dr. Chen would send her appreciation to the low-paid grunt, but she was too busy holding on to her irritation that she was at least a minute into the phone call and still didn't have an answer. She tried to soften her voice as much as possible when she pressed. "Dr. Chen."

"Yes, well, it turns out"—Dr. Chen paused, seemingly unable to help his own propensity for drama—"Rowan White had given birth at some point in her life."

The world around Gretchen rippled, froze, and then snapped back into place. "Before she was murdered?"

"Some time before, yes," Dr. Chen said. "The medical examiner noted the presence of a series of pockmarks along the inside of the pelvic bone that could only have been caused by the tearing of ligaments during childbirth."

"When?"

"It's impossible to tell the date of the birth," Dr. Chen said. "But with the amount of healing and wear evident, it wasn't anytime close to her death."

"Why wasn't this noted more prominently in the report?" It was the only question Gretchen could think to ask. "Why bury that?"

"All supposition, of course," Dr. Chen prefaced, "but I assume because the markings were older and thus less relevant to the case."

The case where they already had a clear suspect. "Because everyone thought I killed her."

"Yes, that is what I meant," Dr. Chen said, in his straightforward way, and Gretchen actually laughed, the shock a thick cloud over her earlier irritation.

Gretchen had found that the best way to continue to get people to do favors for her was to sound grateful, so she managed to force out a shaky thank-you.

"You bring the port next Friday," Dr. Chen said. "And not the cheap stuff."

He hung up before she could agree, and Marconi made a sound in her throat.

"Rowan was pregnant," Gretchen said, answering the unspoken question. "Not . . . not when she was killed, but before."

"Was pregnant or gave birth?" Marconi asked, quick and clever, the way Gretchen liked her.

"Birth."

Marconi's stunned silence cut through the buzzing in Gretchen's ears. "Do you think your parents know where the kid is?"

"Or who the father was," Gretchen said, thinking of the shadow in Rowan's bedroom that night. Maybe that person had been Shaughnessy, but maybe it had been this new player.

"Would they tell you if they did?" Marconi asked.

"No," Gretchen said, pulling a U-turn in the middle of traffic. "But I know someone who might."

"Who are we interviewing?" Marconi finally asked when Gretchen turned into a quiet residential neighborhood.

Gretchen's lip pulled back in disgust as she scanned the passing numbers painted on mailboxes and curbs. "My sister."

Marconi sat up straighter, interest clearly caught. "Ah, the elusive Francesca."

Showing up without calling first had been a gamble, but Fran's shiny monstrosity of a car was there, parked next to her husband's Lexus, in the driveway.

Both Gretchen and Marconi skillfully dodged the rotating lawn sprinklers as they made their way to the stoop.

It took several minutes for Fran to open the door, but by that point Gretchen had figured out it was more a power play than anything else. She could even hear the TV news on in the front parlor.

Her sister had passed forty a few years prior but had the polished, maintained looks of a wealthy Bostonian, her hair perfectly dyed, her teeth bleached, her skin injected with copious amounts of Botox. Despite the early hour, Fran was dressed for the day, down to the pearls around her neck and the slim gold watch on her wrist, which she glanced at pointedly.

When Gretchen just raised one shoulder in a deliberately provocative shrug, Fran sighed, gave Marconi a once-over, and then gestured them inside. "Mother warned me you might come by."

And of course the element of surprise hadn't actually been on Gretchen's side. Bardot would never let her little mini-me charge into battle without alerting her she would need her proper armor. In this case, an impeccable wardrobe and enough makeup to hide any flicker of emotion that slipped through the chemicals holding her face in place.

"What else did Mother say?" Gretchen asked, both their heels clicking on the marble in the entryway. The soft thud of Marconi's boots provided a strange counterpoint to the glamour. Gretchen hoped she was leaving clumps of dirt in her wake.

"Mother advised me to indulge your delusions if you start getting violent," Fran said. "And to have the nine and one ready on my phone the whole time."

Fran led them through the hallway into the kitchen, where she had a mug of coffee waiting. She didn't offer any to them despite the mostly full pot behind her.

"As if you would have time to pull out your phone if I really wanted to hurt you." Gretchen let the malice slide into the words. She was a master at making the world see her the way she wanted it to. Most of the time it benefited her to make people see a controlled, professional consultant. For her family, she liked to present a more dangerous persona.

But Fran didn't pale, simply sipped at her coffee. They'd played these games enough as children for the edge to have dulled for both of them.

"What do you want, Gretchen?" Fran asked, ignoring Marconi.

That was usually for the best, since it let Marconi poke her nose into places that Fran might not want her. This time, though, Marconi stayed put, digging her phone out of her pocket when it buzzed. When she looked at the message, her body went on alert, satisfaction sitting on her face as plain as anything.

Gretchen wanted to grab the phone from her to see what it had been, but she turned her attention back to her sister.

"Rowan's kid," Gretchen said, and that got the first real reaction out of Fran. Quick surprise, there and gone.

"What are you even talking about?" But Fran had looked away, out the overlarge window into the garden that was as carefully cultivated as the rest of her.

"Where is it?" Gretchen asked, ignoring that feeble attempt at deflection.

"It?" Fran turned back, cocked her head like she was insulted on the kid's behalf.

"Her, him, them." Gretchen waved a hand. "I wouldn't have pegged you as being a stickler for pronouns."

"The child is not a dog," Fran said.

Gretchen paused at that. The confirmation that there was a child didn't seem like a slip of the tongue. "I thought you would lie."

"About the existence of the child?" Fran asked. "Why should I? It's not my secret, nor do I care if you find out."

Even though Gretchen had come here guessing Fran was her best chance at getting the information she wanted, Gretchen was still surprised. "You'll upset Bardot."

"I think the days of Mother caring about Rowan's love child are long past," Fran said, the dimple in her cheek teasing into life. It had always made an appearance whenever Fran thought she was being clever. She didn't laugh like other girls, but she did smirk, the superiority that came with her own special brand of narcissism leaving its mark on her body. "Do you really think digging all this up is a good idea, Gretch?"

Gretchen tossed the challenge back at her. "Why wouldn't it be?"

Fran's eyes darted to Marconi. "There's not a statute of limitations on murder."

"Oh, thank you for that lesson in law." She and Fran certainly didn't keep in touch, but Fran was well aware of Gretchen's career consulting on homicide cases.

"You're the one trying to get yourself actually charged this time," Fran countered. "If I were you, I'd take it as a lucky break and move on."

"I'm sorry, but weren't you asleep when the murder occurred?" Marconi finally cut in.

"That doesn't mean I don't know what happened," Fran said. "Everyone knows what happened."

"And you slept through the screaming," Marconi pushed, ignoring the second part.

"I was a teenager." Fran glanced over again, assessing this time. "And I had a prescription for Ambien."

"Which you took that night?" Marconi asked, and Gretchen shot her an approving look. The answer had been worded in just the right way to get around outright lying.

"It was thirty years ago," Fran said, dismissive, just like Bardot. They both seemed to remember everything perfectly until it was convenient to forget.

"I see selective memory loss runs in the family," Marconi said, echoing Gretchen's thoughts.

"How else would I have slept through my dear aunt's murder?" Fran asked.

"How indeed?" Marconi murmured.

"Are you accusing me of something?" Fran asked, unruffled. Fran wasn't on the spectrum for an antisocial personality disorder, but she was hard, with a soul of ice and a backbone of steel. She didn't back down from a challenge; she didn't blink.

Maybe that was the inevitable outcome when you grew up in a household like theirs.

"I'm just struggling to understand how you can know with such certainty what happened that night when you weren't even awake for it," Marconi said, sounding like the epitome of patience and reason, just like she had when facing down Bardot.

There were times in the past when Gretchen had read Marconi as a doormat. Her ability to let verbal jabs land without poking back, the fact that her temper seemed set at simmer, the very easiness with which she navigated conflict by simply ignoring it. But when it was important, Marconi could hold her ground.

Fran's expression didn't flicker from amused contempt, but she did give a half nod of acknowledgment. "Usually finding a suspect holding the murder weapon over the dead body would seem to be enough for most people. But I stand corrected. We can't know for *absolute certain* what happened, I suppose."

The concession came out sarcastic at best, and Gretchen tapped her finger against the granite island top. She didn't care if Fran thought her guilty or not, but Marconi had landed on a point that really was strange. How had Fran slept through all of it?

"Here's the funny thing," Marconi said, deceptively casual. But Gretchen could sense the shark beneath her smooth surface. "I figured rich family, middle of Boston. Even in the '90s there were some pretty good home security systems out there."

Again, nothing showed on Fran's face, but Gretchen could see new tension in her shoulders, her fingers where they wrapped around the mug.

Marconi held up her phone. "And I just had it confirmed. Turns out the system your family had? Still around."

"They wouldn't just give you the records," Fran said, not quite scared. But all the arrogance that had been there before had dissolved into a carefully neutral tone.

"Judges find me quite convincing," Marconi said, as if she'd secured a warrant. Marconi had always been good at coming up with information on the fly—to an impressive extent—but this had Gretchen wondering if Marconi had somehow gotten ahold of Fred's number instead of going through legal channels. "Would you like to know what I found out about that night?"

Fran didn't answer, and that alone reeked of guilt. Marconi had her on the defensive now.

"The system was turned off," Marconi continued. "And it was the only time that month that it hadn't been actively engaged, so that makes me think it was something more than a coincidence. I mean, I can't know for *absolute certain*, but it does make one curious, don't you think?"

Fran had gone completely still at this point. "There's nothing to prove it wasn't a careless mistake."

"True." Marconi nodded, rocking back on her heels. "But since everyone else around here likes to tell stories about what happened that night, I'm going to go ahead and take a shot."

"I should have brought popcorn," Gretchen said, but neither woman looked her way.

Marconi was watching Fran. "I think you were a typical teenager and pretended you were going to bed when instead you were sneaking out to meet your boyfriend."

"I didn't have a boyfriend," Fran said, but to Gretchen's ears it sounded weak.

"You snuck out and left the alarm off just in case you had to crawl back in through a window," Marconi continued. "You weren't even there when the murder happened."

Fran swallowed, visibly.

"So what I'm left wondering here," Marconi said, "is if you were complicit in the scheme or just a dumb patsy."

Gretchen blew out a long breath, but didn't dare interrupt.

"It could have been anyone in the house who left the system off," Fran said, though it clearly lacked some of her confidence from earlier.

"It could have been anyone in the house who handed Gretchen that bloody knife, too," Marconi said, not aggressive but steady. In that way of hers. "But we all know what happened, don't we?"

Fran's eyelashes fluttered too long against pale cheeks, another outward sign that she was unnerved. "Fine, you're right."

"Oh," Gretchen crowed, and turned to Marconi, giving her a golf clap. Marconi just rolled her eyes at the antics. "Well done."

"Please act like the adult you are," Fran said, chastising Gretchen. But Gretchen had studied enough about emotional intelligence to know the woman was exerting control where she could, lashing out because she had been caught off guard, all while thinking she was in charge of the conversation. "I wasn't complicit in anything."

"Which means you were a patsy," Gretchen pointed out, harsh and mocking, conveniently ignoring the fact that her eight-year-old self had likely been one as well.

"Who was the boyfriend?" Marconi asked, not letting up even after securing her victory.

"He told me his name was George," Fran said, slowly.

"Last name?" Marconi prodded.

Fran looked away, a faint blush on her pale cheeks. "He never told me."

Marconi pulled out her phone, typed something in, and then flipped it around so Fran could see the screen. "Was this him?"

Gretchen tilted her head enough so that she could catch a glimpse of the picture.

Shaughnessy.

But Fran shook her head, and when she answered, it was a definitive no.

"Okay," Marconi said, restashing her phone. "Do you remember when you met him?"

"No. A couple of days before maybe."

Marconi nodded. "And do you remember when you broke it off?"

Fran's lips pressed into a thin line. "I didn't see him after that night. There was a lot going on."

"You never saw him during the course of the investigation?" Marconi pressed. "Or that night when you got home? He wasn't in the house?"

"No, of course not." Fran seemed genuinely confused at the question. "He was a teenager."

And that stopped Gretchen short until she realized the kid could have been paid by the killer. That's what she would have done. Cruised by the mall, found a skater boy with too much time and not enough money, and given him a picture of Fran. It probably hadn't even cost that much. Yet it had been a key directly into the town house.

"It doesn't mean anything," Fran said, her voice an icy lash. "You still killed Rowan. It wasn't . . . *him*."

"And you know that how?" Gretchen asked.

Fran just shook her head, her arms wrapped around her waist now.

Knowing they weren't going to get anything else out of Fran on the topic of the boyfriend, Gretchen shifted them back to the reason they'd come in the first place. "Where is Rowan's child?"

At that, Fran looked up, met Gretchen's eyes, that dimple slowly coming back to life. Color flushed into her pale cheeks, her arms dropping from their protective positioning. Whatever Fran was about to say had her feeling assured once more.

"You haven't figured it out," she breathed, the closest thing to giddy Gretchen could imagine she let herself be. "You really don't know."

Marconi tensed beside Gretchen, feet shifting into a boxer's stance.

Gretchen felt the tug of some yawning void, a darkness beckoning her forward.

The dimple was on full display. "Gretchen, darling. It's you."

CHAPTER
TWENTY-NINE

SHAUGHNESSY

1987

Shaughnessy slipped his arm from beneath Donna's head, transferring her over to the pillow with practiced ease.

If she knew where he was headed, there'd be another fight. He was so tired of them these days, so tired of the disappointment his wife no longer bothered to hide.

She wanted him to see it.

That didn't stop him from heading downstairs, skipping the squeaky step almost without thought, crossing through the kitchen of their small row house toward the basement door. He didn't bother with lights until he was sitting at his desk.

He hadn't heard from Rowan White since she'd left his house years ago. She'd stayed for about a week, and then snuck out sometime in the morning on the sixth day without even saying goodbye.

In the time since he'd woken up in an empty house that morning, he'd realized that he'd been projecting so much onto her shoulders. She had been neither strong nor weak, neither the Madonna nor the whore.

She'd just been a girl who had been trapped in a bad life, and he'd been a young rookie with too much imagination.

He'd pictured her as a beautifully tragic victim, fragile as glass and in need of saving. When that illusion had shattered he didn't remember. Certainly, it hadn't happened when she'd pleaded with him to keep her safe.

Maybe it had been later when she'd stopped responding to the beeper he'd run out to buy before she'd left his house. In case her family tried to institutionalize her again, he'd said. Really it had been because he'd wanted a way to maintain contact with her.

For the first few weeks, she'd been good at keeping in touch with him. Then she'd drifted; then she'd cut off communication altogether.

But actually, no, he'd still believed in her at that point. Even when his beeper had sat silent. At first, he'd been terrified enough to try to convince the chief to launch a rescue mission. But Fitzy had just shaken his head, his hand covering his mouth.

"You're still getting mixed up with that family?" Fitzy had asked, disbelief and something far too close to despair coating the question. *"Oh, Patrick."*

He'd felt chastised, truly chastised, with just that damning sigh. *Oh, Patrick.*

And wasn't that his life? He never knew when to quit.

Even after a year of silence, he'd still been expecting to hear from Rowan, had kept his eye on any police reports, had slept in his car too many times just far enough away from the White mansion as to not draw attention. On his personal time, he'd found himself following Anders and spending much of the rest of it in the library, scouring through newspapers.

He'd found nothing.

Absolutely nothing.

Zach Daniels—who had become something like a friend over the years—would grimace whenever Shaughnessy mentioned Anders.

"You got to let it go, man," Daniels would say time and again whenever Shaughnessy seemed primed to bring up the idea.

When Rowan had left, Shaughnessy had tried a different approach with Daniels, unable to get her quiet *That's what they say* out of his head.

"Have you ever seen a case where everyone makes the victim think they're the crazy one?" Shaughnessy asked, one night when Daniels had swung through Boston on yet another book tour.

"Gaslighting," Daniels said, lifting his glass in a little salute.

"What?" Shaughnessy asked, though he was already turning the unfamiliar term over in his head.

"Based on a play from the 1930s." Daniels slipped into lecture mode. *"Though most people attribute it to the film with Ingrid Bergman."*

"Still not helping," Shaughnessy said, trying not to bristle. He wasn't the most cultured person around, he knew. That didn't mean he was an idiot, but it did mean he missed references sometimes.

"Eh, it's about a husband, makes his wife believe she's going insane," Daniels said. *"Makes her think she's stealing, things like that. The word itself comes from the fact that he was using the gaslights in their hallways, dimming them and pretending they were the same level as always. He made her question her own reality, made her think she was going insane."*

Question her own reality. *"Why does he do it?"*

"Uh, the play and the film deviate a little, but essentially he's trying to cover up his own criminal activities," Daniels said with a shrug. *"I think . . . right, I think he was trying to search the apartment above theirs? A wealthy widow lived there. There were definitely priceless jewels involved. He wanted his wife committed so she wouldn't realize what he was doing."*

Committed.

"How does it end?" Shaughnessy asked. He almost didn't want to know. He hated the idea of Rowan locked away from the world, thinking she was the problem.

"Uh," Daniels hedged. "Somehow he ends up tied to a chair, I think? When the husband tries to convince the wife to save him, she tells him that she's too insane to know what he's asking."

"Good for her."

"Yeah," Daniels said, and then sighed, the heaviness of his job apparent in the quiet exhale. "You see it a lot with abusive relationships. Why do you care?"

"What?"

"I'm guessing this has something to do with that serial killer of yours," Daniels said, ignoring Shaughnessy's wince. "And his sister. So. Why do you care about this girl so much?"

"Wouldn't you?" Shaughnessy asked, at a loss.

"Haven't you heard?" There was a dangerous, self-deprecating undercurrent in Daniels's voice. "I only care about the serial killers."

"That's not true," Shaughnessy said on instinct more than belief. Although . . . Daniels was part of the culture where serial killers' names were remembered far more often than their victims. He rode the coattails of their notoriety to achieve his own version of celebrity.

Shaughnessy just hadn't realized Daniels had felt the burn of that hard truth.

"There you go," Daniels said, almost in a whisper, as if Shaughnessy had said his thoughts out loud. "Everyone gets there eventually."

They sat with that in silence, Shaughnessy unable to counter the misery he heard in Daniels's voice. What could he say? The man had made his career on understanding serial killers, not on saving their victims. But in the end, didn't it amount to the same thing? Wouldn't knowing their minds mean they could be caught sooner? The ethics here were gray, but they weren't as damning as Daniels clearly thought they were.

And what did that make Shaughnessy? Did he really care about Rowan? He barely even knew her.

Shaughnessy remembered the way Anders had watched him in the woods, by the shed. The sun on his hair, the amusement in his smile. The careful dance of their conversation. Wasn't Shaughnessy far more hooked by that man than the teenage girl who had been nothing more than a ghost?

Was he any better than Daniels?

"What can you do?" Shaughnessy asked. "If someone is being manipulated like that? To think they're crazy."

"Reality is a funny thing, isn't it?" Daniels said blearily. "There's no such thing as a true reality because we all see it through our own lens. No two people share the same version of reality. And yet we all seem to just accept that we're all having the same experience."

"We're not, though," Shaughnessy said, half comment, half question.

"Did you know when you move your head too quickly for your eyes to focus that your brain just guesses at what's there so you don't get seasick from the blurry images?" Daniels asked, clearly enjoying the slide into his drunkenness. "A good twenty percent of what we see is actually just our brain filling in the gaps."

"We can't even trust our own reality, let alone when someone starts messing with it," Shaughnessy said, easily following Daniels's not-quite-sober train of thought. "What on earth do they have to gain from that type of deception, though?"

"In Gaslight, it all came down to the money," Daniels said. "That's why the villain was messing with his wife's sense of reality."

"Find the reason . . . ," Shaughnessy said.

Daniels finished his thought for him. "And then you've got yourself a motive."

The only thing was, Shaughnessy had been looking for that reason for years now with nothing to show for it.

He knew he should be focusing on his actual cases. He was up for a big promotion after keeping his nose as clean as possible working Vice the past four years. Sure, he couldn't seem to hang on to a partner for very long, but there were always reasonable excuses. One had retired, one had been shot and desked, one had requested a transfer to Arizona because their husband got a job out there. They all made sense. And still his reputation had stuck.

Boyd still gave him shit about it mercilessly, all lighthearted on its face. But there was always a cruel, superior slant to the jokes that had Shaughnessy bristling despite the fact that Boyd was the one officer who didn't roll his eyes when Shaughnessy mentioned Anders White.

Or Jennifer Cross, for that matter.

The chief wouldn't even let him talk about the investigation, shutting Shaughnessy down every time he tried to bring it up.

"Stay away from that Cross case, son. I'm not going to tell you again," Fitzy had said.

"But no one's working it," Shaughnessy had pointed out.

"Because it's cold."

"But—"

"Look, I'll put someone on it when we have time," Fitzy had promised. *"But if I hear even a hint of you sniffing around, kiss that promotion goodbye."*

Politics. That had always been the answer whenever Shaughnessy had too many pints and asked too many questions about why the hell a police chief wouldn't want to solve a murder that had caught national attention.

"The public is going to get distracted by the next shiny thing," Boyd had said. *"But the mayor and city council won't be too pleased when one of their top donors refuses to cough up any more dough because they're being investigated by a rookie cop."*

"Not a rookie anymore," Shaughnessy had muttered, knowing he was beat.

The Whites were too rich, too influential. He was David to their Goliath. Except he was worse off because he wouldn't actually win in the end.

The pipes groaned above Shaughnessy now, and he glanced toward the ceiling, wondering if Donna had woken up. He hadn't heard footsteps, but sometimes she was stealthy about it. Maybe in the morning they'd just mutually pretend he'd stayed in bed the whole night. Back in the beginning they would have fought about his insomnia. It was probably a bad sign that they didn't anymore.

Still, Shaughnessy preferred their relationship that way, preferred the peace and quiet. Donna had never been the love of his life. She'd been convenient, and he'd known that—unofficially—he'd get further in his career if he was married to someone other than his job.

Rowan's face flashed into his mind, but he scoffed at it, shoved it down, buried it deep. She wasn't the great love of his life, either.

No, in some twisted way, he sometimes wondered if Anders was.

Not romantically. But even as one-sided as this obsession was, Anders was intertwined with his life, in his thoughts, even in his dreams, in a way that Donna had never been.

Shaughnessy pulled at the lower drawer of his desk, deciding he was not drunk enough to deal with that damning realization.

Instead he dug out the letters he'd received from Daniels, the correspondence he shared with the man more cherished than most other things in his life. They rarely talked about Anders anymore, but Daniels always had some new insight about serial killers in general.

Daniels enjoyed his own intelligence—that much was clear from his letters. But he was a good guy, and really just one of the thousands and thousands of Americans who were now fascinated by these monsters. He had expertise that others lacked, but he was no different from Shaughnessy or the lady down the street who thought all their neighbors were hiding dead girls in their basements.

"Perverts, the lot of them," the woman always said with a mania in her eyes that Shaughnessy recognized well.

They weren't all perverts, though. That's what the FBI was slowly learning as the agency started to identify and interview more of them.

There are four kinds of serial killers, Daniels had written in one of his messages. Thrill seekers, like Bonnie and Clyde. Then there were the mission-oriented ones, the ones who killed prostitutes or drug dealers because they thought they were ridding society of what they saw as vermin. Visionaries heard God talking to them and killed in his name. And finally there were those who sought power and control. Those were the perverts. The rapists who eventually graduated to more.

What's yours? Daniels had signed off.

What was Anders? If he even was one.

Though Shaughnessy had become obsessed with the man, he wasn't sure he actually knew him. They'd only ever had two conversations: the one when Shaughnessy and Boyd had gone to the White mansion years ago and the time that Anders had caught Shaughnessy breaking into his shed.

Both occasions Anders had been civilized, polite, refined. Shaughnessy couldn't imagine him getting his hands dirty let alone holding down a victim and cutting her open. But looks could be deceiving; he knew that better than anyone.

Shaughnessy glanced over at his wall where he'd pinned every mention he'd found of Anders White in various newspapers. The man had a thriving practice now and took up lots of space in the society columns with his wife, Bardot. There was the article Shaughnessy had found of their engagement, then the two announcements when their daughters, Francesca and Gretchen, had come along. A few gossipy tabloids had run articles on Bardot's difficult second pregnancy—a miscarriage scare that had revealed she was carrying in the first place. According to the reports, the Whites had been trying to keep the pregnancy out of the news until they'd made it past the second trimester successfully. But that hospital trip and then the bed rest for the remainder of her term had made that impossible. There were some nasty captions from when she'd emerged back into society after the birth that dissected all the ways her body had borne the brunt of the difficulties.

Beyond that, there was nothing that didn't scream proper upper-crust family. Bardot was involved with charities; there were rumors

Anders was going to shift into politics. The girls were perfect little clones of their parents, all blonde hair and blue eyes.

And all of a sudden, he couldn't breathe. He closed his eyes, not able to look at the wall that betrayed his own insanity.

Instead, he tried stepping back, out of his own head, his own theories, his own expectations. What if Rowan was just a troubled young girl who'd created a fantasy world to live in? What if she'd run out that one night, bloody without any clothes on, because she was manic and unstable, not because her brother was a serial killer who had been torturing her. What if she'd latched on to Shaughnessy as someone who would foster her delusions?

What proof did Shaughnessy really have that Jenny and Rowan were connected at all? A few marks on Jenny's arms was it.

He'd never found another case with any similarities. If Anders was a serial killer, he'd hid most of the bodies far better than he'd hid Jenny's.

What the hell had he been doing spending four years of his life chasing a fleeting encounter when a disturbed girl had told him to run?

Shaughnessy pushed to his feet, the chair scraping against the concrete, a discordant sound that matched the unease in his belly, in his chest, in his mind.

He crossed to his board in three swift steps, grabbed hold of the photo of Jenny, ripped it off. Grabbed hold of the police report from that night with Rowan, tore it down. He wrapped the red string around his wrists, tugged until the thumbtacks popped out, scattering on the floor, little sentinels felled in his shame.

Creepy, they said, the metal catching the light.

Psycho. Obsessed. Oh, Patrick. Oh, Patrick.

Everything blurred, his fingers numb, his legs unsteady. He heaved in air, but it was so thin it barely made it to his lungs.

In the end, he sat on the ground, the pieces of his life scattered around him, his muscles aching, his jaw sore, his head pounding. And he knew he would never think of Anders White again.

CHAPTER THIRTY

GRETCHEN

Now

For the first time in her life, Gretchen let someone else drive her Porsche.

Marconi kept two hands on the wheel at ten and two and took the corners like someone who'd just gotten her learner's permit. But Gretchen could catalog all that only in an absent kind of way to hold over her later.

Now, she was struggling to form full thoughts at all.

Some uneducated people thought sociopaths were Teflon, fireproof, immune to emotions and shock and any number of things. But just because Gretchen lacked the ability to empathize with those around her didn't mean that she was emotionless herself. It was like a radio. Empaths were flooded with sounds, unable to control the channels. Gretchen often heard more static than music, but she could recognize an opera from a pop song if she paid close enough attention.

And she was paying attention now.

Rowan hadn't been Gretchen's aunt.

She'd been her mother.

Without conscious thought, Viola Kent shoved into her brain front and center. Gretchen had gone on a three-day bender when she'd first heard about the thirteen-year-old girl who had viciously stabbed her mother to death. The only reason Gretchen had been able to pull herself out of that short spiral was because of the difference between Gretchen's history and Viola's present—Gretchen had been accused of stabbing her *aunt*, not her *mother*. It was trivial, irrational even, but Gretchen hadn't cared. The case might have been similar to hers, but it hadn't been the exact same.

Adrenaline coursed through her blood, making everything sharp and tangy, the ringing in her ears loud but not loud enough to drown out the purr of the engine. She sank into that sound, sank into a favored memory, all but feeling the machine jump beneath her hands when she got it up above a hundred miles an hour on an open stretch of highway while the sun rose in the distance. She sank into the memory of the man who'd been in her bed when Marconi had come knocking two days ago, the way he'd sucked on the hinge of her jaw, the way his fingers had tangled in her hair, pulling just a shade too hard.

She sank into the burn of vodka, the pounding of some foreign beat in her chest, the feeling of hands on her hips as she danced and swayed and spun in circles, ecstasy—both the drug and the feeling itself—turning everything syrupy and delicious.

Gretchen chased oblivion because that was what she loved best. She lived her life staving off the need to sink into it, but really all she'd had to do was let go. Every day, she'd clung to the edge of a skyscraper with the very tips of her fingers, and no one, not one goddamn soul, appreciated how hard it was to hold on.

No one appreciated just how easy it would be to fall.

She liked her life, sure. The dead bodies did something for her, let her breathe easier on the days she got to look at viciousness made physical. She liked spending money the way she wanted to, liked the vacations and the nice cars, her apartment and the VIP treatment she got when she decided to indulge in a night out. Gretchen had no interest in jail.

But there was a long way between the perfect, impeccable control she exerted over herself and getting caught in some felonious act.

A long fucking way.

It took a while to notice that Marconi had pulled off the road. Only when the hot sting of Marconi's palm lingered on Gretchen's cheek did she fully come back to herself. The return to reality, to the harsh light of day, to Marconi's steady, watchful gaze.

"Fuck. Off," Gretchen snarled before wrenching the door open. She didn't even know where she was going, didn't care. But she only got three steps before Marconi was there, all five foot nothing, pushing Gretchen back, toward the Porsche.

"No," Marconi said. Her stance gave away the fact that she was braced for a fight, but her tone remained even, cool. The heel of her palm pressed against Gretchen's shoulder again, but this time Gretchen didn't give. "I'm not letting you do this."

"You don't have a say over anything I do," Gretchen said, fingers wrapping around Marconi's wrist. It would take a thought and then half a heartbeat to snap the bone. Marconi would be on her knees in the next heartbeat, clutching her arm to her chest. Gretchen applied pressure so that Marconi would know what she was thinking. The woman didn't budge.

"Oh, Bambi's so brave these days," Gretchen taunted, wanting to hurt her more than she'd wanted anything else in an extraordinarily long time.

"Yeah, well, for some reason I actually give a shit about—" Marconi broke off, looked away. After a moment, she finished, weaker this time. "Solving this case."

She had been about to say *you*. *For some reason I actually give a shit about you.*

It did nothing to soothe the raging wildfire in Gretchen's chest. If anything, it poured gasoline on the flames. How dare this woman she barely knew say anything about Gretchen and her life and her reactions.

"Who the hell asked you to care?" Gretchen spat out. "Christ, you're so pathetic. You have no one, nothing in your life, so you have to latch on to mine like a bloodsucking parasite."

Gretchen yanked on Marconi's wrist, twisted, and in two half steps had the woman pressed up against the Porsche, Gretchen's forearm at her windpipe. "You think I like you? You think I respect you?" She applied more pressure until she could tell Marconi's air supply was dwindling. "You think I would hesitate for even a second to cut your tongue out, cut your lips off, cut your heart out? You're nothing to me." Gretchen leaned close, until her teeth grazed Marconi's ear. A threat. "Nothing."

She pulled back. Marconi's pupils were blown, but her hands were still at her side. Not fighting it. Or, maybe, Marconi was still being a goddamn idiot and this was her version of a loyalty pledge.

"But you know what?" Gretchen asked, finally dropping her arm away from Marconi's throat. Marconi dragged in air, reflexive and inevitable, no matter how calm Marconi thought herself. "You're not worth it."

With that, Gretchen rounded the hood, climbed in the driver's seat, where Marconi had left the keys in the ignition, and drove off without once looking in the rearview mirror.

CHAPTER THIRTY-ONE

TABBY

1993

The shadows started closing in on Tabby when she left her house these days.

Every man whose silhouette caught in her peripheral vision became Cal, dark and looming, thick hands ready to wrap around her neck.

Paranoid again. This time for valid reasons.

Levi didn't notice, didn't care, didn't even blink when she checked that each door and window was locked for the fifth or sixth time. He just lifted his glass and stared blankly at the *Jeopardy!* reruns that had become his solace.

Tabby's skin felt tight with fear from the second she woke up to when she forced her eyes closed at night, and she knew she had to do something.

She had never told Cal where she lived, but she swore sometimes she saw a sedan parked at the end of her street, watching and waiting.

Detective Shaughnessy had promised he'd look into this Cal Hart, but so far there'd been nothing from him but crickets.

It was when she was nearing her breaking point that she saw the help wanted ad in the Sunday paper. Tabby didn't believe in luck or fate or happenstance, but she didn't know what else it could be.

It had been six days since Cal Hart attacked her in that hotel room, six days since Detective Shaughnessy had all but told her he was no longer certain Anders White was Jenny's killer.

Yet, still, she couldn't forget the way Shaughnessy's attention had sharpened after she'd mentioned the man's name. There were things Shaughnessy knew that he wasn't telling her, things he suspected about the White family.

And here that name was again. In print. Not Anders, but Bardot White, his wife. Seeking a nanny—a live-in position at their ritzy town house in downtown Boston.

Maybe Tabby wasn't as savvy as the detectives working her sister's case; maybe she really was just a nobody floundering for answers. But it struck her as strange that the cops hadn't even talked to Rowan White, despite the fact that her name had been in Jenny's schedule more than any of the friends they *had* interviewed. They hadn't contacted Anders White, either, after he'd shown up at Jenny's funeral, despite the connection he would have had through his sister. Even with her little knowledge of investigative work, she now knew a detective should have been there and written down the names of the people who had been kicked out of the church that day.

Detective Shaughnessy had seemed to take the fact that Cal wasn't Anders as proof of Anders's innocence, but Tabby didn't think that was necessarily the case. Anders was a rich man—he could have easily hired Cal to do his dirty work for him. Could have paid him well to keep an eye on Tabby, to take her out if need be. This was Boston, after all. There was no shortage of professionals who would kill for the right amount of money.

From what Tabby could tell, the Whites had plenty of that.

Maybe if Tabby was hired as the nanny, either Anders or Rowan would panic and get sloppy and reveal something Tabby would never have been able to find otherwise.

Or maybe nothing would happen.

But why not try?

For Tabby, the deciding factor came down to Cal. In an almost paradoxical way, she figured that taking the position would help keep her safe from him. If he was operating on his own, she would be far more protected behind the thick walls of the White's town house than she would be in her own place. On the other hand, if Cal was a professional, Anders would likely call him off while she could so easily be connected to the family. A nanny disappearing from the household was a lot more damning than a dead girl who had just happened to go to the same high school as Rowan.

Tabby got an interview for two days after she'd seen the ad. After an internal debate that had lasted far too long, she dressed in her best khakis and cardigan combination to look meek and unassuming. *I'm not here to steal your husband* was what she was going for. The icing on the cake was the low bun at the nape of her neck, effectively hiding her best feature.

When she got to the town house, Tabby realized she needn't have bothered.

No one would steal Bardot White's husband from her.

She was beautiful, and not in an understated way many rich women who could afford nice salons and nicer clothes were. It was the kind of beauty that drew every eye on the street. Bardot wore a white blouse and white wide-legged trousers, her dark, chocolate-colored hair and tasteful makeup flawless, though Tabby could tell she would have looked better than most women even barefaced.

Her red-bottomed shoes clicked on the hardwood as she crossed the room to sit on the couch across from Tabby.

Once seated, she didn't bother with an introduction, simply picked up Tabby's résumé, which hewed a little closer to fiction than reality. Bardot pursed her perfectly painted red cupid-bow lips, tapping a pen against her thigh.

"Your name sounds familiar," Bardot said without looking up.

Tabby glanced around, as if someone would have the answer for her. No one did of course. It was just her and Bardot in the museum-like room. When lying, it was best to hew as closely to the truth as possible. That's what everyone always said. "My sister was murdered when I was a child. It made national news."

The pen paused, midtap. But Bardot still didn't take her eyes from the paper. "My condolences."

"It was a long time ago," Tabby said, shifting uncomfortably on the slick, silky fabric of the couch.

Bardot hummed a little neutral sound and continued to read. The grandfather clock ticked in the corner, so loud, so insistent, so unrelenting that it scratched at the inside of Tabby's skull.

Finally, Bardot tossed the résumé onto the coffee table, sat back, and fully looked at Tabby.

"It's only fair to warn you that we have a daughter with . . . special needs," Bardot said, and something in Tabby sparked with hope. That sounded like Bardot would be offering her the position.

"I'm well versed in—"

Bardot held up a hand. "Whatever you may be versed in, it's not this."

Not quite knowing what to say to that, Tabby kept quiet.

"My daughter Gretchen is . . ." Bardot's eyes dropped closed as she took a deep breath. "She's evil."

Tabby choked on her own spit. "Excuse me?"

"I realize that sounds callous of me," Bardot said. "But once you meet her, you'll understand."

"I'm sorry . . . I . . . ," Tabby managed, not able to do anything but stutter. She'd been prepared for this interview to go any way but this.

"The girl is too young for a formal diagnosis," Bardot continued. "But she will test you and she has no fear of consequences. How will you handle that?"

To say Tabby had exaggerated her experience with kids would be a generous take on what she'd put on her résumé. She barely had experience with other children when she'd been a child. But she was an excellent bullshitter.

"Boredom is the worst possible thing for any child," Tabby said carefully, studying Bardot's face for a reaction. "I would strive to make sure she's actively engaged at all times."

A corner of Bardot's mouth lifted, and her eyes ran down Tabby's body to her beat-up shoes and then back up. "That was actually the best and most perceptive answer I've ever received. I suppose you'll do until she runs you off."

Tabby nodded, not trusting herself to say anything because it sounded like she'd just managed to get herself a position in the White town house.

"You'll start Monday," Bardot said and then stood and walked away without any further instructions.

But it didn't matter. Tabby was in. She didn't know what she would find, but it had to be *something*. It had to be. She'd been investigating this for too long to come upon a dead end now.

She collected herself and then her things, unable to stop the grin.

When she looked up, she noticed a shadow near the door on the opposite side of the room from where Bardot had left.

On a hunch, Tabby inched closer until she was all but standing in the shadow that looked very much like that of an eight-year-old girl.

"Hello?"

"Oh," came a small voice, the door sliding just a bit farther open. The girl was pale and icy, her bangs cropped close to her hairline, her bob sleek and falling to her chin. Her little nose turned up at the end, and she had lips too plush for both her slender face and her age. "You're my new nanny."

"If you're Gretchen, then I suppose I am," Tabby said, mustering up a little smile. "Hello."

The girl blinked at her, and then her mouth curved in a grin far more predatory than anything Tabby had ever seen before. "We will have so much fun, you and I. Just you wait."

CHAPTER THIRTY-TWO

GRETCHEN

Now

Gretchen didn't stop, didn't think, until she was parked outside Shaughnessy's apartment.

At the best of times, her inner voice could be erratic, mercurial, and prone to graphic fantasies. Now it was silent, a thick blanket of rage quieting the chaos.

She came back to herself only when her hand began to ache from pounding on Shaughnessy's door.

It swung open and Gretchen didn't wait to be invited in, just pushed past Shaughnessy with enough force that he grunted at the impact of shoulder against shoulder.

"Tell me everything you know." Gretchen heard herself make the demand, but it came out like she was standing at the end of a long tunnel. The words faint to her, though she knew they'd been forceful.

"And if I don't?" Shaughnessy asked.

She was over playing this game. Maybe Shaughnessy wasn't guilty of anything more than keeping his secrets close to his chest, but he sure as hell was acting like he'd done something wrong.

Gretchen shook her head. "This isn't a threat or an ultimatum. You're going to tell me what you know."

Any fight lingering in Shaughnessy's posture seeped out, his shoulders rounding as he shuffled back with a nod toward the armchairs by the window.

When she crossed the room to sit, Shaughnessy nabbed two tumblers from his liquor cart and a decanter of something amber despite the fact that it wasn't even noon yet. The whiskey caught the light from the window as he poured and then handed her a glass.

Gretchen downed it in one swallow but didn't wait for him for a refill, taking matters into her own hands. On the second go-round, she took a sip, savored it on her tongue, anchored herself to the taste, the burn, the weight in her stomach instead of the way she wanted to open Shaughnessy's arteries just to watch the blood pump from his body.

"You lied," she finally said. Her voice no longer sounded distant in her own head, and she thanked the alcohol for that.

Shaughnessy kept his eyes on his own drink. "You'll have to be more specific. I've lied a lot."

The quiet admission made Gretchen want to hurl her glass at his face, watch it shatter his nose or, better yet, break into shards that sliced at the vulnerable tissue of his eyes. But she wanted the rest of the whiskey more than she wanted that. And he might have trouble answering should she actually go through with it.

That goddamn cost-benefit ratio again.

"You didn't want Marconi reopening my case," Gretchen said, because it felt like a place to start. "Why?"

"Believe it or not, I was trying to protect you, Gretch," Shaughnessy said, and then glanced up like he was ready to fend off a blow. "That investigation should stay buried."

"And just let everyone believe I killed my—" Gretchen tripped over the word "aunt." Rowan hadn't been her aunt. But that's what people had thought. Had Shaughnessy known otherwise?

Something about the way Shaughnessy watched her now made her think that he had.

He shook his head. "You have a successful career. You have a life that's better than one I ever thought you'd have. Why do you want to go digging?"

And with that question, any doubt that he was somehow more involved in Rowan's death than he was letting on quieted. Because she did in fact know Shaughnessy. He was a cop down to the marrow of his bones. She'd seen him before when new information came up about past cases. He wanted answers just as much as anyone, no matter how old or how cold an investigation was. Even if the case had been his, and he might get thrown under the bus in the process of reopening it, he didn't shy away from shining a spotlight on his errors.

The Shaughnessy she thought she knew wouldn't be trying to talk her out of digging around in her own case—unless he had something damning to hide. More damning than a simple mistake or a break in procedure.

Except . . . maybe that Shaughnessy was just a pretty creation Gretchen had foolishly believed to be authentic. For her, he'd always been a bastion of morality. She'd bought into the idea because Shaughnessy bought into the idea. He was a good man, and everyone knew that he was a good man.

But Gretchen had never believed in *good* people or *bad* people, the simple binary options never quite allowing for all the nuance she observed in her world. She also knew that often those who were most immoral thought they were North Stars to be followed. They could justify any sin to themselves and still consider themselves *good*. Not only *good*, but above it all.

How many times had she caught Shaughnessy studying her, watching her, waiting for her to mess up so badly that he could be proven right?

And yet here they were, surrounded by his secrets, his lies, his cowardice.

Where were hers?

People labeled her a monster, but if a life was made up of actions and not thoughts, Gretchen came out ahead of the very people who would look down on her for being *bad*.

"You knew Rowan a long time before she was murdered," Gretchen said, pouring herself another three fingers and an extra splash for good measure.

"Yes, briefly," Shaughnessy acknowledged with a casual nod, as if he hadn't been hoarding that little tidbit to himself for three decades.

"You didn't think that was worth mentioning in the police report?" Gretchen asked. And before he could stutter out some worthless excuse, she continued, "And how about the fact that there was a nanny in the house that night?"

He eyed her, shadows crawling into the deep lines on his face. "You've been doing your homework."

"And you're avoiding my questions."

"I couldn't stop Tabitha from applying for that job," Shaughnessy said, glancing out the window. The second he said Tabitha's name, Gretchen knew this was no simple lie he was hiding, not some obscure connection. There was no way around it—he had covered up the fact that a cold case victim's sister was working at the scene of another murder. "Tabby . . . She was a good girl."

"Unlike me," Gretchen said, softly.

She's just a girl, she remembered him saying about thirteen-year-old Viola Kent, a proven psychopath.

So was I.

So. Was. I.

"I'm starting to think your definition of 'good' shouldn't exactly be trusted," Gretchen mused, finishing her drink. She wanted another, but knew she should be at least somewhat sober for this conversation. This *standoff*. She cradled the glass in her hand. "What exactly makes a girl good, Detective Shaughnessy?"

"Don't do that," Shaughnessy said. "Don't pretend we both don't know exactly what you are."

"A sociopath," Gretchen spit out. "You've reminded me of that every day since I was eight years old."

Shaughnessy met her eyes. "If that's the only good thing I've ever accomplished in my life, I'll die a happy man."

Gretchen flung the tumbler at his face. It was empty, after all.

He blocked it with his forearm, and it dropped to the carpet, a muffled thud.

They stared at each other, just like they'd stared at each other countless times in the past thirty years. He, waiting for her to strip off her mask to show the monster beneath; she, desperately clutching on to the persona to keep him fooled for just a second longer.

Though she'd spent the course of the investigation questioning his moral integrity, she found herself returning to the safety of their previous roles. He, superior; she, trying to prove herself.

"You hold me in such contempt," Gretchen realized. Maybe Marconi was right and Shaughnessy told off other cops for talking about Gretchen behind her back. But what did that matter when he was sitting here staring at her with that expression of mixed wariness and disgust? What did it matter when he said things like that? "Why would you let me work cases if you really believe I'm unstable enough to kill someone in cold blood?"

Because Marconi was right. That really did seem like the giveaway here, a tell almost, one she'd never realized he'd had. Which meant he knew she hadn't killed Rowan and yet let her think she had for her entire life.

The logical reason was that he was trying to distract her—and anyone else who looked too closely—from his own crimes.

"The cost-benefit ratio," he said, as if that was something he really believed in. That was her reasoning, not his. He had never been a cost-benefit guy, not in the thirty years she'd known him. "You know that better than anyone else."

"Did you kill Rowan?" Gretchen asked. She thought she sounded composed, thought the torrent inside her was properly dammed up behind the steel wall she'd been building her entire life.

"I don't understand . . ." Shaughnessy trailed off, glancing out the window once more.

"What?" Gretchen demanded, hating the word and using it anyway.

Shaughnessy shook his head. "I don't understand why you refuse to believe it."

"Refuse to believe what?" That precipice, that yawning void—it lay in wait again.

"Gretchen," Shaughnessy said, almost gentle. "There's never been any doubt. It's always been you who killed Rowan."

CHAPTER
THIRTY-THREE

SHAUGHNESSY

1988

Shaughnessy's resolve not to think of Anders White ever again lasted six months.

Then the knock on his door came.

Another White on his stoop. Anders this time, backlit by the blinding sun.

He was dressed as impeccably as he had been that first time in the White's mansion when Shaughnessy had still been so wet behind the ears, desperately trying to make trouble for himself.

Shaughnessy almost shut the door without acknowledging his visitor, but the obsession that had taken root five years earlier wasn't so easy to shake.

Stepping back, he then gestured Anders inside.

"Coffee?" Anders inquired, as if this were a social call and he the host. As if he didn't know Shaughnessy thought him a monster who tortured his sister and killed who knew how many other girls.

Shaughnessy grunted and led the way to the kitchen, going through the motions.

It had been years since Shaughnessy'd had any real contact with this family beyond monitoring their activities at a distance. If Anders had wanted to slap him with a restraining order, it would have been long before now.

"Can I tell you a story?" Anders asked in that refined accent that must soothe even his most volatile patients. He leaned against the sticky counters as if he couldn't care less about his three-thousand-dollar suit.

"As if I could stop you," Shaughnessy muttered, but it wasn't a real protest. He'd been waiting years for a confession from Anders.

"It's a case study that I think you might find interesting," Anders said, nodding when Shaughnessy held up half-and-half, and then took his doctored coffee. He set it down immediately, though. He wanted his hands free but had wanted to put Shaughnessy at ease at the same time, some distant part of Shaughnessy noted—the cop part, the one that analyzed threats constantly.

"The patient was suffering paranoid delusions," Anders said gently, like he was breaking bad news to Shaughnessy.

Shaughnessy's fingers trembled and he put his own cup down, crossing his arms over his chest to hide any reaction. "I don't know why you think I'd find that interesting."

"I know," Anders said, a tiny, sad smile lurking in the corners of his lips. "This patient lived in his own world where serial killers ran rampant. It's a common enough fantasy these days—you can't open a newspaper anymore without reading a profile on one of these monsters."

Shaughnessy flushed hot. Shame or rage or maybe a mixture of both.

"But it was all projection, you see," Anders continued.

Beads of sweat slid behind Shaughnessy's ears, down into the nape of his neck. He tried not to blink, not to take his eyes off Anders.

"The patient was in fact carrying out the very heinous acts he despised," Anders said, maddeningly gentle still. "He couldn't handle the truth of that, though. So, to protect himself, his mind shattered and he convinced himself someone else was committing those horrific crimes. He truly believed it was someone else doing it." Anders took a visible, steadying breath while Shaughnessy's own lungs clenched against a lack of oxygen. "In this case, he projected these crimes onto me."

Sparks popped at the edges of Shaughnessy's vision, as his body dragged in air almost without his permission. The remarkable, quiet certainty in Anders's voice kicked off a fight-or-flight response that had Shaughnessy locking his knees so that he wouldn't turn and run from all the implications held in the spaces between Anders's words.

Gripping his own arms until his fingers ached, Shaughnessy focused on the uneven rise and fall of his shoulders until he regained control of his own responses.

You're not crazy, he told himself silently.

But then in the dark corners of his mind, the chatter started.

Focused.

Psycho.

Creepy. Bedeviled. Fixated. Haunted.

Obsessed.

He truly believed it was someone else doing it . . .

"I know it's difficult to come to terms with, Patrick," Anders said. "You have to understand, I wasn't certain before. I wasn't sure there were actual victims. But now . . . You've left me no choice."

"I don't know what the hell you're talking about," Shaughnessy said. *Yelled,* he thought. The waves of his voice ricocheted off the tight walls of his kitchen. He hadn't meant to yell.

Anders tsk-tsked, still calm, still composed. "I'll have to go to the cops next, Patrick. If you can't admit to what you're doing."

"I am the goddamn cops," Shaughnessy gritted out. Absently he noted the copper tang on his tongue that meant he'd bit through the soft lining of his cheek. "You can't play mind games with me, White. I haven't killed anyone. It's always been you."

"Just tell me, and we'll get this all figured out." Anders dipped his head, trying to meet Shaughnessy's eyes. "Where is she, Patrick?"

Gentle, so gentle. Yet it stung like a red-hot poker into a fresh wound. Shaughnessy shook his head.

Stepping closer, Anders reached his hands out, like he was confronting a skittish animal.

"Where is Rowan, Patrick?" Anders asked. "What did you do with her body?"

CHAPTER THIRTY-FOUR

GRETCHEN

Now

Gretchen sat in the Porsche parked outside Marconi's apartment long enough to watch the sun slip down below the horizon. She wasn't thinking so much as just being. Breathing in, breathing out.

Surviving.

She'd driven to Marconi's from Shaughnessy's place without really making the conscious decision to do so. It had been instinct.

Marconi wouldn't welcome her in, she knew that. Maybe Gretchen was bad at understanding why people would feel certain ways in situations, but she'd done this enough times, pissed off enough people to know, like a scientist would, the most likely outcome.

If the positions were reversed, Gretchen wondered if she would care about the words she'd spat at Marconi that had been perfectly designed to cut as deep as possible. Gretchen was good with knives, even if they were of the figurative variety.

There hadn't been enough time to catalog Marconi's expressions, to bask in the pain Gretchen had inflicted. But there was no chance it hadn't been there.

Marconi's leniency would have only extended to a certain point, and Gretchen had charged right on past that line, far enough past it that she wouldn't have even been able to see it in her rearview mirror.

The problem was that Marconi was too attached. If Gretchen had pulled that scene even three months ago, Marconi would have likely stared her down, expression blank, eyebrows raised, unimpressed with the tantrum.

But normal people forged bonds. And despite Gretchen's warnings, Marconi's delicate feelings had become involved.

Which meant if Gretchen wanted to keep Marconi in her life, she'd have to grovel.

That had been another realization as she'd pulled up to the curb. She *did* want Marconi in her life. It had been her only thought when Shaughnessy had looked at her with those pitying eyes and told her, *It's always been you.*

The words hadn't been like the ones Gretchen had flung at Marconi. They didn't hurt; they weren't serrated steel that cut into Gretchen's flesh. They just looked like it. Underneath that veneer they were the cheap metal that bent and dinged and flaked. Powerless.

Because she knew them now for the lies they were.

She hadn't truly thought Shaughnessy had killed Rowan before the little scene at his apartment. His behavior had been suspicious, and she assumed he'd been hiding *something*. But it was the continued insistence of her guilt that had her thinking that *something* might be pretty damning for him.

There were too many things that didn't add up about the case for him to be so certain that she was the killer—unless he'd witnessed it himself. And in that case, why wouldn't he have stopped her from actually committing the murder?

No. Either he'd killed Rowan or he was covering for the person who had.

Tabitha Cross?

Fred still hadn't gotten back to her with a current address, and part of Gretchen wondered if that was because there wasn't one.

Had Tabitha been a casualty along with Detective Liam Boyd—anyone who could connect Rowan and Shaughnessy paying a fatal price?

Gretchen didn't know. But she did know Marconi had proven herself helpful, and Gretchen no longer trusted anything out of Shaughnessy's mouth.

That meant Gretchen had to eat crow no matter how rotten the taste would be in her mouth.

Gretchen hadn't brought anything with her to Marconi's, though she thought the protocol here might call for either expensive alcohol or some kind of apology food.

What Gretchen had to offer was nothing but herself.

We need people in our lives who don't expect us to be anything but what we are.

Marconi knew exactly who Gretchen was. Now all Gretchen had to figure out was if keeping Gretchen around had tipped over this morning into *not worth it* for Marconi.

For a moment, Gretchen let herself miss Lena Booker, the woman Marconi ostensibly replaced as a friend. But if Lena hadn't died, Gretchen wouldn't have met Marconi. Or maybe she would have, but it would have been under such altered circumstances that their relationship would likely be drastically different.

Gretchen couldn't rank the two women, and not because of emotion or sentimentality, but because the two brought different things to the table. And in the end, it didn't matter if Gretchen had a preference between the two. She wasn't sure she would take the chance to go back and save Lena, thus losing what she had with Marconi in the process, but the question of whether she would was moot. Time marched forward, whether feeble humans wanted it to or not.

As Gretchen climbed out of the car, she wondered how she would react to Marconi slamming the door in her face, or pulling her gun— even though Gretchen couldn't quite picture Marconi indulging in something so dramatic.

She stopped in front of Marconi's apartment. This was the time to walk away. In this line of work, attachments equaled vulnerability, and Gretchen had done everything in her power never to come off as weak.

And she could do it, too. She could walk away. Marconi was helpful, but she wasn't irreplaceable.

Still . . .

Gretchen knocked.

There had been a chance Marconi would just pretend to be gone. Gretchen had put that at about 20 percent, despite the fact that Marconi was no coward.

And she proved Gretchen right by opening the door.

Marconi didn't say anything, though, just leaned against the jamb, arms crossed, as she stared at Gretchen. The faint traces of purple and red could be seen at her throat. Something deep in the recess of Gretchen's brain told her to press on the bruise to see just how deep it would bloom.

No.

She was more than her impulses.

Gretchen inhaled, exhaled, tore her eyes away from the marks she'd left on Marconi's body.

"You don't have to forgive me—"

"Don't." Marconi held up a hand. "Apologies only count if you mean them."

"But I could say the words if you want me to."

"Maybe later," Marconi said. At a different time it might have shifted toward teasing. This was not that time. "What do you want?"

"I need your help," Gretchen said, forcing the truth out, the aftertaste sour and tacky on her tongue.

"Of course you do," Marconi agreed easily. "But give me one reason I should care about that."

"Because I think you want to know who killed Rowan more than you want to punish me," Gretchen said, taking a chance. This was Marconi. Her curiosity rivaled Gretchen's.

Marconi didn't budge, but that also meant she wasn't shutting the door in Gretchen's face.

"Finish this case with me," Gretchen proposed. "And then you can take me to the gun range and use me as practice if you want."

"Discharging my weapon involves a lot of paperwork. And quite frankly—" She paused, dragging her eyes up and down Gretchen. "You're not worth it."

"Touché." The more verbal slaps Marconi dished out, the more they'd be back on even ground. Gretchen could live with the sting of them. "I'm sure you'll think of creative ways to make me suffer."

A smirk tugged at Marconi's lips, the first real flicker of emotion. "I'm holding you to that."

"Does that mean you'll help me?" Gretchen pressed.

Marconi let the silence hang, and Gretchen could all but see the bricks that had been built back up, the walls that had dropped during the Kent case refortified.

"I'm not helping you," Marconi finally said, stepping away from the door. Before Gretchen could properly react to that, Marconi gestured her inside. "I'm doing it to solve Rowan's murder."

Whatever mental gymnastics Marconi had to perform for herself, Gretchen didn't care. She was back on the case. That's what mattered.

Gretchen would deal with Marconi's bruised feelings when she felt more capable of caring about anything other than this investigation.

Soothing empaths took energy she just couldn't often muster.

And yet, because of who she was, she couldn't help herself as she stepped into Marconi's apartment. "You said I got free passes."

Passes to misbehave, to lash out. Marconi had said that back when she'd stormed into Gretchen's apartment and dragged her out of a perfectly nice spiral.

"Passes don't include assault," Marconi said, a hard edge there, clearly not in the mood to fall back into their easy banter.

"You didn't stipulate that," Gretchen countered, because when had she ever been smart about these kinds of things?

Marconi eyed the closing door like she was considering pushing Gretchen out of it. But she sighed, some of the fight leaving her body. "If you ever lay a hand on me again, I'll press charges. Good luck keeping your consultant gig after that."

The threat was all the more potent for the quiet way it was issued. Marconi wasn't bluffing.

Gretchen's skin felt too raw against her bones. To counteract the *something* that veered too close to fear, Gretchen invaded Marconi's personal space, purring, "But what if you want me to touch you?"

Marconi didn't flinch, didn't blush, didn't stammer. Just stared, unimpressed.

There was that backbone Gretchen had enjoyed seeing when it came to interviewing the White family. It was less amusing when it was directed at Gretchen.

Her tongue felt clumsy in her mouth, and Gretchen swallowed, stepped back. A rare move for her. She knew, *she knew*, this required an apology, and she forced it out. "Sorry."

"I don't want your apologies," Marconi said. "They're not real. What I want is you to acknowledge that you heard me when I said that if you touch me again, I will press charges."

Gretchen chewed on the inside of her cheek, the crisscross of scars there both fresh and scarred over. She managed to get her head to jerk once as she looked away, taking in her surroundings.

"Fine," Marconi said. "Then we can work on the case." She paused. "This case and this case only. After that, we go our separate ways."

For once in her life, Gretchen decided to keep her mouth closed. What she wanted to say was that Marconi was angry and hurt and shouldn't be making decisions like that while she still had bruises on her neck. But if Gretchen mentioned that, she was pretty sure Marconi would send her away.

If it had been any other situation in which Gretchen was getting her first glimpse of Marconi's small apartment, she would have already been exploring shamelessly, touching the frames of the bright paintings on the walls, rearranging the knickknacks, rifling through and then reordering the bookshelf. Leaving her mark on the place just like she'd left her mark on Marconi.

But Marconi clearly wasn't in a forgiving mood, and Gretchen was walking her own tightrope, desperately hanging on to control by the thinnest, most overtaxed thread.

They didn't need anything to throw off this delicate balance they'd just established.

Marconi was watching her now, arms still crossed. But her expression had shifted toward thoughtful. "You found something."

Gretchen didn't know what to do with her hands, her body. But she decided to just drop into one of the overstuffed armchairs that made up Marconi's mismatched living room.

It was always you.

"Shaughnessy killed Rowan," Gretchen said, because she knew that would hook Marconi more than any bland equivocation might. And saying it felt right.

Marconi rocked back on her heels. *Surprised,* Gretchen's brain supplied as if nothing had changed, as if her catalog of Marconi's reactions was something she should even be allowed to access.

"You know that for sure?" Marconi said, tone neutral. But there was curiosity poorly hidden behind the facade.

"Yes," Gretchen said, only a partial lie that was drowned out by the flare of triumph that came with Marconi's interest. "And you're going to help me prove it."

CHAPTER THIRTY-FIVE

TABBY

1993

It took only an hour for Tabby to decide that Gretchen White was a strange child with a penchant for cruel barbs and a mind that feared boredom.

That didn't make her the monster Bardot White had painted her daughter to be, though.

And if Tabby was lucky and played this just right, she might be able to shift Gretchen into an ally.

Rowan White, on the other hand, terrified Tabby.

It was so subtle in those first days to the point that Tabby thought Rowan might just be the older version of Gretchen. Vicious but in a way that could be ignored.

There were little verbal jabs, especially between Bardot and Rowan. But Tabby had assumed that was just the inevitable clash of two grown women who didn't like each other trying to live together.

"Just pour yourself another drink, darling," Rowan had cooed one of the times Bardot had delivered a verbal slap about the fact that Rowan

didn't have a job. *"I know it can't quite numb the crushing self-doubts that come with all the ways you've failed to live up to our name, but you can always try."*

Tabby had attempted to pull Gretchen from the scene, but the girl had watched the exchange with the hungry eyes of someone who thrived on emotional violence.

This family, this goddamn family.

And Tabby wouldn't give a rat's ass about whatever feud Bardot and Rowan had going on, but Tabby soon realized it went beyond some kind of petty bickering.

There was a reason Bardot kept a gun in that study of hers.

It had started on the second week that Tabby was living at the town house. She'd been going over Gretchen's math homework—the child was truly bright even though she lacked social skills. When Tabby looked up, Rowan had been standing over them.

Just watching silently.

She hadn't said anything even after they'd noticed her. Simply stood there for a beat longer before turning and leaving the room.

"She likes you," Gretchen observed, blinking those big, icy-blue eyes up at Tabby.

For some reason that sounded more like a curse than a compliment.

"Why do you say that?" Tabby asked with a forced carelessness to her voice. Showing interest in something was a sure way to get Gretchen to latch on with those baby claws of hers. She wasn't quite old enough, wasn't quite experienced enough to make it hurt, but the sting would still be there.

"You'll see," Gretchen had said. Tabby let it drop. She hadn't wanted to rock the boat, and what did an eight-year-old know anyway?

The next night Tabby woke to her door opening. It had taken her that full week to actually sleep, the threat of Cal still sticking with her even behind the tight security at the White's town house.

Adrenaline pumped into her veins as a shadow moved closer to her bed.

Pale fingers, reaching.

Tabby scrambled back, her spine pressed to the wall, her arms wrapping around her knees to make herself as small as possible.

The hand dropped, the figure becoming the solid shape of a woman. Not Cal.

That realization didn't do anything to settle Tabby's pounding heart.

Rowan stilled by the side of Tabby's bed. "I wonder if you'll beg like she did."

And then she was gone.

Tabby pressed her fist to her mouth to stifle a sob, her body trembling so that she worried she'd fall apart right there.

She thought about saying something to Bardot. But from the way the woman eyed Rowan with a mixture of fear and disgust, Tabby guessed Bardot wasn't exactly ignorant of her sister-in-law's behavior.

Sometimes she wondered if that night had been a test from Rowan. To see if Tabby would push back. Because from then on, Rowan watched her. She touched Tabby when she could get away with it. Just a fingertip along a collarbone, a whisper of lips against the nape of her neck, so light it could be mistaken as a breeze.

Maybe Tabby should have slapped her away; maybe she should have just packed her bags and left.

But she couldn't shake the *I wonder if you'll beg like she did.*

It was a wisp of a theory. Perhaps Rowan was just poking at Tabby, psychologically speaking.

Maybe it was something else, though.

"She likes you," Gretchen said again one afternoon. This time, she elaborated. "She talks to you."

The girl said it almost absently, as she stared at the scissors next to the craft project they'd started that morning. The light caught on the metal, and Tabby swore she could see the answering glint in Gretchen's eyes.

"And she doesn't talk to you?" Tabby asked. Though now that Tabby thought about it, Gretchen was right. Rowan spoke to someone only if she was digging in her own fully grown and razor-sharp claws.

"Oh, she hates me," Gretchen said, without a trace of emotion. The girl picked up the scissors—ones that were far too professional for a child but all Tabby had been able to find—and then pressed her tongue to the very tip of one of the blades.

Tabby lunged across the small table. "Gretchen."

Gretchen watched her with a small, strange smile. "Did I scare you?"

It was little things like these, the moments when Gretchen devoured a reaction like it could sustain her, that offered the best insight into the girl's troubled mind. Gretchen hadn't licked the business side of the shears because she wanted to taste her own blood. Instead it was because she had wanted to see what Tabby would do.

"Yes," Tabby said, deciding it was safe to admit.

"Rowan did talk to me about you," Gretchen said, her little mouth slightly open, panting, high on the buzz of a reaction. Like a junkie, whenever Gretchen got a taste, she craved more. It was why Tabby had learned to stay as calm as possible whenever provoked. Otherwise it made for a long afternoon.

Now, Tabby couldn't suppress the shiver beneath her skin, though she managed to keep her voice placid. "Did she?"

Gretchen nodded, eyes on Tabby's face. "Do you want to know what she said?"

Saying no wasn't the solution here. Gretchen would tell her anyway. And part of her couldn't resist—just as bad as the rest of them. "If you want to tell me."

"She says you look like her," Gretchen said, too young, too gleeful. Rowan would have pressed up against Tabby, her mouth close to her ear, and purred the words. But Gretchen was a monster in training, and she hadn't perfected her delivery yet.

"Well, she's wrong," Tabby said, flat and unaffected.

"Who did she mean?" Gretchen wanted to know, was desperate for it.

Tabby smiled, bland as anything. "My sister."

CHAPTER
THIRTY-SIX
GRETCHEN

Now

"What's Shaughnessy's motive?" Marconi asked, shoving noodles in her mouth in a wholly undignified manner.

They had ordered Chinese food about three hours into rehashing all the information they'd gathered about Rowan's murder.

Gretchen, who had long perfected her use of chopsticks, brought her lo mein up to her mouth without incident. "Like I said, Shaughnessy has never struck me as a psychopath."

"Which leaves rage," Marconi said. "And he clearly had a long history with Rowan where he could have built up a lot of anger."

"Especially if he put her on a pedestal," Gretchen said slowly. "Like you said with the stalker complex."

"He could have easily hired a teenager to get Fran to leave the security system off," Marconi continued. "What would that have cost? Twenty bucks?"

"It would have been so easy," Gretchen agreed. "To get in the house, kill Rowan, leave me there with the knife, and then drive a few blocks away. Wait for the call to come through so he could control the scene just in case he left any evidence. That way he could explain away the possible presence of his fingerprints or hairs. Worst case, he'd get a slap on the wrist for not wearing proper gloves."

"How did you end up in the room, then?" Marconi asked the question Gretchen had been wondering for a while. "Would you have gone with him?"

"No, never," Gretchen said without hesitation. She'd been a stubborn child.

"Would you have gone with Tabitha?"

Gretchen considered. "Possibly, but still probably not. You'll find this shocking, but I didn't like being told what to do."

Marconi's mouth twitched slightly. Not enough to be called anything near a smile, but it was something. "He could have carried you."

"True," Gretchen said with a dip of her head. "But then why lie about Tabitha's presence as a major witness?"

Instead of throwing out a possible theory, Marconi asked, "Do you remember her at all?"

"No. Maybe a plain girl?" Gretchen mused. "They rotated quite frequently."

"Because you're a sociopath," Marconi said, far more bluntly than she would have before. But if she thought Gretchen would flinch . . .

"Yes," Gretchen said. "You can imagine how many nannies I chased off."

Marconi didn't drive home the knife. She wasn't a sociopath, after all. "This has to go back to 1983, right?"

"Rowan White bloody and running out into the middle of the road," Gretchen said. "And then two weeks later Jennifer Cross being murdered."

"Flash forward a decade, and Jennifer's sister is at the scene of Rowan's murder," Marconi said. "And we think it was a rage-based homicide. I mean . . . if I saw those two facts completely alone, you know what I would think?"

"That Tabitha killed Rowan in revenge, because she thought she was killing Jennifer's murderer," Gretchen said, then wrinkled her nose. "That's quite a sentence."

"But Rowan looked like a victim in 1983," Marconi continued. "So, was that an act?"

Gretchen stripped away the empath blinders she usually wore, where she tried to view the world through a logic that was altered by emotions. Instead, she let herself think like herself.

If she had wanted to kill someone, there were a few good ways to get out of it. After living through and then making a living on the criminal justice system, Gretchen had come to the conclusion that would-be killers worried too much about body disposal, as if that were the biggest obstacle for getting away with murder.

You had to assume the body would be found, though. Or parts of it. Bodies were harder to destroy than even the most determined psychopath realized. What was more important was setting up someone to frame for the killing.

Of course, that depended on the circumstances. Viola Kent had made an absolutely perfect patsy because she had a history of killing animals and torturing her brothers. Even if she had proclaimed her innocence, no one would have believed her. To a lesser extent, Gretchen made a good one as well. The lack of notable violence in her past hurt the credibility of the story, but clearly not enough to make anyone doubt she was capable of homicide.

But if she didn't have a troubled child to blame—which, she had to admit, most people didn't—a good way to deflect attention was to make it look like you were the victim of the same perpetrator.

"The arms," Gretchen murmured.

"I've been thinking how strange they are," Marconi agreed. "But it establishes a connection between the two girls where none other would have existed. And that kind of cut is pretty low on the pain scale, relatively speaking."

"Rowan lets herself be found with the same injuries she would then give Jennifer," Gretchen said slowly, feeling it out. "Because she knew it would give her some cover when Jennifer's body was found."

"Gibbs said Shaughnessy got the bug," Marconi pointed out. "He didn't even come close to blaming Rowan for Jennifer's death. He went hunting for a villain of his own making."

"Except, one important fact. Rowan was in a psychiatric facility the day Jennifer disappeared," Gretchen pointed out.

Marconi tipped her head. "Okay, but maybe Tabby didn't realize that. Maybe she was playing private investigator and thought Rowan was the perfect suspect."

Gretchen nodded, feeling that out. "So she figured out a way into the household—"

"But see," Marconi interrupted. "That's what I don't understand."

"Why get Fran to leave the security system disarmed if you're already on the inside?" Gretchen easily followed the logic. "Maybe it really was a coincidence, and Fran just happened to be out that night."

"So if Tabitha is the true killer, why would Shaughnessy leave her out of the report?"

She was a good girl.

"He's still trying to convince me that I killed Rowan," Gretchen commented idly, finishing off her noodles.

"You're just telling me this now?" Marconi asked with a small glance at the clock hanging on the wall.

"How did your skin become so thin so quickly?" The thing Gretchen had liked most about Marconi was that her feathers usually went unruffled.

"Someone tried to choke me out," Marconi deadpanned. "Tends to make me irritable."

Gretchen sighed and eyed the door. But Marconi just waved a careless hand at her.

"Okay, what else did he say?" she asked.

"Nothing of note other than he's *still trying to convince me that I killed Rowan*," Gretchen said, with deliberate emphasis on the part that they could have been focused on if not for Marconi's newly sensitive feelings.

"Well . . . that accusation would actually make sense if Tabitha's the real killer instead of him," Marconi said. "What if Shaughnessy did just show up and see you holding a knife? And Tabitha had already fled the scene."

Gretchen shook her head. "He knew Tabitha was working there. No way would he not ask where she was that night if he just stumbled on the scene."

"Christ." Marconi ran a hand through her hair. "So there isn't any scenario where he doesn't seem at least a little guilty here. At least for leaving out a major witness from the official report."

"There could also be another player we're not seeing," Gretchen offered up.

"Well, especially if you don't think it was Tabitha who did the actual stabbing," Marconi pointed out. "You really certain it wasn't her?"

"I remember her screaming when she found me in the room, and I don't think she had any blood on her," Gretchen said. "She could have quickly changed, cleaned the crime scene, and then lured me in there. Screamed to throw anyone off her scent." Gretchen tried to make that timeline work. "It's possible, I guess, though it doesn't seem like the most plausible scenario."

Marconi pursed her lips. "We also can't forget that there were two lies."

"Tabitha Cross's presence at the scene," Gretchen said slowly. "And—"

"The missing page documenting the fact that Rowan had given birth before," Marconi cut in, almost like she was making sure Gretchen didn't have to say it herself.

Like maybe her instincts to side with Gretchen hadn't been suffocated by the obvious layer of rage Gretchen's attack had provoked.

"Why would Anders and Bardot pretend Rowan's child was theirs?" Gretchen asked. Marconi stilled at her phrasing, at the distance Gretchen was putting between the baby and herself. But Marconi didn't push to make Gretchen acknowledge just who that child had been. "Rowan wasn't a teenager and it wasn't the eighteenth century."

"Maybe she was a threat to herself," Marconi suggested. "And the baby."

"Or Rowan abandoned . . . it," Gretchen said.

"Her," Marconi corrected with a gentleness that grated on Gretchen's skin, already too raw from the past two days. But Gretchen didn't bite out something scathing and hurtful like she might have done even hours earlier. She didn't throw a heavy glass tumbler at Marconi's face like she had with Shaughnessy. It would be a waste of time, and in the end the energy it would cost to navigate herself back into Marconi's good graces was too daunting to contemplate.

Maybe this was what growth looked like for Gretchen. "Her."

Marconi smiled. It was just a hint of upturned lips, but the tiny sign that she might be thawing gave Gretchen incentive to grab hold of her self-destructive tendencies.

"Anders and Bardot thought it would just be easier to raise . . . her . . . as their own," Gretchen continued. "Thinking Rowan was long gone."

"And then she came back," Marconi said, but more like she was reminding herself of that fact. "You said it was about three months before she was murdered, right? She promised she was sober and taking her meds."

"Yes," Gretchen agreed. "But that's my parents' take on the situation."

"Her stays in facilities were well documented," Marconi pointed out. "So there's probably some truth to it."

Gretchen toyed with her phone for a minute, then pulled up a name, hit call.

"Spooky timing," Fred said in greeting. "I was just about to call you."

"What do you have?" Gretchen asked, immediately alert.

"I'm going to email you everything," Fred said. There was a pause, like she was debating something.

"Tell me," Gretchen bit out.

"There's something weird going on," Fred said. "I can't quite put my finger on it. But I'm sending you the files."

"The files?"

"Yeah, about ten of them," Fred said. "All unsolved murders."

Gretchen shook her head, furious, but made sure that anger didn't slip into her voice. Fred wasn't as quick to forgive Gretchen's temper as Marconi seemed to be. "I wanted to know what Rowan was doing in the years she left Boston."

"Yeah," Fred said again, drawing out the word. "And that's what you're getting."

CHAPTER THIRTY-SEVEN

SHAUGHNESSY

1988

"Where is Rowan, Patrick?" Anders asked. "What did you do with her body?"

Shaughnessy stared at him, trying to make the words make sense. Once they did, he shoved Anders away from him with still-shaking hands. "Fuck off. You can't get in my head."

Gaslighting. That's what Daniels had called this. And Anders was apparently gifted at it.

"I'm being serious, Patrick," Anders said, smoothing out the wrinkles Shaughnessy's sweaty palms had made on his shirt.

Shaughnessy heaved in another breath, trying to make his thoughts stand still. It was possible Anders was messing with him. But the bigger takeaway seemed to be that Anders wasn't currently in contact with Rowan. "You don't know where she is."

"You haven't told me yet, no," Anders said.

Focused.

Creepy.

What they needed was a new body.

But no. Shaughnessy had let Rowan walk out of his house only days after he'd had that very thought. Had let her disappear back into her life, despite the fact that he'd thought she was headed back into a villain's lair.

Anders's certain and calm voice from earlier echoed in his head.

The patient was in fact carrying out the very heinous acts he despised . . . He truly believed it was someone else doing it.

What if Shaughnessy hadn't let her walk out that day? What if his mind had snapped? What if he really couldn't tell reality from fantasy anymore?

Shaughnessy shook his head. No. *No.*

He was a cop. He wasn't a killer.

That thought made him glance up and for the first time really look at Anders.

There was one logical explanation for this act—Anders was trying to set Shaughnessy up for his own crime. He could easily see how Anders would do it: he'd go to the chief, spin the same spiel he just had for Shaughnessy.

The investigators would look at Shaughnessy's record, see that complaint from years earlier, the one most people had forgotten about once Shaughnessy had stopped publicly talking about Rowan and Jennifer Cross.

They would interview Zach Daniels and find out that Shaughnessy had been obsessed with the White family all this time, even though he'd made sure to hide it from everyone else.

They would talk to Donna, who would hesitantly lead them downstairs into the basement, where he still kept old information on Anders White.

If Anders had killed Rowan, Shaughnessy had delivered himself as the perfect patsy to take the fall. On a silver fucking platter.

But.

There was another possibility here, too. And maybe Anders was a good actor, but he genuinely seemed to believe what he was saying.

Which meant that if Rowan was missing, Anders thought Shaughnessy had played a role in that disappearance.

Shaughnessy flashed back to that day in the woods. The one where Anders had taunted him, had held a gun on him, had threatened his career.

Remembered that when Shaughnessy had said, *You'll pay for everything you've done*, the emotion on Anders's face had been so starkly different from what he'd expected.

"Why?" Shaughnessy asked, and Anders, for the first time, seemed to really look at Shaughnessy in return.

"Why . . . what?" Anders asked, cautious now.

Why do you think I killed Rowan?

But he didn't say that out loud, not sure of himself or any of his tentative, newly forming theories.

"I didn't kill her, Anders." As Shaughnessy said it, he realized how shaky, how desperate his previous denials had sounded. This one was grounded in absolute fact.

"Patrick . . . ," Anders tried again, but Shaughnessy was at his breaking point.

In two steps, he had Anders pressed back against the wall with the sheer force of his anger.

"Go to the chief." The command came out like snapped teeth. "I don't care."

Anders blinked at him, off-balance in a way Shaughnessy had never seen him before. His eyes traced over Shaughnessy's expression. "You were obsessed with her. It has to be you."

The fight went out of Shaughnessy. He couldn't even deny that. "If you really thought she was dead, you would have gone to the chief first."

"I thought I'd have a better chance with you myself," Anders said, a flush on his cheeks. This didn't look like a cool, calculating psychopath.

Maybe Shaughnessy really had been projecting this whole time, just like he had with Rowan. This was just a man, an intelligent, composed one, but a man nonetheless. One who got flustered, one who could be manipulated.

"I didn't kill her," Shaughnessy repeated, this time on a heavy sigh. "I'd suggest you think about how you came to that conclusion. I know I'm going to." He paused a beat. "Now get out of my goddamn house."

Anders took a half step, paused, shifted. Like his body was instinctively following Shaughnessy's orders, but he didn't want to. "I'm going to the chief."

"You should," Shaughnessy gritted out. "File a missing person's while you're at it. Which, by the way, is what you should have done twenty-four hours after you noticed Rowan went missing."

"She's unreliable," Anders said, though the arrogance that had carried him into Shaughnessy's kitchen was long gone.

"Yes, you've made that clear that's what you think of her," Shaughnessy said. "Now leave."

Shaughnessy was half expecting to physically escort Anders out of his house, but the man finally nodded once and then left. The front door clicked quietly closed.

He didn't let himself think, not really, until he was on the stairs that led down to his basement. Long ago, he'd boxed up his serial killer wall, torn down much of the "evidence" he'd collected. But he'd kept some of it.

Shaughnessy pulled the box off the lower storage shelf where he'd put it several years ago, knocked the lid off, and dug for the journal he'd kept of his own private thoughts on the White family.

When his knees began to ache, he sat down on the concrete, flipping open to the very first page.

His first conversation with Rowan.

They're going to lie.

The message she'd left on that scrap of paper.

There are more girls.

Find them.

Then he skimmed through the years to find the one from that night she'd shown up at his door.

Keep me safe.

That's what they say.

He laughed because there was nothing else to do with the pressure building in his chest.

"*Reality is a funny thing, isn't it?*" Daniels had asked years ago.

Shaughnessy hurled the book at the wall.

He'd been well and truly played.

And going by that confrontation in the kitchen, he guessed Anders had as well.

CHAPTER THIRTY-EIGHT

GRETCHEN

Now

Annabelle. Jessie. Kristen. Chloe. Beth. Margo. Kandice. Liz. Catherine. Laura.

All ten girls had gone missing between 1987 and 1993.

The bodies that had been found all had slit throats and cuts up and down their arms.

Gretchen stared down at their pictures. Marconi had dug around in her closet before finding a years-old printer that miraculously had enough ink left for the files Fred had sent over.

> Traced Rowan's path after leaving Boston. Then found them.

Fred's note had included approximate times Rowan had been in each place. Binghamton, New York. Harrisburg, Pennsylvania. A small town on the Chesapeake shore. She'd worked her way down the coast, ending up in Savannah, Georgia, in the winter of '92–'93. From there she'd trekked back up to Boston, rejoining the White household in late May of 1993. A little over three months before her death.

The email had signed off with **Could be coincidence?**

"That's a pretty active serial killer," Marconi said quietly, the first words she'd managed since she mentioned that she might have a working printer for them to use.

Gretchen just shook her head. The black ink on paper, the faces of the girls, all seemed too bright, too brittle, too fragile, while the rest of Marconi's apartment blurred in her peripheral vision. "What's going on?"

Her phone was in her hand the next minute, Fred's voice on the other end, before Gretchen had even really thought about dialing.

"I don't know," Fred said as she picked up, as if she'd heard Gretchen's question.

Fred continued without Gretchen needing to prompt her. "Binghamton isn't that big—there aren't that many murders outside a drunk college dude beating up another drunk college dude. The same few months Rowan worked there in a local restaurant, a high school student went missing."

Gretchen touched the file. "Annabelle Viera."

"It was big news," Fred said. "And still it wouldn't be enough to raise any red flags for me. But . . ."

"There were cuts on her arms when they found the body," Gretchen said, finishing the thought.

"Yup," Fred said. "Though you didn't hear that from me. That information wasn't exactly obtained legally."

"Like I care."

Fred laughed. "You'd probably pay me extra for it."

"You're not wrong," Gretchen admitted. "Jessie."

"Jessie Turnbull," Fred said, far more obediently than normal. "Harrisburg is similar to Binghamton. Petty crime, break-ins, things like that. They were normal. A murder? Again, not so much."

"Did they find her body?"

"Yeah, but only after Rowan had moved on," Fred said. "Her throat had been slit, and she had the same cuts as Annabelle."

"That can't be coincidence."

Fred exhaled. "No way. And the same goes with the other women. Although some were under eighteen, so 'girls' for them."

"Were they all found?" Gretchen asked.

"No, six were, four weren't," Fred said. "But the disappearances of the four who weren't aligned with the timing of Rowan's visits. I've reached out to some contacts in those places, sent them information about the other cases that might help them find the bodies. It might give the families closure, at least."

Objectively, Gretchen acknowledged that was a kind step to take. But it was one Gretchen would never have thought of herself. Even Fred knew how to consider other people sometimes.

"She killed them." It sounded stupid once she'd said it, hanging in the air, obvious and neon bright. There was something about voicing truth, though, that Gretchen valued. Rowan had killed them. Her . . . *mother* . . . had killed them. She guessed there was something to be said about apples and trees and not having very far to fall.

"I mean there were no leads in any of the cases," Fred cautioned. "And none of the jurisdictions talked to each other back then. But . . . the timing works."

"Is there any chance someone else was with her?" Marconi asked, and it was only then that Gretchen realized how close Marconi was, close enough to hear Fred through the phone.

"Possible, I guess," Fred said. "Everyone I talked to remembered a single woman, though. From what I could stitch together, she usually got work at a diner or bar, flirted with the local boys, made a bit of a fuss, and then left without warning."

"And it's not like they had abundant DNA testing back then," Marconi said.

"The bodies were also pretty clean, from what I could tell," Fred said. "Not immaculate like a pro, at least not the first ones, but nothing incriminating."

"No one thought women were serial killers back then," Gretchen realized. Rowan wouldn't have even been a suspect. Especially if she scouted for her victims in a public, well-trafficked place like wherever she worked. "Christ."

"Preconceived notions and confirmation bias," Fred said. "You know those better than anyone."

Gretchen bit on the inside of her cheek, couldn't think of anything to say, and so hung up.

"Rude," Marconi said, though it lacked any bite. She was already flipping through a few of the police reports. "These girls don't seem to have much in common other than the cuts. There's no clear victimology here."

"No," Gretchen said after she'd skimmed through the rest of the files. "They don't look alike. They come from all different classes. No job similarities, either. Only one sex worker, one runaway. Not nearly enough for a pattern there."

"Even if a cop back then had thought *serial killer*, they wouldn't have connected these girls, not based on some cuts on their arms," Marconi said, tapping a few of the girls' faces. Gently, of course, because it was Marconi. "Not with what they knew back then about these types of murders."

In the late eighties, the press would have been enraptured by the complicated signatures of the flashy male serial killers. Relatively speaking, Rowan's style flew under the radar.

But still, there were things about serial killers that almost always held true. They had rituals that were important to them, and they had their reasons to pick the victims they did. Which meant . . . "We can't see it."

"See what?"

"Whatever it is that connects the girls," Gretchen said. "But Rowan saw it."

Marconi exhaled, and it came out shaky. "It's weird, though. A female serial killer."

"They are certainly the rare breed of monster," Gretchen agreed. "Killing complete strangers is also an anomaly. Most of the time, they target people who were part of their lives. Lovers, parents, children."

"What about ones like Aileen Wuornos?" Marconi asked, and Gretchen nearly rolled her eyes. Aileen was the one every layman knew because of that movie with the beautiful actress who had been "courageous" enough to play an ugly character.

"Aileen's victims were her clients, ergo part of her life," Gretchen said. "But more importantly, she was a high-level psychopath, with a score of thirty-two out of forty on the scale used to measure such things."

"That seems high," Marconi said.

"Ted Bundy's score was thirty-nine," Gretchen said, and then paused for effect before adding, "And mine is thirteen. If that gives you a range."

Marconi's brows rose, but she only hummed a little, not commenting further.

"The bottom line is that there isn't any question why Aileen Wuornos ended up a murderer," Gretchen said with a shrug. "A psychopath with that high of a score may find ways to justify the killings to themselves. But the truth is they get off on murdering people. And so they do it."

"Then Rowan was probably a psychopath, right?" Marconi asked.

"A sadistic one, likely," Gretchen said, in agreement. A shadowy memory crept in, of sharp scissors and bare skin. *I wanted to kill her before I knew what killing was.* Had Rowan been using Gretchen as practice? Gretchen didn't have any scars, but that didn't mean Rowan hadn't made her bleed.

"Sadistic, like Viola Kent," Marconi said slowly. "But if that were the case, wouldn't she have tortured her victims more? I mean, not that a slit throat isn't bad enough, but—"

"No, you're right." Gretchen studied the few pictures they had of the bodies. Considering the frequency of the kills, Gretchen would have expected to see more brutality. It was a smart observation. "It's not something I've studied extensively, and I would need more information, I guess, but the lack of prolonged torture does somewhat fit with female serial killers."

"Aileen shot people in the face," Marconi said, and Gretchen was pleased how easily Marconi followed along. "Which, I suppose while pretty violent, isn't at the level of what you see with male serial killers."

"In many of the cases with female serial killers that I've seen, the women tend to use morphine or arsenic," Gretchen said. "It's almost like the killing itself takes priority rather than the abuse."

Marconi glanced at the papers spread out on the floor. "A slit throat feels like it would scratch a violent itch pretty well."

"It's how you kill an animal," Gretchen agreed, and Marconi, with all her empath tendencies, flinched at that. "But . . ."

Marconi nudged Gretchen's thigh with her foot. "I don't like when you trail off."

It was word for word what Gretchen had said to Marconi earlier in the case, and something about that settled a nervous tremor Gretchen had barely realized had been fluttering against her rib cage since Marconi had greeted her with that stone-cold expression. Marconi might be annoyed with her, but Gretchen hadn't completely scorched that bridge.

"The escalation is strange," Gretchen said, and then shook her head, angry that she had been so imprecise despite the fact that it was only the two of them there. "It isn't strange if you just look at these ten cases after she left Boston." She pointed to the dates the girls had disappeared.

"They start out four months apart and then drop from there, pretty steadily. Any gaps are likely just victims we haven't identified yet."

"So how is it strange?"

"Jennifer Cross's death was in 1983," Gretchen said, glancing up.

"Four years." Marconi rocked back a little bit. "That's a long time to go without killing if Jennifer was her first victim."

"It's too big of a gap to fit the rest of her pattern," Gretchen agreed. "Considering her escalation is textbook starting with Annabelle Viera, it would be odd that she'd killed in '83, took four years off, and then started up again when she left." Gretchen paused. "Unless there are a bunch of unsolved murders out in Boston between 1983 and '87."

"You heard Gibbs," Marconi pointed out. "Shaughnessy probably would have uncovered those. And all he found was Jennifer Cross."

"Right, so it makes more sense that Rowan either was triggered by something here in Boston—and that's why she left to find different hunting grounds—or left and was triggered by that and started killing," said Gretchen. "Either way, it tracks that Annabelle Viera is Rowan's first actual kill, not Jennifer."

"Haven't there been cases where serial killers go dormant?" Marconi asked.

"Yes. BTK is the most famous one," Gretchen said. "But he's a rare case, and even then it was because his real life forced him to stop. More notably, though, is that during that time period, he compiled files on more than fifty potential victims. Psychologically speaking, he was still on the hunt."

"Real life," Marconi repeated. "Like being forced into a psychiatric facility?"

Gretchen's eyes snapped to Marconi's, and she wanted to smack both of them for missing the obvious. She closed her eyes, exhaled slowly, enraged with herself. "Christ."

"What?" Marconi asked.

"Rowan was institutionalized when Jennifer was killed."

Marconi whistled out, low and long. "Well, shit. That's about the best alibi you could have."

"Yeah," Gretchen bit out, trying to rearrange all the details into something that actually made sense.

"They went to the same school, though," Marconi said quietly. "Jennifer was found a mile from your old house. They have the same cuts. They're connected."

Just like they were missing the piece of how Rowan's victims were linked, they were missing something big here. Gretchen couldn't see it, though. So she just shook her head.

"Hey," Marconi said, as if just realizing something. "If she was escalating . . . why did she stop when she got back to Boston?"

"Oh, I doubt she did." That seemed like the most obvious part of their mystery. There was certainly at least one body out there in the greater Boston area that hadn't been found. Likely, there would be marks on the humerus bones. "She got much better at covering it up, though."

"So if she hadn't been killed . . ."

"Who knows when she would have been caught," Gretchen said, finishing the thought. But her mind had already tripped ahead. Or behind. Decades back. To when Rowan had returned to Boston.

She stared at her phone and then thumbed to her contacts. Stared at the name to the point where she felt Marconi hook her chin over her shoulder to see who it was.

Then she stared longer.

Finally, she took a deep breath, hit call.

A deep voice answered. "Gretchen."

"Did you know? What she was?" Gretchen asked Anders. "Did you know she killed all those girls?"

A long silence followed. And then came a simple answer. "Yes."

CHAPTER THIRTY-NINE

TABBY

1993

Tabby called Shaughnessy drunk off a three-hundred-dollar bottle of wine she'd snuck from the White's cellar.

"What if it was Rowan who killed Jenny?" Tabby asked as soon as Shaughnessy picked up. Her forehead pressed into the dirty glass wall of the phone booth, the rain outside beating against the little box. Her wet hair clung to her neck, making her shiver despite the warmth of the summer night. "Not Anders."

Silence greeted her. And then a heavy sigh.

"Are you playing detective?"

The phrase latched into the soft tissue of her survival instinct.

Girls who play Nancy Drew get murdered.

"What?" she asked. The question came out blurred at the edges, and she blinked hard to try to bring the world into focus.

Another sigh. "Tabitha, you need to be careful with that family."

"No, what did you say before?" Tabby forced out.

A pause. Then: "Where are you?"

Tabby hung up the phone, backed away from it like she would a snake poised to attack.

A hand banged on the door.

She yelled, arms flying so that her elbow cracked into the phone box, hard and painful.

"You done?" a voice called.

"Shit," Tabby muttered to herself. She ran a shaking hand through her hair, trying to gather the sopping mess into a bun on top of her head. Then she pushed at the seam of the door. "There you go, asshole."

"Bitch."

That was Boston for you.

At least the man waiting hadn't been Shaughnessy. Or Cal.

Or were they the same person?

Tabby shook her head. No, that didn't make sense. They didn't sound similar. She knew what Shaughnessy looked like.

She scrubbed her hand over her face, swiping at the rain blurring her vision.

It was the wine, that was all. And the separate threats of Rowan and Cal. The wine and the paranoia. And the long week, and the long month, and the long year, and the long life of living with her sister's ghost.

The warning to stay out of the case and let the professionals solve the murder wasn't unusual. Especially coming from a cop.

God, she was tired of herself. And the world.

When she stepped into the town house's entryway, she left the lights off and winced as she dripped on the perfect marble floor while resetting the alarm.

"Where have you been?" a cold voice called from the study's doorway.

Tabby flinched, her hand coming up to cover her pounding heart.

This was getting ridiculous.

Bardot was nothing more than a silhouette, backlit as she was. But everything about her was unmistakable.

"Just making a call," Tabby muttered, hoping that would be it.

"Have I done anything to make you think you can't use our phone?" Bardot asked, all impeccable politeness.

Of course, she hadn't, which she knew well. But it wasn't as if Tabby was going to talk to Detective Shaughnessy on the White's house phone. "Just wanted to get out for a little while. With the girls being at ballet practice."

"In the rain," Bardot observed. But she didn't push it. "Come have a glass of wine."

In any other woman, the offer might be taken at face value. It made Tabby realize Bardot knew she'd snuck that three-hundred-dollar bottle earlier.

The world was already a little too blurry, but if Tabby declined, it would surely be read as an admission. After working with Gretchen, Tabby knew she had more negotiating power than a normal nanny, but it wasn't carte blanche.

Bardot handed over a wide-rimmed glass with deep ruby wine filling up far more than a polite pour.

This seemed to be the equivalent of a parent making a kid smoke an entire pack of cigarettes for the sole purpose of getting sick from it. But Tabby had enough experience with alcohol to hold her own. Her genes came from her father, after all.

Tabby savored the first sip with an exaggerated purse of her mouth. "Good."

"I should think," Bardot said, with a look that seemed caught between disdain and amusement. She took a seat in one of the pure-white chairs that flanked the fireplace. Tabby had always wondered at the point of white furniture. But in a weird way it showed just how much control Bardot could exert over her domain.

Gingerly, and trying desperately not to leave a giant wet spot, Tabby perched at the edge of the opposite chair.

"Tell me, how are you getting along?" Bardot asked, swirling her wine, playing with it almost, but not taking even a swallow.

"All right," Tabby answered, trying to keep this as short as possible.

Bardot eyed her. "Gretchen isn't giving you trouble?"

Of course Gretchen was giving Tabby trouble. That girl lived for trouble. "Not more than I can handle."

"Well, be sure to let me know if that changes." Bardot held up the wine bottle. "A top-off?"

Tabby looked at the glass that now was half-empty and wondered how that had happened. She thought about saying no. But now that she was inside, she had tipped back toward warm, cozy, emotionally numb drunk rather than the jumpy, terrified drunk of earlier.

She held out her glass, and Bardot smiled. In the flickering light from the fire, it looked vicious in anticipation of *something*.

"And Rowan?" Bardot asked, her voice soft and prodding. "Is she staying out of your way?"

Tabby's muscles tensed as she thought about what she'd slurred to Shaughnessy earlier. *What if it was Rowan?*

"Yes," Tabby answered, the easiest way she could. Rowan watched her and Gretchen too closely for it to be comfortable, but she hadn't tried anything. Yet.

Bardot still hadn't taken a drink. "You know, she went to school with your sister."

The paranoia knocked against her chest, but the warning was dull and dim, made weak from the wine. "Did she?"

"Funny coincidence, that," Bardot said easily. "Do you know, I got around to calling your references the other day."

The paranoia howled, became something more tangible and real. "Did you?"

"The curious thing was that none of them were real," Bardot said as if it were some kind of mix-up. But Tabby could tell even through alcohol-heavy eyes that Bardot knew exactly what was going on. "Perhaps you made a typo on your résumé?"

Tabby licked her lips, looked down at her empty glass. Betrayed, she set it down by her feet, tried to stand. "I can leave."

Bardot tilted her head. "Why would you do that? We're just getting started."

CHAPTER FORTY

GRETCHEN

Now

"You knew she was a killer," Gretchen said—accused—and Anders heaved a sigh.

"Yes, Gretchen," he said, tired and annoyed, like this was all just a big bother. "Eventually, at least."

Gretchen met Marconi's eyes, calculated the risks, and then decided to put Anders on speakerphone.

"You took me in."

A startled silence followed that, and then a quiet admission. "Yes."

"Why?"

"Edith made us," Anders said. "My lovely mother made it a part of her will. And then changed it before dying."

And that actually amused Gretchen. If only she could have known the reason for their extreme reactions at the will reading, it would have made it all the sweeter. "I knew I liked her for a reason."

"Yes, well," Anders said. "We got the traits from somewhere."

The tainted traits, the ones Gretchen had assumed had come from Edith's father. Or maybe they still had. "Why did she care?"

"Why do you think she did anything?" Anders shot back. "The family reputation. Rowan having a child out of wedlock on top of everything else? Unacceptable."

Abortion would have been out of the question. Not for the Whites, not in the eighties. "Why haven't you told me in the years since? That seems like prime ammunition."

"That would involve talking with you," Anders said with that casual cruelty of his. "A fate worse than death, let me assure you."

"Ouch. I think I'll go cry into my huge piles of money," Gretchen returned, and Marconi flicked her on the arm. Gretchen mouthed *What?* and Marconi gave her the serious eyes. "Right, back to Rowan. Did she hand me over right away? I thought she didn't leave Boston until I was two."

"She might not have left the city, but she didn't even hold you after you were born," Anders said, and she knew he was trying to be deliberately hurtful. "And then spent those two years getting drunk and high and killing people, possibly."

Genetics might load the gun, but environment pulled the trigger. That's what she'd always said. Maybe Anders wasn't a killer, but he certainly wasn't a kind man. And if Rowan had been as heinous as it seemed she was, Gretchen was starting to count herself lucky to have emerged on the low end of the sociopathic spectrum. "You didn't try to stop her?"

"I didn't know about her victims until later," Anders said, though he sounded bored rather than defensive. "Believe me or not, I don't care. But I only realized how bad she'd gotten when she returned to Boston in '93." He paused. "At one point, I believed that cop of yours killed her."

"That cop of mine?" Gretchen asked, but she knew whom he meant.

"Detective Shaughnessy," Anders said. "He was quite the eager beaver when it came to Rowan. He thought I was a serial killer. I thought he was a crazed stalker who'd killed her in the eighties. Turns out she just ran away, which I thankfully realized before filing a missing person's report. Think of the embarrassment that would have brought us."

Gretchen squeezed her eyes as a throbbing headache started at the base of her skull. "You didn't think any of this was relevant to Rowan's murder investigation?"

"Coincidences happen," Anders said, a shrug in his voice. Like this hadn't defined her entire life. "You were clearly the guilty party. Why dig up anything in the past? Plus it took care of the Rowan problem nicely."

If they'd been having the conversation in person, Gretchen was certain she would have pulled a sharp object on him already. Maybe her shears if she'd been carrying her big bag with her. "Who actually killed Rowan?"

"This is tiring, Gretchen," Anders said slowly. "It was you."

"I'm tired of being told by people obscuring basic facts that the answer is obvious," Gretchen said, making each word snap like a whip. "All of these connections and you still think it was me?"

When he didn't say anything, she pressed forward. "You're a psychiatrist. Tell me why you think I—who had never displayed anywhere close to that level of violence—escalated."

"You were always petulant," Anders said.

"Petulance does not a killer make," Gretchen countered. "You're better than this."

"You hated her," Anders said, his voice gaining strength. "She took attention from you. The timeline fits with her arrival being the trigger. Resentment built for three months, and you seized the opportunity when I was away on business."

"I was eight," Gretchen said, dry as anything. "I barely knew how to tie my shoes let alone 'seize an opportunity.'"

Another pause, longer. Gretchen advanced, sensing blood in the water. "Who killed Rowan?"

"You did." Fainter this time.

Marconi's eyes were locked on Gretchen's face.

"Who killed Rowan?" Gretchen asked again.

"You did." His conviction shivered. Steadied.

"Goddamn it." Gretchen nearly threw the phone across the room. But they were so close. "Who. Killed. Rowan?"

Silence. But she could still hear his breathing. "You're asking the wrong question."

Finally. Gretchen closed her eyes, her hand holding up the phone sagging just slightly. "What is the right one?"

When the answer came, it seemed so obvious Gretchen hated herself for missing it. "Who knew that you would be so easy to blame?"

And yet that still wasn't right. Because Anders wasn't an idiot. He was curious, a psychiatrist to his bones.

Gretchen didn't say it out loud but thought the right question really was, *Why did Anders find it so easy to blame her instead of looking for the real killer?*

Gretchen wanted to pull back, get a look from farther away. But the vines of this case tangled and wrapped themselves around her, pulling her deeper, pulling her into a place where she couldn't be objective if she tried.

She hung up without saying anything else and met Marconi's questioning gaze.

"It's time we talk to Tabitha."

CHAPTER
FORTY-ONE

SHAUGHNESSY

1993

It had been five years since that day Anders had tried to convince Shaughnessy that he was crazy, that he was a killer in denial. Five years since Shaughnessy had come to terms with the fact that Rowan had been playing with him like he'd been an amusing toy to manipulate.

He could only guess, but he thought Rowan might have been playing Anders, too. And Shaughnessy, with his obsessive nature, had helped prove right any story she'd woven about him to Anders.

Had she pointed out Shaughnessy's car whenever it drove by the Whites' place? Told Anders she was worried Shaughnessy had become fixated, dangerous? Told Anders she thought Shaughnessy might escalate to violence if she didn't placate him?

Shaughnessy had cried that afternoon five years ago when he'd read through his notes on the White family with clear eyes, each snippet of conversation revealing the way Rowan had molded his image of her. The way she'd never been too blatant about her fear, denying it when asked point-blank, but making it clear she *was* afraid. Shaughnessy had cried and then drank half a bottle of the cheap vodka Donna kept in the freezer and wondered hopelessly why his life had been so shaped by one encounter when he'd been no more than a kid.

And when he had been drunk enough, he'd been able to admit he couldn't even blame Rowan for it. He'd been complicit. He'd imagined himself a savior of the damsel in distress, painted himself as the hero, and then acted like the villain. She'd been able to play him only because those instincts existed in the first place.

He'd wanted more than anything else to be needed, to be a good cop, to be praised and lauded and acknowledged. Maybe she'd offered a chance at that, but he was the one who took it with both hands.

So Shaughnessy had cried, he'd gotten blackout drunk, and then once again he'd put everything back in that damning box and slid it onto the storage shelf so it could collect dust as it was always meant to.

Once again, he promised himself not to think about the White family.

Once again, he had believed that he'd hold true to that promise.

And he had. For five whole years.

But then Tabitha Cross had called. Terrified, nearly incoherent. Talking about her sister's murder, a man who was trying to hurt her, a quest for answers.

All he'd been able to think was *no. No* and *not again. Please, God, not again.* He was too weak of a person to be offered such a temptation.

Because he was who he was, Shaughnessy got Tabitha's address out of the old file and drove out to the neighborhood. He parked at the end of the street, knowing he'd be watching for any suspicious cars. For this "Cal Hart" who had apparently scared Tabitha so bad she'd reached out to Shaughnessy of all people.

But he wouldn't get involved further. Not this time.

No, he would make sure Tabitha was all right and that was it.

Shaughnessy heard his father's voice, the man who had always told him he'd be a good detective while everyone else had laughed at his dreams. *Be a good man. That's the most important thing. More important than being a good cop. You have to first be a good man.*

It sounded so simple. But life wasn't simple, murder wasn't simple, good and bad weren't simple.

He'd always told himself that he was a good man. That he had made mistakes, plenty of mistakes, but at the end of the day, he tried to help people, tried to make the world a better, safer place.

But was that what counted as a *good man*? He no longer knew, and he was starting to wonder if he even cared.

What good was having morals when all the girls died anyway?

What good did it do the world for Shaughnessy to be a *good man* when bad men ran wild?

Was it possible to fight evil while living on the high ground?

Or did you have to get down in the muck with them, breathe the air they breathed, live the lives they lived?

As Shaughnessy watched a light flip on in what was likely Tabitha's room, he thought he probably knew the answer.

The high ground was for people who didn't have ghosts haunting them every day.

After all these years, Shaughnessy was fine not always being a *good man*.

CHAPTER FORTY-TWO

GRETCHEN

Now

The woman who opened the door at the address Fred had finally been able to dig up looked exhausted by life. Tabitha Cross was only a decade or so older than Gretchen but could easily pass as someone in her sixties.

Still, seeing her now sparked distant, blurry memories, and Gretchen knew they had the right house.

"I've been waiting for you to come," Tabitha said when she caught sight of Gretchen.

"You remember me?" Gretchen asked, stepping into the darkened house. It was heading toward dusk, but none of the lights were on and the windows were small. By the state of Tabitha's appearance—sweatpants, stained shirt, mismatched socks—Gretchen had almost expected to find stacks of old newspapers, empty takeout containers, junk piled in corners. Instead, everything was neat, in its place.

Something felt strange about the atmosphere, though, like the house had been frozen in time and Tabitha existed separate from it.

Gretchen had seen similar things before when working on cases where a child had died.

"You're not easy to forget," Tabitha said, gesturing them to the sofa.

"You said you expected me?" Gretchen asked instead of any other questions she'd come with.

"I've been waiting nearly thirty years," Tabitha said with a little laugh.

There was no use tiptoeing around it then. "Why didn't you ever tell anyone you were there that night?"

Tabitha glanced at Marconi, who had yet to identify herself to the woman. Gretchen guessed that was on purpose. Usually it would have taken Marconi's badge to get them in the door, but Gretchen sensed it would be the thing to get them kicked out in this instance.

"She's not important," Gretchen cut in. "Just my personal assistant."

Marconi didn't even shift beside her, but Gretchen knew if she could, she'd be rolling her eyes.

Tabitha sighed, pushing her hair back into a ponytail, using the velvet scrunchie that had been around her wrist to secure it. "You know about Jennifer?"

"Yes," Gretchen confirmed. "Is that why you came to work for my family?"

Tabitha nodded, a tired dip of her head, and then she stood. She didn't motion for them to follow, but the command was implicit as she started down a hallway. They trailed behind her and stopped in front of a closed door. Tabitha hesitated, her palm flat against the wood. And then she stepped into the room.

Like Gretchen had guessed from the state of the rest of the house, the room still lived in the year that Jennifer had died. This wasn't a shrine or even a memorial; it was a place that existed outside the progression of decades. It was the bedroom of a seventeen-year-old girl.

"I was young," Tabitha said as if there hadn't just been five minutes of silence.

"You thought Anders White was responsible for Jennifer's death?" Gretchen prompted.

"I thought it was a possibility." And then, with a strange smile, continued. "As I said. I was very young."

"What made you change your mind?"

Some emotion flicked across her face and then was ruthlessly constrained into a neutral expression. "I realized I was grasping at straws and I needed to move on with my life."

Gretchen narrowed her eyes on Tabitha's face at that nonanswer. But whatever had slipped through was long gone.

"Can you tell us what happened the night Rowan White died?" Marconi cut in, her voice soothing and nonthreatening.

Resignation settled into Tabitha's body language, the slump of her shoulders, the twist of her lips. "I put Gretchen to bed around eight, which was her normal bedtime. Bardot took a glass of wine into the study to read, and Fran took care of herself.

"I was in my room until I decided to go downstairs for some water," Tabitha continued. "I didn't see anyone in the house. I thought both Fran and you"—that startling gaze once again focused on Gretchen— "were asleep. Rowan's door was open, though. When I saw the blood on the bed, I started screaming. Your mother came up, saw you in the room with the knife, ran back downstairs to call the police. They arrived about ten minutes later."

The recitation of the events sounded rehearsed, but Gretchen supposed the woman had lived those moments over and over in her nightmares. They were likely branded into her brain.

"In those ten minutes, what was happening?" Marconi asked.

Tabitha blinked at her blankly for a second, seeming confused by the question. "Um. Nothing? Gretchen just stood there, and I was too scared to go in the room."

"You thought she was going to hurt you?"

"I don't know," Tabitha whispered, her eyes shifting away from Gretchen as if she were embarrassed. Gretchen thought she should be for admitting she hadn't been able to handle a child.

"And you stood right at the door for those whole ten minutes?" Marconi pressed. "You were watching the scene the entire time?"

Tabitha started chewing on the skin on the side of her thumb. "Yeah, I guess. It was kind of a blur."

Marconi nodded and met Gretchen's eyes.

"Did you hear anything before you saw Rowan?" Gretchen took over.

Tabitha's cheeks flushed as she shook her head. "I was listening to my Walkman."

"Was there anything unusual that night?" Marconi stepped in. "Maybe before everyone went up to bed?"

She shook her head.

"Who questioned you? When the cops arrived?" Marconi continued.

"I don't remember their names."

And there was the first obvious lie. Shaughnessy hadn't hesitated to make clear that he'd known exactly who Tabitha Cross was before Rowan's murder.

Gretchen exchanged a glance with Marconi, who lifted one shoulder. It was up to Gretchen how to play this.

Chewing on the inside of her cheek, Gretchen ran the different scenarios through her mind. Decided to go with confrontational. "But you knew Detective Patrick Shaughnessy before that night."

Tabitha looked away. "Yeah, I guess you're right. I was in shock, though. I don't really remember . . ."

It didn't take a genius to figure out Tabitha wasn't being completely truthful here—or one to realize that the lying made her supremely uncomfortable. So Gretchen decided to apply a bit more pressure to see if she would break. What good was being a sociopath if you couldn't drop a bomb or two? "Did you and Shaughnessy plan Rowan's murder?"

"What?" Tabitha's wide-eyed surprise came on a punched-out exhale, her arms wrapping around herself in a classic defensive position.

"You heard me perfectly well," Gretchen said, shifting closer so that Tabitha would feel threatened, even if just a little.

Tabitha shook her head, staring at the carpet just beyond where Gretchen and Marconi stood. "That's crazy."

"I assure you, it's not," Gretchen drawled.

"We didn't do anything like . . . like plan her death." Tabitha's cheeks had gone pale, her eyes watery. Overwhelmed, Gretchen guessed. But not angry, not insulted, even though her words might have read that way. Her body language, her tone, didn't.

This wasn't what a falsely accused person usually looked like.

There were of course exceptions, but there was no point in looking for them when all signs pointed to guilt as the underlying emotion.

"Then what did you do, Tabitha?"

She shook her head. "What I had to."

CHAPTER
FORTY-THREE

TABBY

1993

Sometimes Tabby would bring Gretchen with her if she had to run errands in public. She hadn't forgotten the feeling of Cal's hands around her throat, that desperate, gasping fear that would likely haunt her until she died.

But Gretchen was her insurance. It was unlikely Cal would approach her while she had a small child in tow.

The downside, of course, was having Gretchen with her.

"Do you think butchers like killing the pigs?" Gretchen asked now, her face pressed up against the glass of the meat display, eyes hungry, devouring the special section featuring a fully preserved pig's head.

Used to these types of questions, Tabby simply said no and placed her order with the butcher, who watched Gretchen, his face pinched in concern.

Tabby sighed and wished the girl were old enough to at least pretend to be normal. Although Tabby wasn't convinced this was a stage, wasn't convinced Gretchen would ever be able to fit in. Gretchen had a long, hard life in front of her, one that would surely be lonely. Kids shied away from her; adults looked on with worry. It wasn't fear yet. But it was with the detachment of a human recognizing the violent *strangeness* of another and then distancing themselves from it. It might not be fair, but it was true.

Lost in that particular grim thought, Tabby didn't notice at first when Gretchen started pulling on the hem of her jacket. When Tabby lifted her brows in question, Gretchen beckoned her down to ear level.

"That man is following you," Gretchen whispered.

Tabby jolted back, her eyes darting around the store. She couldn't see anyone, certainly not Cal.

She leaned down. "Who?"

Gretchen smiled big and wide to show her incisors. "He's gone now." Pause. "Do you think he wants to kill you?"

Tabby closed her eyes, summoned the patience that was buried deep, deep beneath fear. "Yeah, hon. I do."

CHAPTER FORTY-FOUR

GRETCHEN

Now

The thing about people who have secrets—ones that could get them sent to jail—is that they know their rights better than the innocents out there.

Tabitha Cross made quick work of escorting Gretchen and Marconi to the door and directing them to her lawyer, who Gretchen would bet good money didn't actually exist. It made for an effective parting line, though, especially when accompanied by the slamming of a door.

"Was that enough of a confession to trick a judge into thinking it was something more?" Gretchen asked, almost but not quite joking. Marconi lived in the gray areas, but only when the rest of the world forced her to. She tried to color within the lines when possible.

"That wasn't anything, and you know it," Marconi said, sliding into the passenger seat of the Porsche.

Gretchen pressed her thumbs into her eyes.

She was missing something, something big, and she was almost sure she already knew what it was. But she was too involved, her fear and panic and anger slinking into every dark corner of the investigation, blanketing her detached reasoning and logic.

Maybe Gretchen had trouble understanding other people's emotions, but that didn't mean her own weren't there. Sometimes hard to access, sometimes hard to pinpoint, but they were as inescapable for her as any other person's.

Marconi didn't press her into talking, and Gretchen took the moment.

It was there, just out of reach.

Be objective.

There had been something off about Tabitha's answers. Or . . . not off, but the opposite, perhaps. Too polished.

"Did her recitation of the night sound familiar?" Gretchen asked, a wisp of an idea taking shape in her peripheral vision.

"Yeah," Marconi said, squinting out the windshield, and Gretchen knew she wasn't actually seeing anything. "Matched up with Bardot's pretty well."

"That's strange, I think," Gretchen said slowly, trying not to stare at the idea and frighten it away. "Considering how everyone likes to remind us how long ago it was."

"Nearly thirty years," Marconi said, her lips twitching. "Haven't heard that in a couple hours."

As much as it had annoyed Gretchen when Bardot had dodged the question with that excuse, she hadn't actually been wrong. Thirty years was a long time to remember details, even if the experience was seared into the memory through trauma. Even questioning witnesses a few days after a crime meant that you could end up with wildly varying accounts.

But Tabitha hadn't hesitated.

"Tabitha and Bardot rehearsed their versions of that night," Gretchen said. "And matched. What does that remind you of?"

They'd both run enough interrogations to know the answer.

"Accomplices," Marconi said. "Maybe Tabby really had left before Shaughnessy got there."

"She did just say she was interviewed, though," Gretchen said slowly, trying to poke around for the holes in the theory.

"Could have been a lie," Marconi pointed out. "And it would make sense as to why Shaughnessy's so insistent you did it. Bardot pretended Tabitha was out for the night, or something."

But Gretchen shook her head. "He knew she was working there. Even if Bardot made up some lie about her absence, Shaughnessy would have noted that in the report. I've read through old case files of his. He wasn't careless." She paused. The only way to account for both the polished recitation and the missing witness was if Bardot, Tabitha, and Shaughnessy were conspiring to hide something together. "What if . . ."

Gretchen trailed off, but Marconi had always proven she was on the same page.

"What if they're all in on it?" Marconi said, a grim slant to her mouth.

"But why?" Gretchen asked as she stared at the house. A curtain twitched.

Marconi just shook her head. "Any evidence of their plotting will be long gone."

"Right, except we don't need evidence, do we?" Gretchen said as she turned the key to start the Porsche. "We just need a confession."

CHAPTER
FORTY-FIVE
Shaughnessy

1993

Shaughnessy's latest partner had requested a transfer to Florida the past spring, so Shaughnessy had been assigned a young uniformed officer to help on cases until a permanent replacement could be found.

The kid—Nick something—was eager and bright-eyed, and Shaughnessy could all but see his tail wag whenever he was given a task.

This time, though, Nick's ever-present smile faltered. "You want me to do what?"

Shaughnessy reached inside himself for his patience. "Go to the archives and get me the evidence file for Jennifer Cross. It's a cold case from the eighties. I've already called ahead to warn them you're coming."

Nick's weight shifted and his hands tangled together. He wasn't going to get far in his career if he couldn't hide even basic reactions. Shaughnessy just waited him out.

"Okay," he finally mumbled, staring at the ground like he wished it would open up beneath him. Without another protest, he scampered off. Shaughnessy watched him go before crossing to the counter where the coffee maker sat.

"Scaring off another one already?" Boyd asked, as he added a generous helping to his own cup.

"That kid?" Shaughnessy had gotten better at taking the teasing, and it had almost petered off in recent years. But Boyd had always kept at it—and considering they'd settled into something close to friends, Shaughnessy found himself often dishing it out as much as he took it. "Scared of his own shadow."

Boyd chuckled lowly. "Hey, congrats on the promotion."

Shaughnessy ducked his head, embarrassed that he was so pleased about it. Working up to Major Crimes had taken far longer than it should have—to the point that he'd wondered about sabotage on his worst nights—but it had been worth it. "Thanks, now all I need is a case."

"You're not working on something?" Boyd asked, jerking toward the door Nick had exited through.

"Nah." Shaughnessy tried to play it as cool as possible. All he needed was new rumors to crop up about his old obsession. Memories around this place were long, and he had no desire to move into Major Crimes, dragging a shadow along behind him. "Just checking something out in a cold case."

Boyd glanced around, before lowering his voice. "Oh yeah? Not Anders White again, I hope."

And of course Boyd remembered that. *Christ.* Shaughnessy had thought that anyone who mattered had forgotten. He gulped at the too-hot coffee and grimaced. "Nah. Learned my lesson there."

"He'll screw up one day," Boyd said, consoling him with a friendly pat on his shoulder. "And on that day, you'll be there."

He nudged Shaughnessy, teasing, laughter lingering in his face, and pushed off from where he was leaning on the counter. As he did, he muttered, "Incoming."

"I'm sorry." Nick was back, his hands still clutching each other, knuckles white. "That file you wanted? The Jennifer Cross investigation. It isn't there."

"What?" Shaughnessy asked. Out of all the problems he'd expected, this hadn't been one of them.

Nick just shook his head, eyes big, mouth opening and shutting without anything coming out. When Shaughnessy cleared his throat, Nick flushed. "Archives said it wasn't there."

"All right, not your fault, kid." Shaughnessy clapped him on the shoulder like Boyd had just done to him and held back a sigh when Nick full-on ducked. Like he'd been expecting a hit.

"Everything okay?" Shaughnessy asked, studying him closer. This went beyond eagerness to please.

"No. Yes." He closed his eyes, took a visible breath. "Yes, everything is okay. Do you want me to do anything about the missing file?"

"Nah." Shaughnessy sighed. "I'll file a ticket. Thanks, kid."

Nick all but slipped on the tile floor in his scramble to get away from him.

Shaughnessy again watched him go, remembering all too well how odd behavior could stick to you like glue for years.

He wasn't about to tell Nick that he had long ago made his own copy of the Jennifer Cross file. After his little tantrum a couple of years back, he'd moved all that stuff out to a storage facility on the outskirts of Southie and he'd been trying to save himself the trip out there by requesting the official documents. But now he was glad he had the copy.

There were some benefits of being obsessed, he supposed. For him, there were always backups.

CHAPTER FORTY-SIX

GRETCHEN

Now

Marconi raised her brows as she realized they were headed to Shaughnessy's apartment. "Not Bardot?"

Gretchen shook her head as she pulled to the curb. "She won't break. Not yet."

"But he will?"

"But he will," Gretchen agreed, trying to project a confidence she didn't quite feel. "You have your gun?"

Marconi's jaw clenched as she hesitated for a beat longer than she would if it was anyone else they were confronting. "Yes."

CHAPTER FORTY-SEVEN

TABBY

1993

The town house was quiet with Anders gone.

Rowan had locked herself in her room hours earlier, refusing to join them for dinner.

Bardot had retired to her study without even a glance at Tabby.

Gretchen had gone to bed, and Tabby was currently watching Fran cross beneath a streetlamp below after she presumably snuck out to meet whatever boy had been the most recent to put stars in her eyes. For a second Tabby considered resetting the alarm—it took a different code to access it from the outside, one Bardot hadn't let the girls have for this very reason. But that seemed unnecessarily cruel.

Maybe Tabby hadn't had an adolescence of sneaking out to kiss boys, but that didn't mean she wanted to keep that particular milestone from everyone else.

Tabby stretched, rolling out her shoulders, which were always tense these days. She didn't even feel like she could leave the house anymore without assuming Cal was behind her. Waiting for the right moment to strike.

She considered sneaking down into the cellars to pilfer another bottle of wine, but the thought of her dad, passed out on the couch, stopped her.

Instead, she crept down the back staircase to the kitchen, not bothering to turn the overhead lights on as she took out a mug and filled it with water.

After sliding it in the microwave, Tabby leaned her weight against the counter, letting her eyes unfocus as she stared out the window into the darkened garden.

Something shifted beyond the glass.

Tabby took a startled step back, her pulse loud in her ears even as she made herself hold perfectly still.

Listen. Breathe.

Nothing.

The beep from the microwave sent her stumbling back once again, but this time she laughed at herself, not sure what else to do with the adrenaline snaking through her veins.

It would burn out soon, she now knew from experience. Once she realized there was no threat to be found, the crash would be worse than this giddy, sticky high.

A door clicked down the hall, but Tabby ignored it as she took her cup out, careful not to burn her fingertips.

Bardot had a weakness for nice teas, and Tabby grabbed the fancy box from its drawer, thumbing through the options like a card catalog.

One packet promised relaxation, and Tabby laughed. "Can't hurt," she muttered to herself, her voice rough.

She'd just dropped the bag into the water when the hand curled around her throat from behind.

Her mug shattered on the floor, the only noise in the darkened room.

Tabby could no longer scream.

CHAPTER FORTY-EIGHT

GRETCHEN

Now

Shaughnessy opened the door with a glass clutched to his side, hanging precariously by limp fingers.

"We know what happened," Gretchen said without a hint of guilt for bluffing.

He cracked a smile at that, and Gretchen realized how rigid his face had become in recent months. Since Gretchen had started spiraling.

Guilt would do that to a person.

"No you don't," he said, but he stepped back, leaving the door open. He crossed the room—swaying just enough to be noticeable—to sit on one of the chairs by his window. There was no trace that she'd been there only hours earlier.

What was there was a gun. Laid out on the table, temptation made visible.

Marconi had clocked it, too. Gretchen could tell by the way she'd shifted herself so she could lunge for the weapon if necessary.

For some reason Gretchen didn't think it would come to that.

"I know it wasn't me who killed Rowan."

Shaughnessy swallowed the remaining Scotch in his glass and then poured himself another from the bottle on the table. "You don't know anything."

Without hesitating, Gretchen crossed to sit down in the other chair. Marconi was struggling not to react, but Gretchen could see the calculation on her face. Get between Gretchen and the gun or between Shaughnessy and the gun? What was the best way to avoid bloodshed?

Gretchen ignored her, leaning forward, propping her elbow on her knee and her chin in her hand. "So tell me."

CHAPTER FORTY-NINE

SHAUGHNESSY

1993

Shaughnessy stared at his copy of Jennifer Cross's case and came to one startling conclusion that he hadn't been able to see a decade earlier.

It should have been solved.

Something disturbingly close to guilt ate at his stomach lining, burned its way up his esophagus as he realized—it hadn't been solved in part because of him.

There were protocols to follow. The detectives *had* failed at finding leads when Jennifer disappeared, and then had failed again after her body was found.

It had gone cold because of their incompetence. But it had stayed cold because of him.

Because he'd been making noise about how it could be connected to Anders White, and Fitzy had done everything in his power to make sure any waves from that had been effectively contained.

And Jennifer Cross had been collateral damage.

When technology had started to develop over the past five or so years, the department had assigned detectives to work these kinds of dead investigations. As a murder case that had gained national attention, Jennifer's should have been high on the list. But no one had wanted to touch it.

He pressed his palms into his eyes until he could see spots and regretted the better part of his adult life.

"What if it was Rowan who killed Jenny?" Tabitha had asked only weeks ago.

If this was Rowan's work, there had to be some sloppiness in here that would prove her guilt. She would have been seventeen at the time, and this would have likely been her first kill.

There had to be a mistake they were missing.

He glanced at the clock. It was late, heading into evening. But Donna had been staying over at her sister's more and more these days. He wouldn't be surprised if she didn't come home. Hell, he wouldn't be surprised if he found divorce papers waiting for him at the top of the stairs.

He grabbed the file once more.

Read Tabby's testimony. Read it again, and then one more time, trying to figure out what was bothering him about it.

She'd seen a man that her sister had talked to.

The description was in broad strokes, but it was there.

And yet . . .

The detectives had never had her talk to a sketch artist.

Maybe they'd thought her description would be too generic to be any help, especially since she'd been a child, but Shaughnessy remembered those days well. Suspect sketches had been in vogue—everyone had leaped at the chance to order one.

Shaughnessy scanned through the file once more now that he knew what he was looking for. His finger landed on one line, buried among other notes.

Request denied.

The air went thin around Shaughnessy as he stared at the words.

In one swift move he slammed the file down, all but ripping through the pages for the autopsy.

The cuts.

They had never made sense to him.

And now with one word he realized why.

Postmortem.

CHAPTER FIFTY

GRETCHEN

Now

"Why couldn't you have left it buried?" Shaughnessy slurred out, though Gretchen wondered if this, too, was an act.

"Why couldn't you have told the truth?" she countered.

"I did," Shaughnessy said, almost inaudible now, his chin dipping to his chest. Gretchen eyed the gun, curious if that would rouse him from this stupor. But when she looked back, his attention was locked on her face. "Sometimes you can only do what you think is best."

"Who made you the ethical center of the universe?" Gretchen asked, bitterness lacing her bloodstream so that she could almost taste the black-licorice tint of it.

Shaughnessy laughed, hollow and sad and old. "Absolutely no one."

CHAPTER FIFTY-ONE

TABBY

1993

Pounding.

In her head. In her chest. In the palms of her hands.

Tabby's fingernails dug into the flesh of the arm wrapped around her throat.

Blood.

But not enough. Just enough to get her attacker to curse and swipe and tighten his hold.

Light glinted off something in his hand.

A knife.

Darkness beckoned.

She had to fight it.

Had to . . .

Had to . . .

He grunted as he took the full weight of her, her body limp and pliant, as if the fight had been knocked out of it.

Every atom of every cell of every part of Tabby screamed at her to move, but she knew, she knew this was the best—the only—way.

Her attacker adjusted his grip to compensate for the dead weight. *Now.*

Tabby slammed the point of her elbow into his sternum and then brought her foot down hard on his instep. It didn't do much damage since she was barefoot, but between the two blows, the man's arm loosened even further still.

It was enough for her to tuck her chin down, protect her neck, and put her teeth into play.

She sank them into his flesh, hard, without hesitation or remorse.

A howl broke the unnatural quiet of the kitchen as the hand with the knife came up to tangle in her hair. Her head was yanked back hard, and Tabby had a weird sense of déjà vu. Another time, another place when those same fingers pulled at her hair while he groaned in pleasure.

Cal. Girls who play Nancy Drew get murdered.

There wasn't enough air in her lungs to scream, her attempt coming out brittle and broken.

Noise, she had to make noise. She wasn't alone in this house.

Cal had recovered from her feeble attempts at escape. The point of the knife dragged along Tabby's throat as cold as the voice in her ear. "Be a good girl for me and I won't make this hurt."

If she could have, she would have laughed at that. *Make it easier for me to kill you and I'll do it quickly.*

Tabby had spent most of her life chasing oblivion, chasing pain and then the numbness that followed, Jenny's death a shadow that had consumed any will to live a real life. But Tabby didn't want to die.

She didn't want to die.

It shouldn't have come as a revelation, but it did. She didn't want to live only to avenge her sister; she wanted to *live* because she wanted to live.

Cal tugged on her hair to get her attention back on him.

What was his plan? To kill her here? To try to get her to go quietly? Some part of her realized he'd waited until Anders was out of the house to make his move. Some part of her remembered Fran sneaking out, leaving the security system unarmed.

This hadn't been a spur-of-the-moment attack.

The only way she could disrupt it was to fight like hell.

Even as she had the thought, she reached up behind her, dragged her nails along his face, the thumb of her other hand searching out the soft give of his eye.

Her legs kicked out, not back, forcing him to once again take her entire weight while he was trying to fend off her arms.

So close . . . *Just get him two more steps.*

Pain registered dimly. Her forearm. Sliced by the blade. Intentional or not, it didn't matter. Her blood was slick and hot, making his grip on the knife falter.

One more step.

She yelled out, not because it hurt but because she guessed correctly it would make him wrap his arm around her throat once more. Taking the knife out of the danger zone. For now.

And there.

Tabby gathered every bit of strength she had left. She felt him tense against her back, readying for another assault.

But she wasn't going after him.

Instead, Tabby kicked once more, and the massive drying rack that was packed full of delicate crystal glasses, thin china cups, plates, and a heavy frying pan crashed to the floor.

Everything shattered.

Or enough shattered to make it sound like everything had shattered.

The noise rolled over them like a great tidal wave, breaking against the shore, roaring into the deafening quiet and filling it all up.

"Bitch," Cal hissed, and let her go completely. Her knees didn't even try to hold her up, and the next heartbeat she was on the floor, shards of glass making a home in her skin.

Then a cold voice. "Who are you and what are you doing in my home?"

Tabby was behind the island, so she couldn't see Bardot, but she could picture her, rigid and impressive and demanding.

Cal swung toward her, his hand dipping into his jacket to pull out a gun that Tabby was glad she hadn't known he had.

He pointed it at Bardot.

Tabby shoved a fist in her mouth to keep from sobbing out . . . what? A warning? It was too late for that. She'd brought this monster here.

She inched closer to Cal as slowly as she could while dragging her body over jagged pieces of broken porcelain.

"Goddamn it," Cal cursed, and glanced down at her. Tabby froze. "Look at what you're making me do."

His finger twitched on the trigger, as his eyes snapped back to Bardot. This time Tabby did cry out, ragged and desperate, as if she could stop him.

A shot.

Silence.

And then Cal's body crumpled to the floor beside her, his eyes open, his mouth caught wide in surprise, his head smacking against the tile like he'd been a puppet cut from strings.

Tabby pushed herself back, away from him, her palms slipping on the blood that had pulsed from her own body.

In the next heartbeat, Bardot was standing over Cal, her own discharged gun now resting on the island. She studied him as if he were mildly offensive garbage someone had inconsiderately left on her kitchen floor.

Bardot sighed, loudly, and then shifted her attention to Tabby. "This is him?"

Tabby pressed her back against the stove, pulling her legs up to her chest, curling in on herself as much as possible. Shivers coursed through her body, her teeth chattering with the violence of them.

She managed to nod, just one jerk of her head.

Bardot's mouth pursed as she took in Tabby's condition. Then she bent and, without hesitation, dug her hand into the pocket of Cal's jacket.

Whatever she pulled out had her grimacing, the first sign of true distress Tabby had seen.

"Collect yourself, dear," Bardot said, tossing the thing toward Tabby. It wasn't a wallet but a leather holder of some sort. "We're in for a long night."

Tabby's fingers trembled as she reached for it, her body seeming to know what this was before her brain could catch up to it.

The leather was warm from its position stashed against Cal's chest.

Tabby laid it against her thighs, brushing her thumb against the raised letters on the gold badge.

Cal Hart finally had a real name.

Detective Liam Boyd, Boston PD.

CHAPTER
FIFTY-TWO

SHAUGHNESSY

1993

It had been a cop who had killed Jennifer Cross.

Once he looked closely enough, Shaughnessy could see the invisible hand of someone derailing an investigation. There had been nothing overt, nothing Shaughnessy could point to and say, *See.* Even the denial of a sketch artist had come from higher up.

But it wasn't just the file where Shaughnessy could see the manipulation now.

It was the reputation that had haunted Shaughnessy his whole career.

It was the nudge that had started it all—*What does that leave? The woods.*

It was the yawn, the overcasual *Ten bucks says that creep has her chained up in the basement.*

It was the fact that moonlighting as security was a popular way for cops to add a little cushion to their pitiful paychecks and the fact that one of those opportunities was the Phillips Academy's Fall Festival every year.

It was the fact that two weeks after Shaughnessy got it in his head that there was a serial killer murdering girls and cutting up their arms that Jennifer Cross had died in that exact same way.

It was the fact that the wounds had been done as an afterthought, and not torture.

Shaughnessy moved on autopilot then, heading back to the station. Everything at the edges of his vision was blurry and confusing; all he could see was what was directly in front of him.

He made it to his desk in time for his shift, sat, stared at the empty chair on the other side of the room.

There wasn't enough evidence to make it stick.

The scene had been clean. There hadn't been any witnesses.

Except . . .

Except there had been.

A tentative voice cut through to Shaughnessy, and he realized he'd been sitting there for hours, doing nothing as he tried to peel away years of deception, of manipulation, of a friendship that was nothing more than a cover to make sure Shaughnessy never got suspicious.

Shaughnessy glanced up to find Nick hovering nearby. Anxious and tentative as always.

Nick said something that Shaughnessy couldn't hear above the buzzing that had just started in his ears.

A memory of Nick just like that, clutching his own hands, eyes wide and dismayed.

Apologizing for not being able to find Jennifer Cross's file.

Boyd sipping his own coffee as he overheard. Overheard that Shaughnessy was once again interested in the case.

There had been no witnesses. Except . . .

Shaughnessy cursed, grabbed his jacket from the back of his chair, and took off at a run.

CHAPTER FIFTY-THREE

GRETCHEN

Now

"Boyd wasn't a serial killer, wasn't a psychopath," Shaughnessy said, his glass still dangling precariously from his fingertips. He stared out the window as he talked. "He was just . . . he was just a bad guy."

Gretchen glanced at Marconi, whose attention was still locked on the gun. As if Shaughnessy was in any state to participate in some kind of shoot-out. Or maybe Marconi was worried about a different kind of ending.

"Shaughnessy," Gretchen said, her tone sharp. His surprisingly clear gaze swung back to her. "Who killed Rowan?"

He laughed. The high, manic sound of it cut over her skin like a serrated blade.

"Gretchen," he said, putting his drink down next to the gun. Marconi tensed but didn't spring into action yet. Shaughnessy leaned forward, caught her hands between his, voice full of pity, enough that Gretchen distantly heard Marconi utter a soft *no*. "It was always you."

Gretchen's eyes slipped to the gun.

The darkest part of her whispered that she should grab it now while she could. Marconi liked her, sure, but not enough to let her walk free. Not if Shaughnessy could actually prove that Gretchen was guilty.

Could she shoot Marconi?

Yes.

She shook her head.

No.

She didn't know.

"Gretchen." It was Marconi, her voice low, soothing rather than demanding. "We'll figure it out."

Don't do anything stupid. That was the warning underneath.

Her fingers twitched and Shaughnessy laughed again, now mean and delighted at once. Like this was what he wanted. What he'd planned.

And she realized that he no longer held any power over her. So many times in her life the threat of Shaughnessy being proved right had been enough, had been a line in the sand she wouldn't let herself cross.

Now, all she could think was how satisfying it would be to show him that she was exactly who he thought she was.

"He's not worth it." Marconi shifted her body so that it cut Shaughnessy out. This was just her and Marconi, and Gretchen knew she'd used that phrase on purpose. The one Gretchen had spat at Marconi after eviscerating her with sharpened claws.

Gretchen swallowed hard, then, in one swift move, scooped up the gun. Shaughnessy smiled like he'd placed it there on purpose. Like she was a pet who had performed on a silent command.

"You're lying," she said.

"Gretchen." Marconi again, this time her own weapon pointed at Gretchen's head. Gretchen didn't spare her more than a glance.

"Shoot me after I get the information, please," Gretchen said as a droll aside.

"He's not lying."

It wasn't Marconi who said it.

All three of them looked toward the still-open door.

Tabitha Cross stood just inside the apartment. She didn't flinch at the sight of the guns, just met Gretchen's stare dead on and repeated, "He's not lying."

CHAPTER FIFTY-FOUR

TABBY

1993

The frenetic knocking on the door startled both Tabby and Bardot.

Tabby's body was caught in a strange limbo between wired and exhausted. The adrenaline lingered in her bloodstream, sticky sludge, but the pain, the fear, the guilt was all cutting through it, clearing it out, leaving nothing but an empty shell of a person behind.

But no. The empty shell was Cal—Detective Liam Boyd—still lying on the floor, a bullet in his chest.

"Stay here," Bardot ordered and then swept from the room.

Tabby eyed the back door, the urge to flee an unrelenting ache in her legs.

But then she heard the voice in the hallway.

A second later, Detective Patrick Shaughnessy pushed past Bardot into the kitchen. She hadn't seen him since that afternoon he'd stood in her living room and told her he'd catch the man responsible for Jenny's death. She recognized him easily anyway.

His eyes dropped to the floor, to Boyd, before snapping up to her, where she stood over the body, wrapped in her own arms, shaking still. "You killed him?"

She didn't say anything, not sure if answering would get Bardot in trouble. The woman had saved her life; she wasn't about to go pointing fingers.

"It was me," Bardot said, in that crisp, take-no-prisoners voice. She didn't sound even a little bit guilty about it. "It was self-defense. He broke into my home and attacked my nanny."

Shaughnessy nodded once, a curt gesture, but he didn't take his attention off Tabby. "This is the man you knew as Cal?"

Tabby managed to nod, trying not to look at the slack, pale face that had laughed with her, teased her, ruined her. Instead she managed to ask, "Did he kill Jenny?"

It was obvious, of course, that he must have. But she needed to hear it.

"I think so," Shaughnessy said, his lip curled back in disgust as he stared down at Boyd.

"He may have been the one to kill her," a voice said from the doorway. "But make no mistake, I was his muse."

Tabby flinched as Rowan moved into the kitchen, the woman taking in the scene with one sweeping glance.

She crossed the room to Boyd, kicking his pliant hand with her bare foot. "Thank you for taking care of this for me." She glanced at Bardot approvingly. "Very helpful of you, sister dearest."

Bardot eyed her, mouth pursed. "Don't pretend you know everything."

Rowan laughed like she surprised herself with the noise. "I know this is the man who killed Jennifer Cross. I know this is the man who tried to make it look like it was a serial killer who'd done it. The same serial killer who would have theoretically attacked me."

"Anders." Shaughnessy all but growled the name.

"Precisely," Rowan said, with a bright smile. She sobered a little, glaring down at Boyd's lifeless body. "That was quite an interesting day when my own signature showed up unexpectedly on a girl I went to school with."

In one quick move, Rowan crouched and grabbed the knife that Boyd had dropped—one that Tabby realized now seemed to be missing from the block on the island.

"Rowan, drop it," Shaughnessy finally spoke. But it was with all the authority of a rookie cop, not a seasoned detective, and it was easy to see why Rowan was writing him off as a nonthreat.

From the tense way Rowan had her body angled to keep Bardot in her sights, Tabby could tell Rowan thought it was the older woman who could do the most damage here. Tabby couldn't help but agree, the memory of her coolly assessing Boyd's dead body still fresh in Tabby's mind.

"I was curious about how this would all unfold," Rowan said. "But I can't have this"—she kicked Boyd again—"connected to me. That could get very messy, you see. And I don't like messy."

The last bit she said with a contemptuous look at the shattered glass and smeared blood on the floor.

Tabby, again, couldn't help herself. "Why would it get messy?"

Rowan glanced up, studying her closely, clearly trying to decide whether to tell her something. "If people start shining the spotlight into the dark corners of your sister's death? Well, they might find some more girls with similar injuries. Maybe he'd take the fall for all of them, but I can't take that risk. Especially if he's found in this house."

Tabby turned over the words, thought back to her suspicions about Rowan's potential for violence.

My own signature.

Were there other girls? Ones Rowan *had* actually killed? And if so, wouldn't Tabby have eventually stumbled on something that looked like evidence once she'd realized Rowan was a monster and not another potential victim of Cal Hart's?

"You set this up," she realized. "You knew I was figuring things out. Knew I'd eventually suspect you of killing Jenny. Knew Boyd was panicking, too."

"I have been keeping my eye on him since I came back," Rowan agreed pleasantly. "He made his own bed when he decided to cover his ass with those cuts on your sister's arms."

"The cuts?" Tabby asked. "What do they have to do with you?"

"Oh, you hadn't put that together, hmm?" Rowan shot Shaughnessy a chastising look. "You've been withholding information, Patrick."

"We picked Rowan up one night with the same injuries your sister had," Shaughnessy said, without taking his eyes off Rowan. "Boyd was in the car."

"Yes, and he carpe'd that diem when he wanted to get rid of his underage girlfriend," Rowan said, with a little tutting sound. "This time it was me who saw an opportunity and seized it."

"There's no record of me working here," Tabby realized, trying desperately to follow Rowan's logic as if just understanding it could help her avoid whatever fate Rowan had in store for her.

"And Mother pays you in cash," Rowan said with a little approving nod. "Your drunk father would think you ran away if you ever went missing."

"So either Cal—Boyd—would kill me, and stop panicking that he was about to be discovered," Tabby said.

"Or he got killed in the process," Rowan said with a shrug. "I knew you and Bardot were scheming about something. Those late nights in the library weren't as private as you thought."

We're just getting started.

"I'm calling this in, and taking you into custody," Shaughnessy interrupted. His hands were steady on the weapon, but the fact that he was letting Rowan talk at all seemed to demonstrate to them all just how little control he had.

Rowan glanced up at him, face curious. "On what charges exactly?"

"The other girls you killed," Shaughnessy said. "You just admitted it."

"I think you'll find if you replay that conversation that I admitted to no such thing," Rowan said, shooting him a little encouraging smile. "I just said there were more out there, not that I killed them."

"You said your signature." Tabby didn't even realize she'd said it out loud until everyone turned to her.

"I'm quite good at walking fine lines, if you haven't noticed," Rowan said, all arrogance. "My signature can simply refer to the way I cut my own arms."

"What are you doing, Rowan?" Bardot cut in. "Are you just going to kill us all? Two cops included?"

"You already took care of one for me, sister dearest," Rowan said. She pointed her knife at Tabby. "And you're going to finish it."

Her body went cold at that. "What do you mean?"

"You're going to get his body out of the house," Rowan said. "You won't tell anyone, because you'll be guilty of tampering with a crime scene the second you move him. Shaughnessy will cover for Boyd's disappearance, and then we'll all get on with our lives. All our problems neatly solved."

Rowan actually smiled at them at that, like she had just revealed a happy ending.

She was close enough to Tabby now that the knife felt like a threat, despite the way she held it as if it were an afterthought.

Shaughnessy seemed to pick up on her trajectory as well. "Rowan, drop the knife. I won't ask again."

Rowan finally gave Shaughnessy her full attention. "No, you won't."

Tabby recoiled when Rowan moved, thinking she was about to have another arm wrapped around her throat, another tip of a blade against her pulse point.

But Rowan maneuvered herself with a few nimble steps back to the doorway.

She'd been so close to having the power of a hostage, yet she hadn't even feinted toward Tabby.

Something heavy settled in Tabby's gut. The only reason Rowan wouldn't have taken advantage of her position close to Tabby was if the one she was currently in was stronger.

Because even Tabby knew this wasn't normal behavior for someone as clearly psychotic as Rowan. This wasn't the behavior of someone who had delusions of grandeur. This was the behavior of someone who held all the power in the room even if no one else realized it.

Bardot seemed to come to the same conclusion. "What have you done, Rowan?"

"Haven't you guessed?" Rowan asked, something like glee in her expression. "I've been planning this for ages, after all."

Bardot's eyes slipped to Shaughnessy, and she studied his face. Then she gasped, took a half step back, her hand reaching for the gun.

"Ah, ah, ah," Rowan warned. "I wouldn't do that, sister dearest."

"I'm not your sister," Bardot snapped out, but she had stilled. "Anders? Or me?"

Tabby didn't understand the question, but Rowan seemed to. She grinned. "You."

When Bardot simply paled, Rowan glanced at Tabby. "If Bardot says anything about my connection to any of this, the cops will get an anonymous tip about where to find Detective Boyd's body."

If Boyd was found in the woods somewhere instead of in the kitchen, Bardot would lose her argument of self-defense. And the wound would easily trace back to Bardot's gun.

But framing Bardot to make it look like she'd killed Boyd in cold blood would work only if Tabby and Shaughnessy weren't there to give their accounts of what happened. It would take one interview with the cops to land Rowan, not Bardot, in jail.

The heaviness in Tabby's gut turned to lead. Rowan had a plan to control all three of them. One Tabby couldn't see yet, but one Rowan was confident about.

Rowan turned her attention back to Bardot. "Detective Liam Boyd confronted you about killing Jennifer Cross all those years ago and you snapped."

"No," Tabby whispered. Rowan wanted to frame Bardot for both deaths, not just Boyd's.

There was something here Tabby was missing. Something that not only gave Rowan the confidence to say all this, but for Bardot to actually pale at the words.

"Bardot was at the Fall Festival, you know. I can prove it with pictures," Rowan said, as an aside to Tabby. "She and Anders. Anders met Jenny there, started having an affair, and Bardot found out. Killed her rival and has gotten away with it all this time. Until Detective Liam Boyd started investigating the cold case once more and made the connection. I've heard the official file has gone missing. Wouldn't it be lovely to have it returned with just the right evidence to paint that picture?"

Tabby swallowed back a sob. The file was missing because of her. Boyd was here because of her. If she hadn't come into this house under false pretenses, Rowan wouldn't have the upper hand right now.

"That might cover Bardot," Shaughnessy said, breaking the silence. His voice was stronger now, but there was still an edge of doubt beneath it. "But I'd never arrest Tabitha for tampering with a scene when I know she had a knife at her throat. You can't just get us to dance on your puppet strings, Rowan."

"Hmm, I think you *will* dance for me, darling," Rowan said, her smile mischievous.

Tabby watched Shaughnessy falter, watched fear and uncertainty flick across his face before it was snuffed out by a stoic mask. "I don't want to hurt you, Rowan. Drop the knife. I'm giving you to the count of three."

"I wouldn't do that, Detective Shaughnessy." This time the warning came not from Rowan but from Bardot.

Rowan shot her a triumphant smile, then shifted her attention to Tabby. "Go on, darling. You'll find a tarp in the basement you can wrap him in. You and Bardot can take the Benz. Drop the body in the woods near where dear Jenny was found." She paused, assessing Tabby's face. "Chin up. Just do this one thing and all your troubles will be over. The fact that your sister has been avenged is a nice cherry on the sundae, as well."

"No," Shaughnessy yelled, his hand dropping to his belt as if his radio would be hooked there. It wasn't.

"Do it," Bardot murmured to Tabby, and she was caught, not sure if her limbs would take direction from herself let alone any of them.

"You're an accomplice at this point," Shaughnessy warned Bardot.

Bardot laughed, bitter and hollow. "By the end of the night, you'll be, as well."

CHAPTER FIFTY-FIVE

GRETCHEN

Now

Marconi had shifted into full cop mode the minute she'd realized there was a civilian in the room.

Tabitha Cross hovered by the door, her arms wrapped around her waist, her eyes on the weapon Gretchen held.

"Gretchen, put the gun down," Marconi said, her voice taut now. Shaughnessy was no longer laughing, but he wasn't doing anything to ease the new hostility, either.

"Tell me how this plays out," Gretchen said to Marconi, because she knew Marconi would remember her hesitation, the reason Gretchen hadn't wanted to take the case.

"You think you did it." That's what Marconi had said in her apartment only days ago. Both of them hopeful that they could prove that statement wrong.

Gretchen wasn't going to go to jail. Not for this.

"No one has to know anything," Marconi tried.

"You know."

"I don't know jack shit," Marconi countered in a rush. "And considering these two have sat on whatever evidence they've had for thirty years, that probably means it's not exactly pure as driven snow."

The corner of Shaughnessy's mouth slid into a half smile that might have been acknowledgment.

"She's not wrong," Tabitha said quietly from behind Marconi's shoulder.

Gretchen ignored her. "Tell me how this plays out."

Marconi didn't say anything, and Gretchen cut her eyes to her.

"There's no statute of limitations on murder," Gretchen said with a little smile.

They both knew what Marconi would do if she heard something convincing enough. Shaky loyalty be damned, she'd have to take Gretchen in.

She actually had the morals Gretchen had always credited Shaughnessy with, and Gretchen wasn't even angry about it. What good were North Stars if they weren't true?

But she also refused to go to jail for something that happened when she was a child.

"So, what? What's *your* plan here?" Marconi tossed out. "You're going to kill three people in cold blood? Including both of us?" She gestured between her and Shaughnessy. Two BPD detectives. That wouldn't be easily covered up.

"Oh," Tabitha said, as if she was only now understanding what was happening.

Any humor dropped out of Shaughnessy's expression, his eyes locked on Tabitha. "No."

"Gretchen," Tabitha said with the weight of thirty years of secrets. "It wasn't your fault. It was ours."

CHAPTER FIFTY-SIX

SHAUGHNESSY

1993

Shaughnessy edged closer to Rowan, who was watching the scene with a smug, self-satisfied air.

She had a knife, and there were unknown elements in play. But if Tabby or Bardot actually made a move toward Boyd's body, Shaughnessy was going to have to take Rowan down.

His control of the situation was fraying, if he ever had any hold on it in the first place.

"This is what we're going to do," he directed, trying to project as much authority as possible. "Tabby, go to the phone, call in backup."

"No," Rowan said without missing a beat.

Shaughnessy ignored her. "Tabby, go."

Tabby hesitated, her eyes darting between Bardot and Rowan. Shaughnessy had to admit that if Bardot was siding with Rowan, it could get tricky. There was that gun of hers, along with the one Boyd still had in his hand—both of which were far more dangerous than the knife Rowan held. Even if she held it with the ease of someone who knew how to kill with it.

"Mrs. White, you're going to go over there." Shaughnessy jerked his head toward the far corner of the room where Bardot wouldn't be able to easily scoop up a weapon.

No one moved at his directions. Bardot and Rowan were digging in, clearly, but Tabby just looked frozen, staring at Boyd's gun.

Shaughnessy eyed the phone. If he edged toward it, he would lose his straight line of sight to Rowan. That might mean she could have her knife at Tabby's throat before he could get off a clean shot. He could rush her now, but he had a feeling Bardot would go for the gun if he did.

The calculations all came out favoring Rowan.

And each second he let her get a stronger grip on the situation put him more at a disadvantage. He had to do something *now*.

Tabby.

Right now she had to be his priority. He needed to get her out of range of Rowan—not only for her own good but so that she couldn't be used as a hostage.

"Tabby," he said as steadily as he could. She looked at him, face pale, lips pale, eyes big and glazed. Shock. That required straightforward, easy-to-follow instructions. It was why her body had leaned into motion when Rowan had tried to direct her. "Tabby, I want you to take three steps to your left. See the back door? Unlock it and go out to the garden, okay?"

She nodded and didn't move. Shaughnessy bit back a frustrated curse.

Bardot, looking as poised as she would be at a society ladies' luncheon, raised a brow when he turned to her.

"Yes, it was a cop, but you killed him in self-defense, Mrs. White," Shaughnessy tried. "Don't throw your life away for this."

Instead of answering, Bardot glared at Rowan. "Tell him."

"Oh, but I'm having so much fun watching him flail," Rowan said, pouting. "He's like a little puppy dog. Trying so hard for his treat."

Without conscious thought, Shaughnessy's finger twitched against the trigger. He stopped himself. Relaxed his grip enough so he wouldn't shoot Rowan in a careless rage.

"Tabby, go to the door," he tried again, and this time she nodded and took a step. Progress. But Boyd's splayed arm was in her way, and when her foot nearly nudged against his lifeless fingers, she swallowed hard like she had to stop bile rising in her throat.

His attention darted between Bardot and Rowan, and he made a choice. Bardot wasn't a psychopath. She was just making a calculation about the best outcome based on a shit scenario. He had to believe she wouldn't actually go for a weapon to take him out. Not if he was going to eliminate the threat to her.

He shifted closer, closer to Rowan, so he could knock the knife out of her grip, get her in the cuffs he had sticking out of his back pocket.

But the second he took his eyes off Bardot, she had the weapon in her hands.

He cursed. "Mrs. White, she doesn't have any power over you. We all heard her threats—she can't do anything to you."

She laughed again, that bitter, echoey sound that bounced off the walls of the kitchen. "Detective Shaughnessy, it's not me I'm worried about her having power over."

Rowan flashed her one more grin before turning back to the darkened hallway. To someone waiting there. "Come here, baby."

Shaughnessy tensed, knowing somehow that he was about to lose any control he had and unable to do anything to stop the barreling train.

A girl stepped out of the shadows. Young. Seven or eight.

She looked like a miniature version of the woman who was now pulling her close, wrapping an arm around her chest from behind to keep her in place. It would have looked affectionate, protective even, had Rowan not then pressed the flat of the knife blade to the girl's collarbone.

The girl's eyes were curious, big, but not scared at all as she took in the room in a glance.

Gretchen White, some distant part of his memory informed him. He'd had her picture taped to his wall, the one where he'd collected evidence against Anders.

Rowan rocked the knife just slightly to the side, enough to nick the girl's skin. Gretchen wrinkled her nose at the pain. There was something *off* about the girl, about the way she moved. Sluggish, almost. Uncoordinated. But Shaughnessy couldn't linger on that fact. Rowan's threat was easy to read. She'd slit Gretchen's throat before Shaughnessy's bullet could rip through her skull.

If she was going down, she was taking a child with her.

"Patrick," Rowan purred, and he felt the blow coming just from the unrestrained glee he heard in her voice. "I want you to meet your daughter."

CHAPTER FIFTY-SEVEN

GRETCHEN

Now

"Your daughter," Gretchen repeated, her own voice sounding like it was coming from the end of a long tunnel.

"Gretchen, give me the gun," Marconi said. Fast, urgent. Scared for the first time, really.

But Tabitha and Marconi no longer registered to Gretchen. All she could do was stare at Shaughnessy. Shaughnessy, whom she had once upon a time thought of as her equivalent of family.

She didn't know what to do about the fact that she'd been right about that.

"Is it true?" Gretchen managed to get out. "Or was she lying?"

He tilted his head like he hadn't considered that possibility. "It's true."

"How do you know?"

"You look like me," Shaughnessy replied, with a half smile that she wanted to immediately smack off his face. "You have Rowan's coloring. But the chin, the smile. It's me."

"Not good enough," Gretchen said. She wasn't charmed, and she wasn't endeared and she wasn't moved. She was furious to the point that, for the first time since she'd picked it up, she truly no longer trusted herself with a weapon.

Up until this point, holding the gun had been nothing more than a performance to get a full confession out of Shaughnessy, an interrogation tactic that Marconi had played along with beautifully.

Now it burned hot in her hand.

"I know," Shaughnessy said. "I got it confirmed years ago."

A DNA test, then. Which he did without telling her.

In the next breath, she was up, the gun pressed against Shaughnessy's forehead. He didn't flinch, just stared up at her, sad and amused and something else she couldn't quite place with the way her head pounded. Guilty maybe. For lying to her for thirty years. For making her think she was a monster. "Give me one reason I shouldn't put a bullet through your skull."

He huffed out a breath. "Because you want to hear the rest of the story."

CHAPTER FIFTY-EIGHT

SHAUGHNESSY

1993

The gun weighed too much for Shaughnessy's numb fingers. The barrel dipped until it pointed to the floor.

The rational part of him did the math. This was Rowan after all, and she'd proven in the past hour that she couldn't be trusted to have a conscience. He could easily imagine her using her young relative to manipulate Shaughnessy by telling him it was his daughter.

But they'd had one night together. The last night before she left his house all those years ago, when she'd told him *Keep me safe*. He'd tried to erase the memory at the time, guilt ridden and sick, considering her age, his relationship with Donna, the way he'd always looked at her like a victim and not a willing partner. But he'd also been too tempted to do anything but accept her offer when she'd turned left into his bedroom instead of right into the guest room.

He looked at the girl. "How old are you?"

"I just turned eight," she answered without a trace of shyness, without a trace of uncertainty despite the number of weapons in the room.

Eight years. It had been about nine since that night.

He stepped closer but froze when Rowan slid the knife along the girl's neck. Shaughnessy's breath caught in his chest. It would take one twist of Rowan's wrist and his daughter would be left bleeding out on the floor.

Shaughnessy wanted to kneel down, put himself on eye level with her. But he couldn't make himself that vulnerable. He asked, despite the fact that he already knew, "What's your name?"

"Gretchen," she said. Her eyes flicked to Bardot, who nodded once. And Shaughnessy remembered that she was being raised as Anders and Bardot's daughter. Not Rowan's. She looked back to him, her head tilted in a way he recognized from the mirror. "What's yours?"

He blinked fast, realizing his vision had gone blurry from tears. As gently as he could, he said, "I'm Patrick."

This could all be a lie still. But he saw what had Bardot gasping earlier in realization. The chin, the ears. Maybe he was just seeing what Rowan wanted him to see. He knew, though—he knew he couldn't bet on the chance she was lying.

And Rowan realized that. It was why she'd been able to walk in the room unarmed and start giving orders. It was why Bardot didn't trust Shaughnessy not to turn on her once he knew about Gretchen. It was why his gun was no longer pointing at Rowan's chest.

It was Bardot who broke the hush that had fallen over the room. "Tabby, get the tarp."

This time Shaughnessy didn't try to stop her.

Rowan smiled, pleased. "I'm tired of looking at this." She stepped out of the way of the hallway entrance, tugging Gretchen along with her. "Patrick, you come with us."

He eyed her new position and then glanced at Tabby and Bardot.

"Don't do anything rash," he warned them, and Bardot sent him a flat look. He was proving her right, and she wanted him to know it.

Shaughnessy nodded once, hoping to convey his thoughts with that tiny jerk of his head. They could get this cleared up still. Just . . . for now they needed to play along. Once they had backup, once Gretchen was safe, they could sort the mess out. He would testify that Bardot been coerced just as he had.

This wasn't unsalvageable.

Bardot snorted in disbelief and then shifted her attention to the mess on her kitchen floor.

"Lead the way," Rowan said, with a gesture to the hallway. Part of him realized that this was smart—it let her control the situation without trying to actively keep track of three adults with a roomful of weapons. By isolating him, she simply had to trust her threats were effective. And wasn't he proving her right with his compliance? "Up the stairs."

When he passed her, a rush of adrenaline had him calculating the distance between them. If he had the element of surprise on his side . . .

But Rowan clucked her tongue. "You want to chance it?"

He didn't. He couldn't. He wondered if he could get Gretchen to fight back, but she just stared at him with those big eyes that were a bit unfocused. He thought back to the kitchen, those sluggish, uncoordinated movements. Had Rowan drugged the girl into compliance? That would explain the strange, disturbing flatness of her reactions.

"Third bedroom on the right," Rowan called when he made it to the top of the stairs.

He nudged the door open with his foot, stepped inside, didn't bother turning on the lights. Darkness might help, might let him retake the upper hand in some way.

The moon was bright enough anyway, bright enough to spill over Rowan's pale skin, to catch on the steel blade of the knife.

And he was thrown back ten years, driving on a dark, woodsy road. Catching sight of a girl with eyes just as big for her face as Gretchen's were now. The hopeless way she'd mouthed *Run* that had stuck and then burrowed into his skin.

"Did you know Boyd that night?" Shaughnessy asked, and didn't feel the need to clarify.

Because Rowan knew what he was asking. "No. I called in the domestic report, though. To get cops out on the road."

Of course she had. Knowing the way her mind worked now, he shouldn't even be surprised. The uncomfortable presence of her hand directing the entirety of his adult life was clear now.

"Why?" he whispered.

"Like I need a reason?" Rowan asked, lifting one shoulder. But when he didn't say anything, she pursed her mouth. "I was tired of being sent to the facilities. Those quacks drugged me until I couldn't think. I don't like not being able to think."

"You thought to scare your family into doing your bidding?" Shaughnessy asked.

"Cops poking around?" Rowan said. "They would have to be on their best behavior, I thought. Of course, Edith one-upped me. I didn't think anyone would buy that as a suicide attempt. Apparently, it didn't look enough like torture."

"Oh, it did," Shaughnessy muttered, and she grinned, her incisors flashing.

"I was young," Rowan said, and Shaughnessy nearly laughed at how it echoed exactly what he'd said to Tabby weeks earlier. "I've had better plans since then."

"Like this one?" Shaughnessy taunted. There was no doubt that Rowan had been in command of the situation since she'd realized what was happening, but there was also no doubt that it was messy.

"I roll with the punches," Rowan said, but her hand spasmed around the grip of the knife, not unaffected. Shaughnessy fought the urge to shift—either forward to rip Gretchen from Rowan's arms or back so as not to antagonize her further. She shrugged then, as if none of this mattered. "You're the only unforeseen consequence here. But I always had a backup plan for you." She pulled Gretchen tighter as if Shaughnessy wouldn't be able to follow her logic.

And, God, Shaughnessy wished he could think clearly now. Wished he had the confidence, the arrogance, with which Rowan spoke. But he didn't know what the right next move would be. Should he provoke Rowan to get a reaction? Provoke Gretchen to get her to fight back?

If he picked wrong, the consequences would be fatal.

"You must have been livid when you heard about Jennifer's body," Shaughnessy tried, going for *something*.

Gretchen's eyes bounced between them, seemingly fascinated by the byplay. Again, he wondered at the lack of fear. She might not understand how much danger she was in, but most kids her age at least knew knives could cause pain. Even the trickle of blood at her collarbone didn't seem to be enough to faze her.

"Intrigued." She paused. "At first, at least. When I realized it was just some sleazy detective trying to cover up the murder of his underage girlfriend, I admit I wasn't exactly pleased."

"How soon did you figure out it was Boyd?"

"As if it was hard." Rowan tossed her head so that her pale hair swung in the moonlight. "It had to be one of you. Or Anders, I suppose, but he never had the balls to actually kill anyone. If he did, believe me he would have faked my suicide a long time ago."

Some distant part of Shaughnessy laughed at that. The man he'd spent nearly a decade thinking was a serial killer *didn't have the balls to actually kill anyone.*

"You were obsessed with me," Rowan continued. "So I thought maybe you took that out on poor Jenny. But once you started stalking Anders, I realized you'd come to the exact conclusion I'd wanted you to. Like a good boy."

Gretchen giggled at that, a strange, discordant sound in the quiet room that caused both Shaughnessy and Rowan to flinch. If only slightly.

"That's when I realized Boyd must have thanked every God he prayed to that my little stunt was so fresh in his mind when he was trying to cover up Jenny's death," Rowan said. "Between that and your serial killer obsession, it was like a gift from above. Can you even blame him really?"

"For killing a seventeen-year-old girl? Yes," Shaughnessy said.

"Carpe diem," Rowan murmured, with a slight smile. "But he set himself up to be played in return."

Shaughnessy shook his head, not following.

"Those cuts are distinctive," Rowan said. "I like backup plans."

Other girls. She said she hadn't admitted to anything, but this might as well be a confession. Shaughnessy just wished he'd been able to record this. "That's why it became your signature."

"It wouldn't have been my first choice. I just did it that first night because I wanted the theatrics of bloody wounds without the pain that went with deeper cuts," Rowan said with a shrug. "I like things a little more elegant than that. But I do so love covering my own ass."

And the penny truly dropped. Shaughnessy had found one of the 147 serial killers operating in the country. He'd just focused on the wrong White.

His thighs trembled, and he fought the urge to sink to the floor.

"So, what?" Shaughnessy managed to get out. "You were going to make him take the fall for all your kills?"

He spit the last word, disgusted with himself, with her.

Rowan lifted one shoulder in a careless dismissal. "Not all of them. But if someone started sniffing around too close, connecting me to one of my girls, well, they'd get a tip about a cold case up in Boston, an older cop boyfriend and wounds that matched a very distinctive pattern. It would confuse matters enough to let me disappear again."

My girls. The possessiveness, the pride, was so clear. "How many?"

"That's for me to know." She smiled at him, though, like she wanted to talk about it. And wasn't that the Achilles' heel of these monsters? If

Shaughnessy had learned nothing else from his obsession with them, it was that—they wanted to brag.

"That must have been hard," he said, like he was commiserating with her. "Being tied to a signature that wasn't really yours."

While Rowan's expression stayed neutral, her body tensed, betraying her sore spot. "That was just window dressing."

He frantically flipped through everything he knew about her, as if a handful of encounters could reveal a deep rupture in her psychology. But he came up with nothing. "What was important then?"

"That they all wanted to be free," Rowan whispered, and for a second it sounded like compassion. Then he remembered how easily she donned emotions that weren't hers. *Keep me safe.*

Beneath the false sincerity in her voice, he heard the sour glee, the rancid logic of a psychopath.

And he heard Edith's voice that night he'd met Rowan.

This isn't the first attempt at taking her own life.

"They were all suicide survivors," Shaughnessy breathed out. "Like you."

She smiled, clearly pleased he'd followed along. "I could see it in their eyes. The desperation."

"No," Shaughnessy managed. "You saw what you wanted to see. Because you're a monster."

"Their parents were the monsters," Rowan shot back. "Just like Edith. That controlling, manipulative bitch."

Shaughnessy let out a disbelieving laugh at that. "You want to talk manipulative?"

"Yes, I learned it from the best, Patrick," Rowan said, patiently. "You can't look at our family and actually think we came from something other than pure evil, can you?"

He shook his head, helpless, not sure what to say. He had not so long ago thought both Edith and Anders guilty of all sorts of crimes. Could he honestly say he didn't see the taint in the bloodstream?

His eyes flicked to Gretchen. That strange smile, the fearlessness that didn't match the circumstances. Had she been infected as well? By this taint, by this darkness.

"But see, I actually helped my girls," Rowan continued. "I set them free."

"No." Shaughnessy stared at the floor, his vision blurring with unshed tears. "You didn't help them. You killed them because you like killing things."

"Well, that, too," she said with a laugh tinged with mania. "Now, we're getting distracted. As I was saying before, the problem with the good detective downstairs was that he didn't have any confidence in his own plan." Her eyes were hungry as she watched whatever emotions were flickering across his face. "He's lived in fear of being discovered ever since. Tends to make a person do rash things."

She sighed, like this was all just a big inconvenience. "He's not the brightest bulb, is he?" She paused again. "Wasn't."

"Because he's dead now," Gretchen chimed in, her small voice devoid of any emotion beyond curiosity.

Rowan tugged lightly, almost affectionately, on Gretchen's hair as she addressed Shaughnessy's obvious confusion. "She's . . . defective. She can't help it, though. Look where she came from." With that she gestured to the town house as a whole. The White family as a whole.

"How does this end, Rowan?" Shaughnessy asked, without acknowledging that barb. Gretchen was a child. She could be fixed of whatever Rowan—whatever this family—had done to her. He just had to get her out of here first.

One step at a time.

"We're all just going to go back to our lives," Rowan said. "Boyd doesn't have any connection to us. And if someone starts digging too deep, you can redirect them."

"I'm a cop, Rowan," Shaughnessy said, a bit helplessly, his eyes once again dropping to Gretchen. "You know I can't just pretend this didn't happen."

"I think you'll find you can do a lot of things you never thought yourself capable of," Rowan said, in that same sickly sweet, patronizing tone she'd been using in the kitchen. "You wouldn't want little Gretchen here to pay for your stubbornness, would you?"

Gretchen's eyes narrowed at that—the first real reaction he'd seen. Anger, though. Not fear.

He turned it over in his mind. That had to be the play here, right? The only other option was if he could distract Rowan long enough to get off a shot, but his arm just didn't want to listen to him when he told it to lift the gun. All he could see was Gretchen's throat slit, the girl bleeding out on the floor.

"You would kill your own daughter?" he asked.

Gretchen's anger morphed back to confusion, and he cursed himself for the slip.

"You would kill Gretchen?" he hastily corrected.

And there it was again. That spark, that alertness cutting through whatever fog was keeping her docile.

"Darling, I would *enjoy* it," Rowan assured him, the tip of the knife resting in the hollow of Gretchen's throat. He knew it wasn't real, but he imagined he could see the flutter of his daughter's pulse there.

His tongue felt thick in his mouth. But he knew what to say now. Somehow, for the first time in his life, he knew exactly what to say. "How would you do it?"

Rowan licked her lower lip like she was aroused by the question. Probably she was.

"Gretchen here doesn't understand fear," Rowan said. "So it would have to hurt. A lot."

"Would you use that knife?" Shaughnessy asked, sick with himself, but unwilling to stop now.

"And fire," Rowan said, like she was imagining it now. For a split second, Shaughnessy wondered if this would distract her enough for him to lift his gun. But when his arm shifted, she immediately clenched the handle of the blade, her eyes dropping to the shadows where the weapon lay heavy against his thigh.

He needed her attention off him. "With a lighter? Or with hot metal?"

Even as he asked it, acid burned in his esophagus. He'd seen cows get branded before—the smell of hot flesh never left your nose after that.

"Now there's an idea," Rowan said. "I hadn't thought about that." Rowan dipped down slightly to check Gretchen's face. "What do you think, honey? You think that would be fun?"

But Gretchen was watching him. He nodded, once, decisively. Thinking she would slam her elbow into Rowan's stomach, slip like an eel from her grip maybe.

Instead, once given the go-ahead, Gretchen leaned forward, just a tiny bit. And then threw her head back with all the force she could get from her limited position. Her skull cracked against the side of Rowan's face, not enough to injure but enough to surprise. To shock. Gretchen used the moment to slip her arm up under Rowan's to protect her throat.

As Rowan clutched her cheekbone, Gretchen yanked the knife out of her hand and then whirled, in one swift move, sinking it into Rowan's belly. Then her chest.

No hesitation, just raw survival.

Rowan stumbled, falling back on her bed, and Gretchen followed, a bloodlust seeming to take over.

Shaughnessy stood stunned in the shadows, watching, frozen, helpless because of his own weakness.

Horrified, terrified, unable to get his limbs to move, his body to react. To fucking *do something*.

And then it was over, almost as quick as it had started. Rowan stared up at Gretchen, her mouth trying to form words as the life seeped from her body into the mattress.

Gretchen clutched the knife to her chest and swayed.

Shaughnessy finally moved. Just a step. Enough to get Gretchen's attention.

She turned. Stared into the corner where he stood, once again motionless, caught in that terrifyingly blank gaze. She blinked, a fast flutter of pale lashes, but didn't focus on him. Instead it was like he wasn't there at all.

"Gretchen," he managed to force out past lips he could no longer feel. His entire world had just been burned to the ground, the earth salted, every terrible decision in his life seared onto his soul now. Because they had led him here, to this moment, to this wisp of a girl, to this failure.

Shaughnessy could not lie to himself that he hadn't known where provoking Rowan would lead. He'd thought Gretchen would fight to get free, had even taken the calculated risk that one of the two would be injured in the process. But he would never have predicted an outcome this brutal.

"Gretchen," he tried again, though he knew she couldn't hear him.

Because that's when the screaming started.

CHAPTER
FIFTY-NINE
GRETCHEN

Now

Gretchen remembered the screaming. Remembered the sound of someone in the corner, a shadow that had sounded like a whisper.

She closed her eyes, remembering the blood, the knife, the question. *Gretchen, what have you done?*

She pressed the gun harder against Shaughnessy's forehead. Made him meet her steady gaze. He looked back, a challenge in his expression. *Do it. End it.*

No one else spoke. Marconi knew not to, and Gretchen wondered if Tabby could. She didn't seem to be the bravest woman, if Shaughnessy's account of the night could be trusted.

Gretchen let herself picture killing him. Pulling the trigger, the way the gun would jump in her hands, just enough to tell she'd done it. The bullet slamming through bone to sink into gray matter. It would come out the other side, staining the back of his precious wingback chair with blood, with brain, with *bits and pieces*.

She wanted to taste it on her tongue—his death, his body ripped to shreds, his burned soul long gone.

She wanted to be the one who took him from this world, who was his judge, his jury, his executioner. He had been found guilty, and he should pay for his crimes.

She let herself picture it.

And then she stepped back, twisted her wrist so that she was holding the gun out, butt first, to Marconi, who took it as quick as anything.

Tabby let out an audible exhale from behind Marconi's shoulder.

Shaughnessy was watching her, dismay clear in every line of his face.

"You wanted me to do it," Gretchen said. "You've been a coward every day of your life. And you wanted me to end it for you."

He blinked up at her. And she saw him for the first time. A lost, sad little boy who wanted the world to call him the hero he knew he could never be. His mask was thicker, better constructed than most she'd seen, but here he was, stripped bare, deprived of the ending that would have made some poetic tragedy out of a life that had been otherwise marred with mediocre decisions and consuming obsessions that let him ignore all the ways he would never be who he wanted to be.

"You convinced yourself I'm a monster," Gretchen continued. "Because that's the only way you can stomach the fact that you let me believe I'd killed her in cold blood. You convinced yourself I was dangerous, that I was crazy, that I could murder at the drop of a hat."

Her anger frothed and snapped its teeth, but she'd never felt more in control of it. "You convinced yourself that you could give me a gun and a reason and I would be as evil and as soulless as you've told me I am. I would be the monster that *you* created in the first place."

He flinched at that. But he didn't say anything. Because he never would.

"Here's the thing," Gretchen said, ruthless now. "I *am* the monster you told me every day that I am. I am the one you so lovingly created. That gun you put there was for me. Not you. Which means you knew exactly how you wanted this to end." She leaned down, gripped his chin. "Here's the fun part, though. The truly monstrous thing isn't killing you—it's letting you live."

She dug in, wanting blood. "Isn't that ironic? Maybe if you hadn't been so convincing, I would have done it."

He met her eyes, and she saw the acknowledgment there. That she was right.

Gretchen felt the skin give beneath her nails.

And then finally—*finally*—she let him go.

CHAPTER SIXTY

TABBY

1993

Everyone said the *not knowing* was the hardest part.

She'd been to enough grief counseling sessions with the relatives of missing or murdered loved ones to know that closure was key to surviving beyond the deaths.

Tabby had always thought if they'd just known who had killed Jenny, if they'd just seen him brought to justice, then life would finally move forward. Her father would stop drinking, she'd get her life together, they might even box up Jenny's room and turn it into a proper office.

If only he was caught, she'd apply to college.

If only he was caught, her father would find a new job.

If only he was caught, they wouldn't have to dodge creditors and scrounge for coins in the couch just to make the mortgage.

If only, if only . . .

It turned out *not knowing* wasn't the hardest part.

Tabby pressed her hands into the grass by her sister's grave. The slight dampness in the ground soaked into her jeans, but not enough to get her to move.

She'd been there for two hours already, and her legs had that unpleasant tingly feeling of being in one position for too long.

Tipping her face up to the sun, she wondered how normal people just seemed to live like it wasn't hard. How they woke up each day and went to jobs and took care of their kids and breathed and ate and dressed themselves without shattering into a million pieces.

All she wanted to do right now was sink into the cool, welcoming earth beside her sister. To tell her it was okay to rest now. And maybe hear that sentiment in return.

A shadow fell over her, and she blinked the bright spots out of her vision, her body tense, always ready to flee these days.

Bardot White stood just over her right shoulder—dressed all in beige, every hair in place.

"Well that didn't work out as planned."

Tabby snorted at the understatement. The memory of an alcohol-laden night pinned beneath this other woman's sober gaze was as indelible as the memory of Rowan's lifeless body.

Perhaps we can help each other, you and I.

"You got what you wanted," Tabby said, her attention drifting back to Jenny's grave. None of it mattered anymore. Boyd was dead. Rowan was dead. Shaughnessy was blaming an eight-year-old girl for everything.

She didn't know if she'd ever forget the sight of Gretchen clutching that bloody knife to her chest. After Tabby and Bardot had wrapped Boyd in a tarp, Tabby had snuck up the stairs, hoping to catch Rowan off guard. If they didn't remove the body from the murder scene, there was still hope for them.

But then she'd seen Gretchen there, a pale slip of a girl, whose eyes were hollow and unfocused.

Tabby had screamed, having been pushed to the very brink of her control and then over it. She'd screamed, and asked in a horrified voice words that she now wished she could retract. *Gretchen, what have you done?*

Instead, she should have said, *Thank you.*

Instead, she should have said, *Are you okay?*

Instead, she should have said, *I am so sorry I didn't protect you better.*

But then, in the next second, Bardot was on the landing beside her, eyeing the scene. She took immediate charge—and both Shaughnessy and Tabby had been in too much shock to even question her until it had been too late.

Tabby would go dispose of Boyd's body.

Bardot would call the death into 9-1-1.

Shaughnessy would wait for it to go out over the radio and then claim he was only minutes from the scene.

They would keep the story simple, Bardot said. She herself had been reading in the study; Tabby had stumbled upon the room and screamed. Gretchen, who multiple witnesses could attest was odd, was found holding the knife. Shaughnessy would make sure no charges actually stuck.

Now Tabby looked back at that moment, the one where both she and Shaughnessy had decided to follow along and wondered why in God's name she'd listened. Why she'd gone back down the stairs, dragged Boyd out to the garage, loaded him into the trunk of Bardot's Benz.

She'd nearly buckled under his weight, but she'd been moving in a fog, a haze, driven by a single-minded determination to let the earth consume him.

Before she could really think about it, she'd found herself out in those same woods where Boyd had dumped Jenny like she was a piece of trash.

Then she'd dug. She'd dug deep enough that a good rain wouldn't uncover his body. She'd dug deep enough that the worms and maggots and insects and tree roots would relish in the nutrients from his rotting corpse. She'd dug until she'd had blisters on her palms and the sun had well and truly crept above the trees.

Maybe they'd find him. Bodies had a way of turning up, she'd long ago realized. But maybe they never would. Maybe the memory of him would decay back into the nothingness from where he'd come.

By the time Tabby started to wonder why they hadn't just called the cops and explained the entirety of the night, she had already been in too deep. She'd moved the body, destroyed evidence, *buried a detective in the woods.* There was no way she wouldn't go to jail.

So why not just let Bardot wrap everything up in a neat little bow?

The woman had promised to keep her out of the police report, and so far had stuck to that vow. What did it matter to Tabby that the press was ripping apart an eight-year-old who might have ended up killing someone anyway? Wasn't it safer this way? For people to be wary around Gretchen, to know that tiny body held untold violence within it?

Why come forward now all these weeks later?

Not even the most enterprising tabloid reporter had uncovered Tabby's connection to the Whites, just as Rowan had hinted that night. For all anyone knew, Tabitha Cross was just a nobody, living out a sad, little life on the outskirts of Southie.

They didn't know about the dirt beneath her fingernails.

They didn't know about the twisted way her soul settled in her body these days.

"Don't pretend you didn't get what you wanted, as well," Bardot countered.

"Do you know, I got around to calling your references the other day."

The fear that had provoked the night Bardot had plied her with wine seemed so silly and small now.

"Did you?" she'd asked, the paranoia howling in her chest.

"The curious thing was that none of them were real," Bardot said as if it were some kind of mix-up. But Tabby could tell even through alcohol-heavy

eyes that Bardot knew exactly what was going on. "Perhaps you made a typo on your résumé?"

Tabby licked her lips, looked down at her empty glass. Betrayed, she set it by her feet, trying to stand. "I can leave."

Bardot tilted her head. "Why would you do that? We're just getting started."

"What do you want from me?" Tabby asked. If she was being booted out, she needed to know now before she lied herself deeper into a hole.

"Perhaps we can help each other, you and I," Bardot said. It didn't sound like she was about to call the cops. But Tabby didn't relax.

"How?"

"You're searching for your sister's killer?" Bardot asked, though it didn't much seem like she needed it confirmed. Tabby had been sloppy, she realized. Trying to play Nancy Drew. She hadn't even changed her name on the application.

"Yes."

Bardot nodded. "And your investigation brought you to us?"

Tabby chewed on her cheek. "I had thought Anders . . ."

"And then you met Rowan," Bardot said, with the knowledge of someone who had to live closely with the psychopath.

"And then I met Rowan," Tabby agreed.

"There's a problem with that logic, though," Bardot mused. "In that Rowan was institutionalized on the date of your sister's murder."

Tabby's stomach clenched. "There's a man, too."

Bardot straightened. "An accomplice?"

"Maybe." Tabby lifted a shoulder.

"How do you know this?" Bardot asked, her attention on Tabby's face. Tabby told her about Cal, told her about the attack, told her how she was partially using her stay with the Whites to hide from him.

"Does he know you're here?" Bardot asked at the end of it all. It seemed a strange thing to focus on out of everything Tabby had said, but she shook her head.

"That's easy enough to rectify," Bardot said, but beneath her breath like she hadn't meant it for Tabby's ears. "He wants to silence you, yes?"

It was asked without a trace of sympathy. As cold and calculating as Rowan's eyes, as Gretchen's questions.

"Yes," Tabby agreed. Because at the end of the day, did it matter if Bardot cared?

"I wonder what he would do should the right opportunity arise," Bardot mused, again to herself.

"You want to let the man attack me," Tabby realized, a little delayed, as everything seemed to be.

"I do," Bardot admitted, without equivocating. "And then I'll kill him for you."

"A home invasion."

Bardot lifted her glass in acknowledgment. "I'm known to keep a gun in my study, especially when Anders is away."

"What do you get out of it?" Tabby asked. Never in her life had anything come for free.

"I want Rowan gone," Bardot said. "I take care of your problem, you take care of mine. My mother-in-law would suspect either me or Anders of foul play if Rowan died in our care. While she has no love for that little psychopath, she's adamant there be no more scandal attached to our name. Even if I made Rowan's death look like a suicide, Edith would likely punish me for it."

Bardot paused as if Tabby would have anything to say to that. "But you, my dear. You have no connections to us. You don't even officially work here on paper. You will be my perfect little scapegoat to keep Edith from making a fuss. And she won't turn you in to the police, because a murder would be even more scandalous."

Tabby didn't mention the fact that a cop already knew she was employed at the Whites. "You can't . . . you can't actually be serious. How would I even . . ."

Kill Rowan? Because that's what Bardot was hinting at with unsaid words. Tabby didn't think she could stomach killing an animal, let alone a human.

"It's none of my business how you take care of the matter," Bardot said with a delicate shrug.

"Are we playing Strangers on a Train?*" It was the only thing Tabby could think to say.*

Bardot hummed thoughtfully. "Yes, I believe we are."

Tabby hadn't had to wonder when Bardot would collect on her end of the deal. That had all been solved quite nicely.

Because Rowan had overheard them that evening. Had taken their plan and made it her own. She'd hinted as much back in that kitchen on the night that Tabby now remembered as *hell.*

"What did Anders think?" Tabby asked, curious in a detached sort of way.

"What everyone else does," Bardot said, her voice soaked with amusement. "He thinks Gretchen gave into her violent urges." She paused. "*Wants* to believe that. It's the easiest answer, isn't it? We might even be able to institutionalize Gretchen while we're at it."

The way Bardot talked about it so casually made Tabby want to throw up, made her want to scream and claw at Bardot's face.

"Shaughnessy?" Tabby asked instead.

"It's not exactly like his hands are clean here." Bardot lifted one shoulder. "And, legally, I'm his daughter's mother. Rowan isn't the only one who knows how to take hostages to get what she wants."

Tabby almost laughed. Because of course that's how Bardot thought. If the truth came out now, it would rip the White family's name to shreds—at best. At worst, the three of them would face prison time. Bardot wasn't about to let that happen to herself.

And Tabby had seen the power the idea of Gretchen held over Shaughnessy already.

"Will you ever tell her?" Tabby asked. There was no denying that guilt over Gretchen was part of the reason she could no longer sit in silence with her thoughts. The girl had been so young, and yet, surely, this would shape her for years to come. The story had taken on a life of its own, had become sensationalized for a rapt nation. All you had to do was turn on a television and it was in your face.

Eight-year-old sociopath kills her aunt.

"What good would that do?" Bardot asked, without a hint of remorse. "After all, it's the truth. Gretchen killed Rowan, and there's no denying that."

Tabby thought about truth and the ways that you could tell stories that were real but were also lies.

Tabby stood, brushed off her jeans, and turned her back on Bardot. And she hoped, one last time, that one day Gretchen—in all her strangeness and wide-eyed cruelty and somehow uniquely wonderful view of the world—would realize the difference between the two.

CHAPTER SIXTY-ONE

GRETCHEN

Now

Three days after the showdown at Shaughnessy's apartment, Gretchen indulged in the pizza she allowed herself only after closing a case. She'd been expecting solitude, but she'd just slid into the booth when she felt someone looming over her.

She didn't have to look to know who it was.

"You trust me." Gretchen grinned at Marconi in an implicit invitation to join her.

"Let's not get ahead of ourselves," Marconi muttered as she sat down and situated herself, two slices of meat-lover's spread out in front of her on top of greasy, transparent plates. She smiled up at the waiter as he dropped off two sweaty beers.

Marconi clinked the bottles' necks together despite the fact that Gretchen had yet to grab hers, and then took a long swallow. "I like this tradition."

"Is twice a tradition?" Gretchen asked, but unbent enough to accept the beer as the peace offering it was.

"Pizza at the end of a case," Marconi said, and then took an obscenely large bite of her slice. She moaned, exaggerated and deep. "It's a tradition if we say it is."

"Hear, hear," Gretchen agreed, finishing off the crust of her first piece. "So you're not here to arrest me?"

"For what?" Marconi lifted one shoulder. "Self-defense?"

"You could paint it in other ways," Gretchen said lightly. She wasn't exactly a favorite of the local prosecutors—despite the number of convictions she'd helped them secure. At least one or two could easily be persuaded to charge her with a crime.

"I think you've paid enough for your sins," Marconi said lightly. As if this wasn't life or death for Gretchen.

Gretchen tugged at a pepperoni. "Shaughnessy?"

"Well." Marconi sighed. "I'm building a case. But . . ."

"But?" Gretchen prodded.

"Prosecutors are weird about going after cops. Even when they're covering up the death of another one."

That was usually true. But there was one exception that Marconi, being somewhat new to the city, probably didn't know about. "Cormac Byrne."

"Gesundheit?" Marconi joked, and Gretchen rolled her eyes because she would cut out her own tongue before she admitted that she liked having this easy version of Marconi back. There were probably still defenses she hadn't made it back through, but now she knew she might actually get the chance to try.

"He's a progressive prosecutor who has his eye on the White House. He cares more about his long-term political ambitions than pissing off the chief of police," Gretchen said, without going into too many details about how she knew that. Marconi didn't need to know about Gretchen's intimate connection to the man. "You go to him with a slam-dunk dirty-cop case, he'd probably kiss your feet."

Marconi wrinkled her nose, presumably at the image. "But if we make too much noise about this . . ."

"I'll be dragged into it again," Gretchen said, finishing the thought.

She wondered if she cared at this point. Despite what she'd said to Marconi, Gretchen had a very expensive and very skilled lawyer on retainer. If someone tried to spin Rowan's death as anything but self-defense, that lawyer would rip them apart without breaking a sweat, would probably even have fun doing it.

Besides, Cormac wouldn't see any point in going after her.

Legally, she felt safer than she'd had since she was eight.

Her consulting gig with the BPD was a little more precarious. But her record spoke for itself, and she'd been a minor when everything had occurred. Even if someone like Lachlan Gibbs used this to get her barred from any and all cases, there were always private clients. Plenty of people would be morbidly drawn to her story, and plenty of others wouldn't care as long as she could solve their problems for them.

There would still be cases either way to help her scratch that itch.

The press might be vicious, especially coming on the heels of the Viola Kent case.

But they had always been vicious, and she had always survived. Her life had been defined by Rowan's death, why shouldn't Shaughnessy's?

She dug into her bag for a scrap of paper, scribbled out a phone number. "Tampering with a crime scene is a felony if it's during a felony investigation. And Cormac will probably be able to dress it up into something even more damning."

Marconi studied Gretchen's face, as if trying to judge her sincerity. But then Marconi's hand lashed out, quick as anything, and the slip disappeared into her pocket. "Shaughnessy has already put in for early retirement."

Part of Gretchen, the part that had just given Marconi the private line of one of the city's top prosecutors, shouted that it wasn't enough. And yet . . . Gretchen found she didn't truly care. She was so tired of caring about Shaughnessy—about what he'd think, about his judgment, about his life and his priorities and his morals. It was time to let him go.

He wanted to be dead, but he couldn't kill himself because he was too afraid to die. There was some kind of beautiful justice in that. The system had failed her enough times that she wasn't disappointed that he might not be charged. He would live knowing what kind of man he truly was, and for someone like Shaughnessy, that was enough.

"Tabitha Cross?" she asked.

"She didn't do much that we can prove," Marconi admitted around a mouthful of pizza. "According to multiple witnesses, she was attacked and then tried to fight off her attacker. And that was it. We could maybe get her for tampering with a crime scene. But is it worth it?"

"Bardot killed a cop," Gretchen pointed out. "Even the most record-conscious prosecutor has to smell blood in the water at that."

"He was an intruder in her house," Marconi said. She put down her slice of pizza, and met Gretchen's eyes. "I'm sorry I made you dig it all up."

Gretchen sat back against the booth, crowing. "Oho. Is this you saying you were wrong? That you should have left well enough alone?"

Marconi ducked her head. "Maybe not well enough alone . . ."

"But close enough," Gretchen said on a laugh. "Who benefited here?"

"You know what happened," Marconi pointed out. "You know you didn't kill Rowan in cold blood."

"Does that really matter?" Gretchen asked, and it wasn't sarcastic or rhetorical.

And somehow Marconi realized that. "Yes. You've told yourself for so long that you're some villain. And now you know—"

"That I am?" Gretchen cut in.

"No." Marconi shook her head, emphatic. "That you're a survivor."

Gretchen looked away. "You could have taken the gun from me."

Marconi could have easily stepped in at Shaughnessy's place. She was a trained professional who had been no more than two steps away from Gretchen for the entirety of the confrontation with Shaughnessy.

Yet Marconi had let it play out.

Marconi laughed. "I knew you were bluffing."

Gretchen cut her eyes to the woman she was coming to think of as *partner*. "How?"

"I trusted you," Marconi said. Like it was easy.

Except the words branded themselves on Gretchen's skin, painful, raw, indelible. Never once in the years that she'd worked with Shaughnessy had he told her that. "Why?"

"I want to make some grand proclamation here," Marconi said with a grin. "And I truly did believe you were in control of yourself the whole time."

"But?" Gretchen prodded.

"But . . . you never took the safety off," Marconi said with a laugh, and all at once the tension left Gretchen's body. She pursed her lips in a show of annoyance that she didn't actually feel.

"It would have taken a second," she protested.

"A second I could have used to overpower you," Marconi countered, picking up her slice again, eyeing it with something close to lust. She looked up right before she took a bite. "Anyway, I knew you were bluffing."

"How?" Gretchen asked again. Because *logic* said that the fact that the safety had been on was enough. Gretchen shouldn't care about *emotions* or *gut instinct*. And yet, still, she'd asked about it.

"Sometimes the how and the why don't matter," Marconi said, studying her now. Gretchen fought the urge to hide. "Sometimes the stories we tell ourselves are what matters."

"And what story do you tell yourself?"

"That you're a survivor," Marconi said easily. Gretchen flinched, not sure what to make of that. But then Marconi smiled and continued. "And that you're clever."

"I'm not," Gretchen said. "I would have realized exactly what Shaughnessy was years ago if I were."

"You knew he was trying to get you to kill him," Marconi said around a mouthful. "The one thing in the world I've always been sure of is that you want to prove Shaughnessy wrong."

And that was true. It had formed the basis of her moral guidelines for her entire life. "So it's not because you think I'm a good person."

She didn't know why she wanted Marconi to admit that, only that she did.

Marconi smirked down at her plate, like she was amused at some private joke. "You don't believe in the binary of good and evil."

"Touché," Gretchen said, despite the fact that everything in her wanted Marconi to say she was a *bad person*. She picked up a napkin and then began methodically ripping it apart. "You still want to work with me?"

When silence greeted that question, Gretchen jerked her eyes up to meet Marconi's.

"Why did you go to Shaughnessy's?" Marconi asked instead of answering.

Gretchen tried to ignore the way her bones felt achy at the question. "To guilt him into finally confessing."

Marconi nodded like that was what she'd been expecting. "A lesser person would have gone there to seek revenge, to kill him." She paused as if to let the next bit have more weight. "Nine times out of ten . . ."

You do the right thing, Gretchen heard.

"Eight," she countered, just as she had in the car, days ago.

"You're not as terrible or mysterious as you'd like to think, Gretchen White," Marconi teased.

Gretchen thought of the way she'd longed to feel Shaughnessy's gray matter in the palm of her hand, thought of the long minute she'd calculated the ramifications of killing Tabby and Marconi as well.

And she thought about that night in the car, watching Shaughnessy drink away what she now realized was crushing guilt and shame and self-loathing.

If a life was made up of actions and not thoughts, wasn't it the fact that Gretchen had turned over the gun that mattered, rather than anything that came before that?

Gretchen wasn't like *good people* who had simply been born with a moral compass; she had to wake up every day and make the choice to do the right thing instead of the easiest thing. She'd always thought the internal calculations she ran as part of that process made her somehow less worthy of praise. But for the first time in her life, she realized that maybe the end result was just as admirable. Or maybe even more so.

She supposed she had Marconi to thank for that. For knocking on her door and not letting Gretchen scare her away and giving a shit about Gretchen in the first place.

Marconi, who was smiling at her once again, waiting for her to react to gentle teasing that Gretchen probably hadn't yet earned back, if she was being honest.

You're not as terrible or mysterious as you'd like to think, Gretchen White.

Gretchen clinked her beer bottle against Marconi's, almost—almost—believing it this time. "I guess not."

CHAPTER SIXTY-TWO

SHAUGHNESSY

Now

No one told you how scratchy the orange jumpsuits were.

It was only his third day on the block, and Shaughnessy couldn't help but dream of soft cotton trousers that rode uncomfortably into the crease of his thigh. His one-year sentence stretched out in front of him, endless.

Shaughnessy had been surprised when that shark of a politician in prosecutor's clothing had gone after him like he'd smelled blood in the water—had been even more surprised by the relief he'd felt at the verdict. He'd spent his life desperately terrified that someone would uncover his secret, but there was something incredibly refreshing about the idea of serving time. Of a slate wiped clean at the end of it.

The only hitch in that plan was that he knew that it wasn't a one-year sentence he'd been given, not really. As a cop who'd spent a good portion of his life in Vice and then in Major Crimes, he'd be lucky to make it six months with his new cellmates.

He'd take it in stride, he'd decided. Grin and bear it. If the shiv ever found his flesh, he'd be thankful. Until then, he'd endure.

Because that's what he'd always done. Endure.

"Shaughnessy," a guard called. "Visitor."

A rumbling started and then subsided at his name. There would be a reckoning, he knew. Not right away. But soon.

In the meantime, he made his way toward the door that led to the visitor's lounge. A guard checked him—as if he would really be able to acquire a weapon around here—and then let him through.

Gretchen sat at a table near the vending machine, looking as out of place as an orchid in a landfill.

Shaughnessy was surprised to see her so soon after the circus that had been his trial. Before that, it had been six months in which his entire life unspooled, the pieces splashed onto every front page in Boston.

That prosecutor, Cormac Byrne, had been merciless in his case against Shaughnessy, laying out every time Shaughnessy had made the exact wrong choice. Byrne hadn't been able to prove that Shaughnessy had removed the page in Rowan's file about her pregnancy, but it hadn't been hard to lead the jury to that obvious—and ultimately correct—conclusion.

At the end of the trial, Byrne had made such a convincing case that Shaughnessy himself had almost believed it had been him rather than Bardot who had been the driving force for the cover-up even after Rowan's death.

Meanwhile, in exchange for her testimony, Bardot had walked away from the whole debacle with a misdemeanor charge, a hefty fine, and community service.

Tabitha Cross had been spared the hefty fine.

Between the three of them, Shaughnessy had borne the weight of that night on his shoulders alone. And the part of him that had always wanted to be a good man thought that had been the proper outcome, his sins too great to be forgiven with anything but the full weight of justice coming down on him.

The part of him that had wanted Gretchen to end it all that night she'd come to his apartment had also rejoiced. Now there wouldn't be a way out of this mess that wasn't him bleeding out on the floor. He just hoped it would be quick.

His one regret was that Gretchen hadn't emerged unscathed. In his most brutally honest moments, he realized that was ironic considering he had played such a role in dragging her name through the mud her whole life. Still, at some point he'd started wanting to protect her from that, and, of course, he'd utterly failed.

For her it wasn't anything new, though, and he got the sense that seeing him squirm more than made up for that. The steel in her spine was forever a point of pride for him.

Now, Gretchen lifted a brow at him, imperiously. He sat because what else could he do?

She studied him with those cold eyes he'd always known so well. For a heartbeat, he was back in that darkened room, Rowan's knife at Gretchen's throat.

But he blinked, erasing the image. Gretchen had never needed saving.

"You'll die in here," Gretchen said in that straightforward way of hers. Not cruel, but devoid of empathy.

"Yes," Shaughnessy agreed. There was no way he'd survive even one year.

"Good," Gretchen murmured. And he didn't listen to her. She was mean and spiteful and callous, just as he always realized she was. But she was his. So he traced her features, carefully ascribing them to memory.

His daughter.

His.

All his life, he'd been obsessed. Possessive, even. And then Rowan had come along and given him something that everyone in the world would acknowledge he had claim over.

Yet he'd never been brave enough to admit Gretchen was his.

Because she'd been a murderer, a social pariah. One of his own making.

Then he'd paid for that cowardice when she'd become a brilliant consultant with a quick wit, a daunting mind, and a cold demeanor that had rubbed a few people the wrong way.

With a life better than he could have ever imagined for her.

"I'm proud of you," he managed to force out, and something warm uncoiled in his chest at her surprised reaction. He'd always liked that he could get to her. Maybe they had never—would never—have the father-daughter relationship he'd dreamed about once upon a time, but they always had this. They could get to each other.

"Stop it."

But he couldn't. "I am, you know. You've solved so many cases." He shook his head, as always, in disbelief of her accomplishments. "You're so clever. So smart."

"If I was smart, I would have realized . . ."

That Shaughnessy was a shit everything. A shit father, a shit detective. "I told myself a story," he said. "And you believed it. What story do you tell yourself?"

"That I'm more than what you believe me to be," Gretchen said.

"I tell myself that I'm as brave as you are," Shaughnessy confessed, because he knew this would be one of the very last honest conversations that he would ever have.

Gretchen looked away. "I'm not brave."

"Maybe not," Shaughnessy admitted. "But you're true."

His daughter's eyes snapped to his, wide like they were that first night. Curious. Insatiably curious.

Shaughnessy wondered what he would have done differently if he could. Would he have slowed down on those dark country roads so as never to have run into Rowan? Would he have given up his fascination and then his obsession? Would he have pretended to have never heard the name Anders White? Would he have shot Rowan where she stood in the doorway before every terrible thing could have unraveled before all of them?

Would he have changed a single moment to end up with the daughter that he had today? Bold, intelligent, successful. Gretchen had made a life for herself that he had always admired—no matter if he'd let her in on that fact or not.

He reached out now and it felt wrong, awkward. But he let his fingers curl over her unnaturally still hand. Again, he said, "I'm proud of you."

The words landed between them, heavy and unwieldly. Gretchen flinched away from him, like he knew she would. But he'd wanted her to believe it. For every mistake that he'd made in his life, he never regretted Gretchen.

It wasn't *I love you*—it never would be. But it was what he could offer.

He patted her hand once. Then stood, walked toward the door.

The guard let him through, a nasty grin on his face.

Two weeks later he was showering when a blade found its way between his fourth and fifth ribs.

The last thought he had was of Gretchen, in the moonlight, and then in the sunlight. Her face set, determined. And he realized maybe in this godforsaken life of his, he'd done at least one thing right.

ACKNOWLEDGMENTS

It takes a village to publish a book, and I am so eternally grateful to the entire Thomas & Mercer family who worked tirelessly to get the best version of this story out to readers. That includes my fantastic editors Megha Parekh and Charlotte Herscher, production editor extraordinaire Laura Barrett and her team, the fabulous and patient Sarah Shaw, and all the rest of the wonderful people who have a hand in getting my book baby into the world. Thank you so much; I am endlessly appreciative of the work you do.

As always, thank you to Abby Saul, my agent, for being my partner through all the weirdness that came from writing a book in 2020. You are a rock, and I am so thankful to have you in my corner.

On that note, I have to thank from the bottom of my heart my friends and family who were a source of constant support over Zoom and phone calls and texts as we all tried to be creative and somewhat productive in a time of crushing uncertainty and stress.

And, finally, to you, dear readers. Thank you for spending your precious time with my stories, and trusting that I wouldn't lead you astray with a character whose head isn't the easiest to be inside. All of this is possible because of you.

ABOUT THE AUTHOR

Photo © 2019

Brianna Labuskes is the Amazon Charts and *Washington Post* bestselling author of the psychological suspense novels *A Familiar Sight*, *Her Final Words*, *Black Rock Bay*, *Girls of Glass*, and *It Ends With Her*. She was born in Harrisburg, Pennsylvania, and graduated from Penn State University with a degree in journalism. For the past eight years, she has worked as an editor at both small-town papers and national media organizations such as Politico and Kaiser Health News, covering politics and policy. Brianna lives in Washington, DC, and enjoys traveling, hiking, kayaking, and exploring the city's best brunch options. Visit her at www.briannalabuskes.com.